RAGWORT

Also by Sam K Horton

The Eythin Legacy
Gorse

RAGWORT

BOOK TWO OF THE EYTHIN LEGACY

SAM K. HORTON

SOLARIS

First published 2025 by Solaris
an imprint of Rebellion Publishing Ltd,
Riverside House, Osney Mead,
Oxford, OX2 0ES, UK

www.solarisbooks.com

ISBN: 978-1-83786-585-7

Copyright © 2025 Sam K. Horton

The right of the author to be identified as the author of this work has been asserted in accordance with the Copyright, Designs and Patents Act 1988.

All rights reserved. No part of this publication may be reproduced, stored in a retrieval system, or transmitted, in any form or by any means, electronic, mechanical, photocopying, recording or otherwise, without the prior permission of the copyright owners.

This book is a work of fiction. Names, characters, places and incidents are products of the author's imagination or are used fictitiously.

10 9 8 7 6 5 4 3 2 1

A CIP catalogue record for this book is available from the British Library.

Cover art and illustrations by Veronica Park

Designed & typeset by Rebellion Publishing

Printed in the UK

For Bex,

thank you for everything, and for not running all those years ago when you saw all the books...

PART ONE

"I sleep so sound all night, mother, that I shall never wake,
If you do not call me loud when the day begins to break;
But I must gather knots of flowers and buds, and garlands gay;
For I 'm to be Queen o' the May, mother,
I 'm to be Queen o' the May."

Alfred, Lord Tennyson

WITCH'S HAIR

THERE ARE PLACES, where the join between worlds is so thin a person, if they pressed their ears to the moss, could hear the dead talking in their sleep.

Places where there's such thin veneer between above

and below that things can _{*slip*}

A flower petal caught   in the   pages of a book as the reader lies sleeping.
        Staining the story

and marking the page.

Because a story told is a story told, nothing more

Or less.
Truth a shuttle on a broken loom.

                            All the edges fraying.

A story about a magician.
A story about a witch.
A story about a story.

RAGWORT

The truth caught somewhere between them. Settle in.
Trust me.
Listen.

DANDYLION

The High Moor, Cornwall, 1787

THE MOORLAND RIPS apart under a thunderstorm of hooves.

A dappled blue roan mare hurtles out of the small grove of blackthorn that twists out of the mire, Nancy Bligh astride her. White flowers scattering into the black wound of churned up peat. Nancy, face set against the weather, spurring her horse on and trying to ignore the grunts from the figure strapped across its rump.

'Shush! It's your sister I want, you'd be sensible to avoid my attentions, do you understand?'

With a flick of her wrist, Nancy clips her cargo with the leather of her riding crop, the brass snouted top shining in the evening sun. The grunts stop, and though a frown has set hard across Nancy's face—frozen into place by the wind—a smile is creeping out. She lets herself enjoy it for the briefest of moments then her mouth snap back in a hard-set line. She isn't here to enjoy herself.

A steady wind has blown a year's worth of seasons through and now drags its fingers across the bleached tufts clinging to the cotton grass in the marshes. White flags waving as winter surrenders to spring. It has been a busy year for Nancy. Since she lost her father, Pel. Since the chapel fell. A great deal learnt in too short a time. But Nancy has never been the type to shy away from a problem, and there has been no shortage of those. The fall of the chapel, the fall of Pel, has fractured this valley. Where once there were two altars—faith and magic—there are now a thousand. Fractal cults that have spread across the moor like a sickness. The villagers desperate to believe in something have found, without a shepherd, their own stories to tell. The things they saw last year—Callum and his fiery hand, the fire, those killed by the Underfolk—have clarified some things that ought to remain hazy. Nancy knows some sit on the moor and worship the Underfolk like little gods. She knows some still visit the chapel every Sunday and sit in service to a shadow. She knows some, though it sickens her, venerate Callum as some kind of saint. She has broken more than one bogwood effigy, hand dipped in pitch and set to burning. Balance, her father used to say, it was all about balance. Well, Nancy's trying, but it's hard to reset a chessboard with half the pieces missing. And she has far bigger problems at hand.

Problems like this.

Ahead of her, Nancy sees a figure hobble through across the stubby moor grass. It moves more quickly than its shape would imply, rolling forwards in a bundle of rags and darkness, a soft felt hat tied to its head with a shawl. It turns, for a moment, and there is the glint of a gaze under the brim, taking in Nancy as she bears down. The arriving storm is heavy now, and Nancy, lit from the front in the golden sun stands out from the black behind her like she's been cut out from a picture book and pasted onto the clouds. Turning, the creature scurries on, badgerlike.

The creature's name is Hilla, and their brother Stag is strapped to Selkie, Nancy's horse. The pair of them are trouble, but Hilla is the worst. It had been Nancy's friend, Delen Rowe, who'd warned her days ago of the trouble she'd had sleeping. Delen who could barely keep her focus, her eyes trapped under heavy lids. Every night had been the same, waking in the dark with a weight on her chest, a shadow in the room, and Delen unable to move from under it. Nancy had not listened to her friend the first time she had asked for help. The problems of the moor a bag of marbles dropped, each catching on the light as they scattered away from her. Delen had been forced to make her listen. Had visited Nancy in her cottage, dragged her away from a table of notes and charts and taken her for a ride. She had gone to Mirecoombe, the village sat in the hollow of the hills with its boundary ditch and walls built of painful memories. They had ridden through the empty streets and peered through windows at men and women nodding off, sleeping leant against walls. Seen the smith asleep with his hammer in his hand and the hem of his apron catching on the fire. Nancy had listened then. Returning to the cottage, she had taken down armfuls of books from heaving shelves and set to reading. She finally lifted her head as night fell this evening. And with Delen still sleeping had made herself comfortable in the chair by the fire to plan. The same plan that was not going as well as she had hoped.

'Hilla!' Nancy shouts at the figure still barrelling across the landscape ahead of her. The first drops of rain begin to fall, heavy and purposeful from overfull clouds. 'Hilla, stop! Enough of this. It's done. You had a good run, but it is over!' If Hilla can hear her pursuer she gives no indication, on she moves picked out in diminishing sunlight.

Nancy has prepared carefully. Hilla and Stag had entries in Pel's books of folklore, but information on what to do with them was scant. They're nomadic spirits. They don't fit neatly into the known Underfolk. Individual horrors. Ambling around the countryside until they find a quiet town or village ready for them to feast on dreams until full. Until the locals can barely stand for tiredness. Stag has a light touch, swaying gently in the shadows in the corners of rooms, terrifying light sleepers into silence if they wake and vanishing if they move. His sister, Hilla, is a different beast. She hauls herself onto the chests of her victims, clutches tight around their sleeping forms, not moving even if they wake up. Sucks down their hopes and dreams like a wolf laps blood and she has never, not once, known herself full. And now they have found Mirecoombe.

'Hilla!' Nancy is screaming. These two represent something. Her first true test as Keeper. The squabbles of the village and the Underfolk pale against them. She knows that they've walked free for centuries, and she wants to be the one to put them down. She needs to be the one to stop them.

'Hilla, I am warning you this is over. If you escape me today, you'll be alone! I'm sending your brother back whatever happens, however this ends. You might be able to escape the Undermoor together, but you and I both know Stag won't be able to do it alone.' The bundled creature on the back of Selkie tears a howl from its throat which hurls into the rain and just for a second, Hilla slows. Then she's charging on into the cloud choked sun.

Once she had a plan, Nancy had been able to set to work. Leaving Delen sleeping in her cottage Nancy had prepared herself. She was already dressed in her riding trousers and boots. A dress shirt she had altered herself to conceal small vials and a set of knives in a reinforced waist. She had pulled the heavy old coat from its hanger and filled her pockets with twine and bones and charms before opening the cutlery drawer and withdrawing two silver plate forks. Nancy wasn't worried about leaving the girl alone, the cottage had protections carved into the jambs and the sills, had charms mortared in between the granite. Some Pel had left, some Nancy had strengthened. Some preceded them both. Hilla and Stag wouldn't get in. Even so, Nancy considered leaving her dog, Patroclus, behind. Just in case. But the old hound seemed eager to follow his mistress. It didn't surprise Nancy when he stood to follow. He had barely left her side since Pel had died. Her faithful old soldier. Sometimes, just sometimes, she hates him for it. It always passes, Pat's eyes too sorrowful for stern looks, his ears too soft for hard words and misplaced feelings. It's not his shadow she's sick of feeling. She had looked at him, his heavy, jowls, his face, and kissed him on the forehead. Then she had picked up her riding crop, closed the door behind her, and gone out into the night. It was only a short ride to the village and Nancy barely had time to reflect on the task at hand before Selkie was stepping over the boundary ditch, avoiding the small bridge with its stone cross flat across the mud. Pausing only to fret at the sight of a small altar set into the bank— flowers left at its base. On the opposite shore a crude wooden cross. The destruction of the chapel let God out and nobody knows what to do with Him. That night, though, Mirecoombe was silent. The only lights shone from the Mare's Nest Inn, but Nancy could see no customers through the warped glass in the bullseye windows. Only the landlady Madge Gould cleaning glasses behind the bar, her arm still stiff from last winter's break, when Nancy had brought a chimney down on her. A mistake Nancy has not forgiven herself for. Madge was a constant, and the Nest was the only place on the moor other than her own cottage that was so steeped in wards and protections that Hilla and Stag couldn't get in. No need to bother her friend, Nancy had thought, she could do this alone.

RAGWORT

Nancy let herself into Delen's cottage, tethering Selkie outside, taken the forks from her pocket, removed her coat, and had lain on the girl's bed. The room's low ceiling was swathed in peat smoke that drifted from the fire in the kitchen. Nancy coughed. A perk of the job was wood fires, she wasn't used to the fug of burning turf. Patroclus had turned in circles a few times before slumping to the floor at the foot of the bed and falling asleep, Nancy had willed herself to do the same.

She had been dreaming when they arrived. The same dream she had had each night for weeks. A dream of water and creaking wood.

She woke from one nightmare to another.

For big creatures, they had been quiet. And they must have been hungry because both came together. The peat smoke seemed blacker and heavier and through it she had seen Stag, standing in the corner. He was tall and skeletal, long limbs wrapped in dirty rags and, from a face bound tight with the same, stuck two antlers. They had begun to slough, and their bases hung with shreds of velvet, their white tips fading into bloody red, and Stag was picking at them with a hand, pulling the flesh from them as he watched Nancy sleep. She had winced, tried to rise, and only then become aware of Hilla sitting on her chest.

Nancy shudders at the memory. Hard to believe something so heavy was currently outrunning Selkie. But Hilla is. She's still yards ahead and Nancy is not gaining ground. From his bindings Stag groans again, though quieter than before. Nancy feels a pang of pity for him. She knows he misses his sister.

'Tell her to stop then. End this, Stag, its done. You know it as well as I do.'

But the mournful bundle says nothing. And Hilla runs on.

Once Nancy had become aware of Hilla, she had moved

fast. Reaching her arms out, thankfully not fully in Hilla's embrace, she grasped the forks she had placed at the side of the bed. With as much force as she could manage, she had forced their tines into Hilla's flanks and turned her head as the creature screamed at the touch of iron. It was only as the creature detached herself that Nancy felt the loss. It was as though a friend had died. Something had been taken and left a gaping hole, a scrambling sense of panic, it felt irretrievable. And then it had passed, leaving nothing but exhaustion in its place. Hilla had fled, knocking past Patroclus who had woken with the screaming. The old dog had been too slow to catch Hilla, but he had locked his jaws around Stag's ankle. Unused to any resistance, the pitiful creature had frozen, had wailed into the open doorway hoping his sister would return. She did not. Nancy had taken him by the arm, had bound him with rope she found in Delen's cottage and lain him across Selkie's back, trussed like a hunter's kill. Dawn had broken across Mirecoombe, and Nancy had ridden out after Hilla. She had been following her ever since.

'I could do with you now, Pat, could do with some help.' Nancy speaks into the wind. She lost track of the dog when they'd caught sight of Hilla. She'd been ambling over the foothills of Lullaby Tor, two hills distant, but had broken into a gallop when she'd realised that she'd been followed. Patroclus had quickly been outpaced, though Nancy knew he'd be behind them somewhere, steadily following on. Nancy wishes she had left Stag with him; the creature had no fight and Patroclus could probably have guarded him asleep. As it stands, her cargo is weighing her down. Nancy checks her pockets. Hilla is too far ahead for the glass vials and their trapped magic to be much use. Over the past year Nancy has learnt to make all sorts of useful things, but nothing that can help her now. She closes her eyes, pictures the flowers tattooed on her skin.

Every keeper has hundreds of spells to remember, and even the best needs a helping hand. Pel had a book, pressed flowers associated with individual spells that he could picture and call on at will. Nancy has a more personal garden. Tattooed across her body as vivid as life by a girl she still catches herself dreaming of, in quiet moments. She flicks through the spells she has at her disposal. The floral shorthand for her magic, each flower a key to a powerful lock. Her eyes open.

'Stag, do you hear me? If you try to run, I swear you'll go below in pieces. Do you understand?' A muffled cry from under rope and horns. 'Good.' Nancy closes her eyes, pictures a twist of vetch in her mind, then takes her right hand from the reins and bends fingers into the correct shape. Eyes open, she stands in the stirrups, raises a boot and kicks Stag from Selkie, whispering as she does so and flicking her wrist. The creature lands heavily on sodden ground, and immediately attempts to stand, but it doesn't work. It is as though a net has pinned him down. A pale blue fire flickers each time Stag tries to straighten himself and he soon gives up.

'Thanks, Pel,' Nancy mutters under her breath. It's a spell her mentor, her father, taught her. She can still feel his hand on hers, shaping the spell with her fingers. It's not a spell she's had cause for until now. And she has no idea how long it will hold. Without her extra passenger, Selkie gallops faster across the hillsides. Every now and then a hoof strikes granite, and sparks fly, threatening to set the whole world ablaze even in the rain. The distance between Nancy and her quarry is closing now, not quickly, but she is gaining. Hilla turns and shrieks, a deafening yell that causes Nancy to close her eyes, but she'll not stop riding.

'Almost time for it, eh Pel?' Nancy does not like this, her newfound habit of talking to her father as though he's dead. Because she doesn't see him as dead, her mentor, her father. She can't. Not when she knows his spirit, a part of him, is below her in the Undermoor. And nor can she shake the feeling he can hear her, so she chats away. She needs some support for what comes next.

Determined to be a better Keeper than her father, the one her home deserves, Nancy has taught herself a great deal. From books, mostly, but also trial and error. She stood for weeks throwing knives at a wall until a single one stuck. Weeks more until they all did. She has burnt herself, scarred herself, frozen herself and worse learning to pack magic into glass traps. Pages from old books hurriedly put out after a spell gone wrong. She had even made Yestin Calder teach her to fight. Since she rescued him from the Wild Hunt, he had shaken off the worst of his family's dislike of her. He'd seen the truth, seen monsters face to face and finally seen the use of her. His brother, Luk, hated it, but Yestin had agreed to train her best he could. He had been reluctant to spar at first, until she punched him and split his lip—he had revelled in his teaching then—and now, unless he cheated, she rarely lost a bout. But there is one thing she can get no help with. One thing that is hers alone.

'Ready Selkie?' The horse whinnies, possibly in assent, and flattens black ears against her mane. She does not like what comes next. Nor, if she's honest, does Nancy. Raising a hand above her head, Nancy focuses on Hilla, on the little bundle barrelling fast into the dying sun. Focuses on the earth around her. She feels the kernel of her personal magic, her Murmur. The magic she was born with. Pel had hated it. Had demanded she ignored it, that she only used his prescribed magic. Book magic.

Pel's gone.

She has gotten a little better at using it, it exhausts her less, but she can still only manage small, controlled, bursts with any precision. This will take something more. She feels for it, feels it build, feels it get away from her. With a wince, Nancy drops her arm.

'Damn,' she swears under her breath, and watches as the hillside to the lee of Hilla lifts, twelve feet or so, like a sheet across a bed as it's made. Nancy bites back a smile—despite the damage she's causing, a part of her always sings when she uses it—and she watches Hilla fall, the creature's momentum taking her careening to the valley below where she lands with a splash in black, peaty water. She was right not to celebrate; it is a short-lived victory. The ground still shakes and Selkie struggles to stand. The moor swells like an unruly sea and Nancy and Selkie fall, horse and Keeper tumbling fast after their quarry. Nancy hits her head hard against a stone as the rumbling hillside settles and shakes into rest, the horse skidding and sliding on her side. By the time she has righted herself, Hilla is struggling to stumpy feet, but Nancy is on her, pinning the creature to the wet grass. There is a thunderclap overhead as the storm clouds finally overtake them and lightning cracks across the sky. The rain falls heavily now, plastering Nancy's black hair to her forehead and, lungs heaving, the Keeper glares at her quarry. Her head rings from the fall, her vision blurred, but it's the first advantage she's had today and she'll press it.

'Stay down Hilla. Don't make me use it again.' Her voice is built on poor foundations and the cracks are starting to show. Nancy stands on shaking feet. Desperately swallowing each anxious breath as they break from her lungs. She wipes her hair from her face then clenches her fist against the tremors. Squeezes until her knuckles turn white. The Murmur, named for the starlings that pulse across winter skies, still rages in her. She cannot still her cloud of birds, so closes her eyes. Watches the red flashes on her eyelids until the ground feels solid again. When she opens them, Hilla is facing her. Bonnet slipped. For a moment Nancy gets a glimpse of what's beneath. She wishes she hadn't. Hilla readjusts herself, and the horrors are hidden again.

'Keeper.' Nancy had not known what Hilla would sound like, or even if she could speak, but this was not what she would have guessed. The words pour from the darkness like poisoned honey, Nancy can feel her limbs grow heavy. Her eyes close. 'You look tired. Yes, Keeper. Why not sleep? Well done. You caught me. Stag too.'

Nancy tries to blink the sleep away, but it is not working. Her eyes are closing even as she makes her hand into a ward, it fizzles out as she casts it. As her eyes close she can just make out a cream and russet shape tearing towards them. Then the shape barks and she is awake. Wide awake.

'You beautiful hound!' Patroclus wags his tail, barks, then turns a growling attention to Hilla who cowers in the mire. 'Thank you, boy. Right, you. Let's deal with you and your brother.' Hilla makes as if to speak again but Nancy, furious and as awake as she has ever been, is one step ahead. She reaches into her pocket and draws out a silvered glass ball, tossing it at Hilla's feet, where it breaks. It was one of Pel's favourites and fast becoming hers. From the broken shards a blue smoke swirls, and then a thick and viscous substance begins to expand around Hilla, binding her tight.

'You're not getting out of that, Hilla. So don't say a bloody word. All you'll get if I fall asleep is wet and cold.' The creature nods from beneath the hat and Nancy starts to lift her onto Selkie. 'My word you're heavy,' Nancy struggles against the weight of her prisoner but manages to hoist her onto the horse. Once done, Nancy mounts Selkie and they turn back the way they came, past the black scar the fresh-faced Keeper has torn in the landscape. Nancy looks at it uncomfortably. Still, the job was done. Stag is where she had left him, sobbing quietly into wet earth but he brightens when he sees them. His mood is undimmed even when he sees his sister bound.

'I've no room for you, Stag, will you behave?' Stag nods. 'Good, up you get then.' Nancy waves a hand across Stag, keeping the small tattoo of a harebell in mind as she does so and the blue web holding him down dissolves in the rainfall. Stag stands, and Nancy spurs Selkie to walk on. Hilla grumbles, and Stag follows behind. As they ride, Nancy plays with the brass buttons on her coat. Pel's coat. Catching herself, she stops, pulls up her collar, and sets her face against the rain.

THE WORLD IS grey and wet. The lightning has stopped, and the thunder's rolled on but the clouds remain. Night has fallen, and Nancy rides by the light of the moonlight that somehow is beating its way through the firmament. She is wet, mud caked and done with adventure for the evening.

The party arrives at the Fellmire soon after six.

The place makes her shudder every time. The black-watered bog that swallowed her father, that started Callum's journey into and out of hell. Since the fight with Callum and the bog's regeneration, Nancy has used the mire as a point of return. So far, she has only had to use it sparingly, a few spriggans causing trouble, a wish hound that had escaped. Hilla and Stag are her biggest bounty by far. Tethering Selkie to the blackthorn that still grows around Pel's knife, Nancy helps Hilla down.

'Will you go willingly?' Nothing. 'I am giving you a chance here. Both of you. I can make you go, you know I can. You've seen what I can do, Hilla. If I can tear a hillside in two, I can certainly manage you.' Hilla turns to look at her brother, his head hangs down and there is no fight left in either of them. The creature turns back to Nancy and nods.

'Yes.' Her voice has a draw to it, even when she isn't using her magic. 'I'll go, but Keeper, I've tasted your dreams. That head of yours is curdled cream. You've sour thoughts, girl.'

Nancy laughs, a sound hollowed out from within. A lightning struck tree.

'Oh Hilla, you have no idea.' Nancy kneels and takes the riding crop from her belt, the top and cover taken from Pel's old stick, the brass nosed beastie still shining, Nancy's palms adding their own patina to her father's. If she squints, it is almost like she still holds his hand. Brushing sentimental thoughts away, she unsheathes the knife hidden within. She takes a small pouch from her pocket, crushes the dried flowers within and rubs them into the blade. Then she drags it through the blue foam encasing Hilla. The substance falls from Hilla's body like a cast, turning to ash as it hits the floor. Hilla rubs feeling back into her arms, and Nancy takes a step back, lowering a hand to stroke Patroclus who nuzzles his nose into her thigh. Hilla tenses and for a moment Nancy thinks she will have to fight after all. But instead, the squat figure reaches out for her brother's hand and leads them into the mire. The black water bubbles around them as they go and Hilla is almost completely submerged when Nancy asks a question. The question she's asked every person and creature she's met this last year.

'Hilla! Before you go, tell me, who is the Mother?'

The parting gift from her father. A mystery still not solved.

RAGWORT

The world of the Underfolk, the Undermoor, abuzz with rumours of the Mother. A figure she nor Pel know. A figure the Underfolk seem to only half grasp. Spoken with fear, with reverence. Their hushed mutterings uttered like a heresy. A thing half told. A spell half cast. Nancy calls to Hilla and the creature turns her head.

'The Mother?' That voice again, even at this distance Nancy feels its camphor pull. 'Now, then, there's a dream.'

Then, with another step, both are gone. The water returns to its mirrored state and the rain stops. Nancy shouts into the diminishing bubbles.

'Hilla! Damn it, who is She?'

Nancy waits for a few minutes, just to be sure, but she knows the Fellmire, it doesn't return what it takes. She hauls herself up onto Selkie and turns horse and dog towards the fragile lights of Mirecoombe, and home.

THE BAR OF the Mare's Nest Inn is full. Through the windows Nancy can see her friend Madge Gould. Landlady of the Nest. Closest thing to family she has left. Locryn Calder and old Cusk at the bar, two men who have stood in her way at every turn, and still she pities them. Sat there mourning the loss of Calder's middle son, Jan. A son she could perhaps have saved. Another reason to work so hard at being better. To avoid such loss.

She can hear the laughter, the arguments, even through the bulls-eye glass. But she's not looking for company, or arguments, tonight. She hurries Selkie on, glancing up only briefly at the chapel on the hill. The damage wrought in last year's war stark against the sky. Moonlight leaks out of the holes where Nancy fought a monster and brought the chapel down. Calder's two remaining sons, Luk and Yestin, and their crew have been working hard to repair the roof, and there are rumours that a new reverend has been appointed. He'll want to give his sermons without fear of being rained on. The thought of Cleaver's replacement makes her head pound, even more than it already does, but Nancy is done with problems for today. She turns Selkie into the yard at the rear of the pub and stables her in the old barn there. As always, Madge has kept the barn strawed and ready, a net of hay hanging from the hook on the wall. Nancy lifts the saddle from her horse, places it on its stand, and cups Selkie's velvet nose in her hand.

'Good girl, Selkie, you did well. Thank you.' The horse pushes her nose against Nancy's palm and the Keeper laughs. 'Yes, yes, sure, here.' Nancy reaches into her coat for a chunk of carrot and feeds it to a grateful horse. Patroclus, always easily put out, growls jealously at her feet. 'You'll get what's coming to you soon enough boy, shush now.'

As she turns towards the back door of the Nest, Nancy pauses. Somewhere in the darkness, a girl is humming. A song Nancy has heard more and more as the year's gone on. From closed windows, from behind locked doors. Whistled by the workers splitting stone and digging turf. It arrived overnight and has spread like mould. A short refrain that repeats like a folk song. The words on the tip of the tongue.

She shivers, but before she can think any more about it the door opens, and Madge Gould is standing with a warm light seeping out around her. Nancy walks gratefully into the Nest, Patroclus at her heels.

'You look done in Nance, come into the parlour, I've your usual ready. A plate of something hot too.'

'Thank you, Madge. I'm bone tired and soaked through,

Pat too.' Madge Gould takes in her friend. Eyes ringed dark, face flecked with cuts and mud. A bruise spreading nastily across the left side of her face. Nancy's hands, too, are bloodied. Thin. Joints stiff from the cold, Nancy holds them like claws. For a moment, there is a different sentence on the landlady's lips, but it's not the one that's spoken.

'Get everything done then, all wrapped up?'

'Aye, Madge, I think so.'

'In you come then, tell me all about it.'

The door closes, the night grows cold, and deep underground two lost travellers are welcomed home.

Outside on a rooftop, a dunnock teaches a nightjar to sing a song it shouldn't know.

LEOPARD'S BANE

Unlike the main bar, the parlour is heated by an old iron stove, a thick black grate keeping the flames in their place. Nancy is grateful for it as she sinks into the chair. They have become a ritual of sorts, these visits, and Madge knows the score.

'There, girl, drink up. Get warm.' The landlady slides a grass pasty, pastry stuffed with nettles and parsley, potatoes and cream in front of a grateful Nancy and places a pewter tankard heavily down on the table beside it, ale splashing out as it lands. 'I've not forgotten you, Pat,' Madge smiles as she places a heap of scraps on a saucer by the door which is inhaled by the dog. 'Now then, is this a talking night or shall I leave you be?'

Nancy scowls her way through a mouthful of pasty and beer, and Madge turns to leave.

'Why aren't I getting any better, Madge?'

The landlady sighs and wipes her hands on her apron as she returns to the room and takes a seat across from her friend. She knows better than to speak, knows there's more on the way.

'It's been a year, Madge. I've practiced and practiced but I'm not further on. I ripped the side from Lullaby Tor today. Nearly killed Selk. Nearly lost Hilla. Still, I don't know who this Mother is! Hilla taunted me with it as she left.'

Madge sighs, leans over, and takes a swig from Nancy's cup. The tankard was her gift to Nancy, there are two more hanging in this room. One Pel's, one the Reverend Cleaver's. Pewter sided with a thick glass base and Nancy's initials etched into it. Finishing her food Nancy stands, walks to the bar where the other tankards hang, and lifts Pel's tankard from its hook.

'Callum was an accident, Madge. I got lucky. I got lucky with Hilla tonight, as well. And I hear what they say. I know what they do, sat in that chapel still.' Nancy stares at Pel's cup as she touches the ivy inked scar at her neck, the repaired tissue carefully needled with green leaves where it was broken by Callum a year before. Made good by a mad god and the body of her father. 'I'm not ready. Pel should be doing this. He'd have put them down quick. Be halfway to solving this riddle.'

Madge stands and snatches the tankard from Nancy. 'Don't be stupid, Nancy. Pel was arrogant, prideful, and old. He'd not done anything of note for two decades before the business with Cleaver. And he died doing that.'

Nancy takes a swig from her cup.

'He's not dead.'

'He is girl. Please, you need to see that. It isn't healthy. You need to let it out. Let him go.'

Madge pauses, but it needed to be said.

'Whatever he is now, he died. His body rots. He is gone.'

'He spoke to me, he came back, he's still there.'

'Maybe. If he is, then he's out of your reach. He's not been back to talk to you since, has he?'

Nancy finishes her drink and reaches behind the bar for another.

'He listens.'

'Does he, now,' Madge turns and mutters under her breath. 'He never did in life.' She clears away Nancy's empty plate.

'Have you cried for him? Since he died,' she catches Nancy's glower. 'Since he died. Have you mourned him?'

'I've no time for that. I mourned him once already.'

'Aye. But then he came back to talk and gave you hope when there perhaps ought not to be any. Men live, men die. He's a man, Nancy. At the end of it. Your father is still just a man. Take him off that pedestal. He's not suited to it. You are Nancy Bligh, not Lord bloody Hunt and we are all the better for it. Let him go.'

Nancy stares at the fire. A year's worth of tears held back by the flame.

'He's all the family I have, Madge. I can't.'

Madge lays a hand on Nancy's shoulder.

'Look past the end of your nose, Nancy. There's a family waiting. As for this Mother?' There is the sound of breaking glass. 'She's running scared, if she's got any sense.' Madge walks from the room with a furrowed brow towards the bar, where calls for more are lost in a drunken shout.

Alone, Nancy sips her drink and looks at the walls, cluttered with ephemera. Paintings, the taxidermy heads of fox, weasel and deer. Horse brasses and framed knots. Sketches in charcoal that Madge has made. The face of Nancy's father staring down from the wall in ashy strokes. The Reverend beside him.

'I don't want to be alone, Pel.' She sighs and Patroclus looks up from his spot by the fire, coat hot to the touch, and pants a smile.

'I know, boy, I've got you, haven't I? We did good. We'll go on. Whatever comes next.' Nancy sits back down and stares into her drink.

'He's dead, Pat, isn't he?' Patroclus' eyes look balefully up at her. His soft, sloping brows a tangle of curls. He lets out a grumbling whine. She smiles into his trusting face then lets the tears fall. Lets the hollow space she's filled with the ghost of her father empty out until she's left with a weight. A family album, the pictures are all edged in black. The landlady is humming as she walks back in, but the song ends before she enters the room.

'What was that tune, Madge?'

'What, Nancy?' Madge looks at her friend with confusion.

'The song you were humming. I've heard it before. A girl sang it outside.'

'My girl, you're more exhausted than I thought, a tune for an idle tongue, that's all I hum. No thoughts behind it but what's rattling in my head and at the end of a long day that's precious little. Here now, come over and sit with me.' Madge perches on the edge of the low padded bench that runs along the far wall and pats a space beside her. Nancy lets her question go and moves over, lies down with her head in Madge's lap, and lets her friend stroke her hair as her eyes close. Even now at twenty-two, after all she's seen, she hungers for a story. Thinking of Pel, thinking of death, has led her around, again, to her grandmother. The grandmother, she had discovered a year ago, who had been a witch. The source of her Murmur, her magic. Long dead. A secret Pel had kept from her.

'Tell me a tale, Madge. Tell me about my grandmother.'

'Again? Come, girl, look ahead. I told you. Don't go looking for those that are lost. There's those that love you here, now.'

'Not any who are family, Madge.'

She feels Madge stiffen, feels her hand pause on the crown of her head before starting again. And if she sees the twitch at the corner of Madge's smile, the sadness in her eyes, she ignores it. Sitting beside Nancy, Madge begins to speak in a low voice. As she does so, Patroclus hauls himself off the floor by the fire, finally admitting he is too warm, and clambers inelegantly onto the bench.

'Fine, Nance, but remember this is a story. I never knew your grandmother, not really. She died when I was young, I only met her once or twice. This is just a fairy tale, the way my own mother used to tell it.'

Nancy mutters irritably. She's heard this story a lot this year, she knows what it is, and what it isn't. Madge begins, and like all stories too often told she speaks the words without thinking. She has it down pat.

'She was a witch, of course. At least that is what they called her. Because sometimes the words one needs are not the words one has, and people are scared of a woman who knows what she wants. And how to take it.

'Her mother had a little magic. Enough to get by, though her mother had more, because magic travels like a stone skipped across a lake. It doesn't move evenly, and it doesn't play fair. Her father, it was said, was a shadow. He had crept from a fire, and he flickered when he walked, leaving black footprints in the earth. They had met and made love under moonlight, and though there were no clouds above, the houses had shaken as though there was thunder. The Reverend barred his doors and far away, by the coast, fishermen kept their boats moored tight in the harbour. It ended with a lightening flash and the shadow slipped away, back into the darkness, leaving Meliora's mother alone.

'It was always going to be a girl, no boy had been born to that line in a century, and Meliora arrived under a hunter's moon. Her face was covered by a caul that her mother carefully removed and placed, folded, inside a glass vial. She threaded the vial onto a cord knotted with sloes and wrapped the baby round with it. Then she swaddled Meliora and laid her in the hollow hearth of a forgotten cottage, deep in the woods. This done, she died. Meliora was raised by the woods. Ravens taught her to be cunning, wolves taught her how to hunt. She grew strong and learnt many things. She could heal and she could hurt, she knew which bones to crush with which flowers to swell the seas, and which to end a life. They say she had a goat for a wetnurse, and her governesses were ghosts. Her hearth was lit each night by the rasping scales of adders.'

Nancy stirs in her half-awake state. She leans into the story, hoping it will hold her but just like every other time she has heard it, she slips right through.

'What could she do, Madge.' Her voice a whisper.

'Lots of things, Nancy, too many things. She blew fine weather over growing crops, cured children of cholic. She sold women belladonna to make them feel beautiful, and pennyroyal, so they could choose to be free. If they wished. She helped people do other things, too. Helped ships flounder on jagged rocks. Helped horses turn an ankle and throw a rider. It was this sort of help that drew attention. It was the attention that did for her.'

Madge looks down, pauses the story, Nancy is asleep. No matter, the old woman thinks. She has heard it before. She'll hear it again. And Madge hates telling the next part.

'Besides,' Madge speaks to the dark beyond the window, 'it shouldn't be me doing the telling.'

ONCE EVERYONE IS asleep, the dunnock starts up its song again. A dunnock whose wings are arms, with thorny horns on its head. There is laughter between the notes as the singer flits between the windows. It sings into every window where a woman or girl is sleeping and threads its melody through their heads. The song has words, but the singer keeps them to themselves. They'll know them soon enough.

A FINGER OF sunlight breaks through a gap in the shutters and scratches Nancy's cheek. She turns beneath it, dust rising from pillows like smoke in the golden rays as though the touch of the day is burning her. Her brow is furrowed, and she calls out, eyes moving fast behind closed lids. Nancy Bligh is dreaming of drowning. It is vivid and sharp, her lungs heavy with the weight of salted water and she can see nothing in the sea she flails in. Above she can hear the muffled thud of oars, but it is what's beneath that calls her. The sound of iron chains being dragged across a seabed, ancient anchors raising. She is pulled down, fast, and bursts out into an underwater chamber. She coughs out two lungfuls of water so violently it wakes her, and she sits bolt upright expecting the sheets to be soaked, expecting water to still be pouring from her open mouth. But there is nothing. The sheets are dry and it's just her and the dog. The sea as far away as it always is.

A violent start to a beautiful day. Nancy adjusts, slows her breathing, and lays back in the bed Madge must have moved her to. The one she keeps made for nights like that. She could lay here a lifetime, let it all pass her by. The idea of it is intoxicating. She stretches out and watches the light catch her tattoos. She's not grown tired of them yet. The tangle of flowers and leaves that cover her. She runs her hand across the meadowsweet on her collarbone. Remembers the girl who painted her. Her kind, soothing face. The feeling of safety under her needles. The feeling of a kindred spirit.

Not for the first time, she feels keenly the empty space in a bed. Wonders how it might feel to wake next to another.

Someone who might make tea, read beside her as the morning waxed outside. Someone who could fill the space in Nancy's life that seemed so perfect for another. A girl who smelt of hawthorn, who rode without a saddle. With a girl like that beside her?

Perhaps she could just let everything else go.

No.

There is work to be done. Nancy stands, brushing sleep from her eyes that for all the world seems like crusted salt, and opens the shutters. Patroclus is still asleep; no amount of morning sun will wake him until he's ready, and the basket Madge had made for him is warmer than his bed at home. Nancy kicks the corner of the basket, but her heart's not in it.

'Up, Pat, things to do.' Patroclus yawns wider than he seems able and rises on stiff legs and it almost brings a smile to Nancy's face. She makes up the difference with one that's forced and turns to face the day.

Downstairs there is a clattering and bashing of pans. Nancy heads to the kitchen. Madge's brownies, the little spirits of the hearth, are working hard. Cleaning glasses and putting the place in order.

'Hello lovelies, you're up early.' Otter faced brownies peer with glee at their guest and Nancy pours herself a coffee, takes a rasher of bacon from the pan on the stove. 'Don't work too hard, little ones.' Nancy leaves the spirits to it and leads the dog out of the back door of the inn. After the grey black storms of yesterday blue skies seem out of place, but here they are regardless. Shining a light on mud and slate and blinding the rats in the shadows. Selkie is where she was left, quietly eating hay in her stall, and she walks into the sunlight at the sound of the latch.

'Hello girl, sleep well?' Nancy strokes the horse's neck, scratches behind black ears. It takes a moment to saddle Selkie, but Nancy could do this with her eyes closed. Tacked up, Nancy swings herself up by a stirrup and spreads her coat out across the rear of the horse. She clips her heels against Selkie's flanks and the three are off into the streets.

Mirecoombe is usually an early riser, but with Hilla and Stag sent away, the village has had its first good sleep in a week, and the streets are quiet. Only the smith is about, beating metal into shape, scaring warped iron straight. Nancy nods to him as she passes. She's grateful for the solitude. Things are better than they were, but she is still uneasy in the village. Since Pel died and she took up his post, she has begun to understand how he felt. The sharpness in kind words that she worries are spoken in fear. Those who she knows dislike her but still need her help. Not to mention those actively praying to the creature that killed her. No, Mirecoombe is an easier place to be with all asleep.

From walled gardens, behind their stones, geese cackle waiting to be released, and there is the cry of a cat. Nancy rides quietly past the long house, still painful to see, the memory of Salan Dell still haunting it. Its door is closed today, to keep out the rain, the room inside storing last year's grain. Up on its hill, the chapel smiles a gap-toothed grin. In the morning light, the hole in its roof is a gaping maw, held open by the scaffolding that surrounds it. The work to repair it is slow. Arguments are frequent. There are some that would see the whole building razed, see the spectre of last year erased. But you can't remove a stain so easily, not with Nancy riding round in a dead man's coat. Not with Locryn Calder still shaking at night. Nancy turns for home and rides out onto the moor.

RAGWORT

As she clears the boundary fence, two shadows slip from their moorings in the shade of a stone. Their faces are wet though the rain has stopped, and they stink like rotten fish. Their backs are scarred and pitted, stuck here and there with wayward hooks. They follow behind the Keeper, out of range of the old dog's nose, and slip into the brook that follows the path. The fresh water washes the salt from them, and they shiver, but keep on swimming upstream.

MADDER

NANCY GONE, THE peace in the village does not reign long. A cart trundles through the muddy roads of Mirecoombe, pulled by a chestnut cob with blinkers on and a poorly plaited mane. The cart is rough, and one wheel is loose, which causes the whole thing to roll and rock as it passes by the cottages. The driver might as well wear blinkers too. He shows little interest as villagers move aside. He has been here before and though he nods occasionally to people he passes he shows little reaction to his surroundings. His passenger however—sat between cheaply made trunks in the rear—studies every face, every mortared brick, clutching tightly to the books in his lap. Beneath a wide black hat, he has a youthful open face with heavy lashed eyes, though he is older than he looks. With his pale fine hair and placid face, he at first gives the impression of a cow. It is only his eyes that expose the lie. Green and brown and flecked with fire they skewer the village, hold it tight, search for cracks in its armament. These are eyes of the sharpest kindness.

Leaning forwards, with some difficulty due to the rolling of the cart, the passenger speaks with the driver, his words lost in the morning sun. He gets a nod in reply, and the cart draws to a sullen halt, the wheels sinking deep into the mud as they stop. The horse, awakening from his dream, casts his eyes about for food. Blinkers be damned. The passenger alights, leaving all baggage aside from the books behind, and lands in the morass beneath him with an amused chuckle. Worn boots bear the brunt of the muck, a leather overcoat takes on the rest. He turns his face to the driver and smiles, tips his head, but whatever silent question is asked it goes unanswered, and the driver cracks the reins and drives horse and carriage on. Alone now, the passenger turns about, gets his bearings, a weathervane in search of a breeze, and begins to walk towards the chapel, wide brimmed hat shielding him from a cold sun. He takes his time over the journey, each leaf on each tree seems to interest him intently, each carved stone and protection an amusement, the smile never leaving his face. Now and then he asks a passerby about a carving, about a charm, and though few reply he never loses his enthusiasm for the question. There is no shortage of sign and symbol for this new guest to sink his teeth in and by the time he has reached the chapel wall the whole village has been picked over. At the lychgate he sits on the coffin stone, takes a notebook from his library-stack and writes in the shade of the slate covered roof. Considering the enormous care that he has taken to observe everything on his journey up, he shows little interest in the chapel now he is here. Perhaps it is too familiar. He does not look at the shattered roof, the broken windows, doesn't marvel that the bell still somehow hangs on its rope from an unsnapped centre beam. No. He has, it seems, found where he would like to be. Under the shade of the lychgate, making his notes and listening. Listening to the voices he hears echo from inside the chapel, for whilst the door is closed the roof is open and the two men at work have never been the self-conscious sort.

'She could be here, helping. Seeing as she did it. Considering what she can do. I could ask her if—'

'Quiet. We don't need her. Or her help.'

'She's not all that bad, Luk. We could do worse than ask.'

'Ask what, Yestin? She's a witch. You've heard her going on, asking about her grandmother.' It's true, Nancy has been asking around. 'Dad said her grandmother was the worst of them, the witches. Heard this one man she felled by speaking his name into the cup of an acorn. Down he went like a calf under the hammer, told me she kept a man chained by the river, just out of reach of the flow. And he got so thirsty he stretched and stretched 'til he was nothing but throat and slipped like an eel out of his clothes, into the river. Heard she waited until he was deep in the silt then....'

'I don't know about that,' you can hear the doubt in the space between the words, 'Nancy's not a witch, Luk, she saved me, from those things that took Jan. I'd be lying next to him if it wasn't for her. You saw the body.'

Luk Calder shivers, hopes his brother doesn't see. Since that night Nancy has been spending more time in the village, asking around. Each night in the Nest now a contest for the best story, and though none present remember much, it doesn't stop them trying. Without the Reverend, and with his father ill, there is no one to challenge her. His brother lost to her cult like the rest, no matter that without her meddling there'd have been no monster to take his brother in the first place. No, Luk has had enough; he still has a sore shoulder where Nancy threw him into the door of the longhouse. His ego is bruised worse.

'Enough. Get on with your work, that is how you help, our father's near bankrupt himself to bring God back to this valley, we'd do well to remember that without him we'd be saddled again with some Lord. Our working here reminds those who've forgotten just who it is that butters their bread. Gives their idle hands some purpose. Now do your part and stop spreading children's stories. You shouldn't be listening to a word she says. Having anything to do with her. Don't think I've missed that bruised lip, Yestin. You been training with her again?'

Yestin looks away from his brother.

'No.'

'Liar.'

'Am not.' This childish squabbling seems odd coming from men this old. But family cuts through time as easily as a tusker through peat and Luk has hit a nerve. He knows this. And presses on it.

'Do you enjoy them? Her blows? Do you like being made a fool of? Get you going, does it?'

'What? Shut up, Luk. You don't know what you're talking about. She saved dad, that night. Saved me.'

'Saved him from what she brought. Her and Pel.'

The two brothers are amongst the Sunday congregation. Sitting in the pews with their eyes to an empty lectern. Cleaver's sins, the people he killed through his madness and grief, erased in favour of an easier narrative. It is compelling, this seed of mistruth, but it has not fully taken root in Yestin. He's seen the monsters, smelt their breath.

'Maybe,' he whispers it to himself, 'maybe not.'

'What was that, Yestin?' The whisper not quite quiet enough, words echo in this empty house and Luk has heard enough. 'Put down the broom, Yestin. Come over here. If you're good enough to teach that witch, I'd like a lesson too.'

Yestin looks to the shadows, wishing Jan was still here. Jan who had sometimes stepped in to defend him, but he is not. It is only Luk that stands here now. His older brother's mouth is set firm, though it curls into the smoke of a smile at the edges. Yestin knows that look. The ghosts of bruises long vanished reappear and he knows there's no escaping what's next. Luk pulls sacks of rubble to the side of the chapel. Only one pew survived last year's fight and this he does take care with, drags it carefully and leaves it out of harm's way, by the door. The brothers, with some men from the farm, have been working hard and though there is still much to do, they've cleared the rubble, the broken joists, swept the floor clean. The broken stones and splintered wood piled up around the edges leaving a space clear at the centre. A boxing ring whose floor is a patchwork of well-worn tomb tops, ledger stones. Chipped here and there, the slate cracked in places but holding, firm enough to fight on, the one broken the year before replaced with a blank that's yet to be engraved. Luk removes his shirt and tosses it across a broken pew end, his piety only skin deep when he's itching for a fight. And he is burning for this one.

'Come on Yestin, fight me. Show me what you show her. I never knew you were such a bruiser, I'm eager to see it.'

Yestin, fists up, steps uneasily into this makeshift ring.

'What about the bodies? It's disrespectful.' A long shot, a miss.

Luk glares at his brother. His jaw moves as though he is chewing on words.

'They are bones. Bones and dust. Leave them be and I doubt they'll bother you.'

In the rafters above, in the spaces below, bets are made. Ledgers marked. Piskies and spriggans lean back against the stonework and wait for blood to flow. Since the chapel fell, they've luxuriated in their new freedom. They could never enter before. There's usually a crowd here, invisible to most, and today their interest has paid off. They swap bags of quartz stone and play at bookmaking. Yestin, his own shirt removed now, stands in stark contrast to his brother. Though both men are tall and broad, Luk owns and inhabits his body in a way Yestin does not. His body feels lodged in; the rent barely made. They circle each other, as fighting men have always done, and where Luk is looking for an entry point, Yestin looks for a way out.

'Enough, brother. Come on now, please. I'm sorry, I won't train with Nancy again, I won't.'

'You're right. Yestin, you won't speak to that witch again. But a lesson needs teaching before it's learned. Dad should have put a stop to this. I should have put a stop to this.'

Luk lunges, his fist connecting with the side of Yestin's head, and the younger man goes down, hard. For reasons best known to himself—he could lie still and hasten this—Yestin stands and swings back. There is something to be said for being an underdog. After his initial hit, Luk had turned, confident his job was done, so the swinging arm of his brother comes as a shock and sends him sprawling onto a pile of consecrated masonry that is stacked in the corner. Luk grazes his cheek on a granite cross and a scale of lime whitewash, made heavy from years of overpainting, flakes from the west wall.

A peephole for a very old eye. Pressed to the plaster to watch the fight.

There are silent gasps from the rafters and the only piskie to bet on Yestin grins and eyes the quartz. Luk is a man barely held together at the best of times, it would have taken less than this to crack him, and when he turns, he is a thunderstorm. Yestin takes a step back; he had not expected his brother to fall and does not know what to do with the situation. He is still raising hands in surrender when Luk charges, driving arms around his brothers waist and hurling him to the ground.

'What can you be teaching that witch, Yestin?' A fist to the jaw of his brother. 'How to hit a man when he's not looking?

She knows that one.' Another fist, the same face. 'And what does she pay for these lessons with?' He has grabbed Yestin's collar, and his brother hangs limply from his grip.

'She doesn't pay—'

'I know what she pays with Yestin.' Luk pushes his brother down, standing over him. His voice is quiet now and it slides its way into Yestin's ears like a poisoned knife. 'I *know.*'

Where it comes from, neither brother knows, but at this Yestin draws the line.

'Enough!' As he rises, he twists, and Luk is sent spiralling for a second time. He lands heavily against a pillar, carved green men gurning above and underfolk howling in the rafters. The impact was enough to dislodge the bell and it crashes with a toll into the floor, breaking in two on impact. Its dying peals ring in time on the match.

'This is your fault.' Yestin speaks first, voice trembling.

'How?'

'Ours then. Both of us. I *told* you we shouldn't fight.'

Luk scowls at his younger brother.

'It was an accident. Waiting to happen. We should have taken the bell down when we arrived. That's on us. This was an accident, Yestin. Wipe that stupid look off your face.'

'Perhaps Nancy could fix it?'

'I'll not call that witch in here, Yestin. Don't make me explain that again…'

THE MAN OUTSIDE stands. Closes his book. Walks towards the chapel door and heaves it open. He glances up, taking in the state of the ceiling perhaps, the faces in the plaster, but his gaze is lingering long enough to make the Underfolk in the galleries uncomfortable. Especially when he smiles and tips his hat (though he is, reassuringly, looking in the wrong direction). Ignoring the bickering brothers, the man looks at the wall exposed by the falling lime. The startled eye of a deer stares back. He steps unsteadily over the rubble and, taking a pocketknife from his coat, picks away at the edges of the lime, another sheet falls, loosened by the events of the past year, and the rest of the painted deer is revealed. The man makes a satisfied noise and turns, grinning, to the brothers Calder, coated in dust and staring at the intruder they have just now noticed.

'Pardon me,' the man shows no fear though the two men are advancing. They do not like to be disturbed. They pause however, as he slips his coat from his shoulders, hanging it on the only remaining pew. They stare at his throat, at the white bands that are tied around it. 'My name is Pine-Coffin. Reverend Abraham Pine-Coffin. Delighted to meet you, I'm sure. Now, boys, I have two questions. Who painted this,' he points to the deer, 'and what's all this talk of a witch?'

AGRIMONY

DESPITE HER NIGHT at the Nest, Nancy is tired. She stares with naked envy at Patroclus who is, once again, fast asleep by the fire.

'Is there a single worry in that head?' she asks the gently snoring pile, but there is no response. Brownies scurry about her, coffee on and a lunch laid out, a bottle of gorse wine, too. This is a new development. She had left out a book of herbalism and the brownies had taken to the chapters on alcohol. Nancy swallows hard at the memory of previous experiments, the exploding nettle beer and the beetroot schnapps. The wine, however, is quite good. Like the gorse flowers it has been brewed from it is amber, coconut scented and sweet. Nancy sits at the table and butters some bread, then talks into the corners.

'Thanks, loves, I appreciate it.' The brownies do not respond, but she likes to be grateful. They have worked hard, this last year, to help her with the cottage. Her new role as Keeper had meant some changes were needed. The house had been her mother's, and Nancy had lived here as a child before she had died, when she was first apprenticed to Pel. After that she had moved in with the old Keeper, locking the cottage up tight and trapping the memories inside. Even after she had returned, when she had grown up and needed her own space, she had not altered much. She had rarely been home anyway. It was only after Pel died that she felt able to make it her own.

After Pel died.

She knows Madge is right. Knows she has to accept it. She knows his body is beneath the water of the fellmire, the flesh loosening its grip from the bone like a drowning man slips from a wreck, she knows it is gone and even if she knows too his spirit is below, where it ought not be, joined to the husk of a faded god half mad with age it is not here with her. She cannot talk to him. Cannot sit with him of an evening. So fine. 'Pel died' it is. She is Keeper now. Not him. His parting gift to her and she sits here, alone.

'What a thing to leave me, Pel.' She looks around the cottage again. It is similar to those in Mirecoombe, slightly larger perhaps. Unlike its cousins in the village, Nancy's cottage has a separate kitchen. A range instead of a cloam oven built into the fire. A separate living room too, though the settee shares the space with a bath. The walls outside and in are painted white and upstairs are two bedrooms, one hers, the other empty. She has only recently begun to question this. Her mother took in washing, her father worked the fields; this house is more than they ought to have been able to afford. But, with all the people she could have asked gone, she has buried her questions with the dead.

For a while, after Pel's death, after the sinking of his boat, Nancy had tried to make her house like his. To line her walls and clutter her shelves with trophies taken. It had not taken long to know it was not for her. Like his old coat, the life of a Keeper had needed alterations before it would fit. Aside from the fact that Pel's wooden house with its keel hauled roof was larger, more spacious than her own low-ceilinged cottage, she simply didn't have the heart to fill it in the way he would.

Or rather, she had too much of one. The creatures she had put back this last year she saw with love, with pity. Children playing in a garden that was no longer theirs. Where Pel would take a cast of a claw, prise a horn from a skull and hang it on his wall, Nancy couldn't bear it. But she had wanted to remember, so she had asked Madge to teach her to draw. It had been clumsy, at first, but Nancy has given up at very little in her life and now, after a year, she enjoys making her sketches. They hang on the walls, reminders of victories, yes. A reminder too of the world below, and the creatures and spirits that lived there. In charcoal, they range across her wall. The last of the wish hounds – put back with care, it was split from its pack and howling with sadness. There are portraits too, of friends and neighbours. Madge's face sketched one night at the Nest. Delen Rowe and Billy Askell. Underfolk and moor folk side by side, her twin charges. She has drawn Callum and Jacob Cleaver, too. She doesn't want to forget them, either. There is a whole stack of the girl who tattooed her—she can't get the face right, it slips from her mind—but she still keeps trying to catch that smile. She had felt so comfortable with her. They had shared something so intimate, so beautiful. Nancy still wears the blackthorn hairpin she left her. Its two sharp tines remind her of the girl's needles. The wood carries the scent of her hair.

When she had recovered from Callum, from Pel, she had made alterations. Distractions from a hole she's yet to fill. She had a cabinet built, a man from the village came and fitted it against the rough granite walls so the wood and stone joins like a puzzle piece. The lower draws flat and wide and full of maps. The upper ones, small boxes, hundreds of them, fronted with brass handles and an insert for a name card. They are full of charms and wards, full of dried flowers and bones, full of traps. Once the cabinet maker had left the brownies had tinkered, fitted locks, and now the drawers will open at the slightest touch of Nancy's hand and no one else's.

Nancy pulls a stack of rough paper towards her, the sheet's deckled edges like surf on a shore and she reaches for the small tobacco tin, Pel's tin, in which she keeps the sticks of charcoal she draws with; collected from the terrible fire a year ago. The fire that burnt so many of her friends. Each drawing an act of remembrance. Below her charcoal blackened hands, as they move across the paper, Hilla and Stag emerge. It helps, this laying down of marks. Tracing the lines of Stag's antlers, the swell of Hilla's chest and stomach. Pel had not connected with those he was employed to help. Neither the villagers nor the Underfolk. Nancy feels the needs of both pressing on her heart like pins, she is reminded of her duty to them with every heartbeat.

There is a commotion outside the door as the last stroke is finished and Nancy leaves Hilla and Stag on the table. Small hands remove the paper, to be taken away and framed, then hung on the wall with the rest. How the brownies achieve this endeavour, the glazing and woodwork involved, below the floors, is anybody's guess and Nancy long since stopped asking those questions. Crossing to the door, Nancy stops and asks the visitor to announce themselves. She has learnt the hard way to ask first before opening. For every call for help, with a creature like Hilla and her brother, a roaming wish hound, there has been a call for something else. Nancy does not know if it is because she is a woman, and people lack imagination, but she is plagued by requests for charms. Love spells. Curses. Because whilst some of the village use her as their Keeper, there are some that only see her as a witch. She has had men here pleading that she kills another's horse. To make a woman love someone she doesn't. And though she refuses each one, it's not stopped rumours spreading. Not stopped people banging on her door and blaming her for every little misfortune that's befallen them. It is maddening. She even caught Annie Bolan driving a hobnail through her shadow whilst she waited for Selkie to be shod. Said it was to lift the evil eye, stop her family from being overlooked. Silly girl had been lucky the smith had finished and brought Selkie round the front or Nancy might have had stronger words than she did. Not to mention the endless devotees of whichever little cult had most recently emerged. Asking for her patronage, her endorsement. No. She had learnt not to open the door unless she was sure of what waited on the other side. There had been no answer, so she asks again.

'Who's there?'

Nothing but the sound of brawling. Nancy opens the door, hand clawed in the shape of a spell. There, by the brook, three creatures are fighting. Two are covered in lank weed, sopping wet and biting needled teeth into the arms of a creature she knows. A creature trying to wrench something small from wet weedy hands.

'Knot! What is going on?' The scuffling stops, and as the creature known as Knot tears his arm free of the teeth, the two attackers flee. Leaping like two raindrops into the running water and gone into the stream. Knot stands, rubbing bleeding arms, and Nancy waits for an answer.

'Hello mine Ancy!' This is a recent development. A pet name Nancy has worked hard not to be lumbered with. 'I did not see you there.' Nancy narrows her eyes. Knot doesn't fit into any box she's found, and he has shown up sporadically this past year. Rarely in a helpful manner. She believes him to be a pisky, of a sort, though Knot has no wings. And unlike his cousins, whose skin is soft, whose veins shine through translucent skin, Knot seems made of stronger stuff. His skin is like burnished wood laid as a veneer over his organs. Moss grows across him in the semblance of an outfit, and beetles scurry now and then from Knot's back.

'What's going on, Knot? Who were they? They were buccas, were they not? Enough with the Ancy business, too.'

Knot nods, obsequiously.

'A familiarity is all, a slip of the tongue. I recall when all Nancys were Agnes, all Agnes were Annis, all Annis were Ancy. But I understand. You are a modern woman; I shall try and desist.'

'The bucca, Knot.'

'Little wet buggers. Two lost fishes making a sharkful of trouble. I was coming, as I do, to see you mine Ancy, apologies. *Nancy*. And they was sneaking around your door. Trying take advantage of a, forgive me, inexperienced Keeper. Testing the edges.'

The imp skips from foot to foot with his arms behind his back but Nancy sees through him.

'What have you got there, Knot? Show me.' Knot twists and scowls but acquiesces, holds out his open palm to reveal a shark egg, a mermaid's purse.

'I would have given it to you, mine Ancy, I promise you.' Knot sweeps his hands before him in an obsequious bow and Nancy waves him off. Skin crawling.

'Right. Well, you have now. Be on your way.'

'I had heard some more about this, Mother? Was it? Thought you might like to know.' Nancy stiffens.

'What now, Knot? Let me think, what wonderful nuggets have you left me so far? Can it possibly beat "she's in the air" or, "her voice runs in the rock" or my personal favourite "she's the past and future, she's no time at all".'

Knot scowls, his little mossy face scrunching like a tangle of weed. Nancy ignores him. She has asked him repeatedly about the Mother, this past year, and not once has he come close to an answer.

'What is it, Knot? What do you know?'

Nancy shifts in the doorway, a shiver running the length of her spine. Knot has a glint in his eye she likes not one bit.

'She's coming.'

'I know that, Knot. *I* told *you* that.'

'Yes, but now others are saying it. All over. I spoke to a spriggan so old he's fused to the rocks; he says he remembers Her. Scared, he was.'

Knot pushes past her and walks into the cottage, ambling about, tracing a finger across the furnishings. Patroclus growls from his bed.

'He said she was one of the old kind, mine Ancy. Says she's been sleeping but something,' he gives her a patronising look, 'has woken Her.'

This is new. Solid. Information, not the whispers of spirits.

'Can I talk to this spriggan?' Nancy ignores Knot's—clearly deliberate—naming slip. She needs information. Knot turns with a tragedian's mask, face contorted into some foul approximation of sorrow.

'Alas, no. He did not last long after our encounter. Terribly tired, he was, so he left for the Undermoor.'

'Convenient, how often your sources vanish.'

'Oh, mine Ancy, you wound me. I am trying to assist! He did say one last thing though. Will I tell you, or will you keep up this unfortunate attitude?' Nancy clenches her fists and pictures Patroclus tearing Knot to bits. It helps.

RAGWORT

'Please, Knot. Go on.' Knot smiles. An overripe sloe, the skin finally burst. Fleshy, wet, studded with seedlike teeth. It is the least pleasant thing Nancy has seen this week, and that's a high bar.

'There is one who knows more of Her, much more, but they're gone, now. What a sorrowful world!' Knot jumps up onto the kitchen table and sits, swinging his legs. Nancy is going to have to extract these teeth herself.

'Who is gone, Knot?'

Bored again, Knot is down and wandering, trying the drawers in the cabinet, tugging at both lock and magic to try and shake them loose. It is not working.

'Stop that. Behave, Knot. Don't forget I'm the Keeper here.' The creature turns with an impish smile and walks towards the door. Patroclus growls as he passes.

'Is that so, mine Ancy? A Keeper's such a little thing, in such a big world. Mark you might aim higher. I knew your grandmother. She was fond of old Knot. Mighty fond. I knew her well. You remind me of her, I knew it as soon as I saw you riding towards those devils last year. I thought, perhaps...'

'What has my grandmother got to do with any of this? She's dead, Knot.' Then, quieter, 'Everyone's dead.'

Knot swings himself to the floor now and rummages through the jars on the counter. Sucking honey and spices from his probing fingers. Brownies peer out and shake their heads at the impertinence. But they do nothing. Nancy too is silent.

'Was just thinking of her, is all. She used to tell tales about the most marvellous things. I wonder...' Knot sidles up to Nancy's side, face contorted in pantomime thought. 'No. It is no good to dwell. I do worry, though, *Nancy*,' he watches her as he speaks her name. Waits for her to acknowledge his effort. 'Perhaps this Mother comes to take the valley in hand, away from one so…' he looks out through the window and moves to leave, '…young. She's getting closer, She is. I can feel Her, I think. Pressing on my skull, we all can. Oh! It hurts!' He clutches his head. 'Mine Ancy, please, I must go.' Knot bows and scampers from the cottage leaving the Keeper and her dog alone.

'What now, Pat?' The dog looks up with rheumy eyes and whines. Nancy stops stroking him, stands, and with shaking breaths, she forces herself to focus on the dried and brittle mermaid's purse, its tendrils curled at the tips. Nancy lifts it carefully and holds it up to the light. Illuminated, the colour seems painted on in streaks, and something is silhouetted within. Taking a knife from her waist Nancy makes a slit, just a small one, and tips the purse, arm outstretched, ready for whatever new horror lies within. There is a thud as it slides from its casing.

A man's signet ring. Silver. The seal in the setting a three tined spear and on the reverse, engraved in the metal, initials. Pel's initials. Nancy sighs and looks through the wind-stained windows at the tired spring sun.

'What now, Pel? What have you done now?'

WILD STRAWBERRY

THE NEST IS filling slowly, the surrounding moorland funnelling workers into its open doors like water flowing into a drain. The drinkers are tired. They move from door to bar then cluster in corners, separating into their factions of faith and talk quietly amongst themselves. The little cross talk there is revolves around work. Who's grazing what where, whose fences keep failing. Who's cutting turf too early or too much. Who has gone a valley away to sieve metal from stone? They are almost all men. Their wives and daughters, their sisters, at home. Preparing meals or working, still, keeping the year's wheel turning. Though a few would come later. Some to drink themselves, some to collect someone who ought to stop.

At the bar, at the stools they occupy every day, are two old men. Hunched over drinks and not talking quietly. The man on the left is Cusk, his first name is Donyerth, but there's not a soul on the moor who could tell you that. Not even the man sitting next to him, and they've known each other a lifetime. Locryn Calder. Father once to three sons, owner of half the valley and the man responsible for much of its bounty and strife. Cusk is his farm manager. Though the man has not done much to earn his keep in that regard for a decade or two. Nowadays his job is to keep Locryn company while his boys are busy. A job that has been more important than ever this last year. The events of the previous spring, the destruction of the chapel and the betrayal and death of the Reverend have left their mark on everyone here. But the mark Locryn Calder carries—the death of his son Jan, the betrayal of the Reverend—burns like a brand, and it hasn't cooled yet. However much he douses it.

'Another, Madge.'

'Maybe in a moment, Locryn. Your sons will be done soon, wait for them, eh?'

Locryn Calder raises his head and glares at Madge Gould as she dances in front of him, he blinks to steady her in his mind, there are words emerging, but they do so slowly. They rise like gas in his throat. The other drinkers turn to watch. This is not the first time this song has played. But no. Cusk lays a hand on his old friend's arm and looks to Madge.

'Pour him another, Madge. I'll see to him.'

The landlady refills the old man's glass and nods at Cusk.

'See you do.'

The room relapses into the briefest, smallest sliver of peace. Until the door opens, and the Reverend Abraham Pine-Coffin walks into it. He does not wear the leather coat any longer. Though it was fun, wrongfooting the Calder boys at the chapel, honesty is his watchword, and he wants people to see. To see the white bands at his neck, the wide brimmed hat on his head. To see his single breasted, thirty-nine buttoned, lamp black cassock cinctured at the waist with a black leather belt and silver buckle. His white shirt cuffs peering from his sleeves, and his polished black shoes miraculously clean considering the roads outside.

His arrival splits the room like an axe in firewood. Some stand, extend hands and smile to welcome him. Others gasp, a few leave. Considering the dramatic end to their last minister, and the divergences in their resulting faith, it is hard to blame them.

Those who have kept the faith, at least a version of it, draw out chairs and beckon him hungrily to sit. Starved of a confessor, they open to him eagerly. Keen to show this new Reverend they've been doing their best. Spilling their stories uncontrolled. Like children keeping secrets. He sits at every table that wants him, shakes every outstretched hand. He listens, intently, with a smile on his face to every little peccadillo of faith the village has for him. He nods, frowns and smiles at each new twist of devotion and takes out his notebook more than once. Leaving everyone, even those who did not invite him to their table, with the distinct feeling they had been listened to. He does not blanche when old Sawyer Cann tells him of the prayers he speaks to spirits in the apple trees, nods politely as Nell Garner explains just why she makes her dolls. Smiles just as politely at those who turn away, who won't meet his eye. Even stays stalwart when Mervyn Adse spits at his feet. When he is done with his rounds, he takes a seat at the bar with a sigh and a smile and lays both palms on the copper top.

'Mr Calder, a pleasure sir. I've been chatting to your sons, at the chapel. I'm the new Reverend. Some interesting developments I think you'll be most interested in. Lovely boys. They'll be back soon I suspect, I'm afraid I sent them off to my cottage with a package. What are you drinking? May I join you?'

The priest talks at a gallop and if Calder took in a single word, he does not show it, but Cusk extends an open palm behind his friend's back, which Pine-Coffin shakes.

'Cusk, I apologise for my friend. He will want to introduce himself properly to you, I'm sure. In the morning, I suspect.'

Madge does not look up but smiles. Cusk rarely says more

than a word or two in succession so to have been witness to several sentences in one evening is quite the revelation. Pine-Coffin continues unabashed, still gripping Cusk's hand.

'No matter! None at all. The Calders-Two have been filling me in a little on their father's troubles. I quite understand. I was very sorry to hear of Jan, Mr. Calder, I will pray for him.' Calder grunts, and the Reverend turns to face the landlady. 'Mrs Gould?'

'Miss.'

'Yes, quite, a pleasure to meet you. Pine-Coffin, Reverend Pine-Coffin. I have heard much about you too.' Madge narrows her eyes at this. The younger Calders are even less talkative than Cusk, so the wealth of information they seem to have dispersed to the new Reverend in a single afternoon is remarkable, if not outright suspicious. Though if he spoke at this rate to them, perhaps they gave her up just to stop him talking.

'Might I have a drink? An ale is fine, whatever these kind men are drinking. Unless you have wine? No? Ale then, would be perfection.' The priest blushes. She sees him then for what he is, a boy in an oversized suit he's hoping to grow into.

Madge raises an eyebrow as she goes about the business of pouring a glass. She slides the drink across the bar and meets the Reverend's gaze. It is like staring at two gemstones. Even in the dim light of the pub they shine, the flecks of orange catching the light and shining like gold dust. The more she looks into them, the more she likes them, against her better judgement. Dangerous, eyes like that, they remind her of another's gaze and his was dangerous enough with one. These are kinder, though.

'Here, Reverend. On me. You've met the village, then? Don't mind their talk they…'

He stills her with a smile.

'Not at all! The church has a rich history of dissenters and separatists. Why we've seen Ranters and Ravers, Barrowists and Diggers and Grindletonians, not to mention Swedenborg's crowd. It is, frankly, a delight to hear such initiative being taken here. In the absence of other, channels, so to speak.'

'I must say I am surprised. The church isn't often so quick to accept these things. Quick to do anything, in fact. I'm surprised you have arrived so soon.'

Pine-Coffin does not break his gaze but lifts his drink and toasts Madge before taking a drink and barely suppressing a grimace.

'Lovely. No, you are right, Miss Gould, you are absolutely right. An unwieldy beast and slow to turn, that is our church. Quite correct. And were things to have been left to their own devices, I suspect you would not have seen the hint of a cassock until much later in the year. No. I requested this post as soon as I saw it. Snapped it up. Though I did not have to beat off any opposition. And now, here I am. Your parish now mine.'

The Reverend's scattershot conversation has thrown the normally unshakeable Madge Gould off balance, and she has not thought of replying before the young priest is on his feet making the rounds again. Shaking more hands. He is almost done with his ministrations when the door opens again, and Luk and Yestin come in. They look to the Reverend like schoolchildren who have done as they were told and have now returned for a reward. Pine-Coffin does not disappoint.

'Boys!' The two grown men look at their shoes and shuffle awkwardly. 'You're done for the day?' Two heads nod. 'Excellent! Well then, you must let me buy you a drink or two. Your father is, as you said, at the bar. Sit, sit, I'll get them in.' Luk and Yestin move to the bar, glancing occasionally at Madge, who is smirking. They sit, and she places a drink before each.

'Here boys. Mind how you go though, your father might need taking home, soon.'

Luk glances at his father who has not greeted his sons. Cusk twitches out a smile.

'Just the one, Madge, I think.' Luk elbows his brother, and Yestin takes his point. 'Thank you, Reverend.'

Pine-Coffin smiles.

'My pleasure! Do you know, Mr. Calder, your sons have been very helpful today? As I arrived they had discovered, in their vigour, the most remarkable thing in the chapel…'

The Reverend is cut off by a slurring from Locryn Calder.

'The chapel? We're fixing it. For the new Reverend.'

'Yes, quite. Perhaps I was hasty over my introductions. I've been told I speak rather quickly. "Listen faster!" that's what I used to say. Ha-ha, but now I see that I have misled you in my haste. Anyway, this discovery…'

Calder stares dully at Pine-Coffin who continues to prattle on, oblivious, it seems, of the growing confusion and rage in his audience.

'Cleaver? Jacob?' Locryn Calder peers with drunken eyes at the priest.

Calder's sons rise as one, downing their drinks as they do so. Luk places a firm hand on his father's shoulder. The old farmer shrugs him off.

'Dead. You're dead!' He jabs a finger hard into Pine-Coffin's chest, sweat and dirt streaking across the black of the young priest's cassock.

This, at last, stops the Reverend talking. He whitens at the misunderstanding, lays his hand timidly on the smudged black cloth. His excitement at his finds fading in the presence of reality.

'Oh dear, I see, no, sir. Not him.' The Reverend steps back from the bar, as Yestin Calder shepherds his father towards the door.

'Come on dad, let's get you home. Reverend, it was good to meet you, forgive him. He's tired.'

'Yes. Of course, boys, of course. I—I look forward to getting reacquainted with him soon. Mr—Cusk? Was it? Will you help them please, it seems Mr. Calder is a handful even for his sons.'

Cusk glares at the Reverend for questioning his loyalty. He was already getting to his feet. Because Calder was a handful, at times. He was old, yes, but he had spent his decades working hard and the old man's muscles were strong. And when his head was clouded, they worked on memory. And those muscles remembered fighting.

Like some infernal creature, the tangle of Calders and Cusk roll from the Nest in a cloud of blows and curses. A large number of the other drinkers rise to follow. There will be dinner waiting on tables at home and besides, the stage show has been taken outside. Once the dust has settled, apart from one or two quiet drinkers who have nobody waiting at home, it is just the Reverend and Madge in the bar. Madge rubs her bad arm distractedly; after the events of the previous year, the fight, Nancy's accidental injuring of her, she is not what she was. The muscles have knit back together poorly, and they ache.

'My!' Pine-Coffin sits and sips at an untouched beer. 'Quite the thing. I fear I did not help things there, Miss Gould. Not a bit. It is a habit of mine, I fear.'

Madge says nothing, though she dampens a rag and slides it over the bar. Pine-Coffin dabs at the grease on his chest with cautious taps.

'You know, Miss Gould, I have found in my parishes that the local tavern is an excellent place to get to know a community. I hope we will be firm friends.'

Madge continues her work, but her silence does not affect Pine-Coffin.

'I'm sure we will. An interesting name for an Inn, Miss Gould. Where does it come from?'

'My father named it.'

'Ah! Interesting. Interesting. I like it, I like it very much.' The Reverend remains seated as Madge goes about collecting tankards.

'Were you friends with my predecessor? Mr. Cleaver?'

Madge stiffens.

'I knew him, Reverend. Yes.'

'Yes? I did not. I read some of his letters to the Bishop in Exeter, he's a friend of my father's you see. He seems to have been a passionate man.'

'He was that. Yes. He did what he felt best. He believed strongly about the church.'

'An admirable quality indeed. And he died? Suddenly? It was not clearly recorded. I don't mean to pry, I'm just curious, that is all. I thought perhaps we would have a monument to him in the chapel.'

Madge places the empty glasses down and turns to face the Reverend. She will hold his gaze for this.

'Reverend Pine-Coffin. I was a friend to Jacob Cleaver for half his life, and I loved him dearly. But he cost this valley a great deal. I hope you are not here to cost us what we have left. Do what you want in the chapel, those that will come to hear you would like him remembered there. But you've a hard hill to climb if its Mirecoombe's heart you're after, and Cleaver has cast you to the bottom of it.'

There is movement on the Reverend's face, as though he is chewing on a smile, and his eyes flash with something impish.

'I've climbed out of worse, Miss Gould, far worse.'

Madge softens a little. Besides, history is one thing, she can't refuse the business.

'You don't appear to me making much headway on the drink, Reverend. Here, let me pour you another.'

She lifts a dusty bottle from below the bar and pours a glass of claret into an equally dusty cut crystal glass. Pine-Coffin smiles, wipes the rim with his handkerchief and takes a sip.

'Thank you, Miss Gould, but you didn't answer my question. How did the Reverend Cleaver die?'

Madge sighs deeply. Closes her eyes. Behind them she sees broken glass and falling stonework. The jagged memory of Cleaver's son as he lurched across the floor of the chapel. She had not been there, at the end, but Nancy had told her what happened. Cleaver's ending of it. The killing of his son. The sinking of them both.

'He drowned in the mire, Reverend. On the moor. Searching for something.'

The Reverend Pine-Coffin sips his wine and stares at Madge. She can feel his eyes burning her, scouring the shadows for the hint of a lie. But there is none. She told the truth. Or a facet of it.

'A shame. A terrible shame. Well, I shall oversee something appropriate, in his memory. Thank you for telling me, Madge.'

She notices this sudden familiarity. Unasked for, unearned. But she does not mind, and it surprises her.

'Madge, where would I find a Miss Bligh?'

Ah. There it is. The point of this conversation has finally been reached.

'Who?' Madge can't muster the sincerity for deception, but she goes through the motions regardless. Of course those idiot Calders told him about her.

'Miss Nancy Bligh, Madge. I believe the two of you are friends. She is some sort of local—medicine woman? Pellar? Forgive me, I don't know the reginal term.'

Yes, you do, thinks Madge Gould. Those eyes know most things, she suspects. Possibly even before the Calders told them.

'She is our Keeper, Reverend. She does heal, and help, but she does more besides.'

'A Keeper! How quaint. You'll forgive me a moment.' Pine-Coffin reaches into his cassock for the journal he keeps at his side. 'I like to keep track of these, idioms, I suppose. Don't mind me, Madge! It is just a quirk of my character. I do so like to know things.'

'It's Miss Gould, Reverend.' The ease she had felt before is gone now. The void filled with a rushing suspicion that cascades like a torrent in her ears.

'Quite. My apologies Madge—Miss Gould. I must seem appallingly inquisitive. It's a flaw, I'll admit it. I would like to meet her, Miss Bligh that is. Your Keeper. Where does she live?'

You know full well, thinks Madge. Her aversion to the Reverend's gaze has not diminished, but she holds it now.

'On the moor, Reverend. Though she'll be in the village by and by, I'm sure you'll run into her. I wouldn't go off looking though. It's dangerous, the moor. We wouldn't want to lose another minister so soon.' It is an empty threat, and Madge regrets it. But he has penned her in, and she'll go down swinging if she has to, bad arm be damned. But he does not press the point.

'No. I suppose not. Well, Miss Gould, I'll be on my way.' He finishes the wine, straightens the hat on his head and stands to leave. When he lifts his chin, the brim of the hat rings his head like a black halo. His blonde hair shining below, eyes rekindled, and the trace of a smile beneath. 'If you see Miss Bligh, send her my way. I've taken the Reverend Cleaver's old cottage, at the west of the village. And Miss Gould, please call me Bram. Short for Abraham. I am determined, you see, that we will be friends.'

And he sweeps out into the sunshine with a smile on his face. He leaves the door ajar, and Madge listens to him walk away. Listens to the birdsong, listens to the strange melody that is sung through open windows by women cleaning away plates. Feeding the geese with the scrapings. Madge begins to hum it, too, and turns back to the glasses behind the bar.

'This village needs more than a friend, young Reverend. Far more.'

FELONWOOD

CLEAVER'S COTTAGE IS a ghost. A shade. Every room colder than the last. The old Reverend had not lived in it for years, moving himself instead to his anchorite cell behind the chapel. As Abraham Pine-Coffin steps from the sun scorched moor into its dark granite interior, the young man shivers.

'Come now Bram. It is your own, at least.' In the darkness he can make out the shape of his trunk, left here by the cart driver. Charon, Abraham had been privately calling him. His very own ferryman to this dark wet shore. He looks, hungrily, at his notebook, laid on the bare kitchen table. It must wait. Besides, he needs light. Leaving the cottage door open he drags his chest into the rectangle of dying sun that the cottage has permitted inside. He moves his hands across the front of the chest, and after a series of clicks, the lid springs open.

The Reverend smiles every time this happens.

'Most satisfactory.' He speaks quickly and clearly, even when alone. On top of the folded clothes and books is his tinderbox. It is a treasure. Not for him the simple metal cannisters or plain wooden boxes, no. Frankly, little he owns is simple. He makes no bones about his past. Understands his privilege. The allowance from his father quite sufficient to pad the harder edges of the ministry. His travelling cases from Bond St. His cassocks tailored by Gieves & Hawkes. He has travelled, Abraham, too. Far further than he might have made it on the church's coin. His father's endowments, enough to build a small but ornate church meant that Abraham was given free reign when it came to choosing assignments. He has visited countries few in England have heard of, a few that have yet to make it to a map. He has studied the folklore and religions of the world and knows a thing or two. Does not know far more. Has learnt to enter with an open mind and a smile for the shadows. And he has collected things. Idols and carvings, scrolls and books. This tinder box he collected in Holland, and it is beautiful. Carved with intricate crosses, with florid scrolls, it is excruciatingly ornate. Even the base has carved into it his initials and family crest. The top is carved with a stylised flame. He slides the drawer from the base. Inside sits a candle stub, a flint, and the steel. His is fashioned like a whale, the tail curving neatly around his clenched fingers so the body of the beast lies within his knuckles. Beneath them is the folded charcloth waiting for a spark. He gets one soon enough and quickly lights the taper, inhales the sulphurous smoke, and lights the stub of candle. Then he closes the drawer to extinguish the fire and lights the candles in cobwebbed sconces that have waited patiently since the last occupier of the house. The granite walls flicker into existence, framing a dark passageway that leads to the only other room. In this, the living quarters, a rusting range sits in a deep-set fireplace, and other than the table on which he has lain his book and a battered and mouse-inhabited armchair, it is empty.

'Right, Bram. Set to it.' It had been a mistake, perhaps, to have arrived unannounced. He had presented his letter of appointment to Luk Calder at the chapel, and the brothers had shown him here. If he had waited a little longer, as he had been asked, a housekeeper recruited from the village would have been here to greet him. Might even have had a supper waiting. A hot supper. But he could not wait, and it had not been arranged. He finds his satchel, removes a wax paper package and eyes with little enthusiasm the bread and cheese within. He does not eat it. Instead, he drags the trunk through to the dark room he assumes is his bedchamber.

There is a window, the panes obscured by a green that spreads from the moss that lines the iron frames, and through it Abraham Pine-Coffin can just about see the sun as it slinks away below the horizon. He lights the candles in here and stares at the wooden framed bed in front of him. What mattress might once have resided on the frame is long since gone, though here and there a fragment of fabric clings to the slats. He will be sleeping in the armchair, tonight, at least. He sighs and opens his chest. There being no place to hang his clothes he leaves them be. But he rummages, pulls from the folds three little parcels, tied carefully with string. He opens each, and lines the contents up along the windowsill. A shark's tooth. A brass owl. A stone worn smooth. He stares into the corners of the rooms at intervals, startling the brownies as he startled the piskies in the chapel roof with his hopeful, foolish grin. This done, he retreats.

When he returns to the front room the bread and cheese are gone, and there is scratching and gnawing echoing from inside the walls. He peers into the corners but sees nothing. From cracks between the stones, things peer back. Even if the Reverend cannot see them, he's in the habit of hedging his bets. A legacy of his travels. More than once has a myth saved his skin. More than once has a monster almost taken it.

'Enjoy, little ones! Well, if I cannot sleep, cannot eat, I shall work.' He drags the armchair to the table, losing a little more of its stuffing along the way, and pulls his book towards him. He opens it and stares at his sketch with naked joy.

It had taken little effort but much persuasion to get the two Calder brothers to help him clear the rubble and pick away the rest of the lime mortar on the chapel wall. It had only been the bands at his neck and his resolute, cheery insistence that had persuaded them.

The Doom was magnificent.

He had seen many, in his time. These paintings on the walls of churches, designed to illustrate the lessons being taught when the language used had been Latin. Making sure everyone knew that though they might not understand what was being said, their damnation should they not heed the warnings was assured. He had never seen one like this, though. He had sketched it as best he could as the Calder's averted their gaze and worked around him, answering his questions as they worked.

The thing was painted in relief, creamy white showing through a rust red ground. The colour of dried blood. The scene split, horizontally, with a decorative band. Below, giants and fairies danced, devils too, their horns and wings marking them out. Above, men and women working. Smiths beating metal, men splitting stone. Women herding geese. Above them angels and rolling clouds. At either side were the wild beasts, including the deer that had first caught his eye. At the very centre, her body straddling above and below, a haloed figure. Her face bent in prayer; her right hand held up in benediction. In her left she held a staff with apples growing from the head. She wore a wrap of fabric that clung to her body, the same red as the background, as though stained by it. And from the bottom of her shift, the legs of a bird. Long and fine and clawed.

'Saint Reagan, I presume.'

He had seen stranger saints. Christopher with his dog's head, Mary's extra hand. St. Lucy's eyes.

'I do not pretend to understand this, my lady, but I look forward to finding out.' Pine-Coffin draws the candle closer and bends to his study.

So absorbed is he that when the wind gusts and the door and windows shudder, he does not notice. Doesn't notice the candles gutter. Doesn't hear that the scuffling behind the mortar has stopped. Is not aware that from the eaves a creature settles into a new suit of clothes, has a bold idea, and grins to itself in the rafters.

ST. JOHN'S WORT

THE RING HAS prompted it. A re-reading of the books. Nancy had been left with two problems the previous year. A grandmother she had never heard of, and the Mother. She has exhausted the books on the latter subject, so she turns back to the mysteries of her own blood. Over the past year, Nancy has teased those stories of her grandmother from Madge, from Calder when he was drunk enough, from Cusk. All different, as is the way of these things. None, Nancy suspects, true. Madge had told her how her grandmother helped. Calder how she had hurt. Cusk had told her where she had lived, though the old man placed it somewhere different each time he was asked.

Meliora Ray. Queen of the Witches. A monster amongst men.

The Witch Queen was a fairy tale told to children. It had even been told to her, when she was little, though nobody had thought to tell her they were related. When, on the rare occasion she played with children in the village, and they hunted each other in play, whispering about the Witch Queen, she had never made the family connection. She had never liked the games. Over the last year Nancy had questioned why it was Pel had never told her about Meliora. Never told Nancy that the stories she grew up hearing, the stories she spent her evenings reading, were about her grandmother. Her own blood. Madge had not wanted to tell her either, the one person she could count on. How was she supposed to trust them after that? If Nancy hadn't publicly used her gifts the previous year, the landlady would never have said a word. Nancy is sure of it. Perhaps, if Pel had lived, he would have said something one day. She suspects not. Even Calder, who should have had no reason not to torment her with family stories, had held his tongue. Until he knew that word was out. Now everyone knew. Every man woman and child pointed and whispered as she passed them. When they came to her for help, she could hear the question hovering below the one they had asked. Are you a witch, Nancy? Or our Keeper.

Because there is a difference. Nancy knows that. Pel made it very clear. A line between the one and the other. If her Murmur comes from her grandmother, then perhaps she is a witch.

A Keeper helps both worlds, magic and man. They balance both, helping the side with the best claim. They use a magic of books and learning. Matter manipulation. Take one thing, turn it into another. Cause and effect. Pel had enjoyed reading the journals and essays of scientists, had always felt he was one of them. Apples falling from trees, natural philosophies. Lead into gold. He had a bookcase full of heavy texts that explained the world, catalogued it.

Nancy had always preferred the shelf below. The one that held the poets. Milton, Dante, Homer, Dryden. It holds, too, Nancy's favourites. Two slim octavos by a charming radical called Blake. The first a gift from Pel, after a rare trip to London a few years before. He had thought, he'd said, it would be the sort of nonsense she would like. It was. Very much. So much so she had written to the publishers to request notification should the poet write again, and to express her appreciation of his work. The second volume arrived earlier this year. An early edition, a test print, sent out of gratitude for her modest patronage. The glorious, colourful plates accompanying the poems and religious statements transcendent. Sensuous. It had cost a significant part of her savings, and she regrets not a penny. This man, she had thought, saw things as they were. As she does. Nancy sees witchcraft as poetry, the witch as poet. Unlike Pel and his organised thought, his ability to perform miracles and show his working, a witch did what she felt. Pel had not liked that.

'We cannot just do what we feel, Nancy. We need to think about it,' had been hammered home throughout her childhood, her training. And they were one and the same. When her Murmur had started to manifest, she had asked him, straight out, if she was a witch. A smile on her face. He had glared at her, spat out a 'no' and turned back to his teaching. Forbidding her to practice, as though her Murmur would wither and die like an untended shrub.

Some seeds can lie dormant for a century and still bloom.

'You're a damn liar, Pel.' Nancy speaks into the dust as she lifts the book from the shelf. There have been so many stories of her grandmother over the last year she had stopped trying to find her in the books. People placed her in tales she could never have had a part in, children's stories half remembered returning vividly, with Meliora Ray pasted over the text. But that ring, the creatures that had delivered it, that had rung a bell.

The book is heavy. The spine cracked, the gold flaking from the recesses of stamped letters and when Nancy opens it three pages fall out. It is a compendium of collected folklore, covering the whole county, that Pel helped collate years ago. The author turning Pel's vivid memories into fairy tales for children, before Nancy was born, when he still liked to help.

RAGWORT

The story Nancy is looking for is halfway through. She smiles when she sees it. She remembers having read it as a child. So different than the dusty books of rigorous folklore Pel had made her read. She had loved this book, more than all the others, and she is responsible for much of its decay. Little hands flipping pages eagerly, weakening the glue. She had loved how each story began with the first letter alone in a blank square. The rest of the word following a few spaces along. Pel had told her it was because the book was a proof. That when it was finished each letter would be illuminated, illustrated. Nancy had loved it as it was, and each story is covered in her scribbles. Colourful flowers and beasts crawling around the margins carefully delineated in green ink. This story is illuminated too. The 'O' of once surrounded by a thicket of scrawled roses. The story is short and is called 'The Coffin Witch.'

Once there was a witch, who made a nuisance of herself. She lived in a community not often mapped that lies in lightly peaked moorland to the north of the county. The local Pellar, a man of considerable renown, took it upon himself to rid the village of the witch.

Even as a child, Nancy had worked out who the Pellar was. He appeared in most of the stories and was invariably cast in a good light.

One evening, the Pellar went to wait outside the witch's house. Through the window he watched her consort with her badger familiar. When the creature emerged, the Pellar followed through a tangle of trees, and once out of sight of the house had grabbed it with iron tongs. Begging to be spared, the cowardly demon had given up the secrets of his mistress, and the key to her defeat. Releasing the devil, the Peller went home to prepare.

'That's remarkably good of him.' Pel, in her experience, was not usually so relaxed about things such as devils roaming about.

Later that evening, the Pellar had hidden in wait on the road to the witch's house. When he heard her approach, astride her black mare, he ran into the road and cast a spell of containment. Though this did not hold the witch, it toppled her horse, which trapped the evil woman beneath it. Though she wailed, there was nought to be done, and the Pellar threw his magical powder into her face, sending her to sleep. As she slumbered, the Pellar placed her into an iron coffin and bound it with silver chains. For the familiar had confessed the witch could only be killed by water, and so she was to be drowned. Worried she might awaken before his task was done, the Pellar had constructed for her an iron prison. For it is known in these parts that witches have an aversion to it. And the chains wrapped about her were enchanted, to stop her magic.

'There is the Pel I know. Bind them up, take no chances.' Nancy reads on.

Taking his cargo by cart to the sea, the Pellar called upon a sailor to help him with his catch. And together, they heaved the witch into the sea where she drowned, never to be seen again.

The coffin witch was her grandmother. And it was Pel who killed her. A weight has been building in the pit of her stomach and Nancy has gone cold.

'You wouldn't, Pel.' Nancy knows some of the things stopped did not return to the Undermoor, were killed, and held above to stop their return. Could he really have counted her own grandmother amongst their number? No, she won't believe it. Nancy knows better than to trust a folktale. Especially one Pel helped write. She knows her father. Knows his limits. What he's capable of and what he isn't. The book had been written fifty years ago. The woman in the book could not be her, it could not be Meliora. Some other witch or no witch at all. Half the stories in the book are fancies Pel concocted for the teller. Chimeras built from half lost memory. Adventures the old man wished he'd had.

Nancy furiously scrolls through the pages for another account, another mention, but there is nothing. If, and she'll not concede this, it was her grandmother, then these men, her father and the writer, had taken away her name. Still, it was more than she'd had before. She will find a way to talk to Pel, but first she'll call a meeting on the hill. There is too much still hidden. She wants to meet her father with at least a little revealed. She stands, and though she rose late and studied all day it is still light enough for a meeting to be called.

'Come on, Pat, let's saddle up.' Patroclus does not move. Unusual, even for this lazy hound, what does he know? There is a knock at the door and Nancy jumps. She prays it is not that creature returned. She cannot see Knot again, just yet.

'Come Nance. You're the bloody Keeper. Nothing out there to scare you.'

She moves to the door and stifles a scream, standing at the door is a ghost, dressed in black.

'Cleaver?'

The figure turns and Nancy sees it is not him. Not that sad old priest back to haunt her again. Her shock at seeing the cassock had blinded her to the young man that wore it, black hat shading out the setting sun, and eyes smiling out at her from beneath the brim.

'My, you're the second to call me that! A fellow will get a complex. Are you Nancy Bligh? Abraham Pine-Coffin, Reverend. A pleasure, I'm sure. May I come in?' Beneath the volley of polite words Nancy barely has time to nod before the priest is inside, the door closed behind him, and she is trapped within. The Reverend removes his hat, holds it by the wide brim in front of himself and smiles benignly at his surroundings.

'Yes, Reverend. I'm Nancy, please sit down.' Nancy stops when she sees he is already seated. Has already pulled a chair close to the fire. She keeps her eyes fixed on him as she circles the chair, watching for a move out of place. Any hint of attack. She's a hundred spells to bind him if he drives her to it. She casts a quiet cantrip in readiness, the one tied to the Meadowsweet on her spine, then speaks with the ease of an actor. 'Pine-Coffin, was it? Unusual.'

'I suppose so, I suppose so Miss Bligh. There is a story there somewhere, I'm sure of it. Though I've not had the time to look. You live alone here?' The Reverend seems distracted, and Nancy follows his gaze to a dark corner where a brownie sits shaking. He surely cannot see the spirit, but those eyes are shining a light where it is not wanted.

'I'm more than happy to call at the chapel, should you wish to discuss anything. No need to come all the way out here. Uninvited.'

'Bram! Please Nancy, call me Bram. After all, as I understand it, you'll not be sitting in my pews so why stand on a title.

You need not call me Reverend, and I'll not call you Keeper.'

'Where did you hear that word?'

'That is what you are called, in these parts at least, isn't it?'

'In these parts. Not yours.' The floorboards crackle with their meadowsweet charge and the priest sniffs the air. The inside of the cottage charged with the atmosphere that comes before a rain. Floral and bitter and strung too tight. 'Can I ask again what it is you need? I was in the middle of something, I'd like to get back to it.'

Pine-Coffin forces a smile. Looks to Nancy's books.

'So I see. I will not keep you, Miss Bligh. I just wanted to drop by, introduce myself. I know it may be a shock to see a cassock so soon. I have heard some of what happened last year. Quite the business.'

Nancy sets the kettle on the range, as something to do, to give herself space to think.

'Yes. I confess I had not anticipated a replacement arriving before the chapel was complete.'

'No. Well, as I told Madge, I was awfully keen to take the posting, you see. I've been wanting to come here for some time. But my apologies, there are condolences in order. You lost your, guardian? Is that the word for it? The previous Keeper. Lord Hunt.'

The kettle's whistle breaks the tension with a high, shrill cry. Nancy pours boiling water onto the tea leaves but is frozen inside. It is about Pel, then. She thinks. Now we get to it. Few speak his name now and those that do would not offer it freely. Even the villagers, knowing the details, have not offered condolences. She is furious to find her eyes watering. She blinks the tears away.

'Thank you, Reverend.' Nancy passes him a cup. 'Yes, Lord Hunt died last year. Just before your predecessor.'

'Such a shame. I had quite hoped to meet Lord Hunt. Do you know we have letters, in Exeter, that must have been written by his father? Quite the name to hand down, Pelagius! Ruffled quite a few feathers. It's funny, there is no mention of a son and yet, it must be so, how else to account for the age? The letters must have arrived a century ago. Where was his family from? His seat? An island was it not?'

This is too much. Far too much. She barely knows Pel's life story, this shouldn't be possible, and there is a tone in the Reverend's voice that though mocking, Nancy can see is meant to be found endearing. She stamps on it.

'Just what is it you are here for, Reverend?'

Pine-Coffin smiles like a child caught out and sips his tea.

'I'm sorry, Miss Bligh. My father always said I had no nose for people. I invite myself into your home and blunder about like some frightful lummox.'

'You see that, then? Yet here you still are.'

Pine-Coffin does not break his stride.

'He was your, mentor? Is that so? You must miss him. Forgive me, I can get caught up. I had only meant to show that I was interested. Different. I hope you will find me less... oppositional, than the last reverend. In fact, it is with that in mind that I come seeking help. I wonder if you could meet me at the chapel, at your convenience? Something has come to light I would like your opinion on.'

Nancy narrows her eyes.

'You'll forgive me, Reverend. If you know as much as you claim, you will understand my reticence in accepting requests from the clergy, and I am rather busy, at the moment.' Nancy makes a single cup of tea and hopes the Reverend notices the snub. 'Besides, do you not consider all of this,' she waves at the décor, 'pagan nonsense? Heretical?' The

Reverend looks pensively at the table, his hands laid flat upon it.

'Nancy, I believe in God. But I find, having thought much about it, that there is still room left for other things. That is where my interests lie. In the spaces in-between. It is why I'm here. Look, I understand how this must seem, how I must seem. I do not mean to upset you; my interests I assure you are academic. Our interests align there, at least.' He nods towards the books. 'An interesting story, the coffin witch. There is much overlap, I find, in folktales. But that one? That one is quite unique.'

With that the Reverend stands, places his hat back on his head and walks to the door. He nods once at Nancy, once at Patroclus who has been unbothered by his presence, and then once at the shadows where the brownies hide. 'Good day, Nancy. A pleasure to meet you. Please, once your business is concluded, could we meet? My problem is a tricky one, and I'd be most gratified to solve it with you.' Abraham Pine-Coffin tugs on the brim of his hat and steps out into the moor and a lightly falling rain.

Nancy watches him leave, his black form swallowed by the rain and mist. The light from her porch lamps framing his departure in a halo. She blows them out and sends him to the darkness.

'Good day, Abraham Pine-Coffin. Good day.' Patroclus yawns and, closing the door, Nancy slowly goes back to the business at hand. She pulls the coat across her shoulders and picks up her crop. Fills her pockets with charms and wards and opens the door. There is no sign of the Reverend. No sign of much as in the few moments since he left night has fallen and the moon is yet to rise. Nancy turns back, shouts to the dog.

'Well, it seems I have mysteries to spare. Come on boy, let's get to it again.' Patroclus rises and heads with his mistress to the stable.

GOOSE-FOOT

ABRAHAM PINE-COFFIN CLIMBS back up the hill to the chapel with a skip in his step, shrugging off the awkwardness of the day's encounters with a practiced roll, and a hammer and chisel in his hands. He has a hunch that he'll see played out. He has learnt, in his life, that a cassock affords a certain degree of latitude. People tend to assume he has a reason for doing the things he does, beyond simply wishing to pursue a point. So, if any villagers see him dancing up the hill, he is certain they will not stop him. Remark on it in private? Certainly. Stop him, however, they would not. It was amongst the perks.

He had not intended to go into the priesthood, it was just how things were. His eldest brother had inherited the house, the second eldest was now a major-general and he had been sent to the church. He had sulked for a while, then made the best of it. The church, for a start, had a great many books. Many that had been supressed and, as such, unable to buy from even the most esoteric shops at his civilian disposal. And, as he had argued often to the librarians in whose charge these banned books lay, how was one to *oppose* a thing without having read it? He had carved out a reputation, sought out the farthest flung corners of Christendom and learnt everything he could. He was invariably recalled, having no appetite for evangelism or even, frankly, preaching, but not before he'd learnt something. Mirecoombe was already turning out to be quite the choice assignment. The result of gears he'd set in motion several years ago. When he'd first seen the map of the island. That was not the mystery that captivated him tonight, however, this was an escapade of unexpected origin.

The lychgate looms out of the darkness. As is always the case, Abraham wishes someone was beside him to hear his explanations. That *lych* was old English for corpse. That the gate was where the coffin rests, where vigil was kept, waiting for a churchman to start the service. That in this part of the world it used to be called a Trim-Tram. Alas, he is alone, and no one is around to hear him, so he crosses the corpse gate with a sigh. The door is not locked, the church is empty and filled to the rafters with moonlight. He looks up to the roof and watches dust fall on invisible faces, smiles and nods politely. It always pays to be polite to the little folk, wherever one may find oneself. The memory of a Mexican churchyard rises and is hastily suppressed. No point revisiting the classroom if the lesson's been well learned. He places his tools down, and slips his whale strike over his knuckles, lights the candles on the altar. The chapel flickers into life and the shadows illuminate the Doom on the western wall.

'I'm correct, am I not? You are St. Reagan? Tut, Bram, talking to paint.' He lifts a candle and holds it up, watches it catch on the faintest trace of gold leaf, still clinging to the mortar.

'You are remarkably well preserved, my lady. For one, forgive me, so old.' He traces the line that divides heaven from hell.

From the rafters, something coils down a pillar and slithers to a crack at the base of the western wall and sets to listening.

'I've written to Exeter, asked them to send on any books you might appear in. Do you have a hagiography, I wonder? Perhaps you'd like one written.'

The creature slides from its crevice, coiling into something a little more human as it slips behind the priest, gently pries up the ledger stone behind him. The one replaced after the fight the year before. The body that had had lain in it removed and reburied, the tomb is now ready for new guests. Pine-Coffin does not notice, still talking to the wall.

'This is marvellous. Quite marvellous. I…'

A gust of wind winnowing through the open walls surprises both priest and the creature that watches him. It is warm and smells of flowers, Pine-Coffin swoons, steps back, and falls into the open tomb.

Only his pride is hurt. His pride, his ankle, and a number of ribs. His candles extinguished in the fall, he pats about in the empty hollow of the coffin for something to aid his escape. Eyes again the six feet of stone and earth that mark his exit. There is nothing. He is trapped in the hole.

'Oh dear. Saints above, saints right here, I suppose.' He tries to climb, but even without the aching bones, he doesn't think he'd make it. Two steps up and down he comes. He could wait until morning, but embarrassment aside, he is desperate to be home. He cannot say why. Still, Pine-Coffin has never been bashful about asking for help. He tries a trick he's attempted before.

'Little ones, if you are indeed here, could I trouble you for help? I'd be most grateful.' It is a gamble that has never paid off before. Backfired before, yes, many times, but since his arrival in Mirecoombe he has felt something in the air. Something he is keen to acquaint himself better with. No answer. 'I, erm, am friends with someone you perhaps know, Miss Bligh? Nancy?'

Silence, the Underfolk know a bluff when they hear it. Besides, there's a monster with its fingers to its lips. A monster that recognises a win when he gets one. Even if he'd planned a more direct approach. A monster that slips and swings to the floor above the open tomb.

There is a scuffle, and a coil of rope used for hoisting fallen stone, the end still tied to a winch, is nudged into the hole. Abraham beams at the ring of shadow around the grave opening. He stares into empty spaces with glee.

'It worked. Good lord. You helped.' His smile lights the darkness, ironing out the wrinkles so the Reverend is a child again. Watching with rapt hope the end of the garden where his brother told him fairies played.

'Thank you, whoever you are. I will let Miss Bligh know how helpful you were.' With much groaning and suppressed tears, Abraham climbs out from the pit. Ahead of him, still lit with candles, Saint Reagan smiles down and a creature, whose newly devised plan has been set in motion, stifles a smile and slides into the shadows. Piskies and spriggans quaking in his wake.

MOUNTAIN EVERLASTING

Nancy likes to ride at night. Likes to feel the stars on her skin burning freckles onto her face. Echo Tor is a little way from her cottage. To reach it Nancy must skirt below Mirecoombe, she can see the light at the Nest still shining, Madge clearing the inn after a long day. She does not usually call these meetings after sunset. She likes the reinforcement that daylight brings. But she wants answers, and she could not sleep, so here she is riding a tired horse across dark hillsides by the light of the rising moon. Patroclus ambling with measured discontent at her side. Pel's ghost always riding just out of sight. It hurts, calling these meetings. More than anything else since he died. Sometimes she thinks she sees her father's steps etched into the stone. Can still hear the ring of his cane on the granite. She uses the walk to try and set her face. Push the tiredness and grief from her eyes, nudge the corners of her mouth into a confident smile. She gets there in the end.

'Here, Pat, how do I look?' The old dog whines up at her and wags his duster tail.

'Yes, I know I'm not fooling you. It'll do for them, though. Don't worry boy, I'm alright.' She chokes back tears, the same that come unbidden at the most irritating times. The ones she saves for nights alone.

There is a screech from the valley, a banshee wail, and Nancy waits for the sudden swoop of the barn owl. There. Coming from the chapel hill. It glides towards her, and she meets its gaze. Two black eyes in a heart of a face, beak hungry for the creature gripped in feather topped talons. She gasps, there is something familiar in the bird's face, a raggedness to its feathers that seem almost green in the moonlight. A clumsiness to its flight. Once the owl has passed, the silence returns.

She sees the lights from swaying lanterns further down on the moor. Circles of congregants. Scattered prayers spoken into the grass. Nancy's had no time to investigate the cults, each so slightly different, keenly aware she ought to be watching. Keeping a lid on things that might get out of hand. She has no appetite for it, though. Not yet. She knows if she steps in then they'll turn to her for answers, and she has none. Pray to the grass, pray to a cross. She's met the God below and knows full well he's not listening, why should the one above be different? She knows the comfort found in the reciting of words, who's she to deny others of it? She watches the lanterns and heads on her way. Nancy has no light, no lantern, though she could make one if she wished. She could close her eyes, think of the oxeye daisy tattooed on her hip and conjure a little ball of light that would bounce in her palm. But she does not. Aside from the unwanted attention it would bring—Delen has told her there's already a group that have Nancy as the focus of their ministrations—she likes the brightness of the night. The moon hangs directly behind the chapel and the building is silhouetted against its face, as though someone has torn a ragged chapel shaped hole from it, so the blackness of space is visible beyond. She thinks, for a moment, that she sees a figure moving there, but it's impossible; the village is asleep, so she shudders and turns away. She must pass, too, the site that Pel's home stood. His little upturned boat that sank when he left. Even in the moonlight she can still see the whorl of the grass where the moor reclaimed it. She sometimes thinks, if she pressed a sheet of her paper to the grass and scratched her charcoal across it his face would appear. Like a brass rubbing. She's not alone in that hope.

'Who's there?' She tightens her grip on the reins and summons an air of intimidation she doesn't quite feel. The dark shapes on the grass shift uncomfortably.

'It's Cal Hawker, Miss Bligh, me and my son. We were just…'

'I know what you were doing, Cal. He's not a god, you know that? No more than you or I. Go home.'

The darkness shifts as the two men stand and Nancy catches a glint of a knife in the moonlight. Tensing, she calls on the oxeye fire and illuminates a crude altar. A raven dead upon it.

'What's this?' Her voice is knapped to a razor edge. Cal's voice shakes as he answers.

'He's down there, isn't he? Old Pel. We were calling him up. A fellow from Lanson sold me the spell.'

Nancy rides close to the men. So close they have to take a step back to avoid Selkie's iron shoes. She wants them to feel the hot breath of the horse. She positions herself with care, so the moon is her halo, her face in darkness.

'You so much as whisper into the earth and I will show you there myself. Do you hear me, Cal? You've been sold a lie. Pel's dead.' The words taste bitter. 'Besides, nonsense or not, you never know who might hear it.' As the moonlight bleeds around her, Nancy stares at the two men as they shuffle away in a cloud of apologies. When she is sure they are gone she slumps, rubs her eyes and breathes out into the night air.

'Damn you, Pel. How long does it take for the world to forget a man?' Her gut twists at the thought, she has found her grief to be a rolling swell. Missing him as the wave crests, hating him as it hits the floor. Hating herself, for thinking that way. She rides slowly up the hillside towards the Tor top, towards the amphitheatre rocks whilst on the dark grass behind her, a raven flaps its wings.

It is in a Keeper's power to call a meeting of the Underfolk. All must attend. It is a ritual. A ceremony. Tonight, though, something is wrong.

Nancy has not begun her song, the one that calls the gathering, but already a light shines. Burning beacon from the tor. It shines green, the outline of the rocks flickering against the stacks in some dreadful shadow play. Nancy dismounts, shoos Selkie down the hill and creeps towards the ridgeline.

The light is shining from a flaming orb that hovers at the centre of the rocks. Nancy knows what it is, it's the light the piskies use when they are luring travellers astray. A will o'wisp, a jack lantern. Around it, the Underfolk are already gathered. Without her.

'I don't like this, Pat,' Nancy whispers as she wriggles forwards, craning her head to catch snippets of what's being said.

'She's coming. He said...'

'He's a liar. He's a...'

'We know what he is. The things he does. She must have given him the means. She could give them to us. Get out from under the Keeper-God with his rattle-bag head.'

The muttering continues and from the stacks at the back of the tor a shape ruffles its feathers, then steps into the circle. Knot is larger than before, his face broad like a heart and he preens as he walks. Smoothing the moss on his chest. Picking meat from his teeth with a foot that's still a talon before he shakes it back into toes.

'I do not lie.'

The circle of Underfolk shivers collectively.

'She is coming. You must be ready. Because when She returns, She will have questions for you all. I found Her, forgotten, did I not? I found Her and have gained Her trust. I reminded you all of Her. What I do, I do for your own good. To keep you sharp.' Knot is stood behind a small spriggan, Nancy knows them, called Clitter. 'You've all forgotten what it means to have something to lose.' Nancy clamps her hand to her mouth as Knot cracks his neck. It is like watching a dragonfly's wing. He vibrates, the air around him flashes and burns and he is no longer his mossy self. He is a fox. Huge and ragged furred. He leaps in a flash of red then lands, pinning Clitter under a heavy clawed foot.

'I am doing important work. For your betterment. Let me work.' He bows his head and tears a strip from Clitter with his long snout, the spriggan howls as he watches his flesh slip into the great dog's throat. The rest watch on in silence as Knot eats his fill. When he is done, and Clitter lies still on the floor, Knot changes back to his usual self. Larger again, with new thorns and spikes like a blackthorn's ridging down his back.

'I do this for you!' he howls, wide eyed, at the congregation. 'She gave me these gifts to prepare for Her return. She will make me anew; She will help you, but you must help me. The Mother is coming. I have told you that. You've seen what She can do. Does your Keeper-God not fail you? Does He not sit sulking as the ghost in his head scolds?' Nods amongst the Underfolk, the riotous murmur of dissent. 'Does it not rankle that this *Keeeper,* this *dead Keeper* has dominion over you below, whilst his whelp has rule of you above?'

Nancy moves to step in but is frozen in place. Doubt pins her with claws of its own. Patroclus nudges her but she motions him to stay still. Another spriggan, emboldened at the death of a friend steps forwards.

'He says it's a lie, that you lie. Our King would know of Her, would He not? Would have spoken of Her.'

Licking his lips, Knot cracks his neck.

'She *is* coming. Whether He believes it or not. Think on this, too, were you a king, a God, were you to know of another whose power dwarfs your own, would you share it? Or would you ensure nobody told Her story. She is coming, and She will rule us. The one person who might have steered her from that path is dead. Drowned by the fool Keeper.'

Silence.

'What have you to lose? Follow me, follow Her and gain glory if what I say is true. If it is not? He will not have noticed you gone. What, you're scared of your new Keeper? The girl is toothless.' Nancy swears Knot turns to look at her, flat against the tor.

'That poor, poor girl. Old one eye did us all a favour dying, her the most. If she had only…' Knot shakes his head. 'No. The Mother can deal with her.'

Something snaps, and Nancy is leaping into the circle. The wisp fire winking out before her. She raises a hand, holds her daisy tattoo in her mind, and a white light takes the green light's place.

'Oh, mine Ancy! Oh, woe, this is not how it looks, this…' Knot stops, lets his shoulders slump, begins to laugh. 'Enough, then. You do not move as fast as you should, little Keeper. The Mother is coming. Soon. You cannot stop Her. The one who could is gone. Walk away. Do as you're told.'

'What are you, I saw you steal—' Nancy stops. Speechless. Her mouth gaping like a landlocked fish. When her words return, she whispers. 'You took Clitter's matter, did you not? Stole it to make yourself new? Only the God below can do that.'

'See Her power, see Her gift.' Knot spits. 'It is imperfect, but it is a gift. I can patch myself back together with what I take, but I am not what I was. Store a little extra for a special coat or two. Besides,' Knot kicks the limp body of Clitter, 'I always leave enough. He may not be a spriggan again, but a piskie. Maybe a brownie.'

'You are a horrid little vampire, Knot. I'll see you stopped.'

Knot sighs, then flickers again and emerges as a stoat. Nancy is only halfway to a spell when he has torn the throats from six piskies, gulping down blood and bone.

'Speak to your father, girl. You'll not stop me.' Another flicker.

Knot is a bear, his face devoid of flesh, and he roars into the night sky. As the Underfolk run past him, Knot clouts them with his bony snout and hurls them into the rocks.

'Damn.' Nancy sets her feet, turns, and faces Knot. 'Hey!' Knot turns, opens his jaws and yawns. Nancy can smell the rot from across the tor. She pulls a fistful of wards and glass balls from her coat pocket and hurls them at the beast. They explode in a crackle of smoke and flame, but Knot emerges from it unharmed.

'Bugger.' Nancy pictures her tattoos, the flowers that grow across her skin and hold the memories of spells. She pictures too the sigils and signs they grow around. Her fingers twitch, make the shapes. She casts a protective shell, and it seems to hold. Knot, on his hind legs now, is beating down on the fragile shell she has encased herself in, sending a crackle of blue flame across its surface with every blow. Nancy uses the time to see who is left. She sighs in relief as she sees the empty rocks. Even Patroclus is free from danger; she can see him, shepherding the Underfolk down fissures in the stone.

'Good boy.' Nancy does not say it loudly, but the dog lifts his head, wags his tail, and returns to work. Nancy searches for the spell that will free her from this. There is one, marked on her as belladonna, as nightshade. Wrapped around the sigils of a mythical magician, a Welshman, if she remembers right. Who once worked for a king. Pel had shown it to her, just once. It was dangerous, explosive, but her only other option is to reach inside and pull at the power she is so scared of using. The wild and unpredictable gift. The spell could take the tor down, but the other could take down the hill.

As she is deliberating, Knot breaks through. Perhaps it is because she holds both in mind. Perhaps it is just unfortunate. But as Knot swipes a black clawed paw, something gives. And, in trying to choose the safest option, Nancy chooses both. The noise is incredible. The spell has ignited something within Knot, and from the side of his chest a rainbow of flame erupts, scattering bone and blood as it does so, painting the rocks red and black. At the same moment, Nancy raises a hand and the highest stack of Echo Tor, the rocks in which a god once sat, fall to the ground. They land heavily on Knot's ursine form and from beneath the stone an artillery volley echoes as the spell continues unabated. Pel had explained it to her when she was taught it. A chain reaction, each chamber of the body a new reservoir of fuel. The hill shakes and Nancy works hard to focus. She pictures the anchor cross that is tattooed above her heart. The one that always steadies her, and she manages to reign in her own power at least. Though the hilltop still shakes as though it is yet to settle, and stones are now rolling from the other stacks, bouncing like pebbles down the hillside and embedding deep in black earth. Skidding to a halt and tearing up the grass and trees. It does end though. The shaking subsides, the Murmur stops. The explosions cease. The air is filled with fizzing light, with the smell of bitter orange and gunpowder. It is a miracle she has not been hit. She can hear Patroclus barking. The old dog is fine. And she knows Selkie well enough to know she'll have got free. In front of her, beneath the largest stone, the decaying skull of the bear is twitching. A single rancid eyeball staring at her. The jaws open and Nancy prepares herself for the fight. Though there is little left. Using her gift again would kill her, and she is too tired to focus on the forming of spells. A gasp catches in her throat. The jaws are being prised open with small hands and from the open throat of the bear walks Knot. He is smaller than she's ever seen him. Barely larger than a brownie and his skin barely covers his bones. His mossy sides are grey and lichenous, his eyes dull.

'Ha. That was, that was something. She'll be impressed by you, Mine Ancy.'

Nancy takes a step forwards, raises her hand with a spell but stops. Knot has fallen to his knees. Dragging himself towards the cliff edge of the tor.

'Very impressed indeed.'

Nancy is speechless, exhausted.

'You can't stop Her, Nancy. She is coming. Everyone that could help you is too far away to hear.'

Knot, whatever he is, sprite or devil, hauls himself to the edge, Nancy snaps free of her bewilderment. It is too late.

RAGWORT

She arrives in time to see the ragged body fall and burst into a pair of goldfinches that tumble and wheel away on the moorland air. She follows their flight, across the moor, dawn spilling over the moor like an undammed lake. The two birds reach the Fellmire, swooping here and there to some prey on the ground. There is a glint, as though someone has angled a mirror, and even at this distance Nancy hears the splash. It reminds her of something. Of a ritual. She reaches into the inside pocket of her coat and feels for the signet ring she has stored there. Weighing her down.

BINDWEED

If Nancy did not know the way to the Fellmire, she'd find it by the trail of the dead. Twitching piskies and spriggans where Knot has passed by. She does not know how much he needs to be himself again. Less than he has taken, she's sure of it.

Nancy does not come this way often. Hilla and Stag only the fourth time she's had cause to be here since last year. It has changed, the Fellmire. Since it took him. Since it took Callum and Cleaver. The ground around the mire has hardened, what was once illusion can now bear weight. The pool itself confined to a circle at its centre though the water still runs dark. The slate and peat of its banks creating a black mirror. Only the reeds and ferns near the surface break the spell. The tree at the centre still holds Pel's pocketknife tight, the silver of the blade shining in the sun. All the trees are thorn, white or black. All are in bloom. Nancy dismounts under this almond scented cloud of white petals, and tethers Selkie to a branch. The horse lowers its head to graze and enjoy the warming sun. Patroclus is less sure. He moves back beyond the old mire's boundaries and sits guard. Ears back. Eyes sharp.

'It's alright, boy.' But Nancy does not blame him. She feels it too. The wolf beneath the sheepskin. The old beneath the new.

She looks around but there is no sign of Knot, in or out of the water. She knows this was his intention. That he meant her to follow his path, but she sees no other option.

Nancy is not sure how this will work. Before, when Pel came to her, she had played no part. She had been here; her father had come. He's not made the effort again and she's not invited him. She has tried to keep tabs on him. Asking the Underfolk how he's keeping. How things are, below. They have been evasive, 'better' their usual reply. She has not wanted to find out anything more concrete. She is not sure that she has forgiven Pel. Not sure that she should, but she needs his help now. Needs the truth. Though she knows more than most that when it comes to answers, you don't just get the ones you want.

Nancy walks to the edge of the pool and takes the ring from her pocket. It glows in the morning sun. She slides it onto her index finger, already heavy with rings, and closes her fist. She knows roughly how this works, just as Pel did when he came. Just as Callum did. If her father is involved, it doesn't matter that he's dead. She needs to hear it from him. Still, she pauses. It has been freeing, this year without him. Without his voice. Beneath the grief but there. A high, uplifting note amongst the din of the dirge. It is true he was kind, the last time they met. But she knows her father. His forehead's had plenty of time to furrow itself back into a frown. And he's never resisted "I told you so" if he's seen a space for it. She braces herself for what's to come, for the version of help that he'll give her, and continues. It is not enough to ask the mire for help. It has to see you bleed.

Holding the ring to her mouth she whispers, 'I need you, Pel.' Then bites her lip, splits the skin, and lets blood flow into the recesses of the seal with a kiss. Opening her fist, Nancy lets the ring fall from her finger into the bottomless pool. Watches it wink out of sight. She hopes the message will be received; this ritual is a guess. There are no precedents in the books for contacting a dead man who has bound himself to a god. Once the ring has fallen too deep to be seen, Nancy steps back and sits on the grass, wipes the blood from her mouth, and waits. The taste of iron on her tongue, the cyanide smell of blackthorn blossom in her nose and the weight of two worlds on her shoulders.

She hears him far before she sees him.

The sound of bubbles bursting on the surface of the pool. She scrambles over to the water and peers in. The bubbles are rising in a steady column from far beyond the point of visibility. They rise like bubbles in champagne, a close column at the centre of the pool but they are growing. Billowing. They fizz on the surface turning the dark water white. The circle of bubbles moves and twists into the shape of a skull, two ragged holes where the eyes should be though one quickly closes up, and still the fervour is growing. The bubbles piling on top of each other, giving shape and form to the skeletal head which writhes and shakes in the churning water. There is a mouth now, as torn, and wild as the eye, screaming a torrent of water that pours up and over the foam. The bubbles grow smaller and smaller until Nancy is staring at Pel's face. A death mask of it at least. Rotted skin hanging from bone. And then the fizzing stops. Fades to silence. And though his face is pale, he is here. Eye wide and smiling. As though he is treading water beneath with only his face above, his grey hair held like smoke in the water behind his head. Nancy smiles and suddenly she is six again. Waiting at his door with a spell she has botched. An injured piskie she has found. Hands outstretched and waiting for help.

'My Nancy. Oh, my Nancy my love it is so good to see you.'

RAGWORT

Tears form, blurring the world. Nancy had wanted to be severe with him. Start with the hard questions but now, with her father before her she cannot speak. Instead, she takes his face in her hands, leans across the pool to kiss him on the forehead. He slips away, as salt tears fall into fresh water.

'Pel. Who knew it would take dying to get you to learn to swim?'

Lord Pelagius Hunt's face jerks into a smile. Nancy shivers at it.

'You do not look yourself, why are you in the water? Not stood in the light like the last time we spoke.'

'Ah, my Nancy, yes, I am spread thin. I'm sorry to come to you like this, disgusting and rotted. I should go.'

This is new. This self-abasement. It knocks her off balance.

'No!' Nancy flushes, cross at herself. 'You're perfect, I'd take you however you look. Does it hurt?'

The shade of Pel smiles again and Nancy presses down on her revulsion. Wrongfooted again. There is something about him that unsettles her. His flickering mood. He reminds her of the Underfolk. Their capricious, weather wild heads, their stormcloud smiles. She can't catch hold of him. She's about to speak when he beats her to it.

'Forgive me. I find myself not myself. Death takes its toll. I find it hard to keep things in mind.'

She watches, waits for him to settle. Is that it, then? He is becoming like Them? Is that how it works? Is she to lose him by degrees?

'Tell me, why have you called? I'm busy, down here, my Nancy.'

Nancy leans back, wipes the tears away. No. He has settled. Into an all too familiar shape. She is six years old and being shooed away by her father busy in his work.

'Oh, of course. Sorry.'

'I assume it was you, who brought down the tor? You know it fell here too? Your actions have consequences in two worlds. And if you can't control your magic, you should really consider not using it.'

'My Murmur. Pel. It was an accident. Besides I was distracted, I cast the powder keg spell you taught me. They combined, somehow…' She peers into the pool, to a ghost that might well be tapping its feet impatiently. 'It doesn't matter. This creature, Knot, he's tangled up in it all, with the Mother, but something else too. Pel, your ring, it was delivered by a bucca. Knot tried to keep it from me, why?'

The face dips and ripples and looks, almost, to Nancy like it stifles a smile. Just light on the water as the clouds part. As they rejoin, the face is sombre.

'Oh, My Nancy, I feared this day. I must, I suppose, tell you the truth. Of your grandmother and my part in the loss of her. Of what I truly know of the Mother. Of how those things are one and the same.'

Nancy frowns.

'What? You know nothing, you told me so yourself…'

'I lied, my Nancy. It was for your own good. I was protecting you.'

Nancy leans back from the pool as the hillside shakes, her rage opening the cage that holds the Murmur.

'Have we come such a short way down this path? Again you protect me! You tell such stories about yourself, Pel. I was reading the book you wrote with the folk collector. I was reading about the coffin witch.'

The face closes its one eye. Not so easy to turn away when you are held face up in water. Nancy's voice shakes as she talks.

'I had thought you were playing a joke, all these years, that the Pel in those books was a game you played, but it's how you really see yourself, isn't it? The lone protector, the only one special enough, clever enough to help?'

The face twists and contorts, the eye simmering in the pool, but it stays. Nancy gives grudging respect for that. The old Pel would have stormed out by now. It is as far as her charity reaches. She watches blossom fall, watches it land in the pool around her father's face. On his closed eyelid, in the hollow of his lost eye. He exhales and the water ripples. The petals slip.

'Here, Pel, is what *I* know. My grandmother is the Coffin Witch. Meliora Ray. I know that if the story is true then you killed her. Then kept it from me. I do not know how. Or why. I do not know why suddenly everyone is singing the same song. I do not know why Knot is so desperate for me to learn about her, or why he wishes so keenly for me to link her to the Mother. I do not know why your ring was delivered to me by buccas. I do not know who the Mother is, and I do not know why every time I sleep, I dream of drowning.' Nancy turns her head to hide more tears. 'You left me, Pel, you died. And to hear again that you have kept things from me "for my own good" it... no. I'm not here to go through it all again, we've done that.' Nancy's voice, which has been confident till now falters, fades, rage turning to sadness again. 'But you died with a lot of secrets. I need some answers. Just a few, then I can get on with being what you trained me to be and I'll leave you in peace. So please. The truth.'

The face in the water ripples.

'It is appropriate, I suppose, that it starts with a book of stories. Attend, My Nancy, and I'll tell you one of my own, a story that's true, trust me.'

OLD MAN'S BEARD

THE UNDERMOOR SHAKES with the fight above, and in the corner of the throne room, the God of the Mire uncurls in a copse of tangled branches, and a ghost hops free of his nest.

'Off again, Lord Hunt? What a busy little bee you are.'

'I had sting enough for you,' Pel snaps at the ruined King. 'My work isn't done. This place is far from fixed. Sit and sulk, Lord. I care not.'

Lord Pelagius Hunt, last Lord of Eythin, once Keeper of the High Moor, steps out into the blasted hilltops of his Undermoor home and immediately regrets it.

There is already a queue of petitioners. Spriggan, piskie, he sees with a lurch that Hilla and Stag are back, waiting on scuffling feet with the others. They come for audience with their King and though most are here with petty grievances and disputes, one thing unifies all.

The Undermoor writhes with excitement at the Mother.

The hubbub has been interminable. Pel has spent the last months cajoling, threatening and in one unfortunate slip, fighting the Underfolk for more information on who is telling these stories. For that is what they are. Something fills their heads with rumour, and he'd see it stopped. The King agrees. He's not said it in so many words, but the King has no knowledge of the Mother. Pel is sure. Within his temple walls not a soul mentions her, not since the King tore the wings from a piskie who asked about Her. The ignominy of not knowing too much for the broken God. Outside, though, they are not bound by his rules and rumour is rife.

Ignoring the line's gibbering, Pel walks on into the day. Since he took up residence in the Old God's head, he has worked to fix the damage Callum had inflicted. The damage caused when that broken hearted boy had torn through this place on his way back home. The Undermoor's welts, the tears in the grass and hills, are healing slowly. The thatch of new green growth a scar tissue reminder of the damage done.

A rustle in the reeds.

Though he's made peace with this place, and home in the Mad God's head, Pel knows there are things that could hurt him. He curls his hand into a spell.

'Who's about?' He stares into the undergrowth and waits for reeds to shake, for a piskie or spriggan to stir. It is something else. A tiny fluttering creature. Flickering.

'Who are you?'

The little creature flits like a dragonfly.

'Me? Nobody. You can call me—' The creature thinks. 'Pratt. I've no business with you, mine Keeper.'

'I don't like surprises, creature. You don't have to tell me your name, but do you think I don't speak Cornish? You won't trick me, Pratt. I have my eye on you.'

The creature flitters free of the old man's gaze and Pel turns to his other business.

It takes him the morning to reach his goal. The giant, Gogmagog. Two souls kept separate for an eternity before Pel joined them again. They sit, where they always do, wittering to themselves.

A sunny day.

You mean a moon.
Either way it's dazzling.

Pel waits at their rocky foot for them to notice him, their conversation a rockfall that's dust before it reaches him.

'Inane dust,' the Old Keeper, ex-Keeper, mutters to himself and settles into the grass. There is a smile on his face, however, he still loves the Undermoor and its watery sky, its puddle moon. With his empty eye on the giant, he scans the moor and makes a list.

'Give the sisters their heads back. Tame the dog. Visit Cleaver.' It is as he contemplates this last task—one he's come to enjoy, this past year; a gradual mending of a friendship, stitched back together with spiderweb—that he hears a third voice above. A voice he's already heard this morning.

'Brothers! You've heard the rumours?'

We have, little trickster. We see what you're doing.

Nothing gets past us.

Four eyes, four ears, one head. We see through you. See what you are.

What you're not.

Besides. We've not forgotten her. Don't need to work on us. We'll help.

Pel stands and raps on the giant's toe and the mountainous creature shifts. Kneels, holds out a hand. Lifts him to their face.

'Giant, who were you talking to?'

A friend.

Foe.

Matters not.

Pel has spent a year indulging this sort of talk. Gogmagog, of all he's spoken to, the only one to come close to admitting they know the Mother.

'Is this about Her? The Mother? The time is past for evasion, tell me plain if you know something.'

Gogmagog curls their fingers and Pel falls, coming to rest against the granite pad of their hand.

She is Coming. Believe it or not.

And many do not that say that they do.

Everyone's forgotten Her. Even Him.

'But you remember Her, do you? Or have you just been told the story?' There is a knot in Pel's stomach he thought to avoid in death. A story long forgotten; the teller long gone.

We like stories.

'Who told you this one?'

She did. He did. And now we tell it to each other.

She was kind to old Gog.

Magog too.

Terrible what happened to her.

What you did.

Pel freezes. Chicken's coming home to roost. This rooster ghost puffs his own chest up and doubles down on a lie.

'Rot. What did I do?'

Could never forget. A nudge from me.

A nudge from him.

She stayed with us. We'll See her woken.

Sorry.

Gogmagog, moving quicker than Pel's seen them, reaches out a great finger and presses Pel's ghost to the floor. As they do, there is a fluttering, and the dragonfly imp reappears.

'Keeper.'

Pel's fingers curl into a spell, a century or two of practice giving him no need for floral reminders.

'Ah-ah-ah, sorry old man. Can't have that.' The creature flutters to Pel and pins onto his breast a red cotton heart with six bent pins. Sewn into it three nail clippings and a lock of silver hair. Pel's fingers flicker out. 'There we go. A little something to keep you still. Amazing what you find when you do a little digging. The remains of that body of yours is just lying there you know. Anyone could do anything to it.'

'If you think this will hold me, you are an idiot.' Pel's braggadocio is undermined by the worried looks to the heart. Gogmagog releases Pel and the old Keeper stands. He feels it. The absence of magic. He's made quiet. Mundane. Trapped. Still, he tries to act the champion. 'You forget I am bound to a god.'

'No, *you* forget!' the imp flares and flickers and for a brief moment, Pel sees teeth. A long snout. Stripes. And the weight that's growing in his stomach gains once again. 'You think yourself above it all. Even in death—in death!—you still think you're winning. You've learnt *nothing*. Yes, you were bound to a god, but how much of yourself do you leave with him when you go a-walking, Keeper?' He taps hard on the cloth heart. 'You're bound to nothing, now. The part that might save you still stuck in His head. He might be mad but the King's no fool, he'll not come running with the rest of you. You'll walk the Undermoor without power. Until Her plan is through. I hope you've made friends, Lord Hunt. No magic to save you now. Mel sends her love.'

Pel simmers but slides back in acquiescence. His left hand picking at the cotton of the heart. A memory long supressed rises. Of a badger familiar squawking in iron tongs. The screams as it burned. Of a story a friend once told.

'It is you, then.'

The creature smiles.

'Oh yes, Keeper. How did you put it in your story? A quick chat, then you released me from the tongs? You dropped me in the fire! I remember it well. Burnt the stripes right off.'

'Is this all her doing, then? This nonsense of the Mother?'

At the mention of the Mother's name the giant shakes his hand, rolls around the Keeper's ghost like dice. The imp giggles maniacally. Lowers his voice to a whisper.

'Hush, old Gog doesn't like Her to be talked about like that. Awful fond of that story. She is coming. That's all you need to know. The Mother is coming. In one way or another. You tell me, Pel, at what point does a story become the truth? You of all men should know that a legend can get away from you.'

There is a glint, from the rippling sky and a ring is snatched from the air by a little greedy hand.

'Ah, your daughter's finally put the pieces together. What a good girl.'

Knot holds it out to Pel, snatching it back at the last moment. Pel howls as it's taken.

'Knot, leave Nancy be. If it *is* her, it is my mistake to fix. Please.'

'No fixing, Mine Keeper, broken beyond repair. Luckily, I'm good at fixing. Just as She taught me. Now, let's see.' He coughs and tests his voice, it takes three tries but by the end he sounds just like Pel.

'Mine Ancy.' Cough. 'Mine Nancy'. Cough. 'My Nancy.' A crooked smile. 'Let's get to it again.'

The little imp crackles into his mossy, wingless form and Knot is caught by Gogmagog as he falls.

'Up, giant.' Gogmagog stands, raises up his open palm and pushes Knot up and into the sky. To the tipping point where a black stain waits. All that's left of a body long rotted. Most gone to make a daughter whole. All that's left a gossamer shell. A pale sheet of ragged skin and bones in the form of a man. A ghost in need of a soul. He wriggles in like a tape worm. Expands into the semblance of a man. Wears the rotten body like a skin. A fit so close a daughter wouldn't know her father from another. Peers out through the face holes.

Closes one eye.

Pel paces beneath Gogmagog, demanding they reach up and snatch Knot back, but the giant is deaf to him, sat as he always is, slumped against the tors. Basking in the moonlight. Pel beating uselessly at his thigh. He has not been so close to a giant before. The rocky granite skin is painted with lichen. Some as flat and hard as rock. Some glisten and shake like jelly.

'You're a fool, Pel.' He beats his head against Gogmagog's cracked heel before sliding down to lean against it.

'I could have told you that. Did, in fact.' Pel looks up to see the remains of an old friend.

'Cleaver. I—hello, Jacob.'

'In a pickle, I see.'

'Both of us ghosts, now.' Pel smiles as he talks. Death, for both men, has meant forgiveness of sorts. Nothing conciliatory spoken, but nothing inflammatory said. Cleaver's body still waits above, rotting slowly in peaty water alongside Pel's. He remains a shade until his body returns its matter to the mire and the God can work his magic.

'Might I join you?' Pel nods and Cleaver slips down alongside his friend.

'I've sat in more comfortable spots.'

'How is—'

'He's fine.' It is a rare sight to see two spirits tense, but they do. Callum hangs between them as he did in life. Pulling the bowstrings of both men taut. 'It will take time.' Changing the subject, Cleaver taps Pel's cotton heart. 'How did this happen?'

'A woman.'

'Ah. I never took you for a ladies' man.'

Pel might be a shade off top form, but he turns to scowl regardless.

'Her name was Meliora. She was a witch. I—we fought. I won.'

'I see.'

'Nancy is her granddaughter.'

'Oh. Might I…' Cleaver reaches for the heart, but his fingers pass through.

'Thank you, Jacob but it is a witch mark. I'll need another to remove it.'

'Are there no witches here?'

Pel thinks ruefully about the sisters. Their heads still hanging on a branch out of reach.

'We aren't on good terms.'

Jacob Cleaver smiles, swallows a retort.

'Well, we are stuck here, then. Perhaps you could tell me what's happened. Go on, old friend. For old times. Tell me a story.'

'It is not a happy one.'

'Yours never are.'

BLACK SADDLE

As Below

THE GIANT GOGMAGOG's ears prick up; he's never been one to miss a good story either. Let alone two.

Jacob. My friend. I believed what I did to be right.
She was the first person I saw, when I left Eythin.
I washed up half drowned, she said she ought to throw me back, let the sea take me.
She expected me to kiss her hand, which was so like her.
She took me to an inn, introduced me to Jan Fearnaught.
He knew me of course. Knew the island.
She read my future in the cards. The chariot. The magician. The world.
A new start, prosperity, triumph.
When I woke the next morning, she was gone and had left me with the bill.
Jan had warned me about her. It did not bother me unduly.
We had witches on Eythin, I had no fear of them.
It became clear as I moved around the counties that my new countrymen did.
I helped where I could, but magic brought a noose faster than a spell could work.
We saved some, together.
She saved more alone.

RAGWORT

Centuries of senseless murder.
Meanwhile, I lost an eye and gained my sight.
I heard of a post on the moor as Keeper. The incumbent was ill.
I found Mel to tell her, but she was grieving.
I said I'd take the role.
Keep it warm for her.

GLITTERING WOOD

Not Quite So Above

NANCY LISTENS WITH a Damocles heart to a storyteller swinging his words like swords, flinching each time one's spoken.

My Nancy. It was for her own good.
We met when I fled Eythin. Forsook that blasted home of ghosts, washed ashore at Bosmorven.
Mel dragged me from the surf, saved me, though I could have done so alone.
Believed that I, a Lord of Eythin, might deign to kiss her hand.
She led me to a little inn and introduced me to the local Keeper.
My first such meeting.
I let her read my future. One card was upside down.
She warned me it meant arrogance, control. A silly game for women.
I did not say goodbye when she left.
I paid her little mind though I remembered how fondly she spoke of Mirecoombe.
I wandered the country, after that. Watched them burn witches from Scotland to Exeter.
A sad but sometimes necessary endeavour.
I wished I could help, but it was not my place.

RAGWORT

Meliora tried, of course. I thought it foolish. Thought it would burn itself out.
Which it did.
These things do.
As she worked on her project, I sought out teachers.
I heard that the Keeper of the High Moor was ill.
In need of replacement.
I swooped in and took the role.
Right out from under her.

When she returned, Meliora had lost a great deal of her light.
She had lost her laugh.
She helped me a great deal, I can admit that. She taught me how to pack my spells in their glass balls. How to use flowers, brew potions. Nancy's birthright.
She used to tell a story.
I knew it, I had been read it as a child and in my youthful arrogance.
Eyebrows down, Jacob.
I had dismissed it.
Perhaps I should not have.
She drew lines between this story, of a goddess of witches, with others.
Between Perchta, Hecate and Ragana. Women with the feet of birds and several faces.
I see it now. The line between them and the Mother. Should have seen sooner.
It is Mel, Jacob. Telling this tale. I can feel it. From where I left her.
So then. We come to it.
Meliora had grown distant. Sour.
Her time abroad had given her no patience for our work.
She looked for a fight.

The man who governed the valley attracted her attention.
He was a prig, a stupid oaf of a man but there are ways.
I had it in hand.
Locals were dissatisfied with my methods, so Mel took coin to help them.
Spoiled his crops.
Killed his cattle.
He sent a lackey, to investigate. Against my advice.
Meliora killed him.
I'm sure Nance has read the story again now. Put it together.
I asked the creature she held as familiar, a badger.
You've met him.

She returned a while later.
She made herself useful. Did simple tasks I was too busy for.
Women's work. The sort of task I gave to you, my Nancy.
She had a story she used to tell.
A silly tale for children. I knew it, had been read it in the crib.
Had put it away with the other nursery rhymes.
It gave her a simple joy, however.
I ought to have put a stop to it.
Some nonsense about a goddess of witches.
Tried to prove it with other stories as though fiction layered might eventually show fact.
It must be Her. Must be the Mother.
The same Mother that returns now. Meliora was right.
If only...
I did what I did.
Meliora was a liability.
She had no time for the politics of things.
Always picking fights for no reason.
The man who governed us, taking the taxes, attracted her ire.

RAGWORT

He was just doing his job.
I had it in hand.
Mel began to work against him. Local folk paid her to do so.
Reduced yields.
Decreased his margins.
He sent a man. As he ought.
Meliora killed him.
The coffin witch. You know the story.
I tricked her loyal friend, a badger she called Brock.

I threatened him, I had to. Held him with iron over flame.
How might she be stopped?
Water.
I tried to free him, but he sruggled, fell into the fire.
He burnt to ash.
I made a box to hold her, from a storm damaged ash.
Then waited for her by the roadside.
I wished to talk, to stop things if I could.
She wouldn't listen.
I threw my strongest spells.
Chanted incantations not used since, and when we were both spent?
I felled her horse with powdered arsenic.
Trapped her beneath it.
She lay there staring at me as I prepared the salves.
I held firm.
The brews took, she slept.
I bound her in the bed I'd made her. Closed the lid.
It's funny, as I recall it now, I remember.
How strange that one so powerful, so strong.
Should still call out for her mother.
She was too powerful to keep on the moor.

But I could not bring myself to kill her.
I took her to Bosmorven, to Jan's son.
Nicca.
We threw her into the sea.
I carved spells into the wood to keep her sleeping.

> *Held him over a fire, you know me, my Nancy.*
> *They need the rod.*
> *Asked how I could kill her.*
> *Water.*
> *Then I dropped him into the flames.*
> *Ready or not.*
> *I carved her coffin from a lightning struck tree.*
> *Hid by the wayside.*
> *Could only win by treachery.*
> *I struck her when her back was turned.*
> *Used every dirty trick.*
> *Every con at my disposal, then got lucky.*
> *Her horse turned on its leg.*
> *Trapped her beneath it.*
> *Crying out. For her friend's help.*
> *It was too late.*
> *I drugged her, dragged her to the coffin.*
> *Could not look at her as I nailed it shut.*
> *Swore she would return.*
> *With the help of the Mother.*
> *I could hear Her name echoing in the box as it was sealed.*
> *That was not enough.*
> *I could not bear her to live.*
> *I took her to the keeper at Bosmorvern.*
> *The last man's son, Nicca.*
> *We drowned her.*

RAGWORT

> *Or so I'd thought.*

Made deals to care for her.
If it is her behind this talk of the Mother? She has awakened.
Will be coming back to the valley with the story.
Oh, Nancy. Please, if you can hear me, leave her be.
And, if you can, forgive me.

> *This ring, my Nancy?*
> *Perhaps she is still living.*
> *If she is, she can help. Can teach you about the Mother.*
> *Go, if you must, see to the witch.*
> *I don't expect you to forgive me.*

NANCY SITS BACK, looks to the sky as her father's face ripples like weed in the water.

'She's alive. My grandmother is alive.'

'Oh, my Nancy, how you must hate me.'

Nancy's head is a family reunion. A squabbling mess of emotion.

'No, Pel. I can't hate you. Not anymore.'

'No? I meant to kill her. It is error that keeps her alive. I should have taken her talk of the Mother more seriously.'

'I cannot hate you, I said. I did not say I forgive you. Besides. I know how much you changed, in the last year. It is hard, to hear how you were when younger. Crueller, even, than I anticipated. But I believe it. Tell me, though. True. What word, down there, of the mother? Of my grandmother?'

Patroclus, at last woken from sleep, pads to the edge of the water. Sets to growling.

'Pat, enough, it's Pel. Leave him.'

'Yes, mutt. Back off.' Nancy stares at the man in the water. Watches him rearrange his snarl into a grin. 'A joke, good lad, good boy. Sorry, my Nancy. It hasn't been easy, down here. Stop that, though, there's a good dog.'

The dog will not and paws and tears at the surface of the water, jaws snapping at the reflected face that swells and vanishes in bubble and foam. Nancy grabs his scruff and pulls him back.

'Pel, leave him be.'

'If you can't keep that dog quiet, how are you going to keep the moor to heel?'

'What?' The face in the water twists. Every fight with the old keeper resurfacing with it. 'Pel what's gotten into you? I thought we were…'

'What's gotten into me, is that the moor is falling apart. The Underfolk run riot, so do those dolts in the village. The Mother is no story. I was wrong. The air down here is filled with her. She will soon bleed through. If Meliora is alive, has some link with her, perhaps she can intercede.'

'But, how…'

'I've left too big a task for you. Oh, my Nancy, I wish I was there to help.'

Nancy will not cry. She'll not give him the satisfaction even if she is baffled at this sudden reversal.

'This is all new, Pel. You are the one who kept it from me, I could have been…'

'Don't turn this on me. Go, find that witch. See what good comes of it. That sort of magic has no place here.'

'My magic.'

'You know my feelings on that. I thought I'd bred that out of you. Clearly not.'

'I see.'

RAGWORT

'Do you? Do you see what using that magic has wrought? The unpicking of a lifetime's work, girl. If you'd just listened! Applied yourself to the ways I showed you. My Nancy, you have such promise. You're better than this. I made you to be better.'

Nancy sits on the bank, Patroclus still tugging at his collar, and she frowns. Frowns at the dogs curled lip. Frowns at the shadow in the water.

'This doesn't sound like you, Pel.'

Pel stops at this. For a second there is panic, but it washes away with the foam.

'Mine Nancy, my Nancy. I'm sorry. It is just that I worry, down here, impotent. Stuck. Forgive me. I just can't bear to watch you fail, without me there to pick you up again.'

'You arrogant old sod. I've spent a year picking myself up, Pel. I love you, truly, but you need to let go. I can do this.'

Pel, simmering in his pool, flickers between frown and contrition.

'Go then, my Nancy. Find your grandmother, if she can stop the Mother make her do so but know this, my Nancy. If you find her and she gets her hooks in you? It is her or me. I'll not watch her corrupt you.'

Nancy starts, the ultimatum a strike across her face and taking his chance Patroclus wrenches free, leaps teeth first into the pool, but the echo of her father has gone. Nancy speaks to the ripples.

'You're dead, Pel. You don't get to make me choose. At least you've made it easier to let you go.'

BELOW, PEL'S GHOST simmers. Picks again at the heart on his chest. Tears falling down hollow cheeks.

'She is free. Jacob. She will be coming.'

'The Mother?'

'The Witch. It is her doing. I can feel it. I know not what or how she is engineering it, but I know Mel's work when I see it. Cleaver, Jacob, old friend. I have no right to ask this, but will you help me?'

WHITE ALYSSUM

The holes in the chapel wall are closing up, like wounds sutured shut. Abraham Pine-Coffin has been present for every brick laid since his arrival, sleeves rolled up and helping, best he can. It has earned him some grudging respect. His broad grin is hard not to warm to, and he has persuaded a few of the cults to return to the chapel hill, more hands to make light of the work.

His cassock and suit jacket lay folded out of the sun, but he wears his hat as he works, which serves him well as were they not reminded of his higher calling the Calder brothers would struggle to hold their tongues. He is by far the worst builder they have ever worked with. Still, they can't fault his spirit.

'Here, Reverend. Give me that.' Luk Calder takes the large lump of granite that the Reverend is struggling with and lays it on the wall. They have reused most of the stones from before the collapse. Pulling them from crumbling mortar, saving what they can. Abraham hands the stone over gratefully and straightens an aching back.

'Don't forget to leave space, Luk. Your brother's almost done; I think. We can fit it today.'

A shadow passes across Luk Calder's face. A cloud passing over stone.

'And you're sure, Reverend? That it's the best thing to do? He was a good man. It doesn't seem right, somehow.'

Abraham Pine-Coffin gives no impression of having heard the man and walks to the corner, where Yestin kneels by a stone corpse laid out on a roll of fabric. Years of splitting granite fence posts had been hiding a hobby, Yestin has proven himself quite the craftsman. It is the spit of Jacob Cleaver. Eyes closed and cheekbones that cut the air around them into ribbons. Face so severe that you'd find yourself praying before you knew what you were doing, just to be on the safe side. The body, dressed in chiselled cassock and surplice, lies on a bed of stone. Pillow beneath the head and a lamb at his feet. Inscribed on the base:

"The Reverend Jacob Nathanial Cleaver. Died in service to our Lord in the year 1783. May your restless soul lie still."

The Reverend Pine-Coffin stands for a moment and watches Yestin work before laying a hand on his shoulder.

'Lovely, Yestin. Truly. Is it ready?'

'Yes, Reverend. And it's to go where we discussed, not, perhaps—'

Abraham Pine-Coffin holds up a hand. Unlike his predecessor, whose very shadow was a threat, the new Reverend deals in a kinder authority. The men stop, put down their tools and listen.

'It is to go where I said it will go. I did not know the Reverend Cleaver. I do not pretend to understand, either, what happened last year. I have heard a maddening array of stories, and I'll not try and parse them. But I understand he did things that—transcended—the bounds of our faith. Whether those acts were manifested, or of a purely theological heresy they still occurred. So, in honour of those he helped, here he is. In stone. At his chapel. But in honour of those he hurt he will not be placed inside.' Abraham has collected more than stories; he has a notebook full of testimonials. 'You will finish the wall as requested. Place this fine memorial in an alcove on the western wall's exterior. He can be remembered there.'

A thought shared between two heads, but only one has the sense not to speak it.

'It's not right.' Luk cannot hold his tongue. The Reverend stands in an archway that waits for a window and lets the sun stream past his face.

'And you are the arbiter of right or wrong here, are you Luk?' Though his brother smirks, Luk Calder's eyes glisten at the rebuke. 'I am your reverend. I will say what is righteous. You may not always agree. Indeed, if the views of the man we honour here are your own, we almost certainly will not. But you will heed my words, Luk Calder. You will listen. It is a different path to the one you walked before but it leads to the same place, and I will not follow you down a darker one. Do you understand?'

If Jacob Cleaver was an icy night, then Abraham Pine-Coffin is the golden light of dawn. But frostbitten or sunburnt there's a danger to both, and Luk takes a step backwards into the shade. Nods. Helps his brother lift the stone cadaver into place.

As they work, the Reverend walks through the rood screen—by some miracle unscathed—to a dust sheeted object that stands in front of the altar. He carefully removes the sheet and holds the gaze of the brass eagle beneath. It has tarnished a little in the months since its covering, but its eyes still shine. He winks at it, then turns to his newly exposed wall.

'What do you know of your saint, boys?'

The Calders pause, lean back against the stone reverend

behind them. This is not the sort of question they enjoy. They prefer to be told what they believe in, without space for questions. No matter, Abraham is not in need of an answer, all he wants is an audience. 'I have to say I did not know her myself. And I had thought I knew them all. St. Reagan. Fascinating. Did you know this was here?' Neither brother can look at the painting, they bow their heads. Abraham presses on.

'The windows that were broken, was she shown in them? That's a good starting point with these things but I can't see her in those that remain.' More silence from the Calders who, even with a knife to their throat could not honestly say what was shown in the broken glass. 'You know, before the dissolution, church was quite a cheery place, in its way. They used to paint the gospels onto the walls, bible stories, just as these have been.' He taps the worm riddled, dull oak of the rood. Its figures eaten away. 'The wood was painted too, there was colour, light. Gold.'

'We found the pictures before, sir. A few years back. Some plaster fell and there was colour beneath.' Yestin, nodding towards the Reverend's excavations is beaten back into silence by the blows of his brother's glare. The Reverend's jaw tenses. Strains to hold in a thought.

'You did? And they were replastered to preserve them, I hope? Not because you did not like them.' A wry smile. 'At least you did so carefully. It would have been a shame to lose them.'

'No.' Luk sounds angry. 'We did not protect them. The Reverend Cleaver had us wash the colour away with lime before the plaster went back. Nothing was left. That wall was scrubbed clean.' Abraham looks at the scared faces before him. Faces that still cannot look at the wall.

'Oh, I see. Were these the only ones you found and purified?' If he doubts their story he hides it well. If you looked closely, as some of the piskies are doing, you might see the hairs standing up on his neck. Luk speaks with eyes still lowered.

'Can't say you wouldn't find more if you tore the place apart but, with respect Reverend, you'd need to find other men to do it.'

Crestfallen, Abraham Pine-Coffin traces the white plaster with his fingers.

'No, Luk. I've done damage enough revealing these. I see that.' The Reverend's gaze lingers, 'I don't suppose, though, you recall what the other paintings showed? Should there have been more?' Yestin looks to his brother, and it is with the most reluctant nod that Luk tells him to speak. What harm can it do now? A reverend is a reverend. Best keep him on side.

'Flames, Reverend. From above and below and winged creatures. Angels, some at least. Creatures I don't know the names of too. All flying about the moor. There was a lady in the middle, sleeping, though she had been worn away. You could see the stone through parts of her. The Reverend, the old Reverend, told us folk once thought touching images might cure a man. He held no truck with it.' Yestin's eyes are looking beyond the plaster on the eastern wall. Out to the sky beyond and past that too. To wherever he imagines those images were taken from. Luk shuffles uncomfortably and looks at his shoes, but the Reverend is staring at Yestin's face. At the radiance of it. It is happy. He finds he smiles too.

'Thank you, Yestin, for telling me. It is a shame I never saw it, but thanks to you, in a way, I have.' He walks to the man and lays his hands on his shoulders. Squeezing them in thanks then releasing Yestin to his reverie. 'And you know nothing more of St. Reagan? No stories told when you were little, no mention of her in church?'

Emboldened, perhaps, by his younger brother Luk stands forwards.

'She had a feast day. That is, we had one for her. The village. Dad used to talk about it, his dad used to say he'd seen the last. It ended years back. When they messed about with the prayerbooks. We asked the last Reverend once, but he didn't like the idea of bringing it back. Said it wasn't right in a modern church.'

The smile stretches from one side of Abraham's face to the other.

'A feast? A feast! Yes, we will bring that back. Everybody loves a party. Most surely. Quite the thing. When was it, do you recall?'

'May 18th.'

Luk Calder. A man of hidden knowledge. A holy well.

'May 18th it is then. My, only one month away.' The Reverend looks around at the church. The walls though mostly rebuilt are still only held up with earth mortar. They need lime to hold fast against the weather. The missing windows, though they let in the views, need glazing—new stained glass to be commissioned before a congregation can sit here. The hole in the roof still gapes, mouth open at the stars, and the broken ledgestone, covered with planks, needs to be fixed tight against the bodies below. The bell, the pews—a long list.

'We might need some help boys. Put the word out. Ask your father if he can spare more men. I'll write to Exeter, see if the bishop can assist us. In the meantime, did my predecessor leave anything, any books, or papers? There must be some history of the chapel somewhere.'

The brothers file out, the Reverend follows, along the wooden corridor to the far side of the churchyard where Cleaver's hermitage stands.

It does not look well.

The fire must have been fierce, it has melted the lead in the windows and the little diamonds of clear and red glass lie shattered on the path. The door is a crackle of burnt paint and nails and as Luk opens it all four men step back and wait for it to fall. By some miracle it holds, and they step inside. It is black. A place devoid of light, the floor just a noise now of broken, splintered things. On the table is the only thing to survive. Jacob Cleaver's bible. Burnt at the edges but so dense and heavy that even fiery fingers couldn't prise it open.

'What happened here, boys?'

They answer together, the words tumbling over each other into stacks of letters.

'Lightning.'

'Accident.'

This last from Luk who lacks the imagination to lie but is far too savvy to tell the truth.

'I see. A shame.' The Reverend Pine-Coffin plays this game half-heartedly and prises the bible from the desk. A perfect, unburnt square of wood beneath. He smiles, lifts the bible and, just in time, catches the slim volume that was hidden beneath. Clutching the book to his breast he turns and begins to leave, stopping only at the sight of the gorse wood cross burnt black on the far wall. Above the skeleton of a bed. 'Is there anyone else who might have records of the church, the histories of Mirecoombe?'

Yestin steps forward.

'Dad has some things. Madge Gould perhaps. Pel…'

'Madge and our father. Ask them, Reverend.' Luk glares at Yestin. The man steps back against the wall, black streaks rubbing onto his shirt. The Reverend Pine-Coffin considers asking more questions. But he can see the answers are long burnt.

'If I stay here, boys, I can only hope I inspire such devotion on my death as my predecessor has. But please—if it comes to it—go easier on the lamp oil, eh? You can still smell it, really quite strongly.'

'Reverend—' A silencing hand.

'Don't worry, Luk. I don't need to know. But he is gone. You don't owe him anything any longer. All I ask is that from this point, you are truthful with me. Understood?'

The Calders pause before answering, before yoking themselves to another black coated man, but the pull of familiarity is too great. The comfort of a guiding hand.

'Yes, Reverend.'

'Excellent. Back to it, then. We have a feast to ready ourselves for.'

Abraham Pine-Coffin watches the backs of the men as they return to work, then turns the bible over. The small book hidden beneath is a journal, the dates of the preceding years neatly written on the cover. The Reverend smiles and clutches the books tighter, the bible staining his fingers black with soot. He is turning back to the church when he sees her. Nancy. Going into the stables behind the nest. There is a cart and horse in front, her dog, whose name escapes him, wagging his tail at the horse's feet and the landlady lifting boxes out to the caravan. He does not know why but he is smiling and a part of him, a large part, would like to know where this 'Keeper' is going. The same part realises with a start that he will miss her when she is gone.

'Nancy Bligh.' He speaks into the breeze. 'Don't be gone long. I have the strangest feeling we are going to need one another very soon.' He turns back to the church at the tolling of a bell, and he is halfway across the churchyard before he realises there isn't one left to ring.

GROUNDSEL

Nancy turns her head at a noise from the chapel hill. Metal striking metal, ringing in the morning. A Calder at work, she assumes. Not her concern. The cart creaks as it warms in the sun. It was acquired, with the horse, by some complicated scheme as both are owned by Locryn Calder. Nancy has not asked Madge for details, but the landlady has been hinting heavily that the journey should begin soon. Before the owner sees just who he's been lending to, and all hell breaks loose. Madge has filled in the mundane details Pel had failed to give. The location of the village, the way. Madge had told her it all through gritted teeth, but she had told her. Nancy could not shake the idea that Madge had known all Pel had told her. Kept it from her. Another betrayal couched in kindness. Madge had denied it, but Nancy knows.

'Please Nancy, leave her sleeping.'

Since Nancy told her of her plans, the landlady has not slept herself. Though she has other reasons for leaving another woman to her rest.

'I'll not go over this again, Madge. I have family, real family. Family both you and my father hid from me. She can teach me about the Murmur, about my legacy. Why would you keep me from that?'

'Please, Nance, I knew her. Yes. Fine. I did not, I promise you, know she still lived. I would never have hidden that. I don't want to see you hurt. I know I'm not your—please Nancy, I just want you safe.'

'Enough. I'm late as it is. If you'll not wish me well, then leave me be. Thank you, for showing me the way, but I need to go. If I'm to protect this moor, I need her.'

'I could close the Nest, Nancy. I could come with you?'

'What for?'

Patroclus barks, distracting Nancy from Madge's devastated face. She turns instead to Billy Askell, loading Patroclus into the back of the cart with the provisions. Billy who still says thank you every time he sees Nancy. Billy who, to his credit, still delivers the beer, still visits the village. Even with the shadow of a noose round his neck and the wood for his gallows still leant in the corner of the smithy. A little bit in love with her who saved him. A little bit afraid of her too. His interest in magic deepened. He stands back once he's finished loading and, cap in hand, waits to wave her off.

'Thank you, Billy. I'll see you when I get back. Madge, take care of Selkie for me. I won't be long. A day or two at the most.'

'Take care Nancy. I love you; I hope you know that.'

Nancy pauses on the steps of the cart. The words catch in her throat and all she manages is a sharp nod. A wrenching pain in her gut.

She climbs into the seat of the cart and lifts the reins. The horse is a chestnut cob gelding and his tack rattles with a pub ceiling's worth of brasses. Heavy blinkers shielding him from distractions and a white blaze covering one eye. A light touch from Nancy and the old horse moves on. The Keeper draws her coat about her shoulders against the chill morning sun and does not turn back. She's made the preparations.

The moor will be fine without her for a few days. It owes her that. After the shambles of the last meeting the Underfolk are running scared and, though she does not know him, she must hope the new Reverend will keep the villagers in line. There's no point her being here, anyway. Nothing will change without her grandmother back. Knot, and Pel, have made that quite clear. If the Mother is coming, Nancy's no use without her.

Nancy closes her eyes and lets the horse pick his way out of the village, over the fallen cross and stone and out onto the peaty, stitchwort threaded grass. As they pass the boundary of Mirecoombe Nancy opens her eyes and lets out a breath. The weight of it all, the constant weight, lifting ever so lightly. It begins to rain, filling her nose with the scent of the grass and ground, as though she had plugged each nostril with a pinch of moss. It is Nancy's favourite scent in all the world, and she drinks it in as she leaves her home.

Pel had never taken her to the sea. He was Keeper of the High Moor. The highlands, the valleys. They were his. The sea belonged to another Keeper, and he wouldn't trespass without good reason. That's what he'd said.

'You're a liar, Pel. You just couldn't face going back there.' She snarls it into the rain. Nancy steadies her breathing. Calms her nerves. She's angry. At Pel but at herself too. There were things she should have asked. Things Madge can't help her with.

'We'll just have to work it out ourselves, won't we?' She smiles back at Patroclus who is leant against a bag of hay and sleeping already, though Mirecoombe is still in view. No matter. Questions find answers like dowsers find water, in Nancy's experience. Whether you want them to or not. To get to the road Nancy rides over the foothills, cartwheels bouncing on the uneven ground, but as the rain stops, she thuds onto the rough track that will take her off the moor. The last time she was out this way she had met Knot for the first time. Whoever he is.

Thoughts for later.

Nancy turns her gaze to the line of trees that drape their branches over the stream. The branches shaggy with moss and their blossom falling into the water. Apples, sloes and hawthorn berries hiding just behind the petals, waiting for their time to shine. She hears the sound of the tinners a field or two over, sieving pans of stone in diverted hill water that runs through leats dug into the hillside. Shaking out the rocks heavy with metal and discarding the rest. She keeps riding, fantasising about her grandmother. Would she be kind? Could she show Nancy how to use her magic? Would she be pleased to see her? Nancy's memories of her parents are lost in a childhood haze. She can't even picture them anymore, though sometimes she finds a dress in a chest that smells of her mother and she's six again. On her lap in the big armchair, by the fire. Stark contrast with her nights at Pel's, the two of them sat in silence as Pel read and Nancy drew. The closest she got to a hug the day she fell from her pony, hitting her head, and Pel clutched her so tight as she came round, she'd had to shout for him to stop. He'd gotten flustered, his love once again turning to rebuke as he'd told her off for dangerous riding. She's read enough fairytales to know a grandmother's different. Cosy. Warm. Waiting, all this time, barely a day's ride away. A person who is hers. Who knows her magic. Her fantasies curdle into resentment again, as she curses her father's name.

The ground slopes away from the moor, from home. The steep hillsides easing into farmland. Easier to manage with the wind off them they are grazed by cattle and sheep. Tough breeds and horns on both, teeth tearing at the short grass. The cart track

Nancy follows is more even than before, though the wheels of the cart keep bouncing into adjoining furrows. Alongside the trail, violets seep from the banks and white eyebright flowers map constellations in the grass. Nancy tightens her grip on the reins. These fields belong to Locryn Calder. She can see his house on a rise to her left. The largest in the valley. A mock manor of granite built by a man who'd never seen a mansion. Nancy comforts herself with the knowledge the Calder sons are out, working at the chapel. And their father rarely manages to rise before midday. She finds herself humming as she rides by. The tune the Underfolk sang. The tune she keeps hearing in the village. Though she does not yet know the words she can feel them, just out of sight. It gives her a disquieting confidence, this tune. It makes her feel safe, but in the same way carrying a weapon might. A security that will come at the cost of another's.

The problem with feeling safe is that you don't see trouble coming.

'Miss Bligh.'

Cusk. He blends right in with the gatepost he leans on. Grey work clothes merging with the granite though the stone is prettier. Flecks of quartz and tourmaline giving a colour that the estate manager does not possess.

'Cusk.'

'That's a fine horse and cart you've acquired. Can't be sure, but it looks an awful lot like the one I sent to the Wicketts, to use collecting stone.'

Nancy pulls the reins and brings the cart to a stop.

'He was lent to me by another, Cusk. Can't see how he can be yours.'

The old man regards the young Keeper for a long while. Takes her in. Nancy has never thought much of Cusk. Not that she thought little of him, just that he was more furniture than man. Always at the arm of Locryn Calder, rarely saying a word. No children. No wife.

'Where are you riding to on this horse that's most definitely mine?'

'I fancied a look at the sea old man. That's all.'

'Is that so? And is the cart just to carry that lazy dog? You've a fine horse at home, why the need of this one?'

'An awful lot of questions for a man with no right to an answer.'

'Oh, I know the answers, Nancy. These old eyes see more than you think.' Cusk pats the gelding's neck, and he turns to whinny at him.

'See you take care of Foxglove, Miss Bligh. He's a good horse. Don't you go losing him.' Nancy nods to the man and starts to ride on. 'And Nancy?' She turns. 'That's an ugly song you're singing. I'd find another tune if I were you.'

He walks across the fields, hands in his pockets and hat pulled down tight.

'Cusk! What do you know of it?'

He does not break stride, but he does answer, the words carried by a charm of goldfinch that bounce across the grass like leaves on the wind.

'Witchcraft, Miss Bligh. That song's witchcraft. Ask your grandmother when you see her. She'll tell you.'

Nancy goes white.

'My grandmother's dead, Cusk. You should know, you've been telling me her stories!'

'Is she now? Well, that must be right then Miss Bligh. Be careful on the roads to the sea. There's less friendly folk than I out there.'

Cusk raises a hand and waves her on, a dismissal she finds

herself heeding as she lifts the reigns and continues on her journey. With Cusk out of earshot she speaks to herself. Patroclus having slept through the whole conversation.

'Would it be so much to ask, Pat? For just one person in my life to be simple, to just be precisely what they seem. Why is everyone a riddle!'

As the cart disappears over the crest of the hill, down and off Calder's farm, off the moor, Cusk glares out from a new gateway. There's a shout, from the house, and he closes his eyes. Locryn Calder is awake and ready to start drinking. As Cusk turns and walks towards the house, he finds himself humming Nancy's tune. He spits the song out, crosses his chest, and reaches into his pocket for a piece of granite he keeps there, worn smooth by years of rubbing. Two veins of quartz forming a white cross in the black surface. He grips it tight to stop his hand from shaking. The rain, which has been steady until now, falls more heavily. It washes the tears from the old man's face and, for a second, he thinks that is what he tastes. But no, Cusk wipes his eyes and opens his mouth, lets the raindrops fall on his tongue. He stands and soaks in the downpour, swallowing hard. He may still be crying, but he knows seawater when he tastes it. And the clouds are a rolling tide.

PART TWO

"You 'll bury me, my mother, just beneath the hawthorn shade,
And you 'll come sometimes and see me where I am lowly laid.
I shall not forget you, mother; I shall hear you when you pass,
With your feet above my head in the long and pleasant grass."

Alfred, Lord Tennyson

WILD GARLIC

THE MOOR FIGHTS the farmland for several miles. Fields bound in by granite boulders but between them untamed land holds fast. Sheep graze both, stone lined holes left in the hedges so they can pass through, but the cattle stay penned in their field. Nancy, high enough in her seat to look over the banks, takes it in as she rides. Behind her, what remains of Echo Tor and the Queen's Rocks rise above the moorland. Mirecoombe kept hidden between them, a surprise for those that earn it.

A Cornish hedge is a remarkable thing.

Stone built, large at the bottom and smaller going up, and filled to the gunnels with earth. Soil. Rabbit bones. The batter of the hedge carefully shaped to send the water packing and strong enough a bull can scratch its hide and leave it standing. No trace left behind but bristling hairs on a smooth patch of stone. From the top, plants grow and shade the path Nancy rides down. Blackthorn, elder, gorse and, from the gaps between the stones, ferns grow. Little wax discs of navelwort poking from tangles of vetch. Throughout it all honeysuckle twists, a green thread of perfumed flowers that even now, in the morning, are heady and rich like burdock wine. Any later in the day and Nancy would be drunk on it. As she rides, she marks the changes in the top stones. Depending on the builders' whim they are herringbone or tightly packed. Slivers of slate or granite blocks studded like a chessboard with quartz. One field she passes has great slabs stood along the length of the hedge, tombstones leant against a cemetery bank, as though the field it bounds contains a barrowful of dead. Which, after all, it might. The grass in that pasture *is* greener than the rest.

Nancy scans the horizon for the sea. She has seen it from a distance, from the rocks on the hills. A thin line between the blue and the green. But the weather has not let up and all she can see in the distance is mist, the shadow of a woodland sticking like kindling from it. Nancy keeps an eye out for the Underfolk. The spriggans rarely venture this low, these rocks belong to other creatures. The pixies roam freely though. She suspects this is where they come to misbehave. At the edges of things. She knows very little about the woods and fields ahead. These boundaries belong to nobody, no keeper watches them. She has no jurisdiction here.

Foxglove bridles as he enters the wood. Though the rain has slowed, and sunlight breaks through the clouds, lighting up the leaves of the beech trees and bathing the woodland in gold, it still feels oppressive. Like being smothered, but with the finest cloth. The cartwheels crunch over the stalks of the bluebells that mat the floor. A tease of an ocean. A taste of the one to come. At the edges of this florid sea great banks of wild garlic crash against the leaf mould in foamy white splashes and Nancy closes her eyes against the smell. The only woods on the moor are small and wizened. The trees kept low and stocky. This woodland towers over her, the trees run rings around her. The track is easy enough to keep on. Though the beech and oak press close there is a clear path through their trunks. It is a steep path though. A sinking valley, the sides growing closer as she descends. The treetops closing over, a green kiss, Nancy trapped inside. Birdsong echoes and the singers fall from the branches like leaves, fighting each other on the way down. Nancy still feels uncomfortable here. There is rustling she cannot place and too many holes in the trunks of trees that she cannot see into, the hill she's travelled down rising high behind her, no easy way to retreat. So, on she rides. The cart bumps as they descend and even Patroclus can't sleep through it. He jumps from the back and walks alongside Foxglove, who has not settled. She pulls her head from side to side, not trusting the blinkers to keep her safe, and no amount of comforting words seem to be working. Nancy lists creatures in her head.

Adderfoot

The Bone-men

The Root-bound Cat

She knows how to deal with each and yet, what else is in these woods? She has not asked permission to travel. A guest uninvited in a territory not hers. No matter, she tells herself. She has no jurisdiction, but she can use her spells. The Murmur, if she really has to. She may not be wanted but she'll get where she's going.

There is a wind blowing footsteps into the creaking of the trees. But nothing comes close. Nothing breaks cover.

'What do you think, Pat?'

The dog looks up, ears up and forward, and growls at the leaves.

'I know boy. I know.'

Nancy tries to take note of the trees as they pass. Though her tattoos serve the same purpose here as they do on the moor, she feels disconnected. The flowers inked on her skin are the flowers she knows. They don't grow here, not all of them at least. She wonders, idly, if she might get these inked on her skin, too. How she might go about reaching her tattooist. She shivers at the thought of the needle. The hand that holds it. It is not an unpleasant feeling. She's still lost in the thought when the cross appears. For a second, she thinks it is a rotting trunk, a fallen tree. But as the cart draws close, she sees the stone, and a granite cross feels more like home than anything else she's passed today. She pulls Foxglove to a halt and leaves the horse grazing as she dismounts. The cross is tall and worn and covered in ivy. She follows the line of the stone to its base and sees that there, under moss, a wall runs either side.

Sometimes, when looking at clouds, shapes form. Then another. Until all you can see are pictures in the sky. So it goes now. Having noticed the wall, Nancy notices the graves. Poking from the floor and carpeted in moss, their legends covered in a thick shaggy green. A churchyard full. Nancy almost trips then, on the granite slatted cattle grid that once kept livestock out, so moss grown, and leaf filled that it is barely a ripple now. Hardly an obstacle at all. Between them the trees grow. Beech and elm, ash and birch with bark that peels in silver shavings. Oak, too. And in the centre of the copse is a tower. Tall and as green as everything around it, the moss growing all the way to the top and smothering the four stone spikes at its corners. The rest of the church has been torn down by roots and branches. The stone now green rubble, with celandine mapping its surface. But the arched door still stands. The wood intact. Not rotten at all. The iron latch still waiting to be turned. So inside Nancy goes. Nothing left but the tower and the square of church within it. Nothing left there but the font. It is huge. Far larger than any Nancy has seen, and it has a crack running right down the middle. The inside is stained a dark rusting brown.

'Pat?'

Nancy looks behind her, but the dog is not there which means the noise she heard is inside with her. She looks up. Nothing but darkness spiralling up. No staircase. No bell. A hollow tower and yet she knows it is full. Pel was always reluctant to talk of ghosts, but he shared a little over the years. Ghosts are like the Underfolk. They are only seen when they want to be, but Nancy knows they are there.

'What happened here?'

Silence, and then like a death knell, voices echoing down from where the bells once hung.

Peter

Peter

Peter

Then nothing again. Nancy hurries out into fast receding sunlight and climbs back into the cart.

'Pat!'

The dog comes hurrying from whatever scent he'd found.

'Come, boy, this place is a problem for later.' She shivers again, then cracks the reigns to spur their journey on. When the rain starts to fall, washing some of the chill away, Nancy laughs with relief and keeps on riding.

The track climbs out of the church's valley and Nancy feels the weight lift with every step. Though the trees keep pace with the path they seem different to the ones below. Even the birds seem kinder. The path levels out but falls again into another valley. She knows where they are now. She can hear water rushing in the trees to her right, can smell the wet slate. A kingfisher darts across the track and, blinded by the gold and blue, Nancy blinks. When her eyes open, she can taste salt on the air. Hear the boom of waves striking harbour walls and hear gulls calling her down. This is the valley she has been riding to all day. This is where her grandmother was drowned.

ALE-HOOF

BILLY ASKELL DRIVES his cart with little care for the road. His horse, an old grey shire named Cooper, jangles with every heavy step.

Cooper knows the way.

As he rides, Billy thinks of Mirecoombe. A place he loved visiting, before his arrest, his accusation. A place he'd like to love again. There has been little acknowledgement of the events of last year. The men who held him, bound him—constructed the gallows—sit and drink when he brings in the beer. They raise their hands to half-mast to welcome him in, but not a one looks him in the eye. The past is a secret they're bound not to tell. Afraid to open the box and see their own hearts inside. It had been Madge who had pushed him to return. She had written to the brewery, a few weeks after Cleaver drowned. Asked them to send Billy on the next run. Madge Gould could charm a man even through a letter, and after reading it, his manager had firmly suggested he go. He had dragged his feet back there against every instinct. The welts on his wrists healed into thick white scars, and some part deep within him was beyond all hope of repair. And now? He feels adrift, but headed home. Sailing close to the shore in a sea with hidden reefs that have claimed his ship before. Rocks he might not survive twice. Still. Back he comes. For the village. For her. He loves Nancy Bligh as much as the spriggans on the hill, but she terrifies him in equal measure. He thinks that's a part of Madge's insistence on his return. A desire to matchmake. He's not the heart to tell her that she's climbing an endless hill. Nancy might be fond of him, but she saved him out of little more than a desire for justice. She had carried him to safety, deposited him in the rain and sent him walking as a mother does a child, and though a part of him might wish it different, he's proud she chooses to care for him. Proud he's worth her love. No, he comes back for himself, to prove he's undaunted. To show he's not scared. He comes back too for the magic. He dreams of mountains moving, dreams of faces in rocks and movement in the grass. Dreams of Nancy riding roughshod in the sky. Though the part that wishes she loved him differently is the larger part.

No matter. He is content with what he's been given. He blames Madge for these wild, uprooted thoughts. She'd pressed him with a drink before he'd left so while his cart is as empty as his stomach, his head brims with whatever Madge brews under the floors of the Nest.

It mixes amicably with the moonlight. His eyes shine.

'Potent, the draughts that old witch brews, aren't they Billy?'

The voice seems contained within the moonbeams. It hangs from the dandelion seeds. Billy is just drunk enough for his heartbeat not to quicken. But he does lift the reins, for the first time this journey, to spur old Cooper on.

'What's your name then, spirit?'

'You'll not get a name from me Billy Askell. Not for a man so close to the gallows. You've an unlucky air about you. But that could change. How'd you like a little magic in your life?'

Billy rides on but something's spooking the horse, and Cooper bridles on the pathway. The cart creaks to a halt.

'I've no need of your help, spirit. Pass on by.' As he speaks, Billy reaches down and turns his pockets inside out. There is a laugh and Billy wonders if there were quite so many seeds in the air before.

'Now, Billy, am I to be trounced by a backwards pocket? Were you dressed widdershins head to toe I'd not crack the spark of a grin. Stop your fooling. Listen to me. Trust me.'

Billy sits mute in his cart and tries again with the leather reins. Cooper stands immovable before him. The wind has picked up and on its current it carries more seeds towards him. A snowstorm of parasol tufted promise. A future meadow.

'A man's life is a funny thing, Billy. Like the tail of a slow worm. Cut it off and there's the chance it might grow again. The noose can be slipped. A man's life measured in hours to come, now that—that could fill a sky.'

The seedheads swirl now, illuminated by the moon, they shine white in the darkness, catch on Billy's shirt, in his hair. When one lands on his face it is ice cold and he fears it will melt.

'I can give you what you're seeking, Billy. Make Mirecoombe a home, a place to stay. If you'd trust me.'

'Nancy trusts me.' Shaking his head free of seeds, Billy frowns at the air. He knows little of this, but he knows Nancy. He knows a liar when he hears one too.

'I'll not make deals with voices. However pretty their show. Let me be on my way and be done with it. Tempt another. Leave me alone.'

'A man's life, Billy. A slowworm's tail. A thing cut short grown long. And once regrown... well. Who knows how long it might last? She is coming. Billy. The Mother is coming. She can give you magic, Billy. You'd like that, would you not? Mine Nancy might love you, were there magic between you. The Mother can do that, if you'll say her name.'

There is a gust of wind and the seeds swirl around Billy's head, blinding him with feathered edges. And then, in a column, they rise, pulse like starlings, and begin to draw in on themselves. Each seed folding into the next until the storm becomes a shower, becomes a flurry. Becomes a single seed.

Billy opens his mouth, forms an 'M' with his lips, feels his heart between his teeth and swallows it back down.

'No matter, Billy. I'll ask you again, the next time we meet, but be warned. A slowworm can't lose the same tail twice.'

Billy jumps clear of his seat as the nightjar calls. He feels its wings pass by and watches open mouthed as it snatches the seed from the air. When it is gone, he rolls the cart on. Unaware that beneath its wheels the yellow crosses of tormentil push from the ground like a field of floral graves.

TAMARISK

The houses emerge with Nancy as she clears the treeline. They creep towards the harbour slowly—so as not to scare the fish—and Nancy finds that she is holding her breath.

The sea.

More black than blue, more green than black. Each wave another shade of water. There is nothing out there but water. The river flows loudly down the rocks to her left and issues into the sea between the two cleft cliffs. Black slate that seems to have been forced apart by sheer, fluid, determination. The rocks, wet from the waist down, shine where the sea can reach them, and above the tideline plants and flowers cling to the memory of soil. Though the sea seemed calm at first, Nancy hears it boom as it hits the rocks and the spray rises higher than she'd have thought it ought to. Despite the sun and the cloudless sky, far out to sea there is a storm waiting. Dark grey clouds that keep green sea and blue sky apart but buckle under the weight of both. Against this tricolour of weather and water Nancy sees the seagulls circling. They rise and fall at counterpoint with the water and seem to merge with the breaking foam, rising higher than the water's able, silver fish in orange beaks a prize waiting to be stolen. They call at her with mocking tones and dare her to come closer. She is transfixed. It is only the sound of the cartwheels sliding on a too steep path that brings her round. Snaps her free of the seabird's calls.

'Woah! Foxglove, hold boy.' Nancy pulls back on the reins to slow the horse. So taken was she with the view ahead Nancy has let the horse lead her down a dangerous path. An onshore wreck just waiting to happen. She sees a turning to her left that leads between the houses onto a wider, longer path, that snakes its way to the bottom of the valley on a more even keel than the one she's chosen. 'Come then, boy, down we go.'

There are fewer houses here than at home, and these seem more solidly built. Walls bulging under the weight of slate roofs and chimney smoke that smells of seaweed burning. From the mortar ferns uncurl and the granite walls are dripping. The houses are built on tiered ledges, rills beneath steps to let the water flow freely as it pours down the hill in search of salt. The sunlight catches the water and wreathes every house in crystal dusted glitter. As Nancy, horse, and dog descend, they feel eyes on them. See curtains twitch. Though she hasn't passed a road marker or sign, Nancy is sure this is Bosmorven, sure this is where Pel landed. Where her grandmother must reside. She catches a snippet of that everywhere song from an open doorway and hurries on.

At the bottom of the valley the road levels out and runs alongside the river. There are more houses here, granite backed but faces painted white against the weather. Most of the buildings gathered by the water are stores for boats and nets, with the exception of the Inn that towers overhead, crenelated roofline daring a newcomer inside. Its hanging sign long blown down, Nancy is left with the letters in faded gold that seem to sprout from the stone like coral: *The Proserpine Hotel*. Jutting from the seaward side is a huge square clock, the minute hand missing, that shows it to be early afternoon.

Nancy pulls Foxglove and the cart into the hotel's forecourt and dismounts. She looks with hunger at the sea, at her grandmother's prison. She looks at the sky. Sees the dark clouds rapidly approaching.

'Wake up, Pat.' The old dog opens a tired eye and assesses the situation. He takes in the sun that warms his back and is about to decline the invitation when the first heavy raindrop falls beside his nose. Nancy turns away, and by the time she looks back the dog is already under the porchway, waiting. Looping Foxglove's reins through a ring set into the wall, Nancy follows the dog inside.

The Proserpine is not like the Nest. Where that inn is low roofed and dark, crowded channels with the tables clustered together and the paths between them narrow, the Proserpine is the open sea. The ceiling high, no trinkets hanging from the rafters, though there are pictures lining the walls. A great glass chandelier hanging at the centre from a plaster roundel that struggles with the weight. Round tables, chairs at each, stand around the edge of a vast deck of a floor, the grooves caulked like a ship's; the tables edged with a wooden lip in case the hotel capsizes. The rain beats hard at the thick glass windows and seeps under the door. There are men at every table, and they watch as Nancy crosses to the bar, where a man looms over his embroidery. He does not look up when she reaches him, but he does turn his stitching away. Nancy glimpses the rigging of a sinking ship and a black rayed sun in the sky and takes a seat on a stool.

'Lovely work.'

The man does not respond at first, and there is silence at Nancy's back. She is about to speak again when he answers.

'Keeps the fingers nimble.'

Nancy smiles. 'When were you last on a ship? Those are

sailors' stitches.' Pel had a framed example of sailor's needle craft hanging in the boat. The barman keeps working but he talks while he does.

'I bought the hotel ten years ago. Not been out since.'

There is a sadness in the man's voice and Nancy does not press him for answers. Not on this. The questions she arrived with are enough, no need to add more.

'Please. I'm looking for someone. Fearnought.' Nancy hopes the man Pel knew still works here. It must have been a long time, but then, Pel can't be the only one to live too long.

The barman drops a stitch. But he still does not stand.

'What do you want with Dreadnought?'

'You know him, Nicca? He had dealings with my father, years ago. Where can I find him?'

Placing his work down, the barman stands and towers over Nancy. She finds herself facing the knitwork on his sweater. Raised zigzags running down a blue wool front. The sleeves pushed up to reveal heavy wrought forearms and skin-cracked hands. Faded tattoos lost in black hair. Looking up to the man squinting down Nancy clears her throat. Clears her mind. Curls one hand into the makings of a spell. She's ready to argue when the barman speaks.

'Nicca?' Nancy nods. 'He's long dead, girl. Dreadnought's his son. You don't want him.'

Nancy pauses before she replies. She's sensible enough not to lay out each card. But she does need answers. So, she picks at the edges of what she needs to know.

'Is he in the same… line of work, that his father was?'

The barman's scowl deepens.

'He is. Though if help with Them is what you're after I'd not go to him. There are others that would suit you better. There's a fellow on the moor.'

Nancy can't stop the smirk from emerging at the corner of her mouth, but she holds her tongue.

'No, it's a Fearnought I need. Where is he, which house is his?'

A voice pipes up from the back of the room.

'No house here for him any longer. Not for years.'

Nancy waits but no more information is offered. She picks away.

'Then where do I find him? I can wait. I'd take a drink if one was offered. Something small and strong.' Nancy takes a folded note from the pocket without a spell in and places it on the bar. Whispering from the man seated by the window, then three taps on the glass. The barman draws an unlabelled bottle from beneath the bar and pours brandy into a small glass, placing it with a splash on Nancy's bribe.

'On me. Keep your money. He's down the coast a way. Mornader Cove. But don't expect to get what you hope from that one. He'll let you down faster than an anchor reaches sand.'

Nancy reaches for the glass, her tattooed wrist exposed, the twisting violets and alchemical signs purple and black in the lamplight. The barman sees. Reconsiders.

'Ah. That's it then. My warning stands, Keeper,' he waits for a reaction Nancy is not prepared to give. 'Busker Fearnaught earnt his nickname. Nothing but dread to be found in his shack. Doom on every hook. He is nothing like his father. Besides, you won't reach him today, light'll be gone in an hour and a storm's coming in. Keeper or no, you'll not make that trip.'

Nancy downs the brandy.

'I'm more than a Keeper, Jack.' The barman holds her gaze for a moment then laughs.

'Of that I've no doubt, girl, but you've no salt in that hair. No sea wind on your face. Jack-tar I may be but take my word on this. Storm will have passed by morning. Wait.'

Nancy releases the just-in-case spell she's been holding in her palm all this time and nods at the brandy-soaked bill.

'If it won't pay for a drink, will it pay for a room?'

A pause. A smile. Another brandy poured.

'Aye, Keeper. It will.'

The room relaxes and someone produces a fiddle. Nancy turns on her stool to face the seated fishermen, sailors, salts that line the walls, and smiles. She likes this place. She likes this man. She loves this brandy. And she cannot remember the last time she had fun. She searches the tables until she finds Patroclus, curled up at the feet of a fisherman, and calls him over. He is reluctant to move but since Nancy remains seated and they seem to be staying, he walks over. Nancy leans down, scratches his head and whispers into his ear.

'She's been trapped down there long enough she can manage another night, can't she, boy?'

Patroclus growls, but it is half hearted and sleepy, and he slinks back to a warmer corner, away from questions, and closes his eyes. Nancy turns back to the barman as the fiddler strikes up a tune.

'Nancy Bligh.'

'Barzillai Melchor.'

'I am certain I have never met a Barzillai before.'

'Few have. Call me Baz. Nice to meet you, Nancy.' A rough hand is extended, and Nancy shakes it. 'I thought Keepers were all old men. Men, at least.'

'I don't know, Baz. I'll only be meeting my second tomorrow. But I grant you that based on what I've seen it looks like that's usually the way of it.'

Baz lifts a glass.

'To change, then, Nancy. To change.'

Nancy makes the toast. The fiddler plays on.

'Tell me about the Proserpine, Baz. It's an unusual name for an Inn.'

'True. An old pirate made good. Landed here after the Red-Haired Queen had made him bona fide and proper. Made his money sinking the Spanish and set up shop. The Proserpine was his ship. The floor was her deck. She had a figurehead once, mounted at the front. But the salt wind took it down for us, a splinter at a time. She was a beauty though. Clutching a harp and a basket of apples. I think. They could have been something else. Bright red. There's a painting somewhere.'

Nancy sips her brandy and sways with the fiddler's tune.

'I knew a man who lived in a ship once, well, a boat. Your hotel reminds me of it a great deal.'

There is a scuttling at Nancy's feet, and she looks down at shaggier brownies than she is used to. Their coats tufted and crusted with salt. They look gaunt.

'Are you keeping your brownies fed, Baz?'

The barman scowls.

'The coopers? I leave out what you're supposed to, Nancy. Nicca Fearnought told me what to do. 'Fore he died.'

Nancy looks back to her feet and raises an eyebrow at the Underfolk. They smile, stop holding in their guts and race back to the skirting. She had forgotten that the house spirits of the coast were a relation of, not the same as, the brownies she knows. Like the knockers showing miners where the tine lodes lay, coopers—as well as performing the usual house duties—were specialists. Knocking on the floorboards when the owner was due a good catch, hurrying them out of the door to the sea.

'Cheeky beggars.' Nancy mutters. 'He doesn't check in then, your Keeper?'

Baz takes down glasses to polish as he talks. Just like Madge, Nancy thinks. Never a conversation without a task to go with it.

'Busker? No. And "our Keeper" would be a stretch, Nancy. Busker Fearnought is nothing to anyone but himself. He helps when he's paid to, and his prices rise with the tides. What do you want from him, if you don't mind me asking?'

Nancy pauses, turns her grandmother's ring with her thumb. An inheritance, left by her mother, a ring she has worn for as long as she remembers but always as a memento mori. It is something else now.

'He holds something I need.'

'If Busker knows that he'll make you pay dearly, Nancy. Watch yourself.'

Nancy considers the man she's seeking. Turns him over in her mind. The fiddler begins a new tune, and Nancy turns at the sound of dancing. A man begins to sing a song about a whale and outside the rain drums its approval.

'No fishing today, then?' A crack of thunder from outside and Baz looks drolly from behind the bar.

'Not today, Nancy. No. These men are drinking on credit today. Waiting for a sea to get them paid. If you do see Busker maybe you can ask him to come and see me. It's been a week since a boat's been out. Tell him I'll give him what I gave him last time if he helps.'

Nancy skims through her catalogue of spells. Pictures the flowers on her arm. None can change the weather, or still a sea.

'He's done it before?'

Baz nods.

'Aye, after the *Cadwaller* was wrecked he calmed the seas to try and save her. Didn't work, but he did it. For the coin, but he did it.'

Nancy folds this information away for later.

'I'd offer to help if I could Baz, but the sea isn't under my protection. I'm not sure what the etiquette is, but I'm fairly certain it would be frowned on.'

'Don't worry, Nancy. Talk to Busker for me. Maybe meeting another Keeper will make him guilty enough to help. Enjoy yourself tonight, drinks are on me until the excise men appear. Then I might need your help.'

'Deal.'

The fiddler begins a song again. A tune that Nancy knows. The tune she has been humming, the one the Underfolk sang at the tor. She rounds on the musician.

'What is this? What's this song?'

Eyes closed, the fiddler keeps playing. Nancy keeps asking the question, but he does not pause in the tune.

'Baz, what's this song? Why won't he stop!'

Baz is transfixed, and Nancy does not think he is going to answer but then, as though he hears her from underwater, he turns.

'It's an old one, Nancy. There was a woman who used to drink here, before my time. She disappeared. That's the way of the song at least. It's the "Ballad of Old Mel Ray".'

Several dreadful pieces slot neatly into place and Nancy sobers immediately as the fiddler begins to sing. New words hanging on the bones of old tunes.

She winnows the holes in the hard adderstones,
She whistles the wind out to play.
She's sleeping not gone, her legend lives on.
What a beauty was Old Mel' Ray.

RAGWORT

She whispers at night, through the dark and the quiet,
From wherever it is that she lays,
With the ships wrecked on stones, the whales and their bones,
With the ghosts, sleeps Old Mel Ray.
She strains at her chains, sings this merry refrain,
Return me to my loved ones she says.
But she's bound to the deep, in her watery sleep,
On the seabed lies Old Mel Ray.

MARE'S TAIL

The Nest is silent. At least, as silent as an old house gets. The wind feels noisily around its edges, searching for a loose pane of glass, a way through the mortar. It has some luck with the chimney though the heat from the fire burns it back. In the grate the peat has been covered in embers, a long fuse hissing under ash, waiting until the morning to explode. There is a drip from a spill missed, ticking onto the floorboards, and from behind the bar the occasional clink of a glass. The brownies are at work. The place will be spotless when she rises. Madge Gould. Asleep upstairs.

There are six guest rooms at the Mare's Nest Inn, but only the seventh is occupied. In the eaves of the roof. An attic room close quartered and cosy, a deep mattressed bed in the centre, below the window. In it, beneath a tangle of quilts and blankets, gold grey hair spread across a pillow, Madge Gould sleeps and dreams of fish. Great shoals of them pulsing in black water, the murmuration of drowning starlings. And bursting through their middle, something dark and fast moving. Something with teeth.

A creak as the door swings open. A click as it is pressed shut. The sound in the room muffled as though it is underwater. The wind beating on the walls. Nothing above or below. Just an old woman sleeping. Though no longer alone. A little bird has perched on her windowsill, though Madge cannot see it. The voice talks from a shadow it brought from home.

'*Wake up, Madge. There are things to be done.*'

A murmur from below the bedsheets as Madge turns on aching bones.

'Who's there?'

'*You don't recognise mine voice, Madge? I've only been gone a year.*'

Madge rises onto elbows, struggles in the dark for the lamp but the wick won't take.

'Pel?' Madge Gould reaches over and lights the lamp, her face a child's again. There's a gust and the lamp goes out.

'*Come, Madge. I taught you better than that! I'm one of Them, now. Got mine matter back. I took a little extra so you can hear me, but you'll not see me like this. Yes, it's me. Believe it or not.*'

And she does. There is something in that voice, seeping from the shadows like burnt honey.

Why are you here? Nancy, she…'

'*Mine Nancy! We've let her down, Madge. You and I both.*'

'She's gone to get her, Pel. I'm scared.'

'*I know, Madge. It'll be alright, though. There's something I kept from her. Something you need to know.*'

Madge squints at the shadow. Darker than the rest. Where she'd swear she sees a single eye gleam.

'What now, Pel? Have you learned nothing.'

'*Hush woman. You have a new priest, do you not? There's talk of him. Talk too of these rituals, these rites the folk are dealing in. Their faith all spread out. There's a chance here, to fix things. To stop it happening again.*'

Madge stares blankly at the darkness.

'*Division, Madge. Strife. Think—Cleaver and I at each other's throats, what if we had worked together?*

'What do you mean?'

There is a tutting from the darkness.

'Just trust me, Madge. When the Reverend calls. Follow. Help him bring the village together. Under one banner.'

'And whose banner is that?'

'Why, Hers, Madge. You'll see. It might be hard to believe, Madge, but death will change a man. Jacob and I are friends, again, if you can believe it. Please. Don't let the village keep making my mistakes. Follow Her. Trust Her.'

Madge tries to speak, but is interrupted.

'You want to see me, Madge? Once upon a time you could. You'd have been able. As easy as closing and opening your eyes. Would you like that, Madge? To see me again? Follow Her banner when the Reverend reveals it, and it will all be well.'

It is like a wind-up drummer boy, this voice; it hammers out its beat.

'Those days could be these days, Madge. If the right choices are made. Believe me. You could talk to those you've lost, too. Talk to me. Cleaver. Your father even. Whenever you wished. She is coming, Madge. I resisted it, but She will help things. Nancy will know it too, you'll see, she's bringing her Grandmother home. Just as she said. Mel will talk to the Mother. Yoke Her to Mirecoombe's plough. Keep you all safe. Safer than you've been for a long time. They've both been gone for far too long. And they bring a chance for change. Follow her when She calls you, Madge, run to the Mother.'

Madge's heart is beating fast, and she does not know if it's terror or joy. Death is a cycle. What is gone can return. It just takes time. That was what Pel used to say. How long does it take to make a man from dust? How long does a body take to fill with a soul?'

'Madge. When the times comes for things to be done. Do them, for me, do what's asked of you. Do it for mine Nance. Help her. I'd never hurt a hair on your head you know that don't you? Trust me.'

Outside the wind is growing. The window frame jostles against the gusts and the corner pane cracks. Madge tries the lamp again and it flares into light. Every shadow filled; the black cloth removed. Except one. One shadow is as black as it was before though two points sparkle deep within it. Madge only gets a moment to peer closer. The crack in the window deepens, then the whole pane blows in in. The wind howling round like guard dogs released too late, blowing out the lamp. Barking at the shadows that have always been there. In the shriek of the wind Madge can hear the voice. It is everywhere as though riding the gusts.

'Don't worry, Madge. Have a think on what I've said. If you ever feel alone, don't worry. I'm closer than you think.'

Downstairs the brownies have stopped in their cleaning. Glasses have been dropped. And tiny faces shake until the visitor has gone.

SEA BLITE

Nancy wakes with a tempest in her head. She cannot recall making the journey from bar to bedroom, but here she lays. Alone, in a narrow cot pressed close to a whitewashed wall. The curtains are drawn, and a bright light shines through, though with each gust of wind the glass is spattered with sea water, adding to panes already frosted with dried salt. Her coat is neatly folded over a chair, her boots kicked to the side of the room. Lying in the square of sun shining on the floor is Patroclus, fast asleep.

Nancy sits up and rubs sleep from her eyes. Grains of sand falling onto the bedsheets. The room is sparse. Other than the bed and chair the only other furniture is a small table beneath the window. On it, someone has placed a bowl and a jug of steaming water. A towel neatly folded beside it and a small glass of brandy next to that. Nancy stands and the floor lurches beneath her feet, Patroclus opens a single eye and Nancy glares at him with envy.

'Not a word, Pat. Not a damn word.'

Nancy reaches the table with relief and steadies herself on its edges. The smell of the brandy threatens to bring last night's up so she opens the window, tips it out. Fills the bowl from the jug and washes her face. It helps, a little.

There is a knock, and the door opens, the landlord of the

Proserpine poking his head around the corner, eyes closed.

'It's alright, Baz, you can come in.' Nancy's voice is gravelled and low. Her tongue thick and fuzzed like a seaweed covered rock.

'I've brought you coffee. You had quite the time last night.'

Nancy closes her eyes hard and waits for the memories to surface. After the song, her grandmother's song, she had demanded answers and, when none had come, she had demanded different songs. There had been dancing. Brandy. She had not known how much she had needed a release. How much she had felt owed one. She opens her eyes and turns back to the table. Her rings are piled neatly next to the bowl. She has half asked the question as she reaches for the coffee but stops when she sees her hands. Red knuckles bruised and split and aching.

'We made you take them off.' Baz nods at the rings, 'you said you wanted a fight, knocked the tar out of Tristan Ellick. More fool him for agreeing to it.'

Nancy closes her eyes again, but the memories keep surfacing. She drinks her coffee.

'I'm sorry, Baz.'

A smile breaks across the landlord's face.

'Sorry? Don't be, Nancy, it was a great night all round. That crowd, more than most, knows the need to let off steam.'

Baz sits on the bed as Nancy drinks her coffee. Patroclus stands, walks over to him and slumps heavily against Baz's legs, waiting for a scratch. The landlord obliges. As the caffeine drives some of the headache away, Nancy begins placing the rings back on her fingers, one by one. The last one her grandmother's.

'The song from last night, the one about Meliora Ray, I've heard it before. But never the words.'

Baz sits for a moment, focusing on the dog. When he answers, he does so cautiously.

'I was surprised to hear it, truth be told. It's not been played in a long time, not in this bar. It does something to me when I hear it. To all of us.'

They sit with the song between them. Neither speak. The hotel creaks in the wind like the ship it contains. Another splash of water at the window.

'Don't go to Busker's cove, Nancy. Nothing that man touches stays good.'

Nancy puts on her shoes, stands, and puts on her coat.

'He knows how to get where I'm going, Baz. You don't. I'll be alright. I can handle myself.'

'I know Nancy, I saw you deck Tristan. But Busker is something else. You'll see. Come downstairs for breakfast before you go.'

The barman leaves, six feet of kindness in clothes still stained by the sea.

Downstairs, Nancy follows the smell of frying fish. Baz is stood over the stove in the kitchen of the hotel, his back to the door as Nancy walks in. The table is set for two, and as Nancy sits down the fillets are slid onto the plate that waits for them. Butter and eggs on top. A whine is brewing in Patroclus, but it stops as a smaller plate is placed on the floor before him. Fried tails and fish heads which are swallowed before they know what's happening. Baz places his own breakfast down and takes the seat opposite.

'I'll not say it again, Nancy. I won't. But take this with you.'

Baz slides a small fish leather pouch across the table. The fabric is pliant, and the shadows of scales still dance across the surface. Nancy unties the red string that holds it shut and tips six bones across the table. The vertebrae of a fish, three sharp points on each. Tiny. No bigger than a farthing each and the colour of sun on the sea. Nancy looks up, tries to catch Baz's eye, but he is looking away.

'They were given to me when I went to sea. Kept me safe. They'll do the same for you.'

'You know I'm a Keeper, Baz. I've magic enough of my own.' The lightest sting of wounded pride.

'You've got moor magic, Nancy. The sea will knock that right out of you. Magic with salt in it. That's what you need. That's what this is.'

Nancy puts the bones back into their fish skin bag one by one, draws the neck tight.

'Thank you, Baz. For this, and the food. I won't stay much longer. Just point me towards the path.'

Baz begins to clear the plates. There is a set to his shoulders now. His gift given, he's helped where he can.

'Walk to the harbour, the path climbs the cliff to the left. Watch your step. The buccas have taken more than one this year. They'll take you too if you let them. I'll be here when you come back.'

Nancy nods, puts on her coat, and walks out of the back door of the hotel. On the rooftops are thirty or so birds.

'Baz, what are they?'

'Mire-crows, Nancy. Black headed gulls. Sailor's souls.'

Nancy considers. Looks a gull in the eye and sees it cock its head.

'Good or bad?'

'Who knows, Nancy. But they like a show. If they're here, they think they'll get one.'

Nancy turns her back on the birds, on the hotel, on Baz, and with Patroclus at her heels she heads for the harbour.

On any other day she would spend time taking it in. The sea, the stone, the beach. But she's a job to do, last night all the holiday she'll afford herself. Nancy walks quickly and determinedly past the fishing boats, their decks piled with coiled rope and lobster pots. Men with pipes in their mouths and hands busy with work. They do not look up as Nancy passes. All except one, eye ringed with a bruise, who looks up smiling at the Keeper. Nancy smiles back, glad to see Tristan Ellick isn't holding grudges. She raises her hand in greeting and keeps walking. The coast path leads up from the stone harbour wall, its collection of granite slabs and patchwork bricklaying styles wedged into the cove like an afterthought. The path climbs steeply and both Nancy and Patroclus struggle, with hangovers and age respectively. The riding crop useless in her hand, Nancy wishes it was still a stick, and it is with relief she sees the first of the steps hewn into the path. From there, though still steep, the going is easier. Nancy looks back across the harbour, to the woodland climbing up on the other side of the bay. As they reach the edge the trees look as though they've been pruned with a giant razor, the wind slicing the corner of the canopy leaving a hard diagonal cut off at the treeline.

There are no trees on the side Nancy climbs.

There are other things though. Nancy sees the adder just before she steps on it. A young snake newly hatched but coiled in an adult's spring. Waiting to strike. Nancy puts her foot down carefully beside it and gives ground, lets the adder retreat. She watches the grey-brown body with its zigzag back and rasping scales move softly into the undergrowth, under white harebells and mauve anemones.

'Careful Pat, watch that snout.'

The dog withdraws his nose from the snake riddled verges and performs a low, grumbling howl.

'You've had a breakfast of fish, Pat. You'll live without whatever you're smelling.'

Patroclus steps back onto the path and follows Nancy up. They can both feel eyes on them. But Nancy needs to make the Keeper's cove today. She cannot afford more diversions. Whatever is watching, bucca, piskie or just more snakes, they are not her problem.

She has family. Real family. Trouble or not, she'll not keep it waiting.

The top of the cliff takes Nancy by surprise. Focused on not falling she had not been looking up, so she trips over the topmost step. Righting herself she stands, the wind blowing the sunshine through her, warming her face. From this height the sea seems unreal. It is a deep and all devouring blue. The colour of a shanty. Lilting and rolling and shifting shades. The gulls still singing to the water's tune. Nancy walks to the very edge, creeping to the point at which the grass gives way to gravity and peers over at the rocks below, long strips of stone running from beach to sea. There is a shoal of fish, pilchards perhaps, that swim alongside the coast. They shiver in the sunlight, silver points of light as though someone is continually throwing handfuls of coins into the water. You could almost be fooled into thinking it was peaceful, if it wasn't for the wreck wood that is caught in the teeth of the rocks below. As she gazes out her eye is caught by a streak of darkness on the horizon.

An island.

Pel's Island.

Eythin.

The sun plays tricks with land and sea and separates them both. Eythin floating above the ocean. Nancy has read about this, about the refractive nature of light on waves. Still. It is magical how it hangs there—

A bark from Patroclus and a foot not put down. And with good reason, there is nothing beneath. Nancy retreats back to the safety of the path, shaken. She would have tried to walk to the island, would have fallen. She crouches and strokes Patroclus's shaggy head and when she lifts her eyes to the horizon again, the island is gone. There is nothing there but sea and sky and a thin blue line between them.

Mornader Cove is not far along the path, a mile perhaps. The cove itself sits at the base of a great zawn in the cliffs where a sea cave has collapsed, the base strewn with boulders and calcified stone. The path proper curves back inland and around the tear in the rocks, but Nancy's destination is down. The route makes the path she climbed seem horizontal in comparison. Thick iron posts are driven into the stone besides the path. Eyes at the top through which a rope is threaded. Nancy goes first, Patroclus refusing to budge until her head has gone from view and then whatever motivates him—a desire to protect or not be left behind—kicks in and he skitters down the path after her. Though the sky is clear and the path here dry, the climb down to the cove runs with water. A waterfall spring washing the path into the rock. It makes the stone slick underfoot and twice Nancy clutches at the rope to save from falling. Patroclus moves slowly, shaking, every paw placed precisely on its step. Nancy's heart beats faster at every point of the descent. Halfway down there is a space to rest. It is peaceful and Nancy's heart slows until she sees how the platform has been made. A shelf of rock paused in its peeling from the cliffside, a fissure hidden by grass showing the mess of roots and stone that holds their resting point in place. Cautiously Nancy reaches for the iron rope hold, gives it a shake. It comes free in her hand.

'Patroclus.' Nancy's voice is measured. She can't hear it for the blood rushing in her head. 'Let's go boy, come on.' The dog has taken this break as a chance to rest and is reluctant to get up. 'Now. Pat.' She talks through gritted teeth; she needs the dog to get up slowly. Needs him not to panic or worry or worse, think this is a game. He does not. Patroclus rises on shaking legs. Ears back. 'Good boy, good boy.' Nancy doesn't stop repeating it; she needs it more than he does. She moves slowly to where the path continues downwards, and Patroclus follows. The platform lurching with every step. 'That's it, boy, steady now, come on.' The ledge slips, just a little and Nancy stifles a scream at the shift. There is a wide gap now between where they stand and the path below. She takes it in a stride, knees barely holding and knuckles white on the guide rope. Patroclus can feel the ground moving, the shake in his legs returning, freezing him in place. He makes a motion to jump after Nancy but cannot seem to follow through on the intention. Nancy's face pleading at him from the safer point below. The old dog bends his front legs again but as he pushes off, the platform breaks free and his body twists with the falling stone, a yelp tearing from his mouth.

'No!' Nancy screams and lurches forwards, reaching out her left hand, the right clutching to the rope still tethered to the cliff. She catches him by the scruff, his weight yanking her shoulder, tearing muscle but not dislocating. She hopes. Ignoring the pain, she hauls Patroclus up and onto the path where he whines and pants and presses himself against her and the cliff. Nancy listens to the stone crash into the sea below and she slumps with her dog against the wet cliffside, the spring pouring cold water over her hair and face, her body pulsing with adrenaline. Her free hand shakes, and she grips Pat's head to steady it. Pulls him in close. Buries her face in his fur.

'Good boy. Good boy. Good boy, it's all right. It's all right.' Ten minutes pass before either can move again, the rest of the journey spent in tooth-gritted silence. Nothing but the gulls laughing overhead. When they reach the bottom, Nancy wraps her arms around Patroclus and holds him tight, his snout buried deep in the folds of her coat. They stay like this in the sunshine for a moment then Nancy stands.

Mornader Cove.

It's wider at the bottom.

Above her the fissure in the cliff closes up so only a seam of sunlight remains at the top. Here at the base a wide beach, bouldered with enormous stones, stretches out along the cliff line. The sand is black, made up of weather worn slate and studded with quartz. A channel lets the sea into the cave to her back even now, at low tide, the beach she stands on banking up away from the eddying salt water. She is reluctant to leave the blue sky and sea, but she knows the dark cave mouth is where she's going. She knows without being told that's where he lives. The gulls have gone, she can see them sitting on rocks further out to sea. They've had their show and they're quiet for now. Her and Pat will make this last leg alone.

'Ready boy?' A whimper from Pat. He'll follow her anywhere just not back up that path. 'Come on then, let's go.' They walk into the cathedral cave, its roof dripping with spring water. Nancy smells it, first. Before her eyes have grown accustomed to the darkness. The smell of rotting fish. Of seaweed that's been out of the water for too long. The beach is rising the deeper she goes, and shapes begin to make themselves known in the darkness. It takes a while for her to parse them, despite the smell, and when she does, she clasps a hand to her mouth. They are the carcasses of whales, of dolphins. Fat and flesh hacked from their backs and sides, their jaws missing, and their bodies left to rot. As Nancy moves past one, she makes the mistake of looking closer. The black bloody mess of a whale's side writhing with flat, white worms eating away what's left. Nancy gags. Patroclus leans in for a closer look.

'Leave it.' Nancy is stern enough he listens first time and the pair move on. There are barrels lined up against the wall of the cave, black oily stains dripping down the sides. A small boat is pulled up on the shingle, its paint flaked but the vessel clearly carefully maintained, its hull sound, its oars tucked up in their rests. There is a name painted on the back that Nancy can just make out, *Mallygolder*. It is secured to a chain that is tethered to a rock and barnacles cling to both. Nancy leaves well alone. She can feel the wards from here. Can see the faces of bucca peering from the shadows under the keel. The house emerges reluctantly from the shadows. It is little more than a shack. The whole structure a seething mass of poorly constructed planking. Another shipwrecked house, Nancy thinks. Though this one has nothing of the boat or ship about it. Flat roofed, its windows shuttered against the dark, it totters on stilts above what Nancy assumes to be the tide line. Certainly, each post is ringed with green at a point two thirds up, the wood above clean, the wood below a tangle of barnacles and sea anemones with their tentacles hidden. Even in the gloom Nancy can see that the back of the house slants away towards the pool of standing water, like a boat house. It gives the house the impression of some gross ocean insect hauling itself out of the water to dry. She half expects some crustacean to burst through the door like a hermit crab with pincers waving and eyes on stalks. As they climb the ramp, Nancy looks over her shoulder. She can hear the tide turning. Sees the ripples washing up the subterranean trench. Ignoring the signs etched into the woodwork Nancy raises a hand, and the door bursts open.

STAR OF BETHLEHEM

THE CHAPEL IS weathertight again. The last slate laid. Though planks cover the windows that wait for glass, and the door is a placeholder for the new one coming, it is at least dry in the knave. The ledger stones on the floor are swept and cleaned, old names long forgotten lying waiting to be read. The broken slab, the Callum had fallen through, that Abraham had escaped from, has been replaced. The crack joined with lime mortar and after a few hundred years of being walked on, nobody will know the damage is there. The morning sun streams through the glass that remains and in the patch of coloured light by the altar, Abraham Pine-Coffin sleeps amongst his books—Exeter have sent a good haul, the rest scavenged from the village—his dreams a mess of saintly darkness.

Saint Reagan who could walk on the marshes without putting a step wrong.

Saint Reagan who could heal the sick, who could talk to the birds, who wept black bog water in streaks from her eyes.

Saint Reagan who could shape mud into rabbits, turn eels into dogs.

Saint Reagan who lost her head.

Saint Reagan who carried on regardless, her head under an arm, or placed in a basket, until the day she died. It's not the strangest story of a saint he's ever read.

Her hagiography sits open at his side, face down on the ledger stones, and Abraham Pine-Coffin sighs in his sleep. He wakes at the sound of breaking glass.

'Who's there?'

In his bleary state the coloured light swirls like a kaleidoscope but he sees the little shadow moving. Flitting about. Follows it to an alcove beneath a pushed back pew, the end carved into a grimaced scowl. Abraham repeats his summons.

'Who's there I say?' His voice is steady. Eyes bright and focused on the darkness but he can't keep an excited smile from his face.

'I am an angel sent to help you, Reverend.'

'No, you are not.'

A pause. Weighty and heady it fills the church and seeps in tendrils from under the closed door.

'What?' The voice indignant now, with a vein of worry in it though that passes soon enough.

The Reverend pulls himself up into a kneeling crouch, as though faced with a wild animal. To the voice's indignation, he smirks.

'If you are an angel, prove it.'

There is a glint of light beneath the pew as the angel smiles, their lips drawing back across teeth.

'I... No. I won't. Are you not awed? Your God can be vengeful!'

'Our God, surely?'

'Yes, of course, that's what I meant.'

'What are you? Piskie? Spriggan? Other?'

He is reaching, but his blind fingers have caught hold of something. The voice changes tone.

'I am not!' It is flustered, this disembodied voice. Wrong footed. Abraham Pine-Coffin sits down to listen to the show.

'I am here to tell you wondrous things! You read the stories of your saint, I am here to tell you she has another name! Aren't there angels in your books with cloven feet and screaming mouths? With horns? So too your saints. We share a Mother, Brother of mine.'

'Brother, is it? Well, little one, I'll not be rude to a guest. Whoever you may be. You're quite right, of course, lots of delightful overlaps in folklore and the church, I spoke to a bishop from Lyon once, and he swore that—'

'Shut up! My, you prattle.' There is movement in the shadow, the faint sound of footsteps. The Reverend follows the noises, golden eyes tracking the sound. The noises stop below a boarded-up space where the new stained glass will go. *'A perfect place for her picture, no? A few more nights and she'll stand before you. Your saint, our Mother. Fit her to the glass. Pane by pane. Let her watch over you.'*

The Reverend stands, walks to the altar.

'Possibly.' He turns and lifts the paten from the communion cup, the inside empty and dusty.

'These paintings you have uncovered, you see, can you not, that this proves my words? Your saint. My Mother. One and the same. Why do you struggle against it? You wish to heal this village; She is the salve.'

'I believe Reagan was something before she was a saint. I'm not so certain about the rest.'

'Reagan, Mother, Mother, Reagan.' He cavorts and dances, singing his incantation. *'Reagan, Mother, Mother, Reagan.'*

We all start as stories. Made in the telling. There's power in a name.

A floral breeze whips through the chapel and startles both priest and imp. Looking down, Abraham Pine-Coffin sees the cup has filled. A dark, viscous liquid that clings to the gold.

'What is this, what have you put in here?'

'*What?*' The voice is uncertain. '*Nothing. There is nothing in the cup. Look at me! I am an angel!*' Knot's voice whines and wheedles, but Pine-Coffin is barely listening now. He slowly dips a finger into the cup, presses it into the viscous fluid gathering at the base. The wine is so dark as to be almost black and it clings as he withdraws his hand. He sniffs at the fluid and recoils. It smells rancid, a foul ichor, and yet a part of him wants nothing more than to place his finger into his mouth. To taste it.

'*Reverend. What is that? Answer me!*'

Bram stares, transfixed, at his finger. He closes his eyes. He does not know why he does it, but he touches a finger to each eyelid. From the pulsing red and black she emerges. Her face smiling beneath her crown. Her body wrapped in a velvet cloak that spreads behind her into glorious wings and leaves her naked before him. The image bleeds and twists, red clouds on a black sky, but she stays with him. He opens his eyes and the imprint of his vision dances in the light. He moves as though drugged and is reaching for the cup when he sees a tiny creature squatting in the corner of his eye. Dressed, no, made of rotting wood and moss, covered, and laughing at him. For a moment, he forgets all else and starts to laugh. Eyes sparkling at this creature, this magical, wondrous creature. He looks up and sees the rafters filled with others. Faces that peer down. Faces he's bid welcome to each time he's stepped inside in the hope something will hear him. It's only those faces, staring in fear, that snap him back. The Underfolk jabber and point, and the Reverend turns to see Knot bracing to leap. Pine-Coffin hurls the cup at him, the black rotten blood spraying an arterial arc across the newly whitewashed walls. Knot shields his face. Howls in surprise.

'What is this? She told me it was a tale. Mother, if you hear me, I swear it, she told me it was a tale!' He bows, trembling, and runs howling from the chapel.

In the silence, the Reverend stands, touches his hands to his face, and sees he has been weeping. Thick, black tears of peated water that fall in clots to the floor, flowering moss growing where they hit the stone. Looking up he sees again the rafters full of peering faces, not those carved in wood, but creatures crouching in the rafters. Stunned and silent, they know they are watched. Slowly they begin to chant.

'Mother, Reagan, Mother, Reagan.'

Their voices are music. He laughs again, uncontrollably, at the proof of a life's hopeful scepticism and turns to the eastern wall, to the point that Yestin told him the sleeping figure was painted. He knows what to do. Staggers on drunken legs towards the whitewashed lime, grasping for a candle stick on his way, and drives it into the plaster. The wall gives way.

Emerging from the swirling dust is a set of stairs leading down. Pine-Coffin hacks away a larger opening as the Underfolk's chant grows louder.

'Mother, Reagan, Mother, Reagan.'

They silence as he steps into the hole, as he chokes on the sick sweet scent of spring.

PALE BELLIED DOG

Below, there is a sound, the sound of moorland waking. A giant lifts his head.

She wakes.
She stirs at least.
Shakes the dust from her eyes.
Shakes another's face from her head.
The stories are true.
We knew it.

At the giant's feet, Pel sits trapped in thought. Until a ghost arrives to free him.

'Pel, I'm here.' The Reverend Cleaver's shade moves quickly, his eyes darting behind him.

'Jacob, thank you. Did you find who I asked for?' Lord Pelagius Hunt stands awkwardly to his feet. He does not know what the witch's curse makes him. Half ghost, half echo. Completely powerless.

'The two you sent me to, they are rather unnerving.'

Cleaver steps aside and the monsters shuffle forth. Hilla and Stag stand taller in the Undermoor.

'Lord Keeper, you used to be so hard to read, now I see right through you.'

At Hilla's side, Stag rasps out a laugh. Pel forces out a polite smile.

'Quite. Hilla. My friend here made you an offer. Do you accept?'

'Your daughter overreaches.'

'You overreach. We had concords, wretch.'

'You died.'

'Enough of this. I will persuade my daughter to recommit to our previous terms. You will walk the woodland paths again. You may feast on the dreams of travellers. Agreed?'

Hilla shrugs and draws a lump of blackened tallow from her rags. Her brother Stag a striking stone. He rakes it across his antlers and sparks the tallow alight. A putrid black smoke rises, wafted by Hilla up the nose of a sleeping giant whose head fills up with sleep. Slowly, Gogmagog lays back and starts snoring. The echo of it bouncing back and forth between the rocks so it sounds out as a two-gun salute.

Hilla lays a hand on the giant's stony flank and closes her eyes. Drinks in his dreams.

Pel and Cleaver watch her, watch her twitch, seeking answers in a fractured mind. Gogmagog twitches too. Shaken by his dreams. Thrashing out in his sleep and knocking down trees. Pel reflexively seeks to cast a spell, but his cotton heart burns with sulphurous smoke, and he's left to cower in the crook of the giant's knee with Cleaver and the rest. The old Reverend watches his friend. The face creasing into new wrinkles. Fearful ones.

'This is new for you, is it not, Pel? A mundane existence, powerless.'

'No.' Pel's voice is caught on a memory. 'It is not new.' He pauses, picks aimlessly at the heart. He's saved from explanation by the waking of Gogmagog, and the return of Hilla. She chews, as though wringing the last taste from the dream and shuffles across to Pel. He leans forwards, eager.

'Well?'
'She is in his dreams. It's true.'
'Who put Her there?'
'That little go-between. The witch's imp.'

Pel relaxes, shifts back against the giant.

'I see.'

Hilla giggles—a noise so foul that a passing piskie faints—and looks knowingly to her brother.

'There is more, Keeper. There is another voice, in that head. Soft, quiet, beautiful.'

The fear returns to Pel's face.

'Speak plain, wretch.'

Cleaver frowns at the Keeper and lays an arm on his shoulder.

'What my friend means—Hilla is it?—is that we would welcome your help and any more information you are able to provide.'

Pel growls but nods in agreement and Hilla continues.

'Whilst we were there, another joined us. Came to listen to the giant's dreams—there are two sets, you know? Almost the same, just a shade off. Like closing one eye then the other. The perspective shifts—we were watching, simple stories of a goose-footed goddess when another sat beside us. Woken, it seems, by the call of her name. By the repetition of another. Confused. Addled. She is not Her, yet she is. Could be, at least. A ghost in search of a name. Reagan.'

Pel scratches at the curse at his breast, pulls his hand back at the smell of sulphur. Deep in thought. When he looks up, the old spark is back in his eye.

'Well, that is something, then. Magic I may no longer have, but I am a Lord of Eythin. If there's one thing I know, it's ghosts.'

ROVING SAILOR

THE OPENING DOOR knocks Nancy back and she grabs onto the rail, twisting as she does so. A woman in floods of tears bursts from the shack, running howling down the ramp to the beach. From the black behind the doorframe a torrent of abuse emerges like flies from a carcass.

'Go on with you then! I told you it might not work, a man drowns easy enough, can't pin everything on a charm, woman, silly bugger should have learnt to swim!'

The woman does not break stride, just heads on down to the bright maw of the cave. Nancy looks back to the doorway for the briefest moment, at a clattering within, and when she looks back to the cavemouth the woman has gone. Swallowed down by the sea.

'Who the devil are you? Answer, damn you!'

Nancy turns again, faces this man she's travelled to see. Keeper of the Granite Wash, son of her father's friend. Busker Fearnought.

He is a gross disappointment.

Before she can reply, he has turned back inside so she studies his back as she follows, Patroclus growling at her side. Stripped to the waist, the man is covered in tattoos. There are many she knows. The same that Pel had, the same she bears. Marks of office. The rest are new to her. Anchors and swallows, knives and ships all fighting for space across the grubby, sweaty back. The tattoos are of assorted age. The newer ones pinprick sharp on the sea of bleeding blue seeping out of the older images.

'I can feel you looking girl, and you've yet to tell me your name. I don't work for free, so you'd best have some coin on you. Or some other means of payment.' Nancy grimaces and holds a hand to her face. The room is stagnant and stinks of rotting fish, of seaweed left in the sun.

'My name is Nancy, Nancy Bligh.'

No response. Busker is still turned away from her, hacking at some sea beast with a long-bladed knife. His hair is long, falling in greasy ringlets across his shoulders, a deep, rolling black. She waits. The house is a single room divided two thirds of the way down by a sheet of stained, patched sailcloth. The walls are hung with harpoons, with nets. With tools to bring the sea to heel. There are far fewer books than she expected. Those that are here are used as wedges to hold tables level. Stacked on their sides to allow a seal skull to perch on top, the oily bones leaving a stain on the cover. There are no windows. The room is lit by guttering lamps like the ones that stand guard outside, the stench of whale oil burning off them in acrid smoke that twists and turns through a small metal chimney. Even the pollution is desperate to escape. There is a mattress in the corner, the bed unmade, and a chair and table by the stove. The desk that Busker works at is set against the back wall. It is bowed and scored like a butcher's block and rows of knives hang above it, threatening to fall. Eventually the man stops in his work and turns, leans back heavily against the table, and cleans his hands on a cloth. As he does so, she notices the fineness of his fingers. His neatly kept nails. Unlike Pel's and her own, his hands are free of ornament. No jewellery. No rings or bracelets. His face is partly obscured by a beard, as slick with oil as his hair, and it has the unnerving effect of hiding his mouth. This might have prevented him from being easily read if it were not for his eyes.

'And who are you, Nancy Bligh? What do you want? I'm not a man that's easy to reach and yet here you stand. You have heard what I am, what I can do, is that it? Yes, Miss Bligh. I am a Keeper.'

He pauses here, stands up straight, and is such a pantomime of nobility that Nancy cannot stop the laughter bubbling up. It is only a short burst, but it is enough to darken Busker's brows.

'I'm sorry, it's just, I think our fathers knew one another. I'm Lord Hunt's ward.'

There is a twitch at the corner of Busker's eye.

'Pel's dead.'

'I know.'

'It's true then? He passed it to a girl. Gods above, I thought the buccas were lying.' His eyes lose all their fury and instead sparkle like a child amused by some novelty. 'Sit down then, Miss Keeper!'

'Nancy is fine.'

'Oh Miss, I should think you are. Now, it's advice you're after, is it? Quite the task your old man's left you. Sit, take the weight off. Old Pel was a friend of my family, we'll be firm mates too, I'm sure.' As he talks, his passion and emotions pour out of him as changeable as the sea.

Nancy sits in the chair Busker has pulled from a dark corner. She is aware of his appraisal, his looks running across her body, her face. She is used to this, of course, but she'd hoped for a little professional courtesy at least. Nancy closes her eyes and wills herself calm. After the rockfall on the journey down she'll not risk causing a tremor here, however much she'd like to. Patroclus has not stopped growling since they entered, and his ears are flat against his head. Nancy places a hand on his back and whispers softly for him to quieten.

'I hope we will be friends too, Mr. Fearnought. Pel spoke highly of your father and grandfather.'

Busker's face stiffens, but he catches himself and twists the movement into a smile.

'Yes, Pel was apprenticed to Jan, wasn't he? And quite the student. He set the bar of Keeper so high it's all we mere mortals can do to dream of reaching it. Yet still, up our arms go.' Busker mimes reaching upwards, face a mask of pious sincerity. There are cracks in it. 'I never met the man, myself, more's the pity. But here, I am blessed with a prettier Keeper than that old dog. If you're half the man your father was, I'll still not reach the mark, I'm sure.' Busker's mood bobs like a buoy on the sea. Lilting between mockery and sincerity, a darkness roiling beneath. It is exhausting to listen to. But Nancy needs this man, so she does. 'Well then, Miss Keeper, what did your master fail to teach you that you've sought me out, what advice can I give?'

'It's not advice I need, Mr. Fearnought. It's directions.'

Fearnought pauses. Turns. He busies himself with paperwork on his desk. When he twists back his eyes burn holes right through her, distracting from the smile spreading beneath his beard pushing the bristles past slick bared teeth.

'Directions, is it? And where would you like to go, Keeperess?'

There is movement at the back of the shack, the sail cloth ripples, and Patroclus launches himself at the cat that strides through. It is too fast for him and leaps over the old dog's back, hissing as it hides behind Busker Fearnought's legs.

'Pat!' Nancy shouts an admonishment, but the old dog has a new scent. No amount of Nancy shouting or hissing from the cat will call him back.

'Hey!' Busker is striding over with an arm outstretched to grab the dog's collar. Nancy places herself between them. 'Out of my way, girl, or get your dog under control.' Busker is shaking and Nancy can feel the air change. A moment to choose. She steps back towards the curtain, turns, and pulls it back to the sound of fury behind her.

Out of all the things she'd expected, not a single thing came close to this.

The back of the shack is open and slopes down into shallow water. Though Nancy can see from the tideline that stripes the wall it must come close to filling at high tide. The walls are coated with a thick shag of green weed. Gooseneck barnacles. The smell is overpowering though more pleasant than the other half of the shack. Close to the top of the ramp, just behind the curtain, drawers and boxes are stacked. They are all firmly closed, and Nancy leaves them be. There is a murderous energy radiating from Busker already, she won't push her luck. Hanging from the ceiling are lines of dead skate and ray. Their wings cut and pinned back and hung out on racks that must be ready to set out in the sun to dry. Bodies twisted into monstrous shapes that echo the form of a woman. Smiling mouths and wings for arms.

'You're making Jenny Hanivers?' Pel had owned one, sideshow exhibitions, falsified monsters a penny a viewing. Busker steps into the back room, his cat still skulking at his heels.

'What of it? What is any of this to you, Miss Bligh?' Some of the anger has dissipated, replaced by embarrassment but something else too, something that reads as relief. Nancy preferred the murderous anger. She knew what to do with that. 'Is the trade so good up on the moors you can't see the need for extra income? Men pay a tidy sum for these, they come down from London for a bottled merrymaid. Now come back inside and leave my business be.' He turns inside, stooping as he does so to pick up the cat which he begins to stroke, not without gentleness. 'Don't mind Grampus, she's not used to guests and it's turning into a busy day.' Reluctantly, Nancy follows, Patroclus too though he has business with a hatch set into the floor that is stained round the edges and worn from use. If there wasn't a cat to keep an eye on, he would have that open.

Back in the front room, Busker re-hangs his curtain of cloth. Smooths it over as though it would give a greater degree of resilience without wrinkles. Once he is satisfied and the old sailcloth lies flat, he pulls two wooden stick chairs from the edge of the room and sets them in front of the fire.

'A drink, Keeperess?' Nancy scowls and Busker smirks his way into a curtsey. 'My apologies, Miss Bligh. Can I offer you a drink?' Nancy nods and Busker climbs a ladder to a high shelf laden with bottles, with barrels and jars. She recognises the writing on the side of them as French.

'You've the same suppliers as the Proserpine.' Busker does not pause in his rummaging.

'I *am* the supplier of the Proserpine, Miss Bligh. I told you. Ends must be made to meet. Things are not as they were.'

Nancy curses herself for not putting the pieces together. A house in a cave that backs onto the sea, a ramp you could roll a barrel up.

'You don't go across yourself then?'

'No, Miss Bligh. Embarrassing though it is I've not the stomach for sailing. The barrels come to me, and a little bit more besides.'

Grunting, he lowers himself down the ladder and pours them both a brandy. Nancy downs it to a smirk of approval from Busker who does the same, pours another. She leaves it sitting where it is.

'You've no coopers, Busker.' It had been bothering her since she came in. 'No sign of them anyway, I thought they were everywhere, the little ones.'

'They are, Miss Bligh, true enough. But as I am sure you know a cooper makes a house a home and this?' He waves a hand around the planks, the peeling paint. 'This is not home material. Besides, Grampus has a taste for things that live under floorboards.' The old grey cat lazily opens an eye and licks its whiskers with a rasped tongue. 'Before we get to where you're going. A little on where you're from.'

This old salt is changing the subject.

'Please, Busker. I need to be on my way…' He doesn't cut her off, he just ignores her.

'There, on the wall behind you. A gift from your father to my grandfather.' Nancy turns. On the wall is a three tined spear. The outer points hooked over, the centre straight and serrated. A long, polished haft. A spear for catching eel, a glaive. Pel had the same one tattooed on his neck. She has it marked on her skin too. A reminder of him, along with the anchor cross above her heart.

'They call that a grail in these parts. Can you credit it? And that one came from Lord Hunt himself so it's pretty much a relic, give or take. If you get my meaning. Did you see the island? On your way here?'

'I saw something.'

'Disappear on you, did it? Aye it'll do that, Eythin. Tricksy, that place.'

Nancy shifts, twisting her grandmother's ring impatiently as the man bloviates. She opens her mouth to speak but it seems that is what Busker was waiting for as he beats her to it.

'I see your flowers, growing on your skin. I know who put them there too, pretty one that. They help you remember, don't they?' He jerks his head to the workbench, to the space above where a thousand pieces of knotted string hang. 'Those are my flowers, Miss Bligh. I tie my spells in knots.'

'What do you want, Busker? You don't even know why I'm here.'

'You're here to wake the witch.' Ignoring Nancy's whitening face, Busker stands and walks to his workbench, takes down a complex knot. 'Your blasted protector has been here twice in his long, selfish life. Once to be saved and once to be damned. Both times, that witch was involved. So why else would his darling daughter be here? To visit me? To hear my great wisdom? Like hell. I can get you to her. It'll cost you, though.'

Shaking her head, Nancy stands.

'You want money? Gods, Busker you're pathetic. I have no gold.'

'Hush, lass. I've been paid. Your passage has been bought. That's not what I'm saying.'

Busker moves faster than she would have thought the large man able, and he presses his hand to her throat. She has drawn the knife from her belt and has it against his neck as he makes contact, Patroclus is up too and baring his teeth.

'Get your wretched hands off me, Fearnought. You'll not win a fight.'

Busker considers, she can hear the grate of his teeth, and he releases her with a rough shake of his hand. Eyes her with a smile.

'Blood, girl. That's what I need.'

Patroclus leaps, knocks the Keeper to the floor and gnashes at his face, sparks flying from the shield the salty Keeper has cast.

'Get this mutt off me, girl, I misspoke.'

Nancy lays a hand on Pat who stops gnashing but remains sat on Busker's chest.

'A vial of your blood. Given freely.'

'For what purpose?'

'The witch rests with one of Them. Blood opens the way.'

Nancy sees red ink in the still water of the Fellmire as Busker Fearnought extends an oil-stained hand and waits for Nancy to take it. She does, but she is shaking. Every part of her wants to hurt him, to shake this whole cave down, but she cannot trust herself not to kill him. She needs him to show her where her grandmother lies sleeping. Pel made this bed, she won't be the one that lies in it.

'Fine.'

Busker grins, and hauls Patroclus from his chest. He goes to the desk and pulls open a rattling draw from which he takes a glass bowl and what looks to be a penknife. It's only as he opens it Nancy recognises it as a fleam. A selection of short, sharp blades for veterinary bloodletting.

'Gods, Busker at least use a lancet.'

'I have what I have, Keeperess. Sit.'

He motions the chair, and she sits, rolls up a sleeve. Lets him tie a tourniquet around the top of her arm. She does not wince as he finds a gap between the flowers on her arm, as he lays one of the finer points against the vein and gives a sharp tap to the top of the blade.

'Hold this.'

He hands her a rag, and Nancy presses it to the cut as Busker opens the grate of his fire and, using tongs, holds the glass cup in the flame. When it is hot, he carries it carefully to her, motions to remove the cloth and clamps it to her skin.

Her swearing echoes from the hut and shakes the gulls from their roosts.

'My, Miss Keeper. What language. You sure you've never been to sea?'

Nancy ignores him, watches the skin rise under the glass cup, the cut opening and filling the bowl with her blood. When it is filled, Busker wrenches it free without disguising his smile and covers it with waxed cloth.

'With gratitude.'

Nancy stands shakily, closing the fleam's hole with a spell drawn from the picture of yarrow on her shoulder.

'I've done as you asked, Busker. Take me to her.'

'Time enough in the morning, Nancy. It's late and I'm in need of rest. You can take the hammock; I'll take the chair. Because I'm a gentleman, really.'

'Goddammit Busker! Now!'

But Busker is already comfortable, ignoring the constant growls from Patroclus, a blanket over his legs and his cat in his lap.

'No use shouting, Nancy. Get some rest. Besides, I think you'll find we've little choice in the matter. Did no-one tell you, when you visit the coast, that you should always check the tides?'

Rushing to the front door Nancy yanks it open. The arc of the cave mouth fills with moonlight that bounces in rippling light from the sea. The sea that has risen and cut them off, Busker's boat bobbing just out of reach and far, far away on the horizon an island floating on air.

BIBLE LEAVES

THE HOUSE OF Locryn Calder is large and squat and always watching. Broadfaced and hung with slate its windows peer from white painted frames, keeping an eye from the hillside. It sits on the far side of the valley, opposite the chapel so it can take in God and man in equal measure. Around it, in granite walled fields sheep graze between the cattle, and its yards are stacked with fresh cut stone. Even while sleeping this house feels busy. It is a place of hard work and justly earnt rewards. On the ground floor, in a simple room, old Cusk sleeps. He has a home, a house of his own, but since last year has slept here. To better aid his friend. No children, no wife; he upped and left the morning after the chapel fell, and now he lies here every night and dreams of rabbits caught in snares.

Above, two filled rooms and an empty one between, Luk and Yestin sleep either side of their lost brother's bed. Both waiting patiently for a wife, with their eyes closed. No one's thought to tell them they play a part in that search, perhaps nobody will. At the end of the hall, behind double doors, is interred the body of Locryn Calder. Sleeping but not dreaming, alive and not quite dead. Shock and grief have torn his mind to shreds and it's taking an age to darn back together. His eyes are open and glisten with tears and his hands are clenched in fists at his side. On his bedside table sits a bible and a miniature portrait of the woman he loved. The woman who died as softly as she'd lived in the bed where he now lays. The woman who had told him they were young enough for children. That they'd watch them grow together. She had not seen one make ten. Next to her a portrait of Jan, the son he lost. Does he think of them when he lies not-sleeping or is there nothing in that head? The window slides up on its sash as Knot slides in, tickled pink with his revised plan.

'Locryn.'

Nothing. Not a flicker of alarm.

'*Wake up Locryn Calder, there is work for you to do.*'

Across the bedclothes the creature walks until it is sat beside the old man's head, pleased with its new idea. One name has power enough, but two? He thinks himself on to a winner.

'*Quite the number you've done on yourself. I have to say I'm disappointed Locryn, falling at the first like that. Your Mother needs you. St Reagan needs you.*' A pause. The voice unsure of itself. '*They are the same, it seems, after all. No need to worry about the dark anymore, there is nothing but the light. It is a bet you cannot lose. So come, up. Get up. After all the work you've done for her. For the chapel. To fall when She needs you most.*'

A murmur from between dry lips.

'*Come now!*' The voice is shouting, a new tack, '*She needs a bull not a mooncalf! Where are your horns?*'

Another, louder murmur, and a flicker of recognition in long glazed eyes.

'*Aha! He shakes himself awake, a little, at least? Yes. It is a good day, Locryn Calder, your Mother wishes to thank you. To perform a little miracle.*'

The creature places its hands on either side of the sleeping man's head and inside, the tattered mind tears itself straight. Calder's eyes close, and when they reopen, they are crystal clear. The creature moves quickly to avoid being crushed as the man leaps from his bedclothes. His nightshirt and long-tasselled cap billowing in the breeze from the window.

'That's it, Locryn! Go and see the new Reverend. He follows Her too. He'll need the well, for the work he's to do, here let me draw you a map.'

Locryn Calder watches as a crude set of directions is etched into the dust on the floor, marking out a spot he knows.

Out he goes into the hall, clattering on the floorboards and down the stairs to the entrance hall to the large front door which he opens to ring the bell. Its peals echo through the waking house and imagine the surprise on the two boy's faces, Cusk's wrinkled face too, at the sight of Locryn Calder hammering at the bell. Looking up, he sees them staring.

'My boys! My friend! Get your shovels and your picks, we've a well to dig!'

SCURVY GRASS

It is a noise like seaglass breaking and Nancy wakes as though saved from drowning, coughing up imaginary water. Busker's chair is empty. Patroclus still sleeps but there is whispering from behind the curtain. Nancy sits up and tumbles awkwardly from the hammock but manages to land softly. She creeps towards the sailcloth, towards the smell of salt and talking voices. When she reaches it, she stops, stills her breath. Thinks of her flowers. None of them will help her overhear or stop her being seen. The sea crashes against the sides of the shack, and she moves quietly between the breakers. She goes slowly, from hammock to cloth, and peers with one eye through the curtain.

Busker has his back to her. He has gained a shirt in the night, a red and white striped, stained affair with ragged, loose thread edges. He stands at the top of the ramp, looking down into the water which now laps at floor level.

'I don't care what she says, we're due another. The *Cadwaller* was weeks ago. I'm in need. You are too, are you not? Or have you saved enough from our last haul to last?'

There is rippling from the water, bubbles bursting with half heard words.

'Here, hold for a moment.'

Nancy shrinks back as Busker moves towards her and waits

for the curtain to be opened. It is not. Instead, Busker walks to one of the chests on the floor and begins to unlock it. First with a key, then with a spell; Nancy can see his fingers tying invisible knots. As he does, she turns to the water. It looks like a seal at first. She recognises the face as one of the two that delivered the ring. Black eyes in an upturned face only just above the water. The bucca's hair spreads in a cloud of seaweed and jellyfish stings in the water around it and its long tongue dashes out between pinpoint teeth, moistening its eyes. They peer at the shadows where Nancy hides, but their gaze is a flickering thing and soon moves on. Busker finishes extracting what he wants from the chest and moves back to speak with the bucca. It leans up and out of the water in eagerness at what the sea-keeper holds, its smooth and muscular body the colour of serpentine, but Busker lifts his hand away.

'Come now. We've both learned this lesson. I'll not have your glassy teeth in this arm again. And you'd best not have forgotten my retribution?'

The bucca sinks back seal-headed into the water.

'Aye. As I thought. It'll be down the hatch and waiting. But you tell her, a ship is due one week from now, the *Round-Robin*, I'll see it sunk and my bounty brought. Or we renegotiate our terms.'

There are more ripples, that Busker seems to take as assent, and he turns and kneels by the hatch in the floor and drops in the bucca's due.

A human hand, severed at the wrist.

NANCY DOES NOT sleep. She had hurried back to her hammock and turned her face to the wall. Listened to Busker's heavy steps as he creaked his way back to the chair. She has spent the remainder of the night putting pieces together. The wreck of the *Cadwaller* where no man was saved despite the best efforts of their Keeper.

Stories rise of wreckers, cutting the hands from drowning sailors as they reach for a grip on a boat.

Of course Busker is behind the wrecks. Of course he's involved in the mess she's in. Nancy's fists are balled at her side, and she closes her eyes to stop them shaking. She has gotten better at control, but it's a breaking dam, not a lock gate. There is no middle ground. A plan is made as dawn breaks. A simple one. Find Meliora. Deal with Busker. If he keeps his promise, it will be done today. If not, well, she'll find her grandmother alone. When Busker wakes, she feigns a yawn and rubs the lack of sleep from her eyes.

'Good night, Miss Keeper?'

'How are the tides, Mr. Fearnought. Are we able to leave?'

Busker's mouth wrinkles, whatever thought has formed stays unspoken, and he turns towards the door.

'Yes, Miss Keep—Miss Bligh. The tides are fine. But can I not offer you some food to begin your day? I have smoked fish in the stove house outside, I have coffee ready to brew?'

'No, Busker. Nothing. The day is wasting, and I have plans for it, plans that involve you. You promised me passage, Fearnought. Settle your debts.'

Busker chuckles as he pulls on a thick knit sweater. Grampus jumps nimbly down from her bed on the dresser and lands silently next to Patroclus who wakes at the gust of air it brings and snaps fruitlessly after the cat.

'Fine, Nancy.' He drops the pretence of civility with palpable relief. 'Up then. If no time's to be wasted, then we'll be off. I'll show you where your witch went down.' He reaches up, and unhooks the glaive, the eel spear, from the wall. Its haft long enough to use as a hiking stick. He smiles as he pulls on leather boots stained with white rings of salt and kicks open the door. The sunlight burns through the shadows and Nancy has to hold her arm up to shade her eyes. Stepping out onto the still wet deck, the whole cave stinks of high tide. She casts about for signs of the Underfolk, but there is nothing. No piskies or bucca hiding behind rocks. Nothing moves but the gulls. Busker walks right past the base of the path that carried Nancy down, out into the bay, before turning left and walking out along the sand. Nancy follows, aware as she does that the island has returned, lowered now onto the horizon and simmering in the heat.

'Busker, hold! Wait!' But the Keeper marches on. As she follows, Nancy is aware of the shattered wood that nestles between the black slate rocks. These coasts are known for their wrecks, but this cove has seen more than its fair share. She thinks back to the scenes behind the curtain and the knot in her stomach gains weight. How many ships has this man demanded sunk? Who is it that sinks them?

'Come on, Nancy, the day is wasting.' Busker is stood at the base of a gently sloping track, etched lightly into the rock from a cliff fall, as though some giant has pressed his thumb into the rock. It is a far easier way to move between beach and cliff.

'Don't tell me you took the staircase?' Nancy does not answer, just starts walking. But she can feel Busker's mocking eyes on her back. She feels Patroclus' fury too. Busker is silent until they reach the top of the slope, it is only as they reach level ground that he starts talking.

'What do you know of the Brine?'

Nancy knows nothing but she'll not let him know. Pel spoke only of the moor. 'Trouble for others' was his answer when pressed on the other Keeper's worlds.

'Like the Undermoor, but for the Underfolk of the sea.' A guess but a good one.

'Correct, Keeperess. Though They prefer "merry-folk". See Themselves as apart from the others. They aren't that different though, at a base level.' Something in the way he talks sends shivers right through her. 'The Brine is larger than the Undermoor, too. As I understand it. Some of us aren't regularly invited to fairy worlds.'

'How do you know about that?'

'You're not the only one to talk to gods. Though some of us are content to do it by proxy.' Nancy wonders how much of the conversation between the bucca and Busker she slept through.

'I wouldn't say my visit was organised.' Nancy tries to hold her tongue, but it rankles to let him prattle unchecked.

'They never are. In any case. It's the largest by far of what we know to be the under-realms. My grandfather had a map he drew. It's in the shack somewhere. They're layered. One on top of the other. The Æther, The Undermoor, the Motherlode. Whatever lies below. Us trapped between them like a flower between glass.' He stops and turns, points to the floor, 'pick up any quartz you see. Rounded slate too. You'll need them for the journey.' Nancy starts collecting stones as they walk, and Busker keeps talking. 'The Brine runs through them all. Seeps into their edges. Connects them. You know there's power at the edges? Space for things to happen? Well, the Brine is nothing but edge. It's entirely liminal. That's why She's so much stronger than the rest. Stronger than your friend, the God of the Mire. Stronger than the Copper men, the Owl. That's why Pel and my father sent the witch to Her.'

Nancy pauses in her collecting, impatient at this drip, drip, drip of information.

'Sent her to who?'

'The Drowned Goddess. The Queen of Salt. Empress of the Brine. They do love their titles, don't they? Nameless at the end though, like all the rest. Kings and Queens and other despots playing with their toys. She has the witch. It's her you'll need to sweet talk. Though I hear she's keen to be rid of her.'

'And you can get me to Her?' They are nearing the daymark now. A white tower, a single white tooth jutting up and out of the cliffside.

'Aye. I can. Though, Miss Keeper, I've a little thing to discuss before I do. Sleep well, did you?'

Nancy thinks back on the night before. The overheard conversation. The hand.

'Fine. Thank you.'

'Bollocks you did. I'm not the fool I look, and Grampus certainly isn't. She saw you skulking, girl. That cat's a devil for tattletales.'

She thinks of her grandmother, how close she is. Barely a step away.

'You talk to the cat?'

Busker gives a short laugh. 'Ha, I talk to Grampus. Let's leave it at that. I had planned to do this as asked, Nancy. Take you to the shore, have you draw a picture in pretty stones.' He draws the cup of blood from a pocket. 'Give the Bucca their due. You've fucked that, though, girl. Can't have you coming back with ideas above your station. Pel's rules in that head, I'm sure. No wiggle room.' He spits. 'Grow up. You're coddled. You don't know what it's like, not really.'

His smile is gone. Replaced by the face she's seen so often on men who don't like women stood eye to eye with them. He levels the spear at her. Its three tines glinting in the sun.

'Move to the edge, Nancy.' Busker's voice is quiet. Patient. Nancy does not move. 'To the edge, Nancy. Turn, face the water. Raise your arms to the sea.'

Nancy stays put. The stones are heavy in her pockets, and she grips her riding crop tightly. Feels the pressure of the knives in her belt. Feels the sting of the flowers on her skin.

'She's been good to me, the Queen. Gave me the sight. Didn't even have to give up an eye, so I've got one over on Pel there, too. In return I don't work as hard as I might to save those that need saving. Keep the flow of bodies moving. She's the same as the rest. Petrified she'll run out of followers. Between my forefather's and your father, she'd been reduced to living off scraps. Taking only the men who drowned alone. Between Jan, Nicca and the lifeboats, every blasted man was saved.' Busker laughs, a cruel and loud chuckle. 'I've made sure her coffers have been filled. I'll not have you ruin it.'

Busker starts to work a knot with his left hand, glaive still held in his right, and Nancy feels the air charge. Feels the hairs on her arm stand on end. There's little space on the coast path. The sea at her back and heather and rock behind Busker. She pictures campion. Tattooed on her shin. Makes the shape. A blinding flash cracks the air between them.

'Bitch!' Busker staggers back, looses his spell unaimed, and Nancy feels a jolt of searing heat crackle down her cheek. The pain, sharp and sudden, angers her, and before she's thought it through, she's called the Murmur. The cliff shakes, she sees a jagged scar open behind Busker who is as pale as a ghost. Blinking to clear the blindness from his eyes. There's a sickening lurch as the cliff edge drops three feet and Nancy staggers back, feels the air beneath her heel as she braces. Closing her eyes she desperately tries to roost her flock but the cliff's still shaking. Busker, recovered, is scrabbling backwards, up over the heather, using the glaive to haul himself on. He stands, raises it and, distracted by controlling the Murmur, Nancy doesn't move in time to dodge it when he throws. The three tines embed an inch into her shoulder and she's tipping back off the cliff. She sees Patroclus leap, knock Busker back and can just see the snakes, furious at the interruption, slide raspingly towards them. Covering man and dog in a tangle of zig-zag scales.

She crosses her arms across her chest and falls like a petrel into the waiting water, pulled down into the dark by pockets full of stone.

MOONWORT

DELEN ROWE HAS slept well since Nancy put her nightmares down. It has been a tumultuous year for her. Both parents gone. Two faiths rocked to their foundations and no-one to talk to but her memories. She's found a personal peace. Taking a little from the church, a little from the moor. Fully aware she's hedging her bets. She sits, now, in a pool of morning sun that has collected in front of the stove. On the wall her gorse branch cross has sprouted green points from wood she'd thought dead, and she is unsure how to feel about it, so she sits in the sun and waits for explanations.

'Still so many trinkets trapped inside your walls.'

The voice is coming from… well, hard to say. The cross? The stove? Somewhere from *within* the wall. She does not answer. Instead, she bites her lip and wishes Nancy wasn't still away. Wishes the new priest wasn't quite so new. Wishes that she had somewhere to turn.

'Why do you keep them Delen Rowe? Because your mother put them there? Or because she died once she tried to take them out?'

Delen sits silent. Looks to the charms hung above the fire. To the glass cane filled with coloured threads that's hanging in the window.

'3,764'

'Pardon?'

'*In the bottle. That's how many threads. I'll not be kept out by counting Delen Rowe. You'll need more than bottles and pins and coloured string to keep me from stepping in. Besides. You don't want to keep me waiting, out in the cold. Not with what I have for you.*'

Delen curses herself for speaking, but she's in now. No turning back. And her mother always said it didn't do to upset fairies.

'What are you, then? What do you bring?'

'*That's my girl. I am the unification. I am the healing of wounds. Would you not like to sit in church, walk the moor, and not feel torn in two?*'

Delen nods despite herself. Like many in the valley, having been confronted with the power of two ideologies she's fed up with trying to choose. The lure of peace is a strong temptation.

'*You see the cross. New growth from dead wood. A new, green church is blooming, and it wants you, Delen Rowe. A herald is coming, of a saint with two faces. A Mother with two names. Worry not which one to use, you'll know the way.*'

Delen's breath catches in her throat, and she crosses her hands across her chest, as she's seen some people do. It does not feel right and she stops midway, a half-formed sign with the magic seeping out.

'What about Nancy? The moor?'

The voice in the wall laughs with the sound of bird's bones breaking and it tinkles through the house.

'*Why, Delen, Nancy agrees! She's gone to fetch someone ever so special. Someone who will help with the unification. Our Keeper knows her task will be easier, once all sing from the same hymn sheet. Don't you want to show her you've been busy with her gone? Don't you want Nancy to be proud of you?'*

Delen nods again. She wants that very much indeed. But she is no fool. You don't lose both parents young and not learn a thing or two.

'You've not answered my first question. What are you, voice, that speaks so sweetly? This family has been burned before by evil dressed up as a friend.'

Silence.

'I ask again, who are you? Are you a devil, or an angel?'

'I am not.'

There is a change in the air. Despite the furnace stove the room is cold, now. The hair on Delen's arms, the back of her neck, rises. In the pit of her stomach something writhes.

'I do not trust things that I cannot see. Not any longer. I trust in Nancy. I trust her to see things for me. If she returns and confirms what you have said then so be it. I trust in God I think. But I do not trust you. Whatever you are.'

Delen stands and moves to the door, but the heavy bolt draws itself across and bars the way. She looks through the window and outside, across the yard, the great stone that hides the goose hole at night rolls of its own accord into its closed position. There is nothing. Then it rolls away and behind it, in a darkness impossible for such a shallow space, two eyes burn, and teeth are shining. Bile rises in Delen's mouth, but as it does a warmth shoots through her. A flash of memory enters her head, of walking on a summer's day with her mother on the moor. Finding a dead fox. Perfect in its destruction with violets growing through gossamer claws. Then it is gone. The stone rolls closed, and the feeling passes. The heat returns. The bolt stays locked.

'I am but an envoy of the glory that's to come. The Mother is almost here, Delen Rowe. Reagan awakens. When mine Nancy returns, she'll be proud of you. That you helped bring this new way to glory. Do you see?'

'Yes.' She speaks with conviction too fast found.

The bolt shoots back and the door creaks open. On the doorstep are all the charms that Delen's mother had placed in the walls. All those that were too deep to be dug out. Hearts stuck with pins, a leather shoe. A set of keys and a bottle full of hair and dark liquid. But there too are things Delen's grandparents placed there. And theirs. Bones and charms and quartz stones. Things that have not seen daylight in three hundred years. Things that were baked into the fabric of the house. Delen rushes out to see the damage, to see the lime mortar that must be scattered on the floor, to see how long her cottage might stand with such excavations. But there is not a stone out of place. No mortar disturbed. The objects which, now she looks, are clean and pristine have been removed from the wall with no damage at all.

'St Reagan protects you now, Delen Rowe, a new Mother for a girl without one. You've no need of trinkets. Trust me.'

Delen turns, leaving the doorstep collection be and stifles a yelp. On the floor, where she just sat, are thousands of coloured threads. Smoothed straight and lain in rows of ascending colour, the empty glass tube on the floor next to them.

Above the hearth, nestled in between the green spiked leaves a single yellow flower blooms on the cross and the rooms smells like coconut and smouldering ashes.

HENBANE

Nancy blacks out as she hits the water. By some miracle she has avoided the rocks, but the sea breaks her fall like a granite shelf. She hangs for a second, a jellyfish at the mercy of the current then her eyes open and she remembers she is drowning. There is saltwater in her lungs. Seawater in her eyes. She kicks towards the surface but Pel's old coat, heavy enough already, is weighted with the stones she was foolish enough to fill it with and it pulls her down, away from the light. To remove it, she has to wrench the spear from her shoulder, and it slides free in a cloud of dark red blood. She struggles free from the coat, and watches it wave as it sinks from view, but the effort of removal and the blood loss have left her exhausted. She tries to form a spell to save herself but in her entire garden of flowers she can't think of one that will help. Besides, she can't focus enough to think each through. Rocks burst past her from the cliff fall above, sending bubble trails down after her coat. A sharp stone hits her and blood blooms in the water as her chest tightens. As the pressure grows, she tries to summon the Murmur again, tries to force the water like she does the land, but it ignores her completely. Of course it does. Pel had put her grandmother beneath the waves because the water weakened her. Why had she thought she'd be different? Something darts past her, beneath her, above. A pod of dolphins, perhaps. She would have liked to see dolphins, Nancy thinks. She would like to have been able to enjoy the sea. Just for a moment. She lets herself drift. Imagines seeing her friends again. Wonders what's happening on the moor. She thinks she smells almonds then laughs, chokes on the water that rushes in, and tries to picture the tattooist's face.

She's lost in her drowning when the bubbles start. Little pockets of air made by shapes, creatures, that swarm around her. Whatever they are, they draw nearer with every foot she sinks. She can feel them brush against her. She tries once more to kick, to rise up, but her leg feels trapped. Tangled in kelp or weed. Looking down she sees that something does hold her. Something long and muscular that wraps itself in circles around her body and tightens. Then it's gone. She is free again. Her head thuds, red flashes pulse at the sides of her vision and her lungs scream out. The creature is back. And it is only the one. No pod of dolphins or whales. A singular creature. A leviathan, a serpent. Coiling around her, playing with its prey. The bubbles cease, and she passes out again as the creature takes hold.

SHE DRIFTS BETWEEN waking and sleep, though she fears she must be dead. Each time she opens her eyes she is still under the water and yet the pressure in her lungs is gone. She breathes easy. So dead she must be. It does not worry her.

She has been dead before.

Besides, she is not alone. The coiling beast from before. It embraces her tenderly. Does not squeeze too hard. Bucca pass by, their hair drifting in the water and webbed hands waving. The dream continues in a haze of vignettes that ebb and flow with the pulsing pain in her head.

A sunken ship, skeletons still reaching for air.

A perfect ring of standing stones waiting for the waters to recede so they can sing under the stars again.

A column of pilchards swirling to unheard music.

The skull of a giant.

Nancy smiles as she passes them, then darkness returns.

OXYGEN. NANCY BREATHES again. Coughs up water and sits with a splutter. She is in a cavern, lit by the sun through a hole in the roof. Covered with half rotten timbers and hung with rope there are blackthorn trees planted in a ring around it. Blossom drifts down to the damp floor below. From the surface, in the unlikely event it was found, it must look like a mine shaft, long forgotten and worth avoiding. Inside the cave is a vaulted cathedral. Its walls black, wet, slate run through with quartz, so every surface is lightning struck with white veins. Nancy turns at the sound of something breaking water. At the side of the cave, there is a pool, banked by a ledge of slate that pitches straight down into the water which roils with the body of some great snake. No. A conger eel. Its thick, muscular body a reddish purple flecked with dark spots like the coat of a leopard. The fins running almost the length of it a flickering, vivid blue. It is scarred. A survivor. As Nancy sits and watches it, the writhing of the coils slows and the creature dives. Its tail disappearing into the depths. Then, from the blackness, a woman's face appears. Rising up out of the water trailing bubbles from her mouth. Her large eyes are those of a fish—blue, pricked with gold with a very little white showing—and her red lips a tightly strung bow. Her skin the palest blue and translucent. Like fine bone china, blue veins pulsing beneath. She breaks the surface of the water, shakes her green hair, and pulls herself up. She is naked. From the waist up she has the body of a woman but, in the water, Nancy can still see the tail of the eel. It thrashes, helping her rise smoothly from the water. She turns and sits on the edge, tail in the water, body out, and squeezes the water from her hair.

A merrymaid.

The creature looks keenly at Nancy, whose clothes stick to her as she sits on the cave floor, whose hair is full of sand and weed. Then it coils its tail onto the granite and stands on two long legs, the tail disappearing in such a smooth motion that Nancy barely registered the change. The creature that stands before her is magnificent. Seven feet tall and a masterwork of muscle. Each sinew carved from marble, her calves, her thighs twitching as she shifts her weight. As she stands creatures move from the pool and up across her skin, starfish clambering to her shoulders, to her hips, snails with shells of silver crawl across her body creating a lacework of their trails before coming to rest in shining clusters of pearlescence. The merrymaid—though that description seems inadequate now—pushes her hair behind an ear revealing a line of circular gills that curve down to her shoulder. From her parted hair strawberry anemones uncoil red and blue tentacles from spotted bodies and an octopus wraps its arms around her neck. Nancy gazes open mouthed, as terrified as she is drawn in.

'You can bow now.' The creature's lips do not move as it speaks. The sound is inside Nancy's head. Accompanied by a series of clicks, like the sounds that a bat makes.

Nancy coughs to clear her throat. 'Bow?' The creature's head tilts to one side and it frowns.

'Yes. Keeper. To your saviour and your Queen of Salt. Welcome to the Brine.'

Nancy shivers and she is unsure if it is because of the woman in front of her or the cold. But she remembers Pel's advice not to give in to a god and drops into a curtsey, a slight nod of the head. The Queen cocks her head at Nancy's performance and smiles broadly, revealing row after row of thin glasslike teeth.

'Very well Keeper. I'll allow it. You are a lucky person. Where did you come by your charms?'

Nancy looks at her arms, at the flower tattoos.

'They came with the job. Though I confess I didn't know they'd help me here.'

The Queen laughs, the sound of fish driven to the surface by a shark and looks Nancy up and down.

'Not those. Keeper. Not your badges of office. Those mean nothing to the Brine. The bones in the pouch. Those are what saved you. That's why, during my little tour, you did not drown.'

Nancy's hand raises to the pouch Baz gave her, with its tiny fish vertebrae. Still hanging at her neck.

'They belong to a man I met. He gave them to me.'

'He saved your life, Keeper. Those are things from a magic I respect. I've not seen them in these waters. It was a bold entrance you made. There are other ways to get here, you realise. Proper channels.'

Nancy takes a step back from the being in front of her. The Queen is taller than anyone she's seen, other than giants, muscular frame in perpetual motion, her body rippling beneath the skin.

'Your man Busker necessitated a short cut.'

The Queen freezes. Cocks her head.

'My man Busker? The idiot? My, my, Keeper. If you can't cope with him what hope for you?'

'It doesn't matter. I'm here now.'

The Queen turns her back and walks to the ledge leading to the water. She kneels and swirls its surface with her hand. Fish appear and nibble at her fingertips.

'You got my invitation, then.'

Nancy kicks herself.

'The ring. A map would have helped more.'

The Goddess wrinkles her lip, exposing teeth.

'You are young, so I will forgive you this rudeness. Yes. Lord Hunt left it as his mark. With his death our concord is over. Take her and be on your way.'

With her free hand the Queen gestures to the space of the cave bathed in light. There is a crack as the floor opens and rising on a circle of rock is a long rectangular object completely submerged in a tangle of seaweed and netting. Starfish and octopus flee as it rises, furious at this betrayal of bedrock.

'She stopped screaming months ago. I'm surprised it has taken someone so long to come and get her.'

The Queen of Salt rises to her full height and strides towards Nancy who has to tilt her head to maintain her gaze. Nancy shudders once again. Here, with the Queen almost pressed to her, Her bare skin an inch away from Nancy, it is clear that what blood runs through these veins is cold. There is no heat radiating from Her. The Queen takes Nancy's face between her hands and turns it left, then right. With the fingers of her left hand, she traces the raised scar that lies beneath an ivy tattoo.

'You're the girl who died, aren't you?'

Nancy stays silent. Tense beneath cold fingers. Aware of the nakedness of the Queen, of her proximity.

'Yes. This is my cousin's work, I can feel his hand in this.' The Queen closes her eyes, moves her head as though listening to something. 'He gave his life for you, then? Lord Hunt? You are his inheritor, his... daughter?' Nancy starts a question, but the Queen silences her with a raised hand. She is almost through her examination when she stops. As though she has heard a sound she did not expect. There is something approaching fear on her face. 'Ah. Another reason to be here.'

The Queen releases Nancy as though she has been burnt and glowers at Nancy.

'Blood of the Island. Blood of the Witch. A dangerous mixture that you've concocted.'

Nancy holds fast, holds the Queen's gaze, and repeats her question.

'Never mind me, your highness. What did my father give you, in return for your aid? What was your bribe?'

The Queen raises a hand and goes to strike Nancy but stops. Thinks better of it. Lets her words do her thrashing.

'I am a God, Keeper! I am not some fool to bribe. Your father knew that. You should too. It was not about what he gave me. It's what he returned. Pel and Nicca redrew the maps. Restored my tithes.'

'The shipwrecks.'

'Yes, child. The wrecks. We all have our needs. You've met my cousin, in His muddy, earthy home. A god needs subjects. You all forgot that it was I who let you sail my seas all these centuries. You used to thank me. Return your dead to me. Leave a man or woman chained to a rock once in a while for my darlings to feast on. Pel talked old Nicca Fearnought into giving me a ship, once a moon. In return, I was her gaoler. But I am done, girl. Hear me? I suppose he must be dead, Pel, why else would you be here in his place. I should have guessed when she stopped screaming. My deal dies with him. I've accords with Busker now. He's an idiot but he does as he's told. All he wants is gold, no sleeping witches from him.'

Nancy adds these crimes to Pel's lengthening list but carries on. His problems cannot all be hers. And there are matters pressing.

'What do you mean she was screaming? What was she screaming?'

'For her mother, child. The witch screamed for her mother. Pathetic.' Nancy shivers again, in the break of stone above, the gulls cackle.

'What happened, why did she stop?'

'Pel's wards shielded her, nobody knew she was here. They fell when he died. Why does anyone stop calling for help; somebody heard her.'

Nancy frowns. Thinks of her dreams. Of deep seas and chains. But they did not lead her here—Pel did.

'It was not her mother she called for, your highness.'

The Queen pauses at this.

'Child, I have absolutely no idea what you are talking about.'

Nancy frowns.

'A creature I do not trust was very keen I made my way here. He believed the Mother is something powerful. That She is coming, that your prisoner was the key to stopping Her.'

The goddess is silent for a long time. When she speaks, she does so with a shark fin sway.

'There was a tale, once. Told to us when young. Someone is lying to you, Keeper. Filling that head with stories. Take your witch and go.'

Nancy walks over to the pile of weeds and tears the slick, wet greens from the box beneath. It is a long chest of fire blasted wood, and it is wrapped in minute silver chains. They are held at the centre between the jaws of a badger skull with a seal of molten silver poured on top. Nancy does not have time to consider who the skull belongs to, but the memory of Pel's confession lingers. Nancy has no need for magic. With Pel's protections gone there is nothing to give the metal any extra strength, and she wrenches the chains apart like a child at Christmas. Her family waiting inside. The tiny links scatter into the heaped seaweed as she scrapes them from the lid. The box itself is nailed shut and Nancy levers it free with a knife taken from her belt. Once every nail is loose, she hauls the heavy wood free and meets her grandmother, face to face.

Her head wreathed in blond hair, body wrapped in a black velvet cape, a silver wand, wrought in the shape of a ragwort stem laid on her breast.

'Meliora?'

Nancy's voice is a whisper, there is no response. The woman in the coffin has a face as pale as a church tomb effigy. Nancy leans closer, so close she can feel that though faint, there is a heat to her grandmother's skin. When she speaks again, she closes her eyes. Stills her breath. Opens them.

'Grandmother?'

Nancy finds herself staring into her own eyes. The same green flecked with gold. They hold Nancy's gaze, narrow with a precise distrust then widen, no longer focused, staring straight through Nancy. Straight through the sea and the rock. Meliora Ray, awake at last, speaks.

'What did you call me?'

OAK FERN

THE REVEREND PINE-COFFIN shivers against the damp air. Foetid air that stinks of flowers, of curdled sunlight. He has, over the last day, lit a hundred candles so at least it is no longer dark in here. He counts backwards from ten before he approaches the centre of the room.

'Come, Bram. Think of Mexico. You survived that, and that business in Andalucia. This is nothing.' He should, in retrospect, have expected a crypt. It was odd, on reflection, that the chapel did not have one. He has never, though, been in a crypt with only one occupant. The coffin is a rectangular wooden box, painted brightly with reds and greens in the same naïve style as the fresco in the chapel above.

A long way above.

Abraham had counted the steps on one of his trips, three hundred and eighty-four. Spiralling down into the chapel hill. He can feel the weight of it above him. Since his encounter with Knot, Abraham Pine-Coffin has not slept. Everywhere he looks he sees the flicker of magic. Wings and legs and eyes. It delights him. Terrifies him. What scares him most, however, is the debt he might owe to the one who gave him the gift.

'Reagan.' He whispers her name. It's her in the box. Of that, he is sure. Sure, too, that she wants him to open it. He has taken from his home his three totems. His owl, his stone and his box. They weigh him down, tether him, keep him safe. He whispers words he hoped he'd never use and lays his hands on the box. It falls to dust beneath them. The smell of lilies rises again, the body within wrapped in a sheet that seems soaked in perfume, at its head a box. Ivory or bone, pieced with clasps of gold and engraved with papal seals.

'You survived the reformation, then, your holiness. Forgive me.' He lifts the box, and places it on the shrouded body. Sliding his hands under the form, Abraham lifts her, the sainted Reagan. She weighs almost nothing. Blowing out the candles, he does not want to set the foundations aflame, he stands for a moment in the dark. Then he turns to the door and begins the steady climb to the light.

POWDERHORN

PEL HAS LED Hilla through the Undermoor like a bloodhound, letting her feast on dream after dream in search of a story. The Mother is in almost every head, though most a simple fairytale. They dream of walking about on the moor above without a care. Knot's sweet promises of freedom, each image of Her the dreamer's own, piskie, spriggan or giant.

'*She is coming.*' Spoken in Knot's woodsmoke voice.

There are some, though, who share a thought. Just as Gogmagog did. Of a woman with the feet of a bird. An antlered head. A shining smile. In those dreamer's, the message is different.

'*I am coming.*'

Again, and again.

There is one head left in which to pry.

Pel has not returned to the throne room since he lost his magic. Indeed, he only does so now by stealth. Creeping into the shadows as Hilla lights her tallow. Watches as the heavy horned head of the God falls under. He waits for Hilla to start to speak. To describe the dream as she sees it.

'His dreams are barren. Not a trace of the Mother. Of Reagan.'

Pel relaxes, the God at least immune to Knot's meddling, when something shifts. Hilla speaks again.

'She is coming. Into the dream. She tears it like a painting. Horns on her head and a mouthful of copper and tin. A halo behind her head. She stands in the dream and beneath her clawed feet the ground is blooming.'

Hilla, still under the spells of the dream, faces Pel and smiles with absent eyes.

'I am coming.'

Not Hilla then.

'Indeed. And who are you?'

Mother *Reagan*

The two names are spoken simultaneously. The sound of a bell rung twice, and Pel is in the dream. Stood in the dream of the God of the Mire, with the Mother before him. She is a flickering thing. Her face blurred, though he can see the horns, the antlers, clear enough.

'I see. My lady, I have some experience with your kind. You are confused. I think. You've been listening to stories. Reagan you may be, but the Mother? A Saint? Those things are fiction. Let them go. Go back to sleep.'

'Oh, little lord of Eythin. I know who I am.'

The figure, this saint or goddess, laughs. It crackles and twists the air into a snowfall, a dust cloud, a shower of rain and then She is gone.

Pel opens his eyes. At his side Hilla and Stag sleep, these two who have not in all their years, not once, rested. And on his throne, the God of the Mire stares straight at Pel with molten gold tears in his eyes, removes his bone mask and smiles as the Keeper backs away.

Pel sprints down the hillside, past the still sleeping Gogmagog to where Cleaver waits.

'Jacob! The saint. Tell me, what do you know of her?'

Cleaver regards his friend with a squint.

'Why?'

'She is our ghost, Jacob, she is our ghost!'

'What?' Cleaver's face is a flickering candle. The hope of his faith guttering. This, finally, steadies the wick. 'I don't remember a great deal, but I did have a pamphlet, that I requested from the library at Exeter when I took the post. Before, well, I lost my interest in such things.'

Pel shifts uncomfortably.

'Reagan was a simple girl, as her hagiography goes, you know how these things are written. Goodly and wise and kind. An affinity with animals. Turned to God when the rest of the moor was still worshipping stones.'

'Glad we've moved past that.'

'Quite. They executed her, on the site the chapel stands now. You know as well as I do it's set in a ring barrow; it was as important a site for those before as it is now. Supposedly, if you're to believe the apprentice scribe who made this story up, she stood up after the axe fell, collected her head and continued doing God's work. From then on, she could change things, herself included, gave herself the feet of a stork and so on. It gets very colourful. She was supposed to have hollow bones and horns, the legs of a bird, though these things usually end up being unfortunate afflictions misunderstood at the time. I suspect she was a poor girl who liked animals and looked different to those around her.'

Pel considers the story carefully.

'I read a book by a Frenchman once, that spoke of hollow bones, an illness that created *"enfants monstreux"*. Horns, growths of skin and bone, they do occur occasionally.'

'Quite possibly that was it. With afflictions like that it's monster or saint, usually.'

'She is one of yours then?'

'Who knows! God, listen to me. Death does terrible things to faith, Pel. She may have been, she may not. These stories are so old who's to say?'

'Where did she end up, her body, I mean?'

'The chapel was built on her. Under the hill.'

'She is that old? She is who the ring around the village encircles?'

The Reverend Cleaver nods in concession, though he seems reluctant to do so. It is enough for the old Keeper.

'Then the chapel fell… that idiot imp has made a mistake.'

'What on earth do you mean, Pel?'

'The island of my birth, Jacob, Eythin. It has an affinity with ghosts. It's a beacon, of sorts. They're drawn there. Bodies in the ground, in the water, their ghosts travel towards it. They crawl from the sea, shipwrecked sailors, felled knights, who walk a cockstride each day towards it…'

'Ghosts?' Cleaver starts, then looks down at his body. This spectral form. 'Yes, I suppose I must accept that. But what has that to do with Nancy?'

Jacob Cleaver looks to his friend, but Pel is beyond him. His mind filled with the smell of gorse and the call of kittiwake. The tolling of bells from a chantry house, calling an absent son home. He shakes his head and the bells fade away.

'Trust me, old friend. Ghosts are complicated. Powerful. Hungry for stories. And Gods have been created with less.'

'Pel this is nonsense. Gods do not simply appear from nothing.'

Pel smirks.

'Do they not? How many have you met, Jacob? I've three under my belt.'

Cleaver opens his mouth to speak but, thinking better of it, pinches the bridge of his nose instead. Eyes closed. Breath steady.

'You make declarations about faith with an ease I'd have thought even you would be wary of Pel. You told me of your childhood. You see where we now stand. Faith is powerful. God is powerful.' He frowns at Pel's cocked head. 'Gods are powerful. Do not pretend you think otherwise.'

'My life has taught me Gods are nothing more complex than the rest of us. They just shout louder and put on a better show.'

'You believe nothing then?'

'I believe everything.'

'Regardless. A God does not simply appear from the pages of a story book.'

'No? You were awfully fond of yours. That great compendium of stories, told and told over the centuries. The best ones picked and bound. The rest lost.'

Cleaver takes a step back and Pel raises his hands in apology. His friend has come a long way since his death but the band that tethers him to his profession only stretches so far.

'All I am saying, Jacob, is that it helps. The telling of tales.'

Cleaver accepts the concession with a step closer.

'And this creature is telling them.'

'Indeed. Above and below. Stoking a fire with two furnaces. Heating a vessel with no pressure release. Belief building up with nowhere to go because the Mother isn't real. Mel made her up. Tricked everyone.'

'Tricked you.'

'Quite.'

Cleaver sits on the grass, raises his cassocks to keep the hem from the mud.

'Reagan.'

Pel pauses, smiles.

'You have it, Jacob.'

'Reagan is real.'

'Real enough. All saints have a grain of truth to them, I suppose.'

Cleaver watches the horizon. His eyes scanning the past.

'No, Pel. I mean it. I have seen her. She lies under the chapel. In a tomb. In a box. We, I, found her. Years ago. The Calder's found a painting. I found a door. It was beautiful. Strange. Papal. I had it sealed.'

Pel stares at his friend, the slightest twitch of his brow. The slightest spasmodic jerk of what? Anger? Curiosity? Regret at a secret that might once have been shared?

'Indeed. Primed and ready. She lies there still?'

'She must.'

Pel begins pacing. Back and forth across the patch of grass. Wearing it down to the dirt.

'So, Knot needs a plan, decides in his wisdom, to claim Reagan and suddenly, suddenly, all that belief has a place to go because Reagan has been listening. And what does she hear? Reagan is the Mother; the Mother is Reagan!'

'It can't be that simple, religion…'

'That's all religion is, Cleaver! Wishful bloody thinking! And now an actual god believes in Her! My gods, Nancy, I have to help her, I have to warn her…'

Pel doubles over, wails, tears at the cloth heart on his chest. Cleaver rushes across and shakes him but Pel won't stop.

'Good God, man, pull yourself together. It is a story! Surely it can be stopped?'

'You don't understand! Meliora bloody Ray thinks she's been clever! Thinks she can send that dolt of hers to tell a story and she'll ride back into Mirecoombe and rule as Queen! But the story she's telling has gotten away from her, it's telling itself now. None of us can say how it ends.'

SOLOMON'S SEAL

MELIORA RAY RISES with stiff limbed urgency from a very long sleep. Her eyes still wide, she shakes her head sharply from side to side, wincing at senses that have been coddled in her tomb, unused to noise and light and colour. Once upright she closes her eyes tight. Breathes deeply. When her eyes open, she is calmer. Her breaths come steady, and she climbs from her casket. Places bare feet on the wet seaweed piled by her side. She trails long fingers along the edge of the box and considers her prison carefully. Meliora is taller than Nancy. Now that her muscles have relaxed, now that she has shaken off her sleep she has returned, Nancy assumes, to her usual state. She holds herself imperiously, shoulders back, and her long black cloak drapes heavily from them. Her hair is the colour of a lark's breast, and it catches on what little light enters the chamber. Her face is thoughtful. Heavy lidded eyes carefully considering each joint of her prison and as she looks Nancy catches sight of her mother in the turn of Meliora's cheek, the protrusion of her nose. Catches herself in there too. Meliora's lips are pursed, fine lines spreading from her lips. She does not look young, but certainly wears her years lightly. Far lighter than Pel. Nancy has thought about this, they must have been roughly the same age. But whereas Pel, despite his centuries, looked like a man in his eighties, Meliora Ray looks no older than forty-five.

As Meliora moves, Nancy hears a clinking, jangling sound, and peering into the folds of her cape sees it is hung heavy with pewter charms, tarnished by time, but sewn densely across the fabric. There are signs Nancy recognises, but many more besides. Knights on horseback, assorted gremlins and woebegone faces. Pel's cross. They echo the badges given to pilgrims on arrival at their goal, but these badges won't be found at holy sites. Nancy sees that much. Meliora still clutches the stem of ragwort in one hand. She does not look at Nancy as she speaks.

'I asked you a question, girl. What did you call me?'

Nancy gasps and realises she has been holding her breath. Meliora's voice is deep and melodious. Though there is a rasp to it, brought about by disuse.

'You've the marks of a Keeper. You've the marks of a particular Keeper I've considerable enmity towards, so if I were you, I would explain your words very carefully.'

Nancy stutters. She has not thought this plan through to this point. The journey was her focus, not her goal.

'I—yes, I am a Keeper, that's true, and yes I am Pel's heir.' Meliora still does not turn but Nancy sees her shoulders stiffen. Sees her hand clasp the ragwort wand more tightly than before. 'But' Nancy pauses, softens her voice, 'I am also your granddaughter. My Name is Nancy, Nancy Bligh.'

At this, at last, Meliora turns. Nancy does not know what she expected from this moment. She's heard all the stories. She thinks she has a grip on the woman before her even if it's slight, and she is prepared for dismissal. For a refusal of family. She braces herself. Meliora appraises her newfound kin. Looks Nancy over. She does not smile but her eyes soften and the distrust dissolves into something interrogatory. She moves slowly across the room until she stands before Nancy and takes her face in her hands.

'She took his name, then. I see my daughter in you, Nancy. Though you've your father's hair. I never liked that man, what became of him? That you've found your way here?'

'He died, Grandmother. Pisky led. We believe. My mother is gone too, I'm sorry.'

The muscles of Meliora's face tighten but she shows no other sign of distress.

'I see. Pel added you to his collection then. Found a use for you.'

Statements, not questions, but Nancy nods regardless.

'You've found me though, so you must have something about you. And Pel, he is finally dead?'

Nancy looks away, uncertain. Her resolve in her father's mortality shaken by their meeting.

'He is... gone, grandmother. Not quite dead.'

Meliora smiles at this, though she shakes her head as she does so.

'Of course, there was little hope the old bastard would just die. Far enough gone that I'm out of the box, though. I doubt he'd planned for this.'

Nancy brushes her grandmother's hands away and holds her wrists. Looks her in the eyes. Searches for the grandmother she's looking for.

'I found you.' A whisper.

Meliora opens her mouth to answer, but a movement at the back of the cave distracts her and pulling free of Nancy's grip she strides to the dark water lapping at the slate. To the head that bobs there like that of a seal. The Goddess is back in the water, fish below the waist, her tail thrashing in the black sea and her hair pooling in the water around her. Meliora stands above her and glowers.

'My Queen.'

In the water the Queen sinks lower, so only her eyes are visible. Nancy cannot be sure, but the God looks scared.

'Or are you my jailer, Pel's pet? How else should I explain you keeping me here, against my will, for,' Meliora pauses. Tastes the air. 'Fifty years!'

The Goddess' voice is in their heads. Submerged or not, she answers.

'I am nobody's pet, witch. A deal was struck, and I abided by it until the terms changed. Blame me, hate me, I care not. The fact remains I kept you safe. That ends now. You, girl.' Nancy walks and stands by her grandmother. 'You are her kin then. I thought that is what I tasted. No matter. You have made a mistake. I know what you did to my cousin. You and that cyclops. He was too weak to punish you for it, but I'll not see that transgression stand. You survived the journey here with a foreign magic, a magic that is spent. I abide by the usual rules, I'll not attack you whilst you are my guests. Nor, however, will I help you to leave. And you should, very soon. The tide has turned.'

The transformation to eel is as swift as before. The queen disappears and the cavern shakes. Above her, Nancy watches the small hole of sky close up, the last few petals of blackthorn blossom squeezing their way through but falling, now, in darkness to the echo of a seagull's frantic squawk. The pool into which the Queen has gone boils as her coils sink, and then the water begins to rise. The hole that Nancy entered through narrowing too until only a sliver remains through which the torrent flows. Too dangerous to use the Murmur here, only one place for the rocks to fall. She has no spell that will force apart rock and free them. Panicked, Nancy looks to her grandmother, to the witch who nearly bested Pel, who stands wide eyed and shaking at the back of the cave. Pressed against the rocks. The imperiousness gone. Replaced by a darting, hissing tongue.

'Come on then, girl, what are you waiting for? You have ragwort, the salve?'

'What?'

Meliora's face pales as she sees Nancy's confusion. Turning, she rushes back to her coffin, begins to dig frantically through it pulling out rafts of dried wildflowers that turn to dust in her hands. Muttering in frantic whispers.

'You bastard Pel, what was the point of keeping me alive if you didn't give me means to survive?' Nancy stands, arms hanging at her sides and feels like a child again.

'I'm sorry, Grandmother, I didn't know—'

Meliora does not respond, does not look at Nancy, her attentions have turned to her long cape, to what might be concealed there. This is not the family reunion Nancy had hoped for. As she stands in the water, now at her calves, she swallows down regret. If she has learnt anything from Pel, it is that she does not want to repeat the past. She's spent her life following her adopted father, following in his wake, from now on she steers the ship, however unsteady her hand feels on the tiller.

'Meliora. Grandmother. I'm sorry, but we need to go. As I see it,' Nancy glances up at the black roof of the cavern, then to the pool at the back, 'our options have been removed for us. No need to think we just need to go. Can you swim?'

Meliora turns, visibly shocked at this directness, and gives Nancy a stare.

'How dare you ask me that?'

'What?'

'After all who died. All our sisters? Is this a joke? Did he send you to kill me, to taunt me?'

Meliora wrings her hands, backing up to her casket, stepping up on the raised platform in a futile attempt to avoid the water.

Nancy shakes her head.

'No, of course not! Please, Meliora, grandmother, you have to trust me.'

'I will not swim. I will sink. I will sink. Like Jenny Gall. Peg Cawder. Little Annie Kemp.'

As Meliora recites the names, Nancy remembers Pel's books. Remembers the accounts of the trials. She moves cautiously towards her grandmother, hand out as though she were taming a wolf.

'Grandmother, please. I understand. I do.'

Mel's eyes dart up and the cave begins to shake. Nancy checks herself, counts her birds, but this is not the Murmur. It is something else. Something that tastes like copper and rattles the stone.

'Meliora. Please, I need you to stay calm.'

'You'd tie my thumb to my ankle, is that it? See if Old Mel floats?' She spits, pulls on a thread from her cloak. A twist of red cotton. She takes a badge from her cloak, a little pewter branch and begins to wind the thread around.

'With this thread I bind. With this thread I rise above. With this thread I…'

Nancy lays her hand over her grandmother's. Looks into her eyes. The witch stops. The string goes slack. Nancy can see the tears, can see the fear in the grey of them.

'All is well, grandmother. Calm yourself. I know, no, I do not, but I understand why this is frightening. You must trust me. I am not here to hurt you, you must see that. The Queen means for us to die. I do not. I have just found you, after gambling on a story, and I'll not lose you in the next roll of the dice. I cannot swim either, but we either stay or do our best to learn. It may work or it may not but stay or go we drown regardless, so I'm willing to try. Come here, take your cloak off.'

To both women's surprise, Meliora does as she is asked. Nancy takes the heavy cloth and spreads it on a higher platform of rock, a foot or so above the rising waterline.

'Oh...' Nancy is lost in it. The entire inside of the cloak is lined with magpie feathers that shimmer as though still attached to a wing.

'Nancy!' Meliora's frantic voice shakes her from the trance and Nancy sets to. She removes her shirt and boots, places them in the centre of the cloak and motions Meliora to do the same. Her grandmother is reluctant but unbuttons the skirt and bodice she was wearing beneath the cloak. Nancy notices the outdated style, clothes that would have been archaic even at Meliora's entrapment. Both garments are made of red taffeta, both lined with white lace. She hands them to Nancy with her unlaced boots. Sharp heeled and sharp toed. She scans her grandmother's face, pulled into tight pursed poise as though on a drawstring. Even still, Nancy can see Meliora's lips tremble.

'Good. We'll need to be streamlined.'

Nancy stands and, lifting the bundle, wades to the corner of the chamber where the entrance pool is submerged. The water is past their waists now and it is with difficulty that Nancy hooks the cloak around her foot.

'I hope you can hold your breath, Grandmother.' She does not wait for a response, she just dives.

The water is black, and the panic is almost instant. The memory of her death in the mire the year before rises up before her and it takes almost all she has to push it back down. Arms outstretched Nancy feels along the rock until she meets an opening, the fissure through which she entered. Holding onto the edges of the crack with both hands Nancy pulls herself through, kicking as she does so, and she is into the tunnel beyond. Even if there was time there is no space to turn and check Meliora is following, the pressure of the water has a grip on Nancy's head, and she has no clue how far the tunnel extends. She feels the rock press on her chest and her back, no need to learn to swim this is a crawl, Nancy pulls herself along by her fingertips. Her chest is ready to burst, she can hear her blood pounding in her ears and all she wants is to open her mouth and take a breath. The tunnel curves downwards. The change in pressure makes Nancy's ears pop and she scratches her cheek on a row of limpet shells, the brief brush of the warm blood in cold water spurs her on until the tunnel levels out and begins to climb again.

Come on, girl. You can do this.

Her thoughts pound with the throbbing of her head but there is a change, the water which has been still throughout now has a current flowing through it. A pull. The tunnel seems to be widening and buoyed by the space Nancy kicks hard in the water. A mistake. As her head and shoulders shoot forward the tunnel narrows again, gripping her tight around the shoulders. She is stuck.

Shit.

She wriggles, but there is no space, and she can only move an inch or so each way, her arms trapped at her sides and her feet weighted down by the cloak. Though the water is still black she swears there is a lighter point, the deepest navy in a sea of black ink. Her chest feels like it will burst, and she lunges again to try and pull free. It's then, as her head cracks with the weight of water around it, that the Murmur comes. A whisper. Nothing but an echo of itself as though a lone bird has shaken free of the flock and has swum to her alone. The familiar feeling shakes loose and the caves rattle. It isn't a lot but it's enough. As the tunnel walls vibrate Nancy squirms against them and her shoulders come free, then her arms and hips and she is through; it is an effort not to laugh and let the water in. She settles for a smile as the Murmur fades, as the little bird drowns and fades into the sea.

The celebration comes too soon.

The cloak still bound and tied to her foot catches on the same narrow point. Nancy's smile drifts off, drowns like the Murmur. She knows she hasn't the strength or luck to pull off the same trick twice and though the tunnel *has* widened she still lacks the space to turn and unhook the cloak. She is a lobster pot, anchored to the seabed.

Not again. Not like this. Not now.

Nancy has died once. She knows how it feels, it holds no surprises for her. She closes her eyes against the tears that emerge with disappointment to find they swim in an ocean of saltwater. She is on the brink of opening her mouth and ending it when she feels the push. The cloak is bashing against her calf, an urgent knocking.

Meliora. Nancy has not had time to worry about her grandmother, assumed she was behind her, it is the greatest relief to find she is safe and helping. With a final shove the cloak comes free and Nancy kicks towards the patch of blue in a desperate approximation of swimming. She feels rather than sees the tunnel mouth, feels the space of the sea around her and with breaking lungs powers towards the surface. She breaches the waves with a gasp and for a second worries she has breathed too early as her face is wet but laughs to see it is raining, a torrent of water fighting to re-join the waves. A moment later and Meliora's blond hair breaks the surface, awash with panic and gasping relief. Both woman tread water, faces upturned, then Meliora begins to laugh, soft at first, nothing but a giggle then a full-throated cackle of joy.

It catches Nancy at the back of the throat, and she joins her grandmother's merriment.

'Perhaps you are my granddaughter after all, Nancy. It is not over yet, though, girl. We still need to swim to shore.'

Nancy opens her mouth to reply but is cut short, and the question of the swim is answered for her. The thunder and the lightning crack together, the storm directly above, and as the bolt hits the water everything fades to a static, crackling black.

PART THREE

"I thought to pass away before, and yet alive I am;
And in the fields all around I hear the bleating of the lamb.
How sadly, I remember, rose the morning of the year!
To die before the snowdrop came, and now the violet 's here."

Alfred, Lord Tennyson

SAMPHIRE

Nancy wakes to the smell of almonds.

'Hello, my lover, no—don't sit up.'

Nancy recognises her room at the Proserpine. The tattooist is stood at the window, pouring powders into a washbowl set on the table. The bowl is chipped and painted with a frieze of rockpool life, of waving anemones and crab, of guppies in seaweed fronds. Nancy attempts to ignore the instruction, but as she sits pain flashes through her, and she is forced to lie back down.

'I told you.' The girl carries the bowl to the bed and begins to mop Nancy's face with a flannel she soaks in it. 'You, Nancy Bligh, are a marvel. Dead once not enough for you?' Nancy manages a smile; the girl smiles back, and Nancy closes her eyes against the warmth of it.

'What happened?'

'You tell me Nancy. You washed up three days ago with that grandmother of yours—something I have a great many questions about by the way—out cold, with lungfuls of water and skin that electrified every creature that touched you. Both of you lying on a bed of fried crab and crisped seaweed.'

Coughing, Nancy struggles to rest on her elbows, so her head is raised. The memory of her escape is dim, just a press of narrow passages and water, but she remembers the flash of lightning.

'There was a storm...'

The girl pushes Nancy firmly back down and keeps on mopping her brow. Whatever is in the water is really quite wonderful, and Nancy watches the creatures in the bowl's glaze squirm. She looks back to the girl, to the tattooist, caught in the light of the window. She can barely believe it's real. So close to her daydreams. It's only the dull, electric ache that runs down her spine that tells her it is.

'I didn't think I'd see you again, I don't even know your name.'

The tattooist wrinkles her mouth, blushes a little with poorly concealed pleasure and smooths the sheets, tucking Nancy in.

'Hush now, Nancy. Sleep,' then, leaning close, whispering into Nancy's ear so only she can hear, 'I knew I would see you again Nancy Bligh. My name, my lover, is Colenso.'

Nancy smiles, whispers the name, '*Colenso,*' and beams her way into sleep. As her eyes close and the world slips, she feels the soft press of lips against hers and carries the kiss into her dreams.

WHEN SHE OPENS her eyes again, it is night-time. The moon presses its face to the glass, so large she can make out the bags beneath its eyes and sat sleeping in its light is Colenso. Nancy does not say anything, she just watches. The girl's face is enchanting. Almost literally—Nancy can feel its magic from the bed. Her hair, the colour of horse brasses, falls messily across her face and there are pieces of knotted ribbon tied into it. A braid hangs beside her left ear, plaited in a complex pattern that Nancy has not the faintest idea how to replicate, and finished at the end with a flint arrowhead bound in wire. She looks about Nancy's age, about twenty-two, though Nancy knows that's misleading. She tattooed *Pel*. Who knows how old she is. Her face is lightly freckled, like a flea-bitten mare and studded here and then with dark sunspots. The skin beneath pale. Her lips a just-loosed bow. She is still considering her lips when they open to speak.

'You should know Nancy, going forward, that I am really quite hard to take unawares.' Colenso smiles and opens her eyes; they are grey though shot through with dark flecks, white sparks, and remind Nancy of granite with its quartz and tourmaline. It gives her an enormous sense of comfort.

'I'm sorry, I didn't mean—'

'Hush, girl. I'm playing. I am glad to see you awake. How do you feel?'

Nancy considers the question. She does not feel well. Her chest aches, her throat too, and she is covered in scratches from the limpet lined tunnel. There is a ringing in her ears. She can taste metal.

'Fine,' she lies, 'I'm fine.' A thought rises and Nancy sits up, trying hard not to wince as she does so. 'Why are you here?'

Colenso stands and moves to the bed, sits beside Nancy. The hawthorn perfume is intoxicating this close.

'Do you not want me here?'

Nancy pauses on the cusp of replying and then, there, the smile. Twitching at Colenso's lips. She is not used to this, this playful, daylight thing. It's all she can do not to shrink back into the shadows. The tattooist pushes her gently.

'I do other things than give Keeper's their ink. I'm called to witness their deaths. I found Busker, well, your man downstairs did. I came to certify the body. I counted thirty-six adder bites before I decided there wasn't much point to it. Puffed up and dark as a wineskin.'

'He deserved it.'

Colenso walks to the corner of the room where a framed

painting hangs. It shows the harbour, filled with boats, during a storm.

'I daresay he did but picking a fight with a Keeper and a Goddess in one afternoon isn't wildly clever, my love.'

Nancy is not mollified. She has more than one pressing worry and the removal of Busker Fearnought has not allayed the force of them.

'I need to get back to Mirecoombe. Tell me, Colenso, who is the Mother?'

At this Colenso turns, sharply, crossed arms gripping her stomach tight, her open face suddenly sharp. She is about to speak when there is a knock, and the door opens.

'May I have a word with my granddaughter?' Meliora's blond hair spills in with the rest of her. She has recovered her red taffeta dress—somehow unspoilt by the sea—and has darkened her eyes with kohl, stained her lips scarlet. Gone is the vulnerability of the cave, the joy of the escape. Colenso stiffens at the sight of her and then, to Nancy's astonishment, curtseys and leaves the room with a nod. As the door closes, Meliora turns a face of beatific kindness towards Nancy, who shivers beneath it.

'Nancy. How are you?' Her voice a purr.

'Not so well as you, it seems, Grandmother.' Meliora winces at the word. 'You look... radiant.' Meliora moves to sit on the bed with a rustle of silk. Her fingers are heavy with rings, chains running from some to the bangles on her wrists. Around her neck is a flattened silver torc that looks like a knight's gorget. On it, hammered in relief in the metal are wildflowers. Meliora smiles and bares her teeth.

'Do you like it? I had a few things stashed away under the Proserpine. The current landlord was quite surprised.' Meliora's laugh is a breeze through dense forest. 'We witches are hard to keep down, Nancy. But then, you know that don't you?' Meliora strokes her granddaughter's hair then traces a finger across the scar on her neck. 'The tattooist told me what happened. You are an interesting girl, Nancy. Very interesting. I am so glad you found me. You will be of great help to me when it comes to dealing with Her.' Nancy sits upright and firmly takes Meliora's hand from her neck.

'The Mother?'

'The Mother.' Nancy holds her grandmothers' gaze, green eyes fighting blue, and waits for more. Meliora blinks first. 'Pel told you nothing of her?'

Nancy thinks to Pel's face in the pool, made brackish by his tale. It itches at her.

'A goddess of witches. Said it was a story you used to tell.'

'Just so. He never believed me, of course, no room for a woman in that man's pantheon. I told him the stories, passed down from witch to witch. He said he could not find it in any book so what good was it? The fool. The witches remember her. And there are precious few of us remaining.' She pauses, moves to the window and traces the edge of the water bowl. 'Forgive me, girl, for my turn in the cave. I have seen too many of my, of our, sisters drown. Too many burn. Too many break at the end of a rope.'

Nancy moves to take her grandmother's hand, but Meliora recoils. 'No matter. You see why the story of a goddess who might help us was, is, so tempting. It is said She had power over matter, as Pel and his ilk do, but hers was a wilder magic. She could take a thing, make it another. Transmutation, yes, but also the creation of matter. The catch, because there is always a catch, was that to walk above she had to have a host. A woman, always a woman, it was a great honour. But to hold the power of a god, it was, too much. For most.

Many of the chosen lasted only a few days before they were burnt from the inside out. Replaced.'

'What happened?'

'Nobody knows. She vanished.'

'Yet, she is back. Why?'

'Ah, my child. I fear that is my doing. When Pel trapped me, he thought me sleeping. He was wrong. I have lain awake, these fifty years. Screaming for help. It was to Her that I called. When Pel died, I believe She heard me. From wherever she lay. She heard me and now she is awake I must get to her, I called on her to avenge me on those who had hurt me.' She looks again to Nancy. 'With Pel gone, it will be Mirecoombe She visits that vengeance on. It will be hard, but I believe I can stop Her. Perhaps,' she takes Nancy's hand now. Her skin ice cold. 'Perhaps She could be a force for good? I could, with Her help, find peace on the moor again. Especially, darling girl, with you at my side.' Meliora strokes Nancy's cheek and smiles.

'I thought I had lost my family, Grandmother. I'm glad I have found you. I do not understand this story, but I will help. For you and the moor. Of course I will, I—'

'Your magic. I felt it during our escape.'

'The Murmur.' Nancy names her magic with a smile.

Meliora considers the word.

'That is what you call it? It's a good name, I suppose. I never felt the need to give it one. I am able to do it too, you see.'

Nancy feels her magic flutter inside her chest.

'I felt it, in the cave.'

Meliora's eyes narrow, for a moment.

'Indeed. Your magic, however. I was, curious, to feel it underwater. That is quite a talent.'

Nancy beams at this, the first time her Murmur's been praised.

'I can help you control it, harness it. She can help you master it. When we return to the village, when we free Her.' Meliora smiles and smooths Nancy's hair. Her eyes remind Nancy of her mother's. She has questions there too, but she'll save them for another day. They put her at ease, quieten her mind. 'Indeed, we must return as soon as we can, but if we are to calm her, we must be strong. You must rest. Recover. Before we leave, I would like to show you some things too. That tattooist has plans for you as well.' Nancy blushes. 'Yes girl I see it, the thing between you.' The interrogatory look flashes across Meliora's eyes, but the stifling kindness swells in its wake, and it doesn't leave a trace. There is a scratching at the door, then a thud as heavy paws hit the wood and the door flies open. Patroclus comes bounding with the energy of a puppy, but old bones mean he climbs awkwardly onto the bed. He pushes his face into Nancy's neck before settling down to sleep beside her on the mattress.

'Hello boy,' Nancy ruffles his fur, 'I'm so sorry I didn't even check you were safe.' Patroclus lets out a huff, one of his eyes is swollen shut. 'Oh, boy, you were bitten too?'

Meliora seems less keen on the dog than Nancy and stands, brushing his hairs from her dress. Patroclus watches her, and his hackles rise.

'I'll leave you to rest, Nancy, don't worry. Mirecoombe is fine, and we will go home soon. I can't wait to see how it has changed.' She opens the door and looks back to Nancy, already asleep with the dog. Meliora allows a smile to creep across her face and as she closes the door, softly, she whistles the tune that bears her name.

RAGWORT

* * *

Miles away, where the sea is nothing but a line below the sky, the moorland sleeps under the same moon Nancy does.

Mirecoombe does not sleep.

Lights are on at the church, the sound of sawing and hammering ricocheting across the graveyard. The smithy fires still burn and the clang, clang, clang of iron beats into the night. The Nest is still open, Madge at the bar, her bad arm working hard to sew coloured flags in-between serving drinks and at his little cottage, the Reverend Pine-Coffin sits at his table by lamplight, head in his hands and eyes glued to stacks of books, a body of bones laid out on his bed. At his farm, Locryn Calder stands at the window and oversees his sons as they split moor stone into steps, loading each into a cart, and talks softly to his wife and son who shimmer at his side.

High on the Queen's Rocks, a small figure surveys his work and worries. He has seen things, these last nights. Foals birthed too early that stand on breaking legs before dying in the moonlight, blackthorn growing through the feet of roosting birds, and he has a sneaking suspicion he might have overreached.

Looking up, he whispers softly to the starlight and glow-worms fade at the words.

DOLLY WINTER

ABRAHAM ENJOYS HIS puzzle. He has taken the bones from the coffin and laid them out in a heap on the dining table, on a vesperal cloth taken from the chapel—white linen embroidered with beasts, cattle with long horns and rampant wolves—the bones stand out bright against it. They are weightless, almost. There is nothing to them. He has handled bones before, he knows their weight, their honeycomb of marrow. These bones are like glass and when he holds them to the light, he sees the shadow of his hand shine through. These are like the bones of a bird.

They are nothing compared, however, to the contents of the box.

Inside lies her head. Reagan's head.

With its horns. Twisting like antlers from the skull.

He has seen nothing like it, and the Reverend Pine-Coffin has seen an awful lot. He searches the base of the horns for a join, for the mark of a craftsman, but finds none. Whoever inserted the antlers did so seamlessly. The teeth, too, dentistry surely not up to the task at the time of burial, must have been installed post-mortem. The two front teeth tin, flanked by copper, then gold, then tin again. It is with a breath caught in his throat that Abraham realises all the others are quartz.

'Who are you?' He watches the skull for answers, but the

jaw stays shut. It too is light and for a fleeting second, he wants to place a candle inside so the past can shine out, a magic lantern show of memories to light his walls. He does not. He places the skull on the cloth and once again tries to find the mark of a join between antler and bone. He fails again. There is a skitter from the roof above as a resting crow takes flight, black feathers fall down the chimney and set to burning in the fireplace filling the cottage with the acrid smell of burnt keratin. Abraham wrinkles his nose and rummages through a case for an old lump of perfumed resin. He throws it onto the fire and replaces one pungency with another. Turning back to the contents of the box he sifts through the smaller bones like sand. There are some, curved and sharp, that he finds himself reluctant to look at.

It takes the night and part of the day, but it is done. She is complete. Each bone as close to the other as it dares, a table heavy with hollow bones. Abraham Pine-Coffin does not know what he has built, here. The bones he had discarded as offerings have somehow found a place. He finds he cannot look at it but nor will he turn his back. She holds his gaze regardless, grinning with shining teeth.

'Reagan.' The name a whisper. 'Should you have stayed in your painted box, I wonder?' The Reverend looks heavenward for an answer to tumble out. It has not before, and it does not now, but there's an echo from below. The rattling rasp of air, pushing through metal teeth, and the echo of the Reverend's name.

Confirmation or acceptance, no good way to know. The hairs on the back of the young man's neck stand tall and he shivers. An owl calls from behind cracked glass. He traces his finger along the curve of her collarbone, cups her skull in his palm.

'Not the veneration you had expected, I suspect. Still. I'll rebury you, in a grave. I'll sing hymns above you with the rest.' He again runs a finger along her collarbone, and it sings with the clarity of crystal. It takes him aback, there are tears in his eyes. The candle, burning low, gutters and blackens the plaster with soot and he is taken suddenly with the thought of it. That the brightest light casts the darkest shadow. A shadow so black it lingers once the light's gone out.

'Are you the flame or the soot?' He inspects his finger for a dark mark but finds it lacking. *You are talking to bones, Pine-Coffin.* He chastises himself. *Again.* On the table, the saint stays grinning, aware perhaps, of the joke. Of the absurdity of two long legs that end in the feet of a bird.

CANDLEFLAME

THE WITCHES STAND where he left them.

'Ladies.' Pel keeps his voice steady as the headless bodies turn, waits for the answer from the branches. At his side, Cleaver watches, open mouthed, as the witches walk towards them.

'Hold, ladies. I have a bargain.'

The bodies stop and from the trees, three heads speak as one.

'We bargained with you once already.'

'Once too often.'

'Look at us.'

Pel and Cleaver look up to the three skulls tethered to a branch by their hair.

'I am sorry for that.' It is a mark of his worry that Pel concedes this mistake. 'I am in need of help.'

'We see that, Keeper. For a man with so little heart,' she points to the fabric heart on his chest, 'you seem to have a surplus of them.'

It is only Cleaver's arm on his that stops Pel reacting.

'Careful, Pel. If they can help, and you are serious about helping your daughter, speak cautiously.'

Pel straightens, then, to the amazement of all present, he bows.

'Sisters of the Grove, Derowen, Elowen, Kerdhinen. I humbly ask your help.'

The bauble headed sisters confer in whispers, then the oldest, Derowen, speaks.

'And what is our reward?'

'Your heads, in time, your freedom.'

'You will not interfere?'

'I give you my word, as Lord of Eythin, that I will not impede the reunification of your bodies. But you will remove this curse before I return your heads.'

Derowen spits, a glob of black bile that lands at Pel's feet.

'No deal. Heads first.'

'I see. Well now, here is an idea. My friend here will take charge of you, while we conduct our business. He is an upstanding man. He worshipped at your grove in life, in fact.'

Pel can feel Jacob Cleaver bristle at his side and prays to every God he knows his friend will keep his tongue. The faintest nod from the Reverend and the deal is struck. The sisters confer again and the youngest, Kerdhinen, gives their assent. Pel reaches up, unhooks their hair and bundles them into Cleaver's waiting arms.

'Now then, sisters. The pins.'

The heads close their eyes, and their bodies jerk towards Pel's chest.

In turn the knot knuckled hands of each body pulls a pin from the heart. With each, Pel feels himself returning. Feels the crackle of magic once again. Elowen goes last.

'You will keep your promise?'

Pel's mouth twitches impatiently.

'I will not stop you.'

Satisfied, Elowen's body pulls free the last pin and it flutters to the floor. Pel curls his fingers into a crook backed shape and casts a cloud of coloured light. Smiling, he nods to Cleaver who hands each head to a body. The witches cannot keep quiet, so excited are they to be returned, but as each head is placed on its neck there is a fizz, a howl from the mouth of each witch as their heads roll to the floor.

'What is this, Lord Hunt? A promise was made!' Derowen snarls, her body caught between attack and reaching for her head. Pel's mouth is back in its familiar set. A wry, cold smile.

'I have kept it. I did nothing to stop this. My friend here, well, he is not quite who I said he was. He may have prayed in your grove, it is still there in the valley, your oak, your ash, your elm far wider than you remember them. But if he did it was to his own God. My friend is a good, Christian man. Despite all that he's seen. More than that, a reverend. I fear his touch has sanctified those stumps of yours.'

Unable to listen longer, Cleaver grabs Pel's shoulder and spins him round.

'How dare you mock me! Use my faith against me, fragile as it is.' His voice is quiet, sombre. Disappointed. 'I barely know what I believe, here. You know that. We've talked of it often.'

Pel holds his friend's gaze, the muscles in his face twitching, and hopes Jacob can see the pain in his eyes. The tears he barely holds back. He hardly trusts himself to speak but he forces out the words from jaws clenched to stop to mania pouring out.

'Jacob. Know this. I did not do that lightly, but I needed them to help me. I need you, too. But if I am to help my daughter, I must use every tool I have. Please. I know you understand the lengths to which a father must go, and I have not reached the limit yet. Please. Be at my side. When this is done you may hate me again.'

RAGWORT

The two men stand facing each other, ignoring the howls from the witches, and something passes between them. Reverend Jacob Cleaver. Lord Pelagius Hunt. Death binding both men to a daughter's life. It is Cleaver who breaks the silence.

'Very well, Pel. Let's get to it again.'

LADY'S BEDSTRAW

NANCY WAKES WELL rested to the sound of gulls and the rake of rain against the window. She moves tentatively, but her muscles are looser than the day before and she feels close to being able to rise. She hopes Mirecoombe can wait, for a little at least. It owes her that. She's given everything to it twice over, she's died for it, perhaps she is due a rest. There is a knock.

'Can I come in Nancy?' She smiles at the voice, croaks out assent from her just woken throat and smiles as Baz enters the room.

'Thank you for your hospitality, Baz, again. How are you?'

'Still recovering from the shock of finding you.' Sitting upright, Nancy reaches an arm out, pulls Baz over to sit on the bed.

'It was you?' Baz nods.

'Aye, it's been a week of finding things. The day after you left that dog of yours arrived, torn up, swollen and bleeding.' Patroclus, sleeping in the corner, lifts his head and howls mournfully. 'I went looking for you, saw the daymark was ten feet closer to the cliff edge than usual—that your doing?' Nancy pulls a face of guilty admission. 'I thought as much. Anyway, I found Busker. Lying in the heather. Bloated black and blue with venom. He blended right into the flowers. He's downstairs. I didn't know what to do for the best so I cleaned

RAGWORT

Pat up, best I could, and waited. I didn't sleep for three days, then you and Mel washed up on the beach. Pat set to barking and led me right to you. That girl turned up in the night and took over as your nurse.' Nancy considers Baz's face, his open eyes, riptide skin. She trusts him. She is sorry for what she's put him through. She looks to the corner and is more than surprised to see her coat hanging there. Clean and dry with the glaive leant against it. Catching her looking, Baz smiles.

'I told you, a week of finding. They washed up while you were out cold. I've cleaned them best I could too. I've a tray filled with the things from your pockets. Thought it best to leave them be.'

'That was sensible. I won't stay much longer Baz, just until—' Baz shakes his head.

'As long as you need, Nancy. I've no other guests. Besides, that redhead has paid me in gold. Not that I need it, you understand, I'd look after you all for free. I only mention it to settle your mind on the score of debts. You owe me nothing, Nancy Bligh.' Nancy grips Baz by the forearm tightly, stares into his eyes.

'Not true, Baz. I owe you a great deal. I'd have drowned without your fishbones. Thank you.' Baz places his hand over Nancy's, squeezes.

'I am very pleased to hear it, Nancy. Very pleased indeed. They were helping nobody where they were. I'm sorry our Keeper did this, that I sent you to him. He's always been an irascible bastard, but he's never done something like this. Always helped for his fee.' Baz's hand on hers and the talk of Busker rattles something loose.

'The *Round-Robin*, the ship, Baz, has it come in yet?'

Baz's face is a net-tangle of confusion.

'The ketch? It's due in this afternoon, why? The sea is calm.

There is nothing to worry about Nancy, calm yourself.' Nancy ignores him, flings her bedclothes aside and swings from the bed. She can feel muscles, only just knit back together, tear.

'It can't dock here, Baz, it needs to be stopped!' She is out of the room before he answers, lifting limbs that want to stay put and running barefoot down the landing in her nightdress knocking on doors.

'They're on the dock, Nancy but please, come back!' Baz is shouting at the skirting; Nancy is already gone.

The day is soaked. The waves crash against the outer harbour, sending spray into the sky and Nancy cannot see an end to the sea. The water fades into the downpour as though someone has forgotten to paint in a horizon. Despite this, when Nancy bursts from the door of the Proserpine Hotel, Colenso and Meliora are talking, barefoot in the shallow water of the inner harbour, the ripples from the breakers beating fruitlessly against their ankles. Both have heavy cloaks pulled around them. Nancy is vaguely aware she's only in a nightdress but there's more pressing things in her mind.

'Nancy? Get back to bed, for heaven's sake. It's too wet to be out, especially dressed like that.' Colenso's voice holds her worry lightly. She knows Nancy is almost mended, but she's a role to play so she tuts at her patient. Meliora does not look worried, it is curiosity in those eyes.

'What is it, Nancy?' Out of breath, Nancy gasps out the words.

'There is a boat, the *Round-Robin,* it is due in today, but it will not make harbour. Busker made deals to sink it.' Baz, who has arrived just in time to hear Nancy speak, goes white.

'What? That—are you sure, Nancy?' She nods. 'There are good men on that boat.'

Silence. Just the sound of waves over pebbles and the creak of wooden hulls. Meliora is the first to break it.

'Of course we must help!'

Nancy catches Colenso's face, the surprise on it, but has no time to linger.

'Thank you, grandmother, how though?'

Meliora's lip twitches at the familiar address but softens it into a smile.

'Pel taught you a great deal, I am sure. However. You are my blood, Nancy. You are Our Mother's. Pel's magic is parlour tricks. Useful in a pinch, but you have a world inside you. I will teach you to map it.' Meliora's face catches the reflection of the sun on water and shines at Nancy. 'There is a great deal to know, but for now, since time is pressing, we will start with flight.' Nancy's eyes widen. 'Here, these will do,' Meliora wades to the edge of the harbour where a bush of silver ragwort grows. She pulls two stalks free and hands one to Nancy. 'A little unorthodox, field ragwort is preferable, but close enough.' Meliora takes a bottle from a fold of her cape, tips some of its contents into her hand and rubs it along the flower's stem. She hands the bottle to Nancy and indicates she should do the same. 'I'll teach you how to make it yourself when we have time. The important thing is that you trust me. That you believe that this will work.' Once the bottle has been secreted back into Meliora's cape she places the stem between her legs, so the spray of yellow flowers sticks out like a comet trail behind. Nancy, with no little self-consciousness, does the same.

'Are you ready?'

Nancy is not.

'Yes.'

Meliora kicks off with both feet and rises free of the water, rising like a wind-blown leaf.

'Come on girl, let's see if Her grace really does extend to you.' Nancy swallows hard and leaps.

She does not come down.

Baz looks on with eyes wide and a half-hearted crossing of his chest. Colenso squints, rolls her eyes, and folds her arms. Nancy watches her grandmother's face for a reaction, and the blush of what she takes for pride swells her chest. Meliora nods, and the blush fades.

'A quick study then. How do you feel?'

Nancy is rocking with the breeze, knuckles white with the fear of holding on, but she is laughing.

'Free, Mel. I feel free.' Meliora nods, winks at Colenso who does not return it.

'Good! But enjoy it later. We have a job to do,' she weighs the next word, 'granddaughter.' She drops it like a barbed hook and Nancy gladly grabs hold. 'Follow me close, Nancy. The sea won't be kind to you if you fall.' Turning, Meliora pulls on the stem end of the flowers and hurtles out to sea. Still hovering, Nancy looks to Colenso. She breaks her worried face with a smile, but the frown remains in her eyes. What for, Nancy is not sure. She waits for the swell of words she knows is coming. Colenso turns to face the sea.

'I've known your grandmother for a long time, Nancy.'

'And?'

'She doesn't help sailors. Not for free.'

Nancy bridles, cheeks red, and turns to join the tattooist, watching the surf.

'She's changed.'

Colenso narrows her eyes.

'Mel doesn't change.'

'I—'

'Go, Nancy. I'm happy you found her. Just promise me

you'll stay safe. Don't get carried away. Don't make the mistake of thinking she'll stick by you. Not if things get rough.' Nancy frowns and her ragwort mount dips. Colenso broadens her smile, 'Ignore me, Nancy. Go. Help the ship. You'll be fine.' Nancy waits for another sea-change, for some explanation, but none comes. Colenso's smile seen now for what it is. Tape across a crack. The edges peeling. Nancy feels the confusion like a hand pressed to her chest. The joy she had felt at seeing Colenso complicated now. Their next meeting not as simple as she longs for it to be. Nancy matches Colenso's fragile smile then turns. Mimics the movement her grandmother had made. Tugs the stems of the wildflowers and in a roar of wind and salt spray the harbour is gone, and she is miles out to sea, hurtling through the storm. Meliora is waiting.

'There, Nancy, look.' The witch extends her arm and points at a speck on the horizon. The sea ripples like a tablecloth being laid. It continues billowing, the waves growing as the grey sky turns black. The ship rises and falls with the cloth.

'It seems you were correct. Come now, we need to move fast.'

'Will we warn the ship?'

Meliora scoffs.

'No. Nancy. Two witches are unlikely to be a welcome sight. They'd shoot us down rather than listen to us and drown in pig-headed righteousness.' Meliora falls silent and Nancy, hair whipping in the wind, can feel the salt on the breeze.

'Mel?' Her grandmother shakes loose from her daydream.

'No, Nancy we won't go to the ship. We will work our magic here. Another gift, though this one is mine alone.' Meliora reaches into her cloak and withdraws a length of rope. It has three knots tied into it. 'This is not the way this is meant to be used. Things are going to get worse before they get better.' Nancy watches as her grandmother unties the first knot. The wind, that had been gusting and pulling the sea into waves like thickened cream begins to howl. Below them, an outcrop of rock that sits just below the waterline is screaming as the wind passes through seaworn holes in its surface. Limpets are torn from the stone and creatures scuttle from unsafe harbour.

'Mel!' Nancy screams to be heard, 'What's happening?'

'Magic, Nancy. The kind we used to bring. Before that father of yours tidied it all away!' As Nancy squints against the saltwater in the air she can see her grandmother laughing. Her cape billowing out behind her, inverting so the feathers form great wings that ripple in the wind. From within the pewter badges clink and rattle. Beneath her cloak, Meliora is wearing her red dress. She is a giant bird. A swallow, perhaps.

'Mel!' If there is a plan, Nancy needs it to work faster. The *Round-Robin* is larger on the horizon now, Nancy can make out figures on its deck. Its prow turning into the roiling sea. The men on board scurrying about to right the vessel. Mel's eyes still wild.

'We're here to save them, Mel!'

Pulled from her own spell, Meliora Ray unties the second knot. All motion is taken from the world. The wind stops. Nancy clutches at the ragwort and waits to fall, but both her and her grandmother stay put. The sea below them a millpond now, the sails of the distant Ketch hang slack. Nancy watches all impatiently. Meliora has closed her eyes.

'Hold, girl. The Empress needs to make her move.'

In the water below them shadows form. At first, shoals of fish that swarm and pulse in the sea. Their flanks catching in the light. Then a pod of dolphins, backs breaking the surface and ploughing the still water into furrows.

'Here she comes, Nancy, you watch.' Meliora's eyes remain shut, and Nancy watches the water. The whale, when it arrives, is spectacularly large. She knows so little of marine life, has no idea what species of leviathan tracks them from the deep, but the shadow is ten meters long. It takes Nancy longer than she cares to admit before she recognises the aquatic display for what it is.

A royal procession.

The assorted creatures coil around in a long, snaking, train. Their passage creates a whorl, a whirlpool that deepens as it spins and soon a flat outcrop of green rock is revealed. Crabs scuttle across, cleaning the stone of weed and grime until the snakestone table shines as though polished. In the circling walls of water, a new shadow appears, long and sinewed, the Empress of Salt has arrived. She snakes out of the water, Nancy gasping as the slick body of the eel gives way to the woman within. The Goddess stands looking up, huge eyes burning into Nancy's, her glass teeth bared.

'Witches!' The word is hissed. 'You should both be drowned, yet you come back to fight. *Unprovoked.* I will have my tithe.'

'The man you made your deals with is gone, your majesty,' Nancy surprises herself with her answer. She had not planned to speak. 'While this place has no Keeper, *I* protect it. Go. Make deals with whoever comes next.'

The Queen holds Nancy's gaze then raises her arms. As she brings them down the creatures whose swimming keeps the vortex open dart off into the ocean and the sea crashes in to fill the void. The sea is silent once again and Nancy turns, beaming to her grandmother.

'Is it done? Have we won?'

'No, girl. Not yet. I think it is time you showed me what you can do.'

Nancy looks puzzled, but she has little time to consider the request as from the surface of the sea comes a furious bubbling. A head breaks the surface, a bucca, their shark eyes gleaming. Then another. Tens of the creatures clamber up and over each other, making a long and swaying tower of their bodies, their hands reaching and grasping for the ragwort keeping the women aloft.

'Now, Nancy! What did the old cyclops show you?'

Nancy takes her right hand from the flowers, wobbles a little on her mount, and focuses her breath. Thinks through the tattoos that cover her body. A twist of eyebright fills her mind, and from her fingers, sparks fall as though an invisible hammer beat molten metal in her palm. As the embers meet the skin of the buccas the tower shakes and rattles, the creature at the top of the stack tumbling down into the sea. As the sparks peter out, Nancy reaches again for her inked bouquets. Ragged robin. This time the effect is invisible. Each bucca feels their body grow heavy, feels their bones weigh heavy on their frame. The tower falls, each body hitting the water like a cannonball. When the last bucca is sunk Nancy turns victorious to her grandmother.

'Now finish it.' Meliora's eyes are open now. Fixed on Nancy's.

'What?'

'They will come back. Tear the stone down around them. Trap them within. If you want that ship saved, this needs an ending.'

Nancy hangs on her ragwort, searches her grandmother's face for reprieve, but there is none to be found.

'I'm serious, Nancy. Those were fine tricks, but I would have you be better. Show me what you can do. They cannot die, not really, you know that. Besides, they came willingly to the fight. A soldier knows how a battle ends.'

Nancy wavers, but her grandmother does not, so she turns her attention back to the sea. It *is* there, the Murmur. After its unexpected strength during the escape, it has been itching at her.

'Mel, I don't want to hurt them. They aren't making trouble, look, they're swimming away.' It's true, under the water the shadows of bucca, fleeing. Only the ones burnt by the first spell remain. Nancy looks to her grandmother. Her face is fixed in a glare. She looks so much like Pel. The same unyielding schoolteacher. Nancy summons the Murmur. Reaches for it in the rocks beneath the waves, and the sea starts to rattle as tears fill her eyes. Pressed again to kill by a teacher too cruel to be kind. Just as she's ready to let it fly, a hand on her arm.

'Stop.' Meliora's face softens. The storm clouds clear from her eyes. 'Let them go. If that is what you want, I understand.'

'Really?'

'Of course. I'll not make you do anything you do not wish to do. Ever. Let them go.'

'Pel—'

'Is dead. I'm not here to take his place. You found me, girl. You. I've woken from a world without witches to one with you in it. A Keeper witch, no less. We work together, or we don't work at all. Trust me.'

Nancy lets her birds go, lets them scatter into the waves. She surprises herself. This control something new, helped by the presence of her grandmother, perhaps.

'You aren't angry?'

'It's not what I would have done, but then, doing what I think best had me sleeping for half a century.'

The faintest twist of a smile pricks the corners of Mel's mouth. Nancy turns back to the sea, in time to see the merry-folk disappear into the surf.

'Mel—' Nancy looks back, but her grandmother is gone. Nancy can see her halfway to the shoreline. Turning to the ketch, still becalmed out at sea, Nancy sits alone astride her ragwort stems. As she looks around, she sees it, stuffed into the yellow star flowers of her broom: the rope, the one Meliora has been slowly untying. There is one knot left.

'Well Nance,' with no wind the words fall to the water below, 'why not?' She unties the final knot in the rope and a wind immediately picks up. *No.* Nancy feels a familiar panic rise, the sense she has failed. The wind, though, levels out. Remains a constant breeze, and out to sea the *Round-Robin's* sails fill and the small boat heads steadily towards harbour. It passes below her and incredulous faces stare at the girl on her flowers.

'Don't go to Bosmorven!' Nancy yells as they pass, and a terrified skipper raises a hand in acknowledgement. The ship turns, heads to a harbour further down. Once she is sure it is safe, that the sea holds no more terrors today, Nancy turns for home. As she arrives back at Bosmorven, Colenso is on the quay waiting. Nancy lands unsteadily beside her, leaping from the ragwort as she leaps from the saddle. The stem feels brittle, burnt to dust in her hand, and washes away on the wind. Her face beaming, Nancy turns to the tattooist.

Colenso stands ashen faced.

'Did you see me?'

'I saw.'

'We saved the ship!'

'You did, indeed. That grandmother of yours left you to it, I see.'

Nancy's shoulders sag as she searches Colenso's face for the excitement she'd expected. Nancy reaches for her, places a hand on each of her cheeks but the tattooist pulls away.

'I don't understand, what's wrong? We saved them.'

'Did anything happen out there? Anything strange?'

Nancy gives a stilted account, her voice clipped as she recounts the rescue. She mumbles past the part where she tried to use her Murmur, races to Mel's change of heart, but she sees Colenso's lips purse.

'What?'

'She was testing you. Wanted to see if you could do it. Could use your magic out there.'

'I stopped.'

Colenso turns to face her.

'And if she hadn't let you? If she'd pushed?'

'It's irrelevant.'

Colenso takes Nancy's hands in hers and kisses her gently on the lips. The salt stinging her wind-pricked skin.

'You're nothing like your grandmother, Nancy. Don't let that change.'

Colenso turns, walks away, and for the first time Nancy feels the thorns beneath the blossom.

From the roof of the Proserpine, Meliora Ray regards her granddaughter with cut-glass precision. As she does so, a ripple runs out, shakes the tiles on the roofs. It is all that the old witch can muster. Even this leaves her panting.

'Too much in you by far girl. We'll have to even you out.'

CODLINS AND CREAM

Abraham Pine-Coffin is beating the bounds.

An old custom, usually done in a crowd, that today he's enacting alone. The walking of the parish boundary. The checking of the edges. Making sure nothing gets in, or out. Though, as is often the case with him, he has a more fluid purpose.

His head hurts. Since he drank the ichor in the chapel, he's felt hungover. As though the world is just a little too bright. Even on this overcast day he squints against the glare of it.

Since his laying out of the bones, the sheen has worn off his newfound sight. Reality, this new form of it, is setting in. He has always prided himself on his optimistic scepticism. A belief in belief, even if he could not muster faith himself. He had joined the church for its books but had envied his colleagues' devotion. Their following of the unseen. Deciding Christianity did not have all the answers, or at least that he had more questions than it could manage, he travelled in search of more of both. Became a missionary. Taking posting after posting in far off lands, technically in service of an ever-expanding God, in search of proof. He was always recalled quickly. Other missionaries noted that rather than reading the good book to the unconverted he spent quite a lot of time reading theirs. Listening to their stories, their gods and monsters.

Finding space in ceremonies he'd been tasked with ending. South America, the East Indies, the sub-continent. Not once had he felt what his hosts had felt, but he always hoped. And now?

Proof.

And with it, the crushing burden of belief.

For if the stories of this place are real, if, as he now sees, piskies and spriggans do roam the moor, if then he is to take it every tale is true, that Black Annis eats children in her Leicestershire cave, that kelpies and selkies roam the waterways of the north, if yokai roam Japan, then what of God? If he sits in his heaven with his son at his side and a devil below what then?

What must he think of his servant forsaking him.

He dwells as he walks his parish, the broom of gorse he has collected sweeping his doubt into the cracked and peaty earth.

He passes the base of the Queen's Rocks and watches spriggans stacking stones. He waves and they eye him with suspicion. He bats away the hand of a piskie that reaches for his pocket. Halfway up the lower slopes, he sees three men, knelt by a standing stone.

'Good day.'

Pine-Coffin lays his gorse broom down and raises a hand. The men stiffen, the look in their eyes the same as the spriggans'. The central man nods in reply.

'Reverend.'

No explanation is offered, so Abraham requests it himself with a smile and a little shake of his head.

'We're praying, Reverend. This is the grave of Hocken Darrow.'

'You pray *to* him? This is a new one on me, I have to say. Even here.'

'No, Reverend. To Them. To keep him safe. To Her. To watch over Them.'

As the Reverend parses this, a spriggan climbs unsteadily to the top of Hocken's grave marker. The creature catches the Reverend's eye and beckons him with a tip of its head. Draws the priest towards him on unsteady legs, the men shuffling back on their knees to make space. The spriggan leans forwards, hungrily, his voice the breaking of stone.

'Priest. You hear us, too?'

Pine-Coffin nods.

'She has given you this gift, so She must wish us to see you as you see us.'

The Reverend chooses words with care.

'She must. Tell me, what is this, what are these men doing?'

'Their friend, he is with us below in the Undermoor. They ask for him to be safe.'

'Might he not be?'

The spriggan shrugs.

'Maybe, maybe not. If they want to give me apples, a nice meat pie then I will see to it he is. Whether he would have been or not.'

'You have quite the confusing patter, little one. Does She know you take their offerings?'

The spriggan rocks back on the stone and crows.

'She told them to do it, did She not? Her little chattering thing at least. He that told us of Her, them of Her, you of Her. She is coming, priest. I'll not be left behind.'

'You have always known of Her, though, have you not?'

The spriggan shrinks into himself, looks up from squinting eyes.

'Well. Not as such. She has been sleeping. He said She has been sleeping. We know Her now. She comes to us in dreams. She is coming.'

'I see.'

Abraham Pine-Coffin backs away and the spriggan grabs his

offerings with relief, scampering down the back of the stone and away. The men, rising slowly, look to the Reverend.

'It is appreciated, your understanding.'

Pine-Coffin shifts uncomfortably on his newfound faith.

'Quite. Good day to you, sirs.'

He takes up his broom again and heads on his way. He has met others, on this walk. Talked to a group making a cross on the moor from fragments of quartz. To three women bathing in a peat black pool.

A field further on, he finds Madge Gould kneeling in the reed grass.

'I did not expect to find you out amongst the dissidents, Miss Gould.'

'And you haven't, Reverend. I'm here on my own business.'

She stands, revealing a basket in her arms filled with rushes.

'I'll make a rushlight or two for yourself, if you like?'

'I'd like that a great deal, Miss Gould. I have to say it is a relief, I feared I may have lost you too.'

Madge smiles, reaches out a hand and accepts Abrahams help in hoisting her up.

'Don't worry, Reverend. I've got it in hand. I'll keep them in line.'

'Thank you.'

'Besides, I know all about Her.'

Pine-Coffin's heart sinks.

'You do?'

'Oh yes. She is coming, but I know too She will save us. Nancy's bringing Mel, Mel will help us talk to the Mother. We can all sit in that chapel of yours, Reverend, and sing to Her.'

Abraham sinks to the floor, dazed. *Is this how it is? Is it really just a matter of belief?*

'I cannot tell you how it gladdens me to think I can be of

help to that girl of mine. And to you, of course. I'm quite giddy at the thought of the festival. I've opened the Nest to all who wish to use it. Banners and costumes, I'll provide the drink and food. And Locryn is making such wonderful progress on the well.'

He stands at this. Scrabbling to his feet and scratching his hands on the gorse.

'The what?'

THE VALLEY RINGS with the sound of scraping stone. The Reverend hears it two hills over and by the time he reaches it he is exhausted. There they stand, down by the valley floor. Three Calders hard at work, two bowed heads and the oldest shouting out the pace. Cusk stood apart. Arms folded with his back against the moor.

'Come lads! Dig!' Locryn has the wide-eyed stare of the evangelist, his muddy mind washed clean with fresh sprung water. Water he knows is here. Under the earth. His two sons swing their mattocks against the thatch of reed grass. The flattened blades scraping across the granite trapped beneath. They have already found stone. Huge carved pieces lying under the grass, long covered. A puzzle of granite. They lifted each piece and laid them out carefully, a problem for later. They have not stopped digging since.

The Reverend clatters down to the worksite and the digging stops. Locryn Calder stares at the Reverend as though he were a cow, wandered in and getting in the way.

'Locryn, I'm told you've found a well, how, may I ask?'

The old man's eyes snap into focus, and though the Reverend's faith may be new, he recognises the stare of a true believer.

'Sainted Reagan. Her messenger showed us the way.'

'Did he now.'

Locryn nods, fervently, then calls to his sons to start digging again. It is on the third swing of Luk's axe that they hear water. Locryn runs from his overlook, past the Reverend, down to the tangle of grass. On hands and knees, he tears roots from earth and stone. A long stone slab emerges. The water sounding from below. Ripping the vegetation back another three slabs are revealed. A cover. A well cap. Even Cusk allows his eyes to widen. Pine-Coffin moves to stand by the men. Keen, at least, to be present at the opening. There are marks carved into the stones, erased by time and the feet of fieldmice, but recognisable as crosses. Digging their hands around the edges, the Calders find each is set with a recessed hand hold. The stones take a heave to shift, a long set grout of mud and grass seed fusing them shut, but they shake loose in the end. They are lifted then lain to rest on the excavated greenery. There is a wonder of a space beneath. The sound of a river rises from the pit. Steps, alternating granite and quartz veined slate, leading down to the dark water. Abraham Pine-Coffin steps cautiously into the well. Behind him, Locryn Calder calls for candles and places them in the sconces carved for that purpose, lighting the waiting cavern. Broad enough for twelve men to stand, the walls made of undulating rock and earth propped up with wood that time has scared stiff, the floor a careful fretwork of flagstones. The river running through it. Copper, seeping from the stone, has dyed everything it touches. The stone is blue, the wood is blue, the river inky black.

'Well done. She will be pleased. Sing your praises to your twin faced Saint, sing your praises to the Mother.'

Knot's voice is a trick of the light. Even with the sight allowing him to spot the imp, perched in an alcove at the back, Pine-Coffin struggles to focus. The voice seems to come from all directions at once. Locryn falls to his knees and sets to praying, his sons and Cusk descending tentatively behind.

The Reverend, pulling Locryn to his feet, holds the old man steady as he speaks to him.

'Mr Calder, your sons and you have done fine work, fine! Might I ask you to leave? I'd have words with this herald.'

Locryn's brow furrows but he sees the sense.

'Of course, you must, you must. A man of God and a gentleman besides. Of course, sir. You must speak to the angel. Come, boys, come.' He leads his little flock away and the Priest and voice alone.

'*Hello Mine Reverend.*'

Knot's voice wavers, now they are alone.

'Hello again. You left quickly, at our last meeting.'

'*I work the magic of the Mother. She sends me where I need to go, She knows what must be done She...*'

'She meant for this?' He points to his eyes. 'Shall I go up into the light and paint these good people a picture, creature, shall I tell them what you look like?'

Knot chokes on his fragrant lies.

'Ah. As I suspected. This was a surprise?'

Knot's face churns in fury. The Reverend can see him bite the inside of his cheeks.

'*It matters not. She is coming. The villagers have listened. They will make Her welcome when She arrives.*'

'Who? Come, beast. You call yourself angel, herald, what is Her name? I have heard at least two. I heard a new one today. Meliora.'

'*Who told... no. You'll not trick me again.*'

'Has this story changed in the telling, imp? Do not forget I see you.'

Abraham is piecing something together but he's not as confident as he sounds.

'I hear you, too. Repetition, repetition. Mother, Mother, Mother. Tell me, have you played the game that young folk play? Stood before a mirror?'

'*I don't play games.*'

'I think you do. I think you've lost, you've at least not won. Names, imp. I've read enough to know they hold power. You spoke two, to me. In the chapel. Who have you called, who is it, that is coming?'

'*The Mother. Reagan.*'

'Meliora Ray.'

Knot hisses, a screech of rage as he beats the stone.

'*Don't say her name!*'

'Why? You hold no sway over me, imp, though I thank you for this.' He touches beneath each eye. 'I came here following a story, you know? Not this one, but a story, nonetheless. I *know* how stories work.'

'*It doesn't matter. She's coming. The feast will be had, the well will be christened. She'll see to you.*'

'And Nancy? What of your Keeper?'

Knot's laugh is hollow and twisted like a lightning struck tree.

'*The girl's sat safe on her grandmother's lap.*'

'Grandmothers aren't always safe from their granddaughters. Nancy strikes me as the sort that might own a riding coat. She certainly seems the sort to see through a person's lies.'

'*Maybe, Mine Reverend. Maybe. Are you willing to bet on how long that might take? A lot can change in this valley in the flick of a horse's tail. Have you found out, yet, how the last priest died?*'

There's a gust, and the candle wicks snuff out. Leaving Abraham once again completely in the dark.

TANSY

Nancy wakes alone. A night of thinking has led to no answers and the morning is grey. A light rain mists the window, even the gulls are quiet.

'Morning Pat.' The dog is still sleeping and gives no response but a cooper, the coastal brownie, slips from a shadow and walks cautiously up to Nancy, lying in bed. She strokes the creature's cheek. It is shaggier than its inland counterpart, though its nose still lies flat on its face. Its eyes are different too. Not the red glow of coal, the cooper's eyes glow blue green, like phosphorescence on waves.

'Hello, love.' The cooper, mute as the brownies at home, nestles into Nancy's hand. 'A pleasure to meet you.'

'Be careful with her.' She didn't even hear the door open. Colenso is stood, wrapped in a bright satin dressing gown printed with chinoiserie flowers. The hem is lined with tassels in a deep purple trim. Colenso walks to the bed, sits beside Nancy.

'The cooper?'

'No.'

'She's my grandmother, Colenso. I don't know what you think you know but—'

'I know your grandmother Nancy. Have known her longer than Pel did. Knew her as a girl, as a woman. As a witch.'

Nancy turns her face away, but Colenso pulls it back, gently, looks her in the eyes.

'You never called; I'd hoped you would.'

'I didn't know how.'

'Sure you did. The wee ones like nothing more than a message to send.'

Nancy pulls her face free from Colenso's hand with a shake.

'I wanted to get things straight. Get settled. Show you who I could be. Take the moor in hand.'

Colenso laughs and punches Nancy softly on the shoulder.

'Gods, girl, if that was your yardstick thank the stars Busker died, or we might never have seen each other again. No matter. I'm here now.'

From downstairs comes the noise of Meliora's laughter, the sound of drinks being poured, and Nancy leans towards the door.

'Don't fall for her, Nancy.'

Nancy's look is reproachful.

'She's family, Colenso. Family I never knew I had. Is it such a bad thing to want to get to know her?' Colenso leans in, kisses her, her skin a copse of hawthorn blossom. Nancy closes her eyes against the scent of it and feels a little of her sadness fade away. Replaced with a ripple of something new—she can feel the sting of the tattooing needles beneath it.

'You have more that love you than her, Nancy. More who care.'

Nancy nestles in, but Colenso sits up, pushing her away. Her face serious.

'Come now, up. Let's go for a walk.' Colenso jumps from the bed and throws Nancy a blue smock dress with white stitching picking out the crosses on the front. Nancy is not sure what this is, this thing between them, but she grabs at this light in the darkness.

'Wait! I need to put on my boots.'

'No, Nancy, you don't!' Colenso's voice echoes down the hall and Nancy hears the back door of the hotel open and shut. Patroclus still sleeping, she follows Colenso outside onto the cobbles. They are slick under her bare feet and though the rain is still mizzling, there is a warmth to the air. Colenso is walking determinedly away, up and around the looping coast path, the opposite direction to the way Nancy went before. Away from Mornader cove and Fearnought's shack. Nancy runs to catch up, feels the change on her feet from wet stone to mud as she climbs up the cliffside. Colenso waits for her at the top.

'Thanks.' Nancy smiles but Colenso's face is set in stone.

'Come on, we've a way to go.' Colenso takes Nancy's hand, the first time she has done so, and Nancy squeezes tentatively. She is more relieved than she'd expected when Colenso squeezes back, but her heartbeat still quickens, she feels a fight coming. The familiar gut wrench she always felt when she'd disappointed Pel. Waiting for the shouting to start. Colenso does not shout. Colenso seems comfortable with silence. Seems to be revelling in it, in fact. It is somehow worse.

Nancy takes a breath.

'I like your gown.' She immediately regrets speaking at all but to her surprise she is still talking. 'The tassels are nice, the colour too. It's a lovely fabric.' She swallows hard and looks up at the sky, but it has turned a grey and impassive back to her, shaking out the rain, and all she gets is wet. 'I don't understand.'

'I know it must be hard to hear but you can't trust her.'

'She's all I have.'

'Grow up, Nancy.' Those thorns are back. 'I know you think you need her—you don't. Meliora is complicated. Don't lose yourself following her, she'll not thank you for it.'

'Has she not earned some kindness? Tell me that.'

'I'll tell you this.' Colenso stares at Nancy. Fixes her with storm cloud eyes. 'Your Grandmother has a cruel streak as deep as the Undermoor. I sat with her, once, watched her listen to a man petition for her aid. He hadn't enough food for his wife and child. He hadn't enough gold to pay her, so she took what he had and said she'd deal with it. He couldn't see the shadow that tore from her eaves. Couldn't see it latch to his neck. But I could. He lasted a week, then dropped dead. More than enough food for them now, she said.'

Nancy listens in silence. Bites her lip.

'She has suffered, Col, seen terrible things.'

'She's not alone in that.'

Nancy does not want this debate. Twists and pulls against the barbs as Colenso starts to descend a natural staircase that winds from the top of the cliffs. Each ragged edged step carpeted with hard and calcified shells.

'No. True. I do not condone it, but you must see how it affected her? Those she lost. And then, she returns home to her friend, to Pel, and he betrayed her. He thought he had killed her, he wanted to kill her. He told me as much.'

Colenso looks up at this. Furrows her brow as she descends the last stone step to a wide plateau of weed paved slate.

'He did? That's not the way I remember it. Whatever his plan, did it cross your mind at all that he was right to do it?' Colenso drops Nancy's hands and strides to the edge of a tide pool. Long and deep and crystal clear even in the mizzle, its sides a mop of pink and green weeds, anemones, and urchins. The sea breaking over the edge and running in ripples across it.

'Meliora did terrible things. Wonderful things too but—you know she calls herself Queen of the Witches? She gave herself that title. She knew full well she was one of the last. The years she spent watching her sisters die up country changed her. Took away something the world won't give back. Everything she was, good and bad, has calcified on that seabed, Nancy.'

Nancy walks to the water's edge and sits, lets her bare feet drift in the saltwater, seaweed fronds. Colenso remains standing.

'I've read the stories, Col. I know who she is. I owe her help. As her granddaughter and as a Keeper.'

'You owe her nothing!'

They lapse into silence, the black headed gulls enjoying the production, wheeling overhead.

'Truly, Nance. You do not.'

The fine rain has soaked them both and Nancy is very aware that the cotton smock is clinging to her skin. Colenso's gown clings to her, too. Nancy mumbles, as she shoots Colenso a look.

'Where did you get it, the gown?'

'We don't need to fill the silence, Nancy.' Nancy listens for it, but the smile has yet to return to Colenso's voice. It softens a little though. 'I made it. I'll make you one too.'

The wind picks up, the fine rain a salted balm and they sit in a more comfortable silence. Nancy reaches out and picks at Colenso's hand with her fingertips until the tattooist relents, lifts her hand and lays it down over Nancy's.

'I know I only met you the once, Nance, but I got the measure of you, I think. Do you still wear the hairpin?'

Nancy nods. Her two-tined blackthorn clasp one of her most prized possessions.

'I liked you, Nancy, did from the moment you opened that

door. Most folk bridle when they see me, or look about for whoever I'm with, but you? I could see it. You took me as you found me and let me in. You've a strength, Nancy Bligh. A rare and beautiful strength. Don't let anybody make you forget it. Gods, you didn't even flinch when I passed the needles over your hip.'

Colenso laughs, and Nancy warms in the rain. For a second, lets herself see that empty space beside her filled. She wants to tell Colenso about the life she's seen. Caught in the morning light. Trapped between the sunbeams. But she doesn't. Can't. She hasn't got the words.

'I like you too.'

'Your grandmother is not as powerful as she likes people to think, Nancy. I suspect you are quite capable of standing up to her, if it should come to it. Which it will.' Colenso shivers, shakes her head crossly and peels her gown from her skin, standing naked in the rain. Nancy can feel her cheeks prickle even in the chill.

'I don't want to fight, Nancy, that isn't why I stayed. Come on, if you're going to keep antagonising sea goddesses, it's high time you learnt to swim.' Colenso steps carefully into the pool, walking down a natural stair formed by the rock. Once she is in, she swims to the centre and turns, treading water. Waiting. Nancy lifts the smock over her head cautiously. She had no time to dress properly before they left, and she has only a shift on beneath. It is soaked through; Nancy's tattoos show through the wet fabric. *To hell with it.* Nancy discards the shift with the dress and walks to the water's edge. She puts a foot in and shivers, but she's made up her mind and keeps walking. The weeds that line the steps are soft underfoot, and as she reaches the last ledge the waterline laps at the base of her ribcage. She finds, without the adrenaline of her escape from the Brine, that the idea of taking that last step into the water, of having to swim, is terrifying. Colenso sculls effortlessly over and takes her hands.

'Here, trust me.'

Nancy does as she's told, steps off into deep water and gasps as she sinks. Colenso catches her just before her head dips below the water and Nancy holds on tight as the other girl treads water.

'Lie back.'

Nancy lets her legs float upwards, feels Colenso's hand on the small of her back, feels her other arm cradle her neck. The fine rain patters on her face, her shoulders, the rise of her chest above the waterline.

'You're my best work, Nancy.' She drifts her fingers across the flowers on Nancy's stomach, counts each petal.

'What are you, Colenso?'

The tattooist, still holding Nancy afloat, moves to her side.

'Does it matter?'

Nancy moves her arms and gently eddies the water around her.

'It does if this is to continue, whatever this is. Yes. My world is constant questions. One after another. Never any answers. I want you to be the one thing in my life that I *know*.'

Colenso pulls Nancy to the side of the pool, sits with her in the shallows. Anemones pull bright blue tentacles into soft crimson bodies. She swings the Keeper around, pushes her against the rock. Nancy can feel the shells of sea life press against her skin. The nettle sting of the anemones. It is a hard kiss, which moves from her lips to her neck, the notch beneath her ear. Colenso whispers.

'You would *know* me? Would you?' Nancy turns her head to kiss her, but the tattooist bites her ear, lightly, and pushes away, diving under the water and reappearing on the far side of the pool.

'Swim to me.' Nancy stays where she is. 'Come here.' Nancy's whole body is tingling, only part of it from the stinging fronds at the edge of the pool and she pushes off the rock with force. It feels like flying, it feels *better* than flying. She turns in the water, then loses confidence and sinks. Colenso pulls her up and into another embrace, both women laughing, giggling in the pool. This close Nancy can count her freckles, her skin a sky of them. She presses her face to Colenso's neck and breathes in the smell of her. The almond blossom scent, but the salt washed sting of her sweat too. Colenso lifts her, wraps her legs around her waist, leans back and takes in her prize.

'I remember drawing this.' She traces the curve of Nancy's breasts, the twist of briony that's drawn there. She leans in and kisses the ink, her hand moving along the line of Nancy's hip, catching on the notch of it and tracing it down. Lifting her head, she holds Nancy's gaze as her fingers follow the wildflowers that snake around her thigh.

'Is this—' Nancy nods and her breath catches as Colenso's hand finds its place. A heat spreads across Nancy's chest, and with one hand she pulls the small of Colenso's back to her, hard enough to leave a bruise. With her other she draws Colenso's face to hers, kisses her until she cannot breathe, then presses her cheek to Colenso's neck, her hand entwined in her auburn hair. Colenso moves, leans against the sea wall next to Nancy who is still calming her breath. When she feels able to speak, Nancy turns.

'That was,' Nancy cannot find the words so settles for a kiss, 'but I can't help feeling you avoided the question. Tell me who you are, Col.' The tattooist smiles at this nickname, brushes sweat and sea slicked hair from Nancy's face and takes her hand.

'Very well. I suppose I'm what you might call a fairy. In a broad sense. Other people might once have called me a nymph, or dryad. Depending on who was telling the story.' Nancy stifles a gasp; she has read the books in Latin and Greek Pel had strewn around the boat. The almond scent makes sense now, too.

'You're a hawthorn.' Colenso cocks her head, eyes sparkling, and smiles.

'Yes, Nancy, that is, a hawthorn is my home. I act as a sort of neutral agent, in this mess of creatures we're lost in. I'm from somewhere similar to Cornwall, but far enough away I've no horse in the race,' Colenso's eyes darken briefly, 'at least I hadn't. What this is—Nancy it's new to me too. I don't want you to think I make a habit of this.' Nancy turns to look into Colenso's storm cloud eyes. Watches the lightning flash. 'It's not supposed to happen. I am not supposed to have favourites.'

'I'm your favourite?' A smile flickers across Nancy's lips, she bites it back. Colenso leans in to kiss her but moves at the last minute and tips Nancy into the pool; she rises spluttering, indignant. She doesn't even notice she's treading water. Colenso laughs and dives forwards to join her, wraps her legs around Nancy's, pulls close. Kisses her again, Nancy tastes the salt on Colenso's lips and reciprocates, kissing the dryad along her neck, revelling in the mineral tang of it.

'I told you. I've thought of you a great deal, Nancy.' Nancy doesn't answer, simply draws Colenso close, out to the middle of the pool. She runs her hand across Colenso's back, down to the dip of her spine. Over her bottom. She thinks again of eyebright, but fleetingly, a small jolt of electrical energy running out from her fingertips. The dryad gasps and the water around them flashes with a brief phosphorescence.

'Oh, you think you can swim now?'

Nancy giggles, nods, and traces her fingers around the circumference of Colenso's thigh.

'I do, Col,' Nancy whispers into Colenso's ear, 'besides, no time for this when I return to face the Mother.'

Colenso pulls back, looks into Nancy's eyes and the water feels cold.

'Why do you think this Mother is returning, Nancy? Did Mel tell you she was?' Nancy pulls her knees to her chest and sits on a rock shelf at the edge of the pool. Stares sullenly into the water.

'No. The moor is full of it. Below, too. Things have happened. There is a creature, Knot, who....'

'The Mother is a story, Nancy. Someone is playing with you.' Colenso's voice is soft, the lilt of her accent as amiable as always but Nancy senses something sharp within it.

'That's what Pel said. You agree?'

'I know the story.'

'Can you tell it to me?'

Colenso pushes back, treads water in the centre of the pool as the rain falls.

'Fine, let me tell it the way it was told to me. Here, get settled.' Colenso sculls back and pulls Nancy to her, lets her nestle in the crook of her shoulder.

'Once, long ago, before I was born, so who knows the truth of it, there was a Goddess. She could touch a thing and make it another, could twist the sea into sand, the sand into sea. Could make an acorn blossom into a flock of sheep, could make a man a monster. She made other gods, made whole worlds. Made people. She had her favourites, gods always do, and for her it was usually a woman—not always, mind, but someone often at the edge of things who might need a little extra magic—and she would teach them a little of what she knew. Gave them a gift, or two. In time these people became known as Witches. The Mother, trusting her daughters, stepped back into the shadows, and was never heard of again, though it was said she'd return if she was needed. Choose a witch to carry her soul. Fight for what was needed.'

'Mel thinks...' Colenso stops, sighs, turns to face Nancy.

'Does she. Please, Nancy. Listen. The Mother is a story, I am literally telling it to you. Full of the same beats and twists as a hundred others. Your grandmother, Nancy, was very fond of it, and Meliora Ray is no fool. She used to tell the girls she found waiting for the gallows. A story to give them hope. She knows full well what power a story has for those that choose to tell it.'

'She says we come from her, our power, my Murmur, she can do it too...'

'Have you seen Mel use it? Has she shown you?'

'In the Brine, she shook the cave walls.'

'With intent? With purpose? Or just with rage?' Nancy says nothing, waits for more.

'Your grandmother can do a lot of things, Nancy. Terrible, wonderful things, but I am beginning to think you can do more. She won't like that, not our Mel. She's a storyteller, and they tend not to take kindly to those that tell a better one. I do not know what her goal is, whether she believes in the Mother or not, but I promise you it will not be good.'

'She's my grandmother.'

'She's complicated.'

Nancy swallows, then pulls herself up and out of the water, taking up her clothes and dressing as she walks away.

'Nancy! Please come back. I'm trying to keep you safe! I know you think you have found your family, and I'll not stop you getting to know her, just… do not give all of your heart to her. She will not appreciate you for it. Trust me, please!'

Nancy does not look back as she walks, speaks through gritted teeth.

'Pel believes it! He told me. Came right up from the Undermoor to tell me. Meliora's story's true and to find her, that's what he said. Go and get her. Bring your grandmother home.'

Over her shoulder the dryad hauls herself from the water. Stands dripping on the stone.

'What? Nancy he can't do that. He can't leave the Undermoor and if he did, he wouldn't say that. Nancy! You're being lied to. You have to trust me. Trust what we've shared today. I told you, I do not give myself easily, Nancy. I have given myself to you. I believe in you. I trust you.' Nancy can feel Colenso's eyes on the back of her neck. Can hear the waver in her voice. 'Very well, then. But Nancy, if you will not trust me. Please, trust yourself.'

If Nancy hears, she gives no sign, grateful that her tears are lost in the falling evening rain.

WATER BETONY

'What I don't understand is how the saint figures in this. It should not have been enough, even with Mel spreading her word. It takes more than a week to wake the dead.'

Cleaver, sat on the shore of an underground pool, coughs.

'I fear I am to blame.'

Pel dismisses his friend with a wave of his hand.

'No, Jacob, mentioning her name for whatever little sermon you'd concocted wouldn't do it. It would need to have true intent behind it.'

Cleaver stands. His fine, sharp features a duelling blade and he's in with a riposte.

'Good God, you are an insufferable prig. I at least am trying to learn from my mistakes! I should have known Lord Pelagius Hunt was too arrogant to grow. Perfect at birth, is that it Pel? How dare you, how dare you again belittle my faith. I allowed it with those hags, but I'll not sit here and listen to it again. Little sermon? Did you once hear me speak? Did you listen to a single service?'

Pel, taken aback by the blindsiding—despite the regularity with which they happen—stands mute. Shakes his head.

'No. You were so focused on your way, weren't you? Even before I transgressed, before I allowed my grief to warp my devotion you picked at it. I used to remember our fireside talks fondly, do you know that? I missed sitting with you as you told me how things were, as you saw it. Told me tales. When we found ourselves here, together, I was pleased! Fool that I am. Thought we might walk our way back there. I see it now. I was another feckless dog, sitting at your feet. Lapping up your wisdom like so much spilt milk. It is sour, Pelagius. Rank. I gave, the church gave, Mirecoombe something you never did. Hope, Pel. Where was the light in your darkness? I tried, when I spoke, to show the light that could be reached.'

'How did that end for you?'

'Enough!' Cleaver roars, and a hill over, his son lifts his head from his exile. 'I am sorry for that. More than you care to acknowledge. I took what was good and right and broke it. I need you to listen, Pel. To what I am trying to say. My words mattered. What was spoken in that church mattered as you yourself are saying! Reagan's name *was* spoken. Over and over. In sermons, which carry a weight of their own, but in private also. When Callum returned, he brought the books he'd stolen from you. You know that. I believed God had sent him back to me, so I adapted the rites. Wove prayer into the rituals.'

Pel narrows his eye, and Cleaver can see him choosing his words like a book from a shelf.

'I see. You are right, my friend. It was unfair to dismiss you. Perhaps, had I known your feeling, I would have made more of an effort to listen.' Cleaver lowers his guard just enough for Pel to strike. 'Then, you might not have made such a mess of things! What did you do?'

'I asked my God for help, and those who might assist Him! Not having a friend to call on closer by. I invoked the saint of my church. By name.'

'Idiot.'

'Good God, man, enough! We are both fools, Pel. I at least have sense to admit it.'

The two spirits sit by the pool in silence, their words floating like petals on the surface of the water, and they watch as they drift away. It is Pel who breaks the silence.

'That may have been enough. To wake the ghost of Reagan, to catch her attention at least. This nonsense with the Mother could have sealed it. You may have done us a favour, Jacob.'

Cleaver, burnt once already, does not respond. Though he does incline his head, a fraction of an inch.

'I doubt Mel intended her Mother to be conflated with Reagan. I doubt, indeed, she intended anything to happen at all. She's arrogant enough to think she could win the valley with words and violence. If you, and she, have woken something else? Well. The more pieces on the board, the easier it will be to win.'

Cleaver leans back, lets the moonlight bathe his face.

'You are right. Perhaps, had you spoken more, I would not have made the mistakes I made with my son. I am trying to make amends for that, now. I have paid, though, Pel. With my life. Do not think I need you to add to my suffering. I have plenty enough as it is.'

Pel, leaning forwards, content with the moonlight reflected back from the water, closes his eyes in the heat of it.

'Oh, my friend, I am sorry. What purgatory I have exiled us to. I have no wish to make it hell. We will talk, when this is over. I promise. Until then, there is work to be done. And no rest for dead old men.'

'More pieces to place on the board?'

'Indeed. And I know just the pawn.'

DOG MERCURY

The headache wakes her before the sunlight does. Cracking right through to her dreams, and shattering them into a thousand pieces, her skull a mess of broken glass. Colenso had not returned to the Inn, and Nancy had drunk herself blind with the regulars in the bar. She opens her eyes and is more grateful than she has ever been to find it's raining. The window is open and drops of water hitting the table are misting the air, cooling her face. A single gull is peering in, but a glare stops it from squawking. She mutters newly learnt curses and twists in bed, her arm meeting an empty space that ought to smell like hawthorn.

Colenso is gone.

Of course. It was too good to last. You're on your own again, girl.

Patroclus rises, nose already sniffing. There's breakfast on the air. Nancy smells it too and it drags her from bed to the kitchen where Barzillai Melchior stands frying hog's pudding, potatoes and eggs.

'Morning Nancy. Here, this'll set you up.' He plates up a dish of hash and sets it on the table with a coffee. 'I can pour you some hair of the dog if you need it.' Nancy blanches.

'No, Baz, thanks. I don't remember much of last night, I'm afraid. You look very spry.'

'Not my first lock in, Nancy. You had the eyes of a girl drinking to forget. Far be it from me to get in the way, but I see we're down a guest. She'll be back, mark my words. Don't fret.' Nancy smiles, flops into her seat, and the jar to her head blinds her with pain. It is not helped by the arrival of her grandmother in a sweep of black velvet and feathers.

'Come on, Nancy. It's well past time to leave.' Baz turns back to the stove without offering the old witch breakfast.

'Fine, grandmother. I'll get my bags.' Nancy wolfs down a breakfast she'd intended to savour, stands with a sigh and heads upstairs to dress. She had packed light, this trip already three times longer than it was meant to be, so there is little to bring down. She finds the cart and horse ready and waiting for their departure. Gulls circling above. Her eyes scan the ridgeline where a hawthorn grows. Stood tall where the others are bent.

'Can we not fly?' The idea of a lurching cart is not sitting well.

'No. I've no salve left. Besides, we have things to talk about. You,' she points at Baz, 'lift that lazy tangle of a dog onto the cart.' Baz complies, Patroclus nuzzling his neck as he's lifted.

Nancy walks to the landlord and wraps him up in a hug.

'Thank you, Baz. For everything. If she comes back, tell her I'm sorry.'

'I will, Nancy. I will.'

'Enough, Nancy. Their sort is fickle, don't lose your head to a tree, it's unbecoming.'

Meliora, saying goodbye to no one, is already sat in the driving seat. Nancy is getting used to her moods, changing like shade under a tree as the day goes on, and she shrugs it off, climbing up beside her grandmother. Patroclus is once again asleep in the back. Foxglove, carefully kept by Baz for his stay, ambles up and out of the valley. Nancy can still hear the gulls even once they enter the forest, the steep slope of waterlogged houses long behind. The coast does not feel like the moor, which seeps into the surrounding fields and copse feeling for escape. The forest makes a clean break with the sea, soft worlds with sharp edges. They ride in silence, Meliora's hands gripping tightly to the reins.

'Looking forward to going home?' Nancy regrets speaking as soon as she does so, she can see her grandmother's knuckles whiten as she grips tighter. The cart has rolled twenty feet before she answers.

'Do the flag iris still flower in the marsh?'

'They do.'

The conversation falls under the cartwheels and the birds fill the silence with song.

'Here, take the reins girl.' Nancy takes the leather straps from Meliora. 'We have time enough on this journey, time enough for a lesson or two. Your *spells*,' Nancy can hear the scorn, 'the tricks Pel taught you, are fine in a pinch but you've more at your disposal. Why is getting you to use it like pulling teeth?'

'I can't stop it, after a certain point. It's like pouring a jug of water into a glass, if I focus, let it out drip by drip, it is fine, but after a certain point it tips, and I flood the table.' Meliora lifts her gaze to the clouds.

'Enough extended metaphors Nancy, I don't want to hear him in you. Listen. You ask about the Mother, what she is? She is everything. She is all. She is gone. Still, she left us something. Our little bit of power.' Meliora lifts her hand and to her left a tree shakes and lets go of its leaves six months too early. She lays her hands back in her lap to hide the fact they're shaking. 'We control this gift. It does not control us. He should have had you practicing since you could walk. You are underdeveloped.' Nancy turns to protest, mouth full of fallen tors and torn up graveyards. Mel stops her. 'Any child can make a mess, Nancy. It takes no skill at all to knock things down. To shake a field but leave the cows standing? *That* takes skill.' Nancy bites back a retort. She has tried to tell her grandmother of her triumphs, the trauma of the past year, but she has no interest. So she listens, waits for the lesson.

'Pull over here.' It is a tombstone walled field, like the one Nancy saw on the journey down. Meliora jumps down to the grass and calls her over. 'You call it your Murmur, yes?' Nancy nods. 'Fine. It comes down to visualisation. For myself, I see it as blood in water. I see it bloom, see it dissipate. That is the image I hold on to. I can make it short, and sharp. The drop just entered the water.' Meliora raises her hand, and a tombstone hedge stone is pulled into the earth before shattering. 'Or it is a soft, voluminous thing. The drop expanded, a cloud of blood.' A hand again and this time the row of stones rise as though passing over a wave. 'You must use your birds, Nancy. Hold them in mind, you control them. Their shape. How many are in the flock.' Nancy pauses, unsure quite what to do next but a click of impatience from Meliora spurs her on. Taking a few steps forwards she pictures a murmuration. Pictures the poppy tattoo she sees as the leash of the Murmur.

'Steady, now, Nancy. Think what it is you want to achieve. Knock down a stone.'

Nancy tries to tell her birds to form an arrow, but there are too many, the Murmur hits the wall like a cannonball. The bank of earth and stone shatters into a cloud of brown and black, the field shakes.

'Again.'

'Mel, I—'

'Again.'

This time she pictures a single starling. The Murmur seems unsure, unused to restriction and tempts her to picture more. The bird is not enough. She adds another. Another. More birds until she has a cloud, though far smaller than before. She forms them into a point and this time they break the stone. The ground beneath it rising quickly enough to split the granite. But the fissure left is three feet wide and deeper than she is happy with. She sees rabbits, their warrens suddenly laid bare, tumbling into the darkness.

'Again.'

Nancy concentrates. Holds both her flower tattoo and her cloud of birds and forms the latter into a dart. A helix of birds she allows to flow smoothly around their axis. This time, she does not waver. She drives them through the earth at a stone slab, and as they approach, she narrows them. The earth vibrates in a sliver of soil and the stone splits in two under the quaking. Neatly, no soil disturbed. Carried away she lets the Murmur blossom, the birds flock, and then, as though whispered from within the earth, a voice.

Yes, daughter.

The voice fills Nancy with a sudden clarity, a sudden awareness of the Murmur. She pictures her birds again. Sees them as needles with trailing threads and with them she sews the fissure from her last attempt shut. Pulls the earth together.

Something new.

She feels more than the earth. She feels the roots of the grass and in her newfound visualisations she lets her birds take them in their beaks and wind them around their broken other half, a graft of grass. The ground rattles into quiet and the moor is unbroken.

It is the most focused the Murmur has ever been, the most powerful she has ever felt, and Nancy turns round beaming. Her grandmother is stony faced and there is the whisper of a frown on her brow. She restores her mask, but not quickly enough.

'Good, Nancy. A quick study. Back in the cart, it's time we got on.'

Nancy still stands beaming, waiting for praise, for something. Patroclus nudges into her leg and wags his tail. She'll take it. Once they are back in the cart and the wheels are rolling again, Nancy turns to her grandmother.

'You didn't tell me we could control the grass? What else can we do?'

Meliora sits silent for what seems like minutes before she answers.

'We can't, Nancy. I have never seen that done before.'

Nancy, a girl who has grown up in a world with unending, magical surprises, takes it in stride.

'Perhaps I'll teach you!'

Meliora does not answer.

RAGBAG

Gow, LAST OF the maneaters, leans on his staff as he watches his herd. They have fattened in this passing year. Skeletal cattle putting flesh on their bones. Gow smiles as they pass. The light catching on their golden horns and hooves. As they move, he sees a flicker, stood in the centre of their mass. A flicker with a single eye.

'Keeper. I warned you about visiting me.'

Pel scowls up at the giant, Cleaver in his shadow.

'This talk of the Mother. Do you hold with it?'

Gow leans on his staff and thinks.

'A story for the little ones. Though they believe it. It clearly scares you. Her name echoes from every hill.'

'Yet she doesn't talk to you. You'll not run to her when the time comes?'

In all his experiments with Hilla, Gow is the only creature who does not dream. It had been Cleaver who'd realised why.

His cattle need tending to.

Gow never sleeps.

The giant leans down and blocks out the moon.

'I'd kill to feel the sun on my shoulders.'

'For the second it took to turn to stone?'

'Don't lecture me on my own kind, Keeper. I know a giant's lot. Yes, though, even for as short a time as that.'

As Pel talks, Cleaver circles a cow. There is skin on their bones again.

'Fine beasts, giant. How many do you have?'

'A thousand head.'

'You must be proud of them.'

They have worked on this routine, the Keeper and the priest. One more comfortable with this stage than the other. Cleaver plays his part well, laying a hand on the glistening flank of a cow as she passes.

'I'm surprised to hear people talk so poorly of you. Above, the farmer is prized. For all he does for the community.'

Gow rumbles in the sky.

'Who talks poorly of me?'

'I misspoke.'

'Who?' The thunderclap. Cleaver, still not ready to accept he cannot truly be harmed down here, blanches a little at the reverberation. Clears his throat.

'There is a little creature, called Knot. He was laughing with the spriggans. A poor show, I felt. You deserve it as much as they do.'

'Deserve what?'

Pel steps in, takes the stage in the only role he's happy in. The starring one.

'Why, to be present at the Mother's rebirth, Gow! Don't tell me you've not been told?'

Gow straightens, leans on his staff and eyes the two men suspiciously.

'Of course I have.'

Pel's eye glitters.

'Apologies. I had just not heard your name amongst those who will be there to greet her.'

'I do not sleep, Keeper. I see it all. Hear it all.'

Cleaver, emboldened by Pel's confidence, pipes up.

'Yet not Her, it seems.'

Gow's staff comes down hard by the Reverend, tipping him to the floor in a shower of mud.

'She knows I am faithful, does not need to whisper in my ear.'

Pel, helping his friend from the floor, hopes the giant cannot see his grin from such a distance.

'You will run to her then, should she decide to call you? My friend here is right. The little ones laugh, say you're not fit to meet a Queen. That she has no need for cowherds.'

Pel is feeling this as he goes. The laying of plans, the hedging of bets. If there's one thing he's learnt in a long and tricky life it's that when your back's against the wall there's worse you can do than cause chaos.

'What? Who says that? My cattle are the jewels of the Undermoor. I'll drive them over those little wretches' bones when the time comes. I'll race to her side. And you, Keeper, will fall in the mud with the rest of them. You hear me, my Mother!'

Gow turns to face the puddle moon and when he looks back, his cattle walk alone again.

YELLOW FLAG

As they approach the edge of the woods, its palisade of trees and dark hollows, Nancy's nose wrinkles. A sour, sweet scent that fills her nose and drives the smell of rain and flowers from it. It is all consuming, so strong that it wakes Patroclus from his sleep, and he is on his feet in the wagon barking. Wagging his tail. Pointing towards the base of a tree not far from the track. Beneath the white blossom and new green leaves of a blackthorn tree the sheep bloats. Wool stretched tight over near-bursting skin. Eyes an inch from their sockets and staring at Nancy and her grandmother. Nancy's heart beats faster but she does not flinch. She looks steadily at the creature emerging from behind the sheep. A man. Drenched in blood from top to toe and shining in the sun and it is good, in a way, that he is doused as he is. Because beneath the blood there is nothing. A space where the man should be, his shape only visible where it's red. At least this way she sees him. Nancy holds her breath.

'Be ready, Nancy.' Meliora steps down from the wagon with the grace of a queen and walks to face the phantom.

'I know you, bloodstain.'

'Aye, you do, witch.'

Patroclus stops barking but has not lost interest in the sheep. He considers the possibility it could be his while

Nancy dismounts. Walks to the corpse. The smell, though pungent and rank, has something in it that is almost alluring. As heady in its way as the honeysuckle.

'It's been in the heat too long, cut itself raw on a sunbeam.' The ghost's words startle her from her reverie.

'Don't talk to her, Peter. Talk to me.' Mel drags the ghost's attentions back to her with sheer force of will and Nancy, though impressed, would like a say in the matter.

'It's alright, grandmother, I am a Keeper after all. I can handle myself.' Mel bridles but keeps quiet as Nancy turns to the bloody ghost. 'Peter, was it? Who are you?'

'Me? The man's voice has a light, singing quality that reminds Nancy of a puppet show she saw once, as a child. 'I'm Peter, Keeper. Peter Joule. Don't mind me.'

'It's a little hard not to, Peter. Dressed as you are. What happened to the sheep?'

The man smiles. At least, Nancy thinks so, the blood on his face lifts into some semblance of a grin.

'Not me, Keeper. Honest. This one died alone. Too cold, too hot. Matters not.'

In Nancy's experience it never bodes well when the Underfolk start rhyming, she hopes it was an accident.

'And the blood?' She gestures vaguely towards Peter. 'Where is this from?'

'Not her, Keeper. She's a bubble not yet popped. Peter's blood is eternal. A little reminder.'

'To whom?'

'Me. Keeper. To me. I'll take my leave if that's…' Peter's eyes move nervously to Mel, but Nancy is not done with her question.

'I'm not leaving a ghost covered in blood alone without knowing more, Peter. Answer me, what's your business here?'

The creature climbs onto the sheep, which quivers underneath his weight and sits, smearing blood on her fleece. The melody in his voice is dulled now.

'I am here, Keeper, because I was sent here. By one of you. I'll not say I'm proud of the man I was, but this? Seems a little much. I'm to stay here until I'm called back. Eating the dead.' Nancy chokes down a retch as the creature bends to the carcass of the sheep and begins to tear it open. 'I don't kill folk, Keeper. I'm like them up there,' he gestures to a skyful of buzzard bashing crows. 'Carrion. That's my treat. One hundred years. Then one for luck.'

'For what?' Nancy stares at the creature. Waits for an answer. It is undeniable now, Peter is grinning.

'I was a curate. Tended the souls in the churchyard in the woods.' A gesture to the trees behind him. Mel laughs.

'You lying wretch, Peter! Do you forget I knew you?' Peter's face contorts into a clot.

'Fine! I took a little more than I had a right to. Lived a little longer than I ought to. But they were dead! I wasn't tasked with their souls and their bodies were fair game. A bath of blood under moonlight keeps the grey hairs away. Did you know that, Keeper? It's true. It is. Frowned upon by those that've not tried it, but a tonic still. Anyway. A member of your order stopped it. Drained my bath. Didn't last much longer. Him above washed his hands of me. Them below didn't want me, sent me back. Nothing to work with, you see. A mannequin of blood and dust. Nothing holding me together, so I fell apart. Not spirit, not ghost. It was the Keeper who blooded me. To keep an eye on me he said. The curse was his too. You lot can be mighty preachy for folk without religion.'

Mel stands with her arms folded.

'Peter was and is a monster, Nancy. He was foul when he was a man, and he is foul in death. Do not listen to him. We should be on our way.'

Nancy considers.

'What was the name of the Keeper, Peter?'

'Saundry Pencast. Old bastard.' Peter looks down at his hands, wrist deep in the sheep.

Nancy has read the histories. Saundry Pencast has been dead a very long time. The keeper before the keeper before Pel. Let down by a Keeper again, but at least it wasn't her father this time.

'I think you might have served your time, Peter.'

The creature looks up from his lap.

'What?' The spaces where his eyes should be look hopeful. He leans forwards, starts at the possibility of freedom.

'Think this through, Nancy.' Meliora's frown is felt, not seen, but it presses, nonetheless. It takes an effort for Nancy to dislodge it.

'I think you're due for release. I give you my word I will ensure it. Mel, you say you knew him. Do you know how to end this?' Meliora Ray is very quiet as she answers. Her mouth barely moves.

'I do. Take us to your church, Peter.'

Peter climbs into the back of the wagon, his hands and feet leaving bloodstains where they meet the wood, and he sits opposite a hackle risen Patroclus. The dog's teeth bared and a steady growl coiling from his mouth. In the front, Meliora leans in close.

'Do you have experience with ghosts?' Nancy shakes her head. 'Ghosts are a tricky lot, Pel should have taught you that, they're his inheritance after all.' She looks across at Nancy who looks at her hands. They keep rolling until a cartwheel hits a stone and the tower looms out from the green. 'You should not have promised to help him. The living don't owe the dead anything, Nancy.'

'I promised him help. I will help.'

Meliora draws the cart to a halt under the shade of a whitebeam and looks back to Peter, stretched out at the very back of the cart, his blood slowly drying in the dappled forest sun. Satisfied he is not listening, she continues.

'Once, when I was young, I found a wolf caught in a trap. It was near these woods. Wire wedged in the bone. It was a pitiful thing. All that power reduced to nothing more than a howling pup. What would you do, for that wolf, granddaughter?'

'Free it.' Nancy does not have to think.

'And when it had regained its strength, when it came for a sheep, for a child?'

They are interrupted by the mossy ivied tower sticking up from the woodland floor like the stump of the world tree. Peter shrieks in delight at the sight of it.

Meliora jumps from the cart, Nancy pulled in her wake. The old witch walks with determination towards the ruined tower, to the echoing voices cascading from the belfry, keeping up the bats.

Peter

      Peter

  Peter

An endless tolling of the dead. Nancy had forgotten the name the bells rang.

'I've been here before.'

'Stay behind me, girl. You, ghost. At my side.' The passengers disembark and enter the dark door of the church. Nancy's eyes adjust slowly to the empty tower, the cracked font still lying like a broken nutshell on the floor, the bowl stained with blood. It's clear to Nancy now that's what it is, she is surprised she couldn't smell it before. The whole tower smells of metal, she can taste it in the air.

'Come on, dog.' Patroclus seems unconcerned at his un-naming and follows happily along as Meliora scours the towers corners. 'It's funny. You'd not think the smell of lichen and moss, damp stone and leaf mould would be something you miss.' Meliora kneels and scrapes windblown leaves from the floor. 'I remember coming here when I was younger.' There are words emerging from the soil scattered floor. Carved in arcing, scrolling gothic font, their impressions shallowed out over the years from the feet of mice and foxes. Readable still, in parts at least.

Here lies the Rev. Peter Moule
May he remain undisturbed.

Beneath the text a skeleton, grinning. Caught mid dance. The ledgestone cracked down the centre, a little slice of black peering out.

'Look, Peter, here you are.'

Peter's gaiety has soured a little, he darts looks at Nancy as he hops from foot to foot.

'Keeper, you promised your help, not that of the witch.'

'I trust her, Peter. You will help him, will you not Mel?'

Sitting back on her legs, Meliora smiles, then loses interest in the slab. She is focused on Patroclus, pawing interestedly at a pile of leaves. Nancy hisses at him.

'Back, Pat. What have you got there?' She kneels besides the whining dog, his tail wagging in excitement. She is brushing the leaves aside when she gasps, sucks on a bleeding finger. In the leaf mould is a coiled hedgehog, sleeping. 'Poor thing. You should be awake.' She can feel, in her hand, the ball of prickles breathing in short rhythmic breaths. She pulls it away as Patroclus snaps at it. 'No! Leave it, Pat.' Nancy places the hedgehog back under its leaves and shoos the dog further back. She does not miss Peter's anguished look at the creature, nor his relief when it is returned to the leaves. Mel, finished with her investigation, stands. Faces Peter who still implores Nancy from the doorway.

'Time to set things right. You gave me your word, Keeper. Keep it.'

'I trust my grandmother, Peter. She'll set things right. You've earnt your rest.'

'Rest? That one-eyed narcissist has raised my granddaughter a fool.' The shadows move and Mel's scorn is back. 'Have you missed the clues, Nancy?' She pauses to raise a single finger to Peter, inside the church now. 'Do not take one step closer to it, Peter. Not a bloody step.' Peter pauses, looks over to its tomb. 'He's not asking for death, Nancy. He's asking for a change of terms. Let me.' Meliora raises her hand and when she brings it down there is the sound of grinding stone. The crack in the ledgestone closes like two sides of a wound pressed together. Peter screams, the literal sound of blood curdling and Nancy jumps at the sound of fists beating on the underside of the stone.

'Fetch the hedgehog that dog found, Nancy.' It takes a moment for the words to sink in, then, in a daze, Nancy picks up the sleeping creature from its leaves. 'Give it to me, your knife as well.' Nancy does as she is told, withdrawing the blade from her riding crop and handing it over with the animal.

'Do not do something you will regret, witch.'

'Please, Peter. Did you really think anyone intended that deal to be honoured? A lazy, old Keeper made you someone else's problem. Unfortunate, I agree, that I am here. That I am old enough to remember you. What you did. Already dead, my foot.' Meliora turns the hedgehog over in her hand, revealing a neatly sewn line of catgut stiches. Using the curved blade, she nicks each one and the hedgehog opens like the case of a chestnut. Inside is a human heart, beating. Nancy lifts her hand, begins sifting her mind for a spell that will help, but she feels powerless. Even the Murmur feels futile here. She doesn't know whose side to take, or what to do.

'Hold. Witch. I've had three centuries of hunting. Three centuries of scavenging. The deal is done. A deal made with her line, not yours. Not my fault they couldn't kill me then, a deal is a deal!' The blood that coats the phantom's skin bubbles in the half light. Nancy lays a hand on her grandmother's arm.

'He's right, Mel. I promised him. Help me release him. If he finds a way to hurt again, we'll stop him.' Meliora looks Nancy up and down then pulls the heart from its case, reverses it, and presses the heart inside. Closing the skin around it tight, spines pointed in. An organic iron maiden. The bloody form of Peter does not change but whatever was hammering on the tomb top is screaming, the stone thudding with each bruised fist. The tower shakes and the voices, ceaselessly ringing out the Reverend's name, have stopped. Nancy feels them more than she sees them. The shadows from the tower reaching down, hands wrapping around Peter's bloody echo, hoisting him into the belfry like a marionette whose strings have tangled. Meliora drops the hedgehog bound heart to the floor.

'I killed that wolf, Nancy. I drove an iron spike into its skull and left it pinned at the boundary line for all wolves that came after. There is no virtue in a monster saved. None at all. I let you have your way out to sea, but a bleeding heart's a liability. All it does is leave a trail.'

Nancy takes a final look up into the dark, then follows her grandmother and dog back to the waiting cart. They ride in silence, just the creak of the wheels as they move over stone. She feels the press of Colenso's thorns. *Mel doesn't change.*

'Here, take the reins girl.' Nancy takes the leather straps from Meliora. 'Time we were home.'

KNOT LIFTS HIS head. He feels the sea-change on the air and giggles as he swings between the houses of Mirecoombe. Belly full of little creatures, a store of matter he's ready to disgorge. Whistling the song he's been whistling since the one-eyed wizard died. *Her* song. He has sung it to old and young, man and woman. It has burrowed into the ears of all. Preparing the ground. He's laid the traps. Spread the word. Taken only the slightest of liberties. He tastes the air again and turns a somersault as he swings from the Mare's Nest to the barn to the blacksmith. Landing on the roof he climbs to the brass weathervane, hammered into the shape of a kestrel at rest. Knot lifts his head, flits into the shape of the wind-turned bird and leaps into flight. Turning in widening gyres above Mirecoombe he finally, after all these years, gives words to the tune, gives the village the power of names…

Her house on the tor doesn't stand anymore,
Her memory's faded and grey.
But what's broken can mend, you can patch what was rent,
She's a marvel is Old Mel Ray
She's here to give help, to teach one-eye's whelp,
For your saint and the Mother she prays.
It's their story she'll tell, down the old stony well
Sit and listen to Old Mel Ray.

MOTHER-OF-MILLIONS

MIRECOOMBE FLUTTERS IN the wind. Every house and tree garlanded with long cotton flags, the village the back of a tapestry, a tangle of coloured threads, the image trapped beneath them. Nancy has never seen it so in motion. So alive. People run back and forth, arms laden with boxes and fabric, breaking into smiles as they see the carriage arrive, rushing inside shouting. As they dismount from the carriage, Nancy is knocked into by a man with the head of a weasel, a rough sewn mask made of deer hide. It seems the tide of people are washing back and forth between two points: the chapel and the pub. It is to the Nest that Nancy turns. She leads the horse to the stable, knows that Madge will see it returned, and she leaves the cart in the yard. Nancy walks to the backdoor and knocks. For the first time in her life, it does not open. Nancy turns and sees Meliora has dismounted, turned her cloak inside out so that her feathers are on the outside, and is stood wating.

'I believe we should use the front door, Nancy.'

Nancy looks at her grandmother. Her eyes are bright and there is a smile on her face that Nancy cannot, truly, say she is comfortable with. Something wriggles in Nancy's stomach, but she nods, leads her grandmother to the front of the Nest and pushes open the door.

Every table has been turned into a workbench. Piles of costumes, threaded needles sticking from masks, midway through stitching eyes onto snarling faces. In the aisles bent willow and hazel frames wait to be covered, wooden masks wait to be painted into the abstract of a horse. At the bar, Madge Gould stands smiling, her eyes bright and wide, and gathered before her, all eyes on the door, is the rest of Mirecoombe. There is a hush, then Madge starts to sing Mel's song, then Delen, then Billy, then every soul of the village. Even Locryn Calder and his sons sing, ringing out deep and tenor, though Nancy sees that Yestin's heart does not seem to be in it, and Cusk's lips are sealed. The verses go on, elaborate rhymes of Reagan and the Mother, of Mel and her life.

When the song is done, Meliora steps past Nancy and raises her arms. It takes Nancy a moment to realise she's waiting for her to remove the cloak. Nancy lifts it, lays it over a chair. Chokes on a feather.

'Mirecoombe! How happy I am to see you. It has been many years since I was banished. My... is that? It cannot be! Young Maddy Gould! My girl, you are shining, look at you.' Madge beams. Madge who warned Nancy of bringing back the witch. Madge who looked so sorry at her leaving, and at the back of Nancy's mind, Colenso's warnings about Mel start picking at the stitches of this newly patched family. Letting in the breeze through the heavy down quilt.

'And, no, it cannot be! Locryn? Stand tall, man, let me see you.' Locryn Calder pushes himself up from the bar and sets his jaw.

'Mel, you're a sight! Here, these are my boys...' He pushes Luk and Yestin into the light, and they squirm like embarrassed children. Nancy is waiting for Mel to pinch their cheeks.

"Ansome boys Locky! You must be proud. I am sorry to hear of Jan, though.'

Nancy bridles at Mel's sudden joviality. It sits on her face like an ill painted mask. And she hadn't told her about Jan.

'I hope nothing like that will ever happen again.'

'Thank you, Mel. We're so glad you're back. To set things straight. We've been divided too long, to hear that you come to rejoin our fractured saint! To heal this valley's faith, why it's a tonic. It is.'

Meliora's white skin pales.

'Your saint? I thought I heard a new name in the song. I have been called back to intercede on your behalf with the Mother.'

'It has been explained, Mel, don't worry. The angel said you would be coy. We have learned about Reagan, her two faces. One of our Father's, one of the Mother's. We understand. She watches us, doubly.' He crosses his chest and looks skyward as Mel's eyes scour the darkness. Coming to rest in a dusty corner and burning holes into the shadows.

'I see. Yes. That's it. I have come to… heal this division. Deal with this split saint.'

Nancy pulls at her grandmother's sleeve.

'Mel, what are they talking about? What is this about the saint? Who's been speaking to them?'

Meliora yanks free from Nancy's grasp with annoyance. Leans in close and whispers loud enough to hurt.

'Silence, girl. They are simple dolts, they have been confused, that is all. The Mother's message taken as something holy. Is that so hard to believe?'

'But who—'

'Silence.'

Nancy steps back, tells herself that Mel has earnt this

homecoming. That emotions were sure to run high. Stands, listens, as her grandmother continues.

'Tell me, while your Keeper has been fetching me, how has she made herself known?'

'Her creature sent Pel to me, told me to look to you.' Madge Gould.

'Her angel told me to look to the chapel, that you would yoke the moor to the church.' Locryn Calder.

'Her messenger told me you would calm her, heal the damage done.' Delen Rowe.

Even without her cloak of feathers, Nancy can see that Meliora is ruffled. So is Nancy. She brushes it from her, but her disquiet is like static and won't lie flat, this talk of a messenger, of a voice of a friend. It itches in the same way Pel's face did in his pool. If Meliora feels it too, she shows no sign. Her speech unbroken.

'My. What a busy, clever little friend I have. I'll be sure to thank them, just as soon as we're alone. We must hurry, however, who knows how long we have.' She pauses, but when nothing happens, she turns back to Madge. 'This,' she waves towards the costumes, 'is for her?'

'Her feast day! Yes. We will welcome Reagan back. With you at our head!'

'I see. It might be best if we do not continue to use her saintly name. The Mother is primal, angry, she may lash out.' Meliora waits, like an actor whose partner's forgotten their lines. 'She will, I'm sure, make herself known to us.' Her voice rises at the end of the sentence and the Nest falls still.

In the silence, all can hear it.

A pulsing, fluttering beat. Starlings. Out of season. Nancy feels her grandmother relax. Meliora bites down on the smile that creeps from her mouth. Chews it into a frown.

'It is Her! Come, all of you, gather with me.' As the crowd moves to Meliora, Nancy walks to the window. There is a rush, a rattling of glass, as the murmuration passes. She has not seen this many birds before. Her own murmuration, her magic, pulls at her, asks her to let it join the birds outside, but she holds it tight as the flock passes again.

'Grandmother, it's a message! For me. It's the Mother, it must be. Welcoming us home.'

'Hush, granddaughter. She is beyond you. Come here.' Nancy pulls against it, but the draw of the birds is stronger than she expects, and she joins the throng pressed against the glass. Outside the birds swirl round and round the Nest in a tornado of starry wings, then silence.

The Nest creaks like a ship in dock. The throng, still bound by Mel, begins to relax when the flames of the peat fire gutter. Patroclus cocks his head at the breeze and a thousand birds come pouring from the chimney.

They wheel around the pub, wings on fire and feathers smouldering. Their beaks cutting cheeks, tearing clothes. Talons ripping at hair and hands in the birds' panic. In the centre of the pub, Meliora turns her back to the flock and draws her ragwort wand from her dress. Winding it around her and drawing a thin blue green veil over the villagers to shield them.

'Hold, my friends, it will pass! The Mother is testing us!'

The birds beat against the shield and rattle at its bars. Yestin, edging around the group, sidles close to Nancy.

'Nancy, help us!'

Yestin's eyes are wide, and despite Meliora's instructions, Nancy has tricks up her sleeve. She closes her eyes and thinks of celandine. Feels the tattoo on her shoulder blade, remembers how the ink felt going in, and she curls her hand into its spell.

It bursts from her hand like a meteor shower. An expanding net of crackling yellow light that burns the birds to dust as it hits them. It grows, pushing the flock to the corners of the Nest then beyond. In her hurry to help, Nancy has not bound it and she cannot stop its growth. Outside of the Nest, pigeon and lark fall to its expansion. A heron loses a foot as it frantically flaps away, and Nancy prays everyone in the village is in the Nest.

They are, almost. As the net crackles towards the chapel, the Reverend Pine-Coffin sweeps the floor and whistles as he works. Oblivious to the sudden combustion of a robin that had been perched on a gravestone.

'Enough, Nancy, the birds are dead, stop it.' Meliora looks furious, her blue eyes black with anger. Nancy closes her hand and the net crackles into the air. At the chapel, the Reverend lifts his head at the smell of burning feathers.

'I can help, grandmother, I'm a Keeper after all.' Meliora sighs.

'Quite, but Nancy, from everything you've told me, isn't that the problem?' Before Nancy can answer, Mel releases the crowd.

'My friends, I see we have very little time indeed. The Mother is close, she will arrive on the day of your Saint's feast, yes, I feel it. That is when it will happen. Do not fear Her, this was not an attack. She wished to make herself known. She needs me. I will join Her fractured faces again, make the moor safe. Look to the future, and new solutions. For now, I must prepare. I will see you all again soon.'

Nancy moves to follow, but Mel pushes her back.

'No, stay, see your friends. I will find you when I need you. I will need your help, and we can't rely on your little tricks. See you soon, granddaughter.'

Nancy watches sadly as her grandmother leaves, kneels to lift the body of a starling from the floor. It's so light it shocks her. A feathered breath. She's pulled from her reverie by the embrace of Madge Gould.

'Nancy!' She grips the Keeper by the shoulders and pulls her tight. 'Where have you been, girl? You've missed the preparations!' Wriggling free of the embrace Nancy holds her friend at arm's length.

'Madge, what's going on? I thought you said Meliora was trouble, what—'

'Here, take my hand, look Agnes has sewn the 'oss skirt. We found a book, Pel had lent me, with so many pictures.'

'Madge...'

'Have a cake. Saffron and hazelnut. Or we have nettle-bread.'

'Is this the new Reverend's doing? I should have known he'd be trouble, however different to Cleaver. What creature have you spoken with?'

Madge hears not a word. She drifts between the workers, hands lingering on fabric. Nancy grabs her hand and pulls her through to the back bar, sits her down.

'Madge. Look at me, what is happening?' Madge's eyes clear, and she seems, for a moment, to recognise Nancy's distress. She places a hand on the girl's cheek and speaks more calmly.

'I was visited, Nancy. By Pel. He explained what Mel is, what the Mother is. She is our saint! One name trapped beneath another! This village can be whole again; can you believe it?' Nancy cannot. 'The Mother is going to fix things. Take us back. Join us.'

Shaking her head Nancy stands to pour a drink. The others may well be confused by a voice on the moor, unable to tell goddess from saint, but Madge? Nancy knows her friend. She's not so easily fooled.

'Pel wouldn't say that. The Mother is the Saint? Is that what you're saying? Where is the Reverend? Surely, he should be—'

'It's the Feast Day tomorrow. Locryn found the well. The Reverend is leading us there.'

'What well? Madge, please, can you tell me what's happening. Why are you going to a well?'

'To join them. Reagan and the Mother. Two sides. Just like the Underfolk and us. We are to reconnect. Listen, Nancy! I can't keep explaining it. It will be better for you, you can rest, finally! Mel will take things in hand. We're doing this for you.'

'The Reverend is happy with this? It's heretical, surely.' Madge smiles, her face creased into a child's grin, and she winks at Nancy.

'The Reverend doesn't know that part, Nancy. He serves only one of her faces. We serve both. Only those she spoke to, Delen, Billy and me, but others in the village too, know the whole truth. A way for us to be joined in our difference. Worship them both.' Nancy has seen eyes like this before. The Reverend Cleaver's shone the same when he spoke about his son. She'll not fight this friend.

'Good, Madge. That sounds good. I'm going to go and see if anyone needs help. Then I'll go home. I'll visit you before I go, though, here.' Madge nods as Nancy leaves.

When she is outside, she looks about for Mel, but her grandmother is lost to the crowds, or already gone to the moor. The stream of people has already turned back to the chapel, so that is where she heads, but she's not taken three steps when she's called from inside the longhouse.

'Nancy! Miss Bligh!' From the darkness, Nancy can make out the Reverend's young face, disembodied above the black of his cassock.

'Reverend?' Nancy steps into the dark cautiously. She's not

had long enough with the man to know if she trusts him. And the madness outside is muddying that. Still. There is something in his eyes that holds her gaze, draws her in. He looks tired, worried. Fiddles with his cuff and the bands at his neck.

'Miss Bligh. You've returned. Things have gotten away from me, and I would dearly like your advice.' His candour is unexpected. So is the request. Nancy does not know what to do with it, so she leaves it lying between them.

'Reverend. I, forgive me but I don't understand any of this. There was no mention of a feast when I left and now this,' she gestures to the noise and colour outside the open door. 'It is a lot.' The Reverend smiles apologetically and sits on the slab table that had held Salan Dell the previous year. Nancy cannot bring herself to join him.

'You recall our conversation, before you left?' Abraham Pine-Coffin waits for Nancy to nod before continuing. 'There was more I had hoped to show you. If I'd known you'd be leaving, well, no matter. Would you come with me?'

Against her better judgement, but then this Reverend seems to inspire this in her, Nancy allows him to lead her to the chapel. The door is open. It is new and brightly painted, studded with nails newly killed. The font which had been on the east side of the chapel is now at the west. Otherwise, the chapel has been rebuilt the same. Entering the knave Nancy treads carefully on newly laid stone, the memory of the fight here still fresh in her mind. Above her head newly carved faces stare down. She starts at the sight of them. They are the faces of the Underfolk. The Green Men replaced with spriggans, brownies and piskies. Some craftsmen must have been inspired by their renewed presence, their faces seeping into their tools. The faces they are modelled on are absent today, however, the rafters empty. The sun breaks through the clouds and Nancy is bathed in coloured light from the other change to the chapel. The old window shattered; the new one has been installed. A woman shrouded in black, A sword in one hand and flame in the other. Her head haloed with a disc that could be the moon. If it were not for the gothic Latin text claiming the image for religion, Nancy would feel sure she was one of the Gods below. The Reverend leads her to his prize.

To the Doom on the western wall.

'Our Sainted Reagan.'

'Madge, others, believe her to be an… earlier figure.'

Pine-Coffin laughs and the ease with which he does so, and the generous nature of it, disconcerts Nancy far more than dismissal would have. She is unused to this from churchmen.

'The Mother.' He doesn't acknowledge Nancy's surprise. 'Yes, I daresay she's right. Is that such a bad thing though? That's the question.' Nancy steps back, glances about for the trap. 'Oh. She thinks I do not know. Is that it? Believe me Nancy, and no offence to your friends, but they are poor spies. I know Madge and her group are working towards an adjacent goal. I don't mind. I tried to explain to you before you left, Miss Bligh. I am not my predecessor. If I can unite this parish under an image, whatever that is, then I would try to do so. I am a historian, as well as theologian, and Reagan would not be the first pagan to find veneration in a church. However. Things have progressed faster than anticipated. The villagers have taken to the festivities with a vigour that, if I am honest, I find alarming.'

This, at last, brings a smile to Nancy's face.

'Yes Reverend, I'm sure they have. Mirecoombe has had a dark year. If you have offered them some light, they will have jumped at it. Especially if it offers a cure for their division.

Tell me though, you strike me as a confident man, why are you hiding in the dark with the grain and ghosts?' Pine-Coffin turns a rueful smile to the keeper.

'As I say, none of this would be something to cause much alarm. I've seen similar elsewhere in fact, it's quite exciting. No, it is another, outside agent, that has concerned me. I was spoken to. A voice that would have me think it an angel. A shadow with a great deal to say. Talking of a Mother, of our saint. He has spoken to others, rather good at voices. It was keen on these celebrations, and I do not know how to feel about the endorsement. You've been told of the well?'

'In passing.'

'Locryn Calder, madness gone, marched his sons into the valley and found the parish holy well. Lost, according to the records, since 1241. He says an angel sent him.'

'You do not believe in angels, Reverend?'

Pine-Coffin freezes, just for a second. His eyes clouding.

'I don't know what I believe. If there are angels, however, I do not believe they threaten their prophets, Nancy.' Twice now he has used her name, she adds it to his tally of black marks and would mention it, but his face is stern, so she focuses on the issue at hand. 'Besides, I saw him. That is, perhaps, the greater thing I should tell you. He was small, covered in moss and wood.'

Nancy freezes. A problem presented and immediately doubled.

'You *saw* him?' Nancy casts her eyes about the long house but there are no Underfolk in sight to test the claim.

'Yes. I seem to have gained quite the gift. I have long wanted it, but the manner of its delivery has left me really rather vexed. I think it was Reagan, whoever she is. I do not know why it was given but I don't think it was the outcome the voice was after.'

'I will check the books I have, Reverend. My grandmother is,' she cycles through lies, 'newly returned from foreign travel. She knows of the Mother. The figure your Saint might share a face with. I suspect she is also acquainted with your angel. I'll talk to her.'

'I fear she is, Nancy. The creature did not like it when I spoke her name.'

'There will be a reason, I'm sure of it. My grandmother will have a plan.'

'I'm sure of it. Of course. I would like us to be friends, Nancy. However long that takes. There is a lot I'd like to talk to you about. Your father, especially.' He is making it hard for her to trust him, yet, somehow, Nancy does. 'There is another issue, too. I have one more thing for you to look at. If you'd be so kind.'

Abraham takes her and helps her down the stairs to the crypt. Her breath clouds in the cold and she is drawn to the stone slab, the wreck of painted wood. Though it is empty, and the body sits at the Reverend's table, she kneels by it, traces her hand across the stone. There is a magic coming from it. She feels that strongly enough. If her Murmur is a cloud of birds, then this tomb is a place to roost. She could lay down here and sleep for eternity. She knows it to be true.

Daughter.

A word in her ear. There is a fizz of static on the stone, and she pulls her hand away.

'Her body, it is unusual, I moved it. I did not know what might happen if it was found whilst the village was in such peak. If you wish to see it, it is at my cottage.'

Nancy tears herself from the coffin stone and stands.

'Come to my cottage this evening, Reverend. We have two days left before the feast and I would like us to both be prepared.'

Nancy leaves the Reverend in his isolation and walks into the chapel yard for air. In thought, she wanders to the eastern wall. To the effigy of Cleaver now installed there. He lays in sight of the graves of his wife and son, the cold granite as expressive as the man himself ever was. She stops at his side.

'What would you make of this, Cleaver? This colour and laughter? Not a great deal, I suspect. Frankly, I am a little concerned you'd be right.' She follows his stone gaze to the chapel wall and notices a stone placed outside of it. Walking across she gasps, holds her hand to her mouth. A standing stone, small but prominent, has been erected past the boundary. PEL engraved on the top of it.

'Friends above and below, it seems.' She wonders who installed it and is grateful to them.

'Nancy.' She had not heard Yestin Calder arrive. 'That was quite a thing, at the Nest.' She chuckles at his stating of fact; a trait of the young man's she has grown to find endearing.

'Yes, Yestin. Don't worry, Mel and I will deal with it. You've been busy I hear, building a well?' The man does not answer. 'Your father, he's recovered?' Silence. Tears are streaming down Yestin's face. Over the last year he has helped Nancy and though she's not quite brought herself to call him a friend she'll not see him sad. 'What is it?' Yestin wipes his face.

'He's not recovered, Nancy. Just lurched from one madness to another and taken Luk with him.'

'The Reverend mentioned he was spoken to, a voice?'

'His angel? No angel berates a man to drive his family to exhaustion. I hear it too; I've sat at his door and listened to its poison. It teases him, mocks him. Uses his grief against him, and that blasted well! I have dug until my hands bled, torn the moor apart, it was buried for a reason, Nancy. I don't care how long ago it was lost, there was too much soil on top of the cover.' Nancy's stomach sinks. There is something in his words that rings a distant bell inside her.

'Does the angel have a name, Yestin?'

'It plays games with dad, tells him to guess and then after every attempt it cackles and says "No, it's not" It's a devil, Nancy, and dad is leading the whole village to it'. Another sliver of worry has worked its way loose and Nancy feels sick.

'I'm going to set things straight, Yestin. Trust me.' He nods and Nancy knows he does. She feels the weight of that trust. It is a heavy load and she's nobody here to share it with.

MELIORA RAY STANDS at the edge of the Queen's Rocks with a squirming, flickering, tangle of limbs in her outstretched fist.

'Enough, settle!' The creature known as Knot fixes himself into his mossy shape and hangs from the witch's grasp, eyes turned away.

'I did as you asked!'

'Did you? What is this about the saint? She was not the plan.'

'It is good! Mistress I swear, it is good, listen, they are together now! You can have them all, you've been gone, the magic has left this valley! The Keeper's share has dwindled. It is better this way.'

'Hmm. Perhaps. There is power in names, though. Be more careful with them.' She pauses, then swings Knot back onto the stone.

'I've missed you, dearie.'

There is a simper from the creature at her feet as Meliora shoots it a wink.

'I've missed you too, mistress. It's been a hard half century without you. A lot has changed. I wept when I heard your call. When the magician died.'

'You've changed too I see, where is your lovely face? What's this wooden skin and moss-grown back, my love, my Brock. Where are your beautiful stripes?' The creature snarls, spits against the wind.

'He took my face. Dropped me in the fire. I did not give you up, Mel. I died for you. Thank the stars for mad gods. I learnt to make myself anew when the ancient fool's back was turned. Read your books. Watch!'

Brock cycles between shapes.

'Very clever, that was you, then? The cloud of birds at the Nest? I was worried it was something more.'

Plucking a stem of ragwort, Meliora Ray, Queen of the Witches, sits astride it, rises six feet into the air. As she does so, Knot drops his head.

'What is it, my pet?'

'That was not me.'

Meliora comes down to earth.

'Also, my Queen, the priest. I was working on him, and he saw me.'

'Well. No matter. Some have the sight, after all. Unfortunate, but it is good to know. Come. Let's see how things are going.'

'You don't understand, he—did not have it, then he did. She gave it to him.' Mel dismounts, leans close and grabs Knot at the throat.

'She? Tell me exactly what happened.' Knot recounts his conversation in the chapel, the chalice and the wine. Meliora's face grows graver with every word.

'And you promise it was not you, in the Nest?'

Knot shakes his head.

'We are building a puppet, Brock. I thought you understood that. You'd best not have handed over the strings.'

FOXTAIL

Nancy is staring at the fire when the Reverend knocks. She rises stiffly, the bruising of the waves not yet fully healed, and though the brownies could open the door she wants to be the one to let him in.

'Nancy.'

'Miss Bligh, or Keeper, Reverend. Come in, please.' Nancy turns and lets the priest shut the door behind him, manoeuvring a box under his arm. As he walks to the fire, where two glasses of gorse wine are waiting, he admires the pictures on the wall, Nancy's charcoal sketches.

'These are lovely, Miss Bligh, truly.' He pauses in front of the portrait she made of Pel. He stares straight out from the paper, the hollow of his missing eye a deep, dark black. She had tried to capture his glare, easier to hold on to than his kindness, but she was not sure she had managed to do it. She felt like the drawing was disappointed in her, was planning on redrawing it.

'This is Lord Hunt, yes?'

'Have a seat, Abraham. Are you hungry?' She guides the priest from the pictures towards the fire, but Pine-Coffin crouches, leans close to a terrified brownie that looks to Nancy for direction.

'You do see them, then. That is fascinating. Truly. Leave

the brownie be and come sit by the fire, Reverend.' Freed, the brownie races back to the shadows.

'Bram, please. Thank you, Nancy.' The young man takes his seat and removes his hat, his ringlet curls spilling out from beneath. He has the look of an aged cherub. His cheeks round and blushed from the walk. Lifting the glass of wine, he shudders as he drinks it. Nancy has no clue what proof the mixture is, but she rarely has more than a glass or two.

'Rev—Bram. I do not know what to make of you. You know too much. Too much by an acre. And yet I am to trust you?' She pauses, hears Colenso's parting words echoing in her head. *Trust yourself, Nancy.* 'Very well. Hear this, though, Reverend. It is not in you I trust, but in another's trust in me. Do not let me, or her, down.' It is done. Leap of faith, blind hope, she's stepped off the edge and fall or fly there's no changing it. 'Now, tell me. Who are you?'

'Me? I am just a man who likes a puzzle. Likes to know things. Not, you understand, for power or to hold it over a fellow, just for the love of it. My education gave me a curiosity that needed sating. My privilege the means to sate it. The priesthood gave me ample puzzles, ample information. The keys to doors even my family money would not open. An invitation to spaces otherwise closed. Folklore, though, Nancy. Ah, now there is a thing to sink your teeth into!' The Reverend looks to Nancy, tired and impatient Nancy, and changes tack. 'But you know that, of course. I found his letters,' Abraham tips his head towards the picture of Pel, 'in the archives at Exeter. I suppose being able to sign 'Lord Hunt' meant nobody looked into it much. Assumed a son, then another and so on. I noticed the handwriting, the turn of phrase, all the same. He used to write an awful lot, you know, years ago. Trying to get the church to step in or aside during witch trials. Correspondence on exorcisms of creatures that turned out not to be the devil. He signed them as Keeper, a role I had not come across.'

'He did not write about Eythin.' Nancy's lips have been tightening as he speaks, this feels like her failing, though it was Pel's indiscretions that have brought the man here.

'No, he didn't. But it was there, between the words. As I said, I like a puzzle. He was on no roll of honour, had no seat in the house of lords. No country pile. Do you know the year he was born?'

Nancy shakes her head, Pel would never tell her.

'1521. Can you believe it? I came across, in our records, a copy of a letter of congratulations to a Lord Eythin, on the birth of his son. Very few people christened Pelagius at the time, and he is the only one I have found that has no date of death. Once I had that I went in search of Eythin. I found it in a book older than I thought we possessed. The illuminated manuscript of a monk, entitled: *EYTHIN, being an account, strange and wonderful, of an island*. It was quite the read.'

'I should like to read it.'

'I've no doubt. I have a copy—made at my own expense—at my cottage I will show you when you visit. You see, I hope, why it was a riddle too delicious to leave be? The book ends with a deed of promise, an exchange of goods in perpetuity. A map. I'm getting ahead of myself. When the Reverend Cleaver passed, I applied before the ink was dry on his death note. I had expected Mirecoombe to be... interesting, but I confess it has exceeded expectations.'

Nancy sits with the information. Downs her glass of wine.

'What do you wish to do with this knowledge?'

The Reverend's eyes dim, anguish spreading across his face. 'Oh, my, you think me sinister. Again, it happens! Miss

Bligh, Nancy, forgive me. My curiosity has often been a curse. How rude I must seem, prying where I have no business. A product, I am afraid, of my profession and my upbringing. You'll not find a fellow so comfortable in another's space as a member of the English aristocracy. I admit, my initial reasons were selfish. I wanted to know more. Wanted to meet a Keeper. My whole life I have searched for proof, for something more than the books can give and now I have it! This wonderful, terrible valley has given it to me, and I wish to help! Perhaps,' he gestures to his eyes, 'with this new gift, I can.'

'Indeed. Perhaps you can, Bram. Let's talk about this gift. You said it worried you?'

Abraham recounts his experience at the chapel, the ichor in the chalice, the voice inside his head. Nancy knows old magic when she hears it.

'You are a lucky man, Bram. Pel lost an eye for that gift.'

'And you were born with it?'

'Aye, near enough.' She'll keep some secrets. 'This celebration, this feast. It worries me. These bones of yours too. Did you bring them?'

Pine-Coffin smiles and lifts his box. Unwraps it so the bone and gold catch the firelight. Opens the lid. Inside is the skull, and a single bone.

It is the skull she lifts.

'My. My oh my.'

Abraham is too giddy to hold his tongue.

'I cannot fathom it! There is no join I can see.'

Nancy turns the skull gently in her hands.

'You found these on the bier you showed me? Then this could be her, it could be Reagan.'

Daughter.

Both Reverend and Keeper look up. Shiver in the heat of

the fire. Nancy replaces the skull and lifts the bone which, to Abraham's horror she snaps in two and examines.

'It is black inside. Burnt. My grandmother, she mentioned women who acted as a host for the Mother.'

'Your grandmother. Have you had chance to speak to her?'

Nancy lays the bone down and adds another log to the fire.

'No. If she means me to know she'll tell me. I trust her. I think. May I borrow this?' She holds up the fractured tibia. 'I am scratching at two closed doors Abraham, and neither's giving an inch. I wonder if they lead to the same room.' Abraham's face becomes serious, earnest. His eyes a flickering intensity.

'I agree. So let me knock at one, whilst you knock at the other. Leave the Sainted Reagan to me. I'll leave the Mother to you. And your grandmother. If you are right, we will meet in the middle. We can compare notes, at my cottage, tomorrow night. The day before the feast.' He closes the box, extends a hand, and Nancy smiles as she takes it.

'Deal, Reverend. Deal.' After sealing it with more wine, too much wine, she stands and leads him to the door, which takes longer than normal as he asks her to name each face in her pictures so he can greet them should he see them on the moor.

'And this?'

'A spriggan, that a piskie, that a wish hound but please, if you see them do not engage them. At best they are trouble and at worst fatal. They play rougher games than you are used to, Abraham.' The wine has gone to both their heads, and she finds herself laughing.

'See you tomorrow, Bram.' The priest bows, replaces his hat on his head.

'Adieu, Nancy, goodnight.'

Nancy stands in the starlight to see him safely down the

path that he seems unable to stick to. Once he is past the gate, she smiles.

'You cannot trust him, Nancy.' The voice is stitched into the shadows, Nancy hears the threads snap as her grandmother steps from the darkness. Knot at her feet.

'He is yours then, Mel?' Knot smiles at her.

'Yes, girl, are you planning on inviting me in?'

Nancy steps aside to let the old witch pass but blocks the imp's way.

'I would talk to her alone, Knot. Stand guard.' The door closes in the creature's face and Nancy leaves him at the mercy of the wind.

'That seems unnecessary, granddaughter.' Mel has poured wine into the glass the Reverend left and drinks it without reaction.

'That creature, Knot, I do not like him. He's done things, Mel. Hurt people.'

'He is overenthusiastic, that's all. He knew that if the Mother were to reappear, I would be needed. He did what he thought best to ensure that.'

'He has killed innocent creatures.'

'I'm sure he felt he had no choice.' Meliora sits, in Nancy's chair, and looks into the fire. 'What did the priest want?' Nancy ignores her and sits by the fire. Knot being her grandmother's ally changes things. Knocks them askance at least. There is a creeping sickness at the base of her spine, a curdling in her stomach.

'Colenso says the Mother is a children's story. Tell me straight, Meliora, is that what this is? Are you telling stories?'

'Does it matter?'

Nancy straightens in her chair, watches Meliora move to the fire and stand over it, her hands on the mantlepiece.

'Is it true?'

'Come, girl. What's magic but stories? Repetition and intent. Pel knew it, if he taught you, then so do you. The difference, between him and I, between him and you—is that his stories just persuaded things that Pel was right. That coloured light could hold or hurt. Our magic, Nancy, can create. Your Murmur, it comes from you. That power that shakes the hill is you, girl. Why should it not come from a Goddess?'

Nancy closes her eyes. Wishes the heat from the fire would warm her. The chill runs too deep. A wind running through the space where a hawthorn grew before she cut it down in anger.

'This is your plan then. Laid, what, as you slept?'

'Brock, Knot as you know him, was given instructions. When Pel dies, prepare for my return. Spread the word of the Mother, of the Witch that could direct Her.'

'And me?'

'A wrinkle.' Meliora catches herself. 'Not an unpleasant one, Nancy. What I said above the ship holds. I am delighted to find I am not alone any longer.'

'So what comes next?'

'The plan continues. Don't tell me you wish things to stay as they were under Pel? Keepers, Nancy, are a dying breed. Pel loved to talk about balance but where did that get him? Hmm? Underground and dead or not there's little comfort in the distinction. Besides, balance is just another word for control, of magic, of the moor. Of women. It is a club for men who tinker at the edges.'

'And you would be different?'

'Why must I be? Why must we, be?' Meliora's face flares in anger. 'You're right, I am some of those things also. I can't deny it. Why should I suffer, and he live? We both held power that could hurt. Hell, every lord in the country carries a sword and pistol. Do they have those taken from them, just in case? No. Men walk around, trusted not to kill unless they must. At their discretion. Not us. Not witches. Not women. No, when we showed power they killed us. Fire, water, and rope. It is time for change. That is what the Mother brings. Story or not, She is the root of our power, she lets us fly. She has been gone a long time, perhaps it is time she was back.'

'And what of Reagan?'

The wind goes from Meliora's sails. There is a brief guttering of certainty, but the flame renews.

'Knot overreached. He was not made for independent thought. However, if it is useful to add her to the fiction then we shall.'

Nancy opens her eyes and stares at her grandmother.

'You're adamant it is a story then?'

'I am.'

Nancy stands, retrieves the bone that the Reverend left and hands it to her grandmother.

'Then what, Meliora, is this?'

BLOODY WARRIOR

ABRAHAM PINE-COFFIN CANNOT sleep, and it is not just because a skeleton occupies his bed. Since gaining his sight, he has discovered his brownies, and they delight him greatly. Even the prospect of the feast day, whatever terrors it may bring, cannot dim his joy. He has his own copy of a book on the Cornish pisky and their kin, knows a little. But their otter faces, coal burnt eyes and utter surprise at his seeing them have him transfixed.

'Little ones! Ah, you are a treat. Here.' He lays a plate of bread and cheese down. 'Thank you, for your service.' They still regard him strangely, but they'll not look a gift horse in the mouth. The boldest gestures to his stove—he has not gotten it working since he arrived, rather wrapping in extra clothes each evening as he waits for the year to change.

'You'd light it?' A nod. 'Please, please, I would be most grateful.' There is a roar as coal takes in the chamber and the old range shakes into life. Sat in the armchair—he has made peace with the mice—the Reverend rereads his books. Seeing the brownies is indeed a delight, but finding he has the audience he always hankers for is truly wonderful.

'May I read to you?' Mistaking the shrug for enthusiasm, the Reverend begins to read. He reads stories of the Underfolk, of giants, and mermaids and ghosts. Once done with the volume he rummages for another. Pulls out the diary he found beneath the bible in Cleaver's shed. He starts strongly enough but finds he cannot continue the show. The brownies sense the change, quietly cleaning around him, pushing a plate of food and a coffee to him where they are hastily consumed. He has reached the point of Callum's rebirth.

He had told me what I must do, and I have done it, May God forgive me, yet it did not work. My son lies weak as the day he returned. I will try again tomorrow.

God spoke to me in the night. Gave me the piece I was missing. Tonight, I will try once again. Callum calls to me but I tell him patience, the Lord needs time.

It is done. As my Lord said, in his whispers, I carried Callum—he could no longer walk—to the tomb stone beneath the altar. Laid him upon it. As the moonlight reached in, colouring itself on the glass I could tell He was with me. Guiding my hand. I felt it, rising, His power. That heart, that stolen heart, it beat! My boy was returned. His vengeance can commence. Hers too. He made it clear, my God, that his Love alone was not enough, nor his son's. The Holy Reagan herself has joined them, their family reuniting mine.

Praise be our Lord, and St Reagan.

Abraham lays the diary down.

'Well. That is troubling, most vexing indeed. Little ones?' He cannot see the brownies; they must have moved as he read. He stands, realising he is still dressed, and walks with light steps to his bedroom, pauses, takes it in. Around the bed, the bones still daintily laid, are the brownies. Gazing up, eyes closed, in a ring. They lift their arms in what he sees is clearly prayer and he backs from the room. He lifts the other half of Nancy's broken bone from its space on the mantlepiece. Traces the charred edge. Without thinking he slips it into his coat pocket. He immediately feels better. Sitting back down in his chair, he slips into sleep and dreams of the wings of birds and arrows whistling past his ears. Dreams of running, of white stags and the piercing pain of iron in his chest. The brownies, done with their reverence, walk back in to find him crying in his sleep, a smile on his lips and a hand on his heart.

PART FOUR

*"All in the wild March-morning I heard the angels call,
It was when the moon was setting, and the dark was over all;
The trees began to whisper, and the wind began to roll,
And in the wild March-morning I heard them call my soul."*

Alfred, Lord Tennyson

VALERIAN

NANCY FINDS HER grandmother at the summit of the Queen's Rocks. She stands with the morning wind whipping her hair to gossamer. Knot, to Nancy's relief, is absent. She cannot reconcile his presence on the side of, what? Good? Something is wrong. She cannot quite see what.

'Good morning grandmother. How did you sleep? I dreamt of burnt-out bones.' A lie. She dreamt of grandmother's knees. Big ears. Long noses. Sharp, sharp teeth.

'I've been sleeping long enough, Nancy. And the dead do not concern me. Have you thought about what we spoke of?'

'I don't see the need for the story, Mel. If Pel's ring would have found its way to me regardless, if the Empress of Salt would have delivered it to have rid of you, I would have helped. I would have rushed to find you. And is the bone not proof of…'

'The bone is nothing. Are you so easily tricked? A goose's foot. Nothing more. Leftover's from some prankster's plate.'

Nancy scours her grandmother's face for a twitch of a lie but sees none.

'I thought, Abraham thought…'

'A whelp of a priest tells you to follow and you go with him? Come, Granddaughter. See better, Nancy.'

Mel turns to face the moor.

'My house stood there.' She points to a patch of ground taken over by blackthorn. Nancy knows it. Has seen the ruined walls in the copse. 'I was born here. Raised here. Saw our Keeper work. He was the same as Pel, in a lot of ways, a little kinder perhaps. I went to him when I discovered my magic. He turned me away. I learnt my trade on Lullaby Tor. Went every night to stand on the rocking logan stone until I could climb it without it shaking. Listened to the wind blowing teachings from women further down. Went back to the Keeper to show him what I had learned and still he turned me away.'

Nancy walks to stand beside her grandmother.

'I'm a different kind of Keeper.'

'Maybe, but I did not know that girl, when I laid this plan.'

'It's not too late to change it, the world is a different place to the one you knew.'

Meliora takes a seat on a slab of granite. Pats the space next to her.

'Is it, Nancy? If you had seen what I have seen... do you know the smell of bodies burning?'

Nancy remembers Hugh Dell. His head a flaming lantern. Meliora must see it, in her eyes, the flickering remembrance. Nancy sees the tilt of the witch's head. The narrowing of her eyes in recognition.

'This world does not change for the likes of us. If we wish to live freely in it, we must yoke it. Bring it to heel. Enough. Put it from your mind. Let your grandmother teach you. As I've said, your *spells,* they are charming enough, but I can teach you practical magic. You saw my knotted rope; you saw Peter's hedgehog heart. The ragwort stems we ride on. Witchcraft is worked through metaphor and intent. I will teach you a little, so you do not have to rely on that old fool's tricks. Yes?'

'Yes, grandmother.' Nancy's tattoos prickle at Meliora's dismissal of them.

'Good. There is little cap on what a strong witch can do with a little preparation and forethought. Pel knew it too, I see those filled pockets. I taught him how to pack those glass balls. They are the least of it. Let us take the rope.' Meliora takes a length of unknotted rope from a fold of her cape and holds it, laid flat, on her upwards facing palms.

'To knot the wind, you need to see it. Close your eyes.' Nancy does as she is told. 'Feel the wind, its ebb and flow. Try and picture it, as though it is a smoke that billows around your head.'

Nancy concentrates and wills the image into her mind.

'Good, now open your eyes and take the rope. Do not lose sight of the wind. Now, wrap the rope around the smoke and tie it tight. See it. See the wind whip and buck against it.'

Nancy does, and the rope whips from her hand, coiling onto the floor as the smoke dissipates.

'Again, Nancy.'

Three times Nancy tries and fails to tether the wind. Then...

'I have it! Grandmother I have it!'

'Good! Tie it again. Twice more!'

Nancy quickly, deftly, knots the rope, and the wind that buffeted the tor top drops. The air stills. Then rekindles on the third tie. Gentler than before.

'Good! There. The power of the winds in your hand. A gale, peace, a breeze. To use or sell as you wish.'

'You sell this power?'

'Life has taught me one thing over and over again, Nancy. None will thank you for taking sides, you'll always be thrown over by the victor in the end. This power of ours is our livelihood. Take the heart of a dog, stick it with pins, bind it to a man's affection. Make a poppet of a lover's rival. Drag a ploughshare through the fields at night and think of failing crops. You can change the world, Nancy. Name your price.'

'I help for free.'

'Then you are a fool. This is the barest taste of your potential, Nancy. Do not give it away. Why, take a man's hair, tie it to a fabric heart and pin it to his breast and you could take down even the most powerful magician. Think about it.'

Before Nancy can, Mel has brought a small vial out from the lining of her cloak.

'Here, a gift. Some of the salve we use to fly. Made from a scrape of the mould that grows on wheat, six of the downy feathers that line an owl's nest and the yolk of an unhatched wren. A drop each of mandrake, nightshade and wolfsbane. Pick those stems of ragwort, granddaughter.'

Meliora's misdirection works, Nancy's thoughts already in the clouds, and she plucks the sprays of starry yellow flowers from the grass.

'Always ragwort?'

'If you've any love of tradition. But no, anything will do. Just not, for the love of all witches, a broom. Here.'

Meliora hands Nancy the vial and directs her as she smears it along the flower's stem. As before, Nancy jumps, rises into the air, and the magic of it is undimmed by repetition. She angles the stem and rises, high above the Queen's Rocks until the whole valley is a map below her. Meliora rides alongside her, and together they circle the parish.

'What if She is real, Mel. The Mother?'

Meliora does not react, keeps flying steady, but Nancy sees her knuckles whiten on the stem.

'Then we are truly blessed.'

'Indeed. Perhaps, Mel, we might help the village without lying to them? I have been working, this year, to repair the damage Cleaver and Pel—'

'You are cauterising a wound that is already infected. Those limbs must come off, girl. Follow me or don't, that's up to you. I told you; I won't make you do anything you don't want to do. But I'll not let you stop me.'

'The village is better than you give it credit for. If you just explained I am sure they would welcome you as you are. The Reverend, too.'

Meliora's laugh is hollow.

'I've known Mirecoombe far longer than you, girl. I know what they are and are not capable of. The truth is an empty promise. Stories will keep them fed.'

'And your stories, of the things you've done. Turning men to eel, burning crops. How much of it is true?'

Meliora does not answer. She stays mute until they have circled the ruins of Echo Tor, until Mirecoombe is in view again, when a sigh escapes from the old witch's lips.

'See if anyone needs help, Nancy. I must go and prepare for the Mother's arrival.' Meliora twists the stem of her ragwort and sails into the clouds.

Alone in the sky, Nancy closes her eyes and listens for the voice again. She does not hear it, but the ragwort stem dips with the weight of another. She shivers and turns for home.

THE PREPARATIONS FOR the festival have reached an end early, the people of Mirecoombe so excited that they have sped through their work. The village flutters under flags, every table in the Nest is heaped with costumes, and nobody knows quite what to do with themselves. Across the valley, the newly found holy well has been restored. The cut granite stones that had covered the pit have been exhumed from their bed, revealing a steep staircase that leads to the water. In a miracle of masonry, the same puzzle cut blocks that capped the well have been lifted, scrubbed clean, and pieced back together in new formation and resurrected into a doorway for it. Interlocking without the need for mortar into a pitched roof portal. Seven feet high, three feet wide and deeply uninviting.

Nancy arrives at the chapel as people buzz about putting finishing touches to finishing touches. The pews have been pulled back to their positions, each carefully set. There are new pew ends. No longer scenes of the Passion, they now show the moor. The new Reverend had not asked for this, but it is what he's got. Frogs and toads, newts. Foxes and rabbits. Wildflowers, waving in meadows. The craftsmen that made it adding their own flourishes and biases. So, one pew end is carved with Pel's anchor cross. Another with what might be recognised as Callum though draped in the clothes of a devil. There are dancing skeletons, wild dogs and mermaids all facing inwards to the aisle. On each seat a kneeler. More of the same though picked out in cross stitch. Someone has embroidered the sign of the Nest. The black horse sat in its reeds. Another shows St. Reagan, as the embroiderer saw her. Her halo moon shining. A church, faith or no, is a folk museum. An archive of a people. Each mason's mark, carpenter's cut. Each dropped stitch. There, in front of the altar, are set glazed tiles. Each showing a different flower head. Bordered in squares of slate set on their ends and tightly packed so they feel like the top of a horse's tooth when you run your finger along them. The murals have been finished. Every wall now painted just like the one recently rediscovered. Not for Mirecoombe any old scenes of doom, of sabbath breakers and trees of sin. No. There is the moor, the stacks of the tors rising up and out of the grass. There the wish hounds, chased all about by the Hunt. There are horned figures in the long grass and men with the heads of cattle. A lion headed fish with the shell of a turtle. Overseeing all, lit by the yellow rays of a painted sun, is Reagan. She offers her hands, though the painting does not make it clear if she offers the scene as a warning or salvation.

It sticks in Nancy's throat.

Easy enough to forget the chaos under the masonry during the rebuilding. But now? The stage has been reset. The play goes on.

There are people all around her, but Nancy has never felt so alone. She even thinks, for a moment, of praying.

'Pull yourself together, girl. You've knelt to no gods yet, don't start now.'

Her mind is a sail torn apart by wind. Her grandmother's face painted upon it. Since finding Meliora a hard knot has sat at the pit of Nancy's stomach. She lifts her hand and lets her Murmur out, just a little, the way her grandmother had shown her. She finds, if she concentrates, she can rattle individual tiles on the newly laid floor. She is so lost in the distraction it takes a crack to bring her out of it. A crisp bright glaze split in half. She hears the whispered voice, a gentle *tut* in the back of her head and, shaking her head, Nancy twists her hands around the memory of goosegrass and knits the tile back together. A year ago, it would have been impossible to work any spell in the chapel. Clearly whatever she had broken then was not possible to fix. A thought rises, and she turns to the painted saint.

'Did I wake you, Reagan? Is this my doing? Or,' she lowers her voice to a whisper, an idea barely formed given vent, 'is this truly just a story we've all decided is real?'

Nancy takes the coral tooth that hangs around her neck in her hand and toys with it.

'What to do, Reagan?' If the other occupants of the church notice their Keeper talking to herself, they do not say. 'Do I tell Abraham not to worry? That his saint and the mother are the same, and one or both may not exist? Or do I tell him nothing. Do I make my grandmother see that her stories have come to life.' In the candlelight, the image of Saint Reagan dances on the wall, flickering and jumping. Nancy closes her eyes.

'Can you hear me? Reagan?' The candles gutter in a draft from the door, 'Mother? Is it you who speaks to me?' A gust blows through the chapel and Nancy shivers in it. Shivers as it blows an answer by her ears. Two voices, one word.

YES

THE WALK TO the cottage is not one she's made before. She has lived on this moor her whole life but never had cause to go. When she was young, because of her aversion to Callum, and by the time she was older, Cleaver had moved to his shack behind the chapel. Nobody went there. It was an empty shell full of ghosts nobody spoke to. A dare set between children.

Even in spring, the air feels cold in its garden.

'Nancy!' The door swings open, and Abraham Pine-Coffin stands in his shirtsleeves. 'You came, please, come inside.' He ushers her into the dim front room with flapping arms. 'Here, sit, let me show you what I've found.' In his excitement at his guest, the Reverend does not notice her melancholy. Nancy sits quietly at his table and waits for him to tire himself out. When he does notice, he is full of contrition. Hands folded, brow furrowed, and the intensity of his expression makes Nancy laugh, just for a moment.

'Oh, Bram. Why should I trust you? Tell me, please because I need to know. I fear you and a friend I should have listened to are right. My grandmother is involved. I may need help, in the coming days. The church is not a comfortable place to look for it.' The Reverend blushes and reaches for Nancy's hand. Holding it across the table.

'What is it you wish to trust me with? We had a plan laid out, only yesterday, what's happened?'

'My grandmother. She came to see me after your visit.' Nancy explains Meliora's plan. The story of the Mother and her part in it. The voice in the chapel. Abraham listens closely, thinks before he speaks.

'I would be a hypocrite to say that a story holds no power, would I not? I have quite the book of them balanced on that golden eagle. Perhaps your grandmother invests less power in them than she ought to. I have treated much of my life as an investigation, so let us lay out the facts. First, there is this.' He taps his temple and flutters his eyes. The ease of him is a comfort, her decision to trust him, for Colenso, a salve on a broken heart. 'Who gave me this?' Laughing, Nancy shrugs.

'Reagan? A reward for your piety, Reverend?' Cocking his head Abraham frowns.

'Perhaps. Though it would be an unusual gift. Option one then. Option two, it was the Mother.'

'Option three, they are the same.'

'Quite. I would place my money on the third. Regardless, this gift is proof of something.' Nancy thinks of the tomb at the church, of the feeling of power within it. The voice. 'What is it, Nancy?'

'I think you are right. I felt something. At the chapel. Something I recognised.'

Abraham stands, rummages on a shelf behind him and

drops a book in front of Nancy. It is Cleaver's diary. Abraham keeps on talking, but Nancy does not hear a word. When she finishes reading, she sees Abraham, stood across from her, eyes wide and waiting for an answer to a question she hasn't heard.

'Sorry, Bram, what did you say?' For a brief moment the Reverend seems put out, but he brightens quickly at the prospect of talking again.

'Do you think it was Her?'

Nancy shakes her head.

'It can't have been. If the Mother is awake, it was last year that woke her. She has risen to fix what Pel broke. What I broke.' Abraham looks crestfallen, but it does not last. He raises his head, bright eyed.

'Perhaps, Nancy. Perhaps. But we all talk in our sleep, do we not? Why should She be any different?'

'Perhaps.' Nancy rubs her eyes, feels them pulse with tiredness.

'You see what this means? She, whoever she is, was at least listening when that boy was brought back, perhaps she believed herself part of it! The chapel in dedication to her, the village in dedication to her. It's a machine of reverence, a chamber built to sustain belief, if a person hears their name enough, or at least the name they assume is theirs, would it not make a person a little big headed?' Nancy does not see why he is so pleased.

'What are you saying? That whoever it was that lay beneath the chapel is the Mother now, Reagan now, because it thinks it is? Magic and faith are two sides of a coin, but only one side ever faces up.'

'Perhaps.' Abraham's mouth twitches in an excited smile. 'But the events of this year, the stories your grandmother is telling have flipped that coin. It's spinning, still, and I'm not sure it's coming down. You ask why you should trust me? I do not know. Perhaps, Nancy, it must be a leap of faith.'

'Very well, Bram. Gods help me, I do trust you. I need to. Please,' her voice softens, 'please do not make me regret it.'

Abraham Pine-Coffin's face is grave. He nods and crosses his heart. This done, the familiar smile cracks through.

'Follow me. I have Reagan in the next room. See if you can find something I've missed.' He turns and walks into the bedroom. Nancy raises an eyebrow at a cleaning brownie and follows him though.

'Why are you showing me an unmade bed? Bloody hell Bram, what are you doing in here?' There is nothing there. No bones, no claws, no antler crown. Just a dishevelled vesper cloth with a stain in the shape of a body in the centre. The Reverend stands mute, and for the first time since Nancy's known him, he stays that way. She lays an arm on his shoulder.

'Bram, get some sleep. This must all be very exciting, the gift you've been given, the new job of the festival. But I have been doing this for years, trust me. I will talk to Meliora, work this out.' Abraham nods and Nancy leaves him to himself. His cottage is no great walk from her own and she takes the opportunity the cooling night air brings to think.

'What would you do Pel?' As soon as it is whispered, she regrets it. She does not need ghosts; she has her grandmother. Here, now, and she has helped her more than Pel ever did. She lifts her hand and shakes the rocks that line the brook. Sends them splashing into the water.

'What will I do?'

She's home before she's given herself an answer.

RUSTY BROOK

Jacob Cleaver knows his role. He walks quietly between the hubbub of the Undermoor, a ghost amongst the ghosts, dragging a cart behind him. Most of the Underfolk ignore him completely, they remember what his son did. What he did. Refuse to welcome him to their home. If not for Pel he would be the pariah that Callum's become. He sees his son, sometimes, in the far distance. Callum's mangled mind seeking some kind of peace, out in the moonlit marshes. Even now, though, even after everything, the Reverend does not regret what he did. Cannot. What father would not do all he could to save his son? He has kept this from Pel. The old hypocrite would not see any parallel between Cleaver's actions and his own. Cleaver helps now not because Pel has told him to, though he knows it's what Pel thinks, but because he understands the desire to ruin worlds if it saves a single soul.

So far, their investigations have been fruitful. Confident the Mother, Reagan, is the ghost Pel believes her to be. A story made flesh. They must trust Nancy to deal with her above but they have plans for those below. The creature, Knot, has promised the Underfolk a new dawn. A future where they once again roam unrestrained above. They do not know how this is to be brought about, but they work to stop it happening.

RAGWORT

He reaches the copse where the witches wait, under a midday moon, and scuttles past with his eyes down.

'Ladies.'

They hiss at him as he kneels and drives a short torch into the ground. The rags around the top stinking of Hilla.

'What are you doing, priest?'

'You think we won't tell?'

'We'll see you gutted, ghost. When She returns, we'll see you made flesh and see you gutted. Flensed. Immolated.'

Cleaver ignores them, plants another torch as they detail the damage they'll do when their newly remembered Goddess comes home.

They echo after him as he makes his rounds, torches every few steps.

One by the wish hounds, sleeping in their kennels.

One by the bone arch entrance of the beast of Bodmin moor, still licking its wounds from its fight with Pel a year before.

When he has placed all that he was asked to, he makes his own trail. Places torches closer together in a line out onto the Undermoor. A watcher would not see pattern here, but Cleaver knows where he is going.

He always knows exactly where his son is.

'My boy.'

He enters the cave, head bowed, and walks towards Callum. The boy, his leather hard skin tight across his bones, is curled on a mat of furs. Cleaver nestles in beside him, wraps his arms around his son and holds three torches tight in his hand.

'I'm here, son, stay with me. Will you do that?' Callum turns, curls his head into his father's chest and nods.

Jacob Cleaver holds his son tight. Night light in hand. Because night time is coming. And his son is afraid of the dark.

GOLD DUST

It is time. The feast day has arrived.

It starts at sunrise. Nancy wakes with a seasick dread, a stomach that just won't settle, to the sound of a beating drum. She jolts at the rhythm, it's in lockstep with her heart. There is no sign of Meliora. She has not seen her grandmother since the tor top lessons. She had searched well into the night and found not a trace—of Knot, either and she's still not certain of their plan. Whatever Mel tells her, something doesn't fit.

Nancy stands and dresses. She pulls on the clothes she's come to think of as a uniform—Pel's coat and regimental trousers, her reinforced shirt—and has slotted her knives, potions and traps into their places before she's had time to think about it. *Why are you going to a feast dressed for a fight, girl?* She has no answer for herself and slides another vial into her pocket. The day is strange. The sky a mat of low hanging cloud. No birds flying, no wind. She opens the door as the brownies make coffee and stands on her porch, frowning. Nothing. No sheep, ponies, or cows. No rabbits. Though there are flags hung in the trees. Scraps of fabric, and fires are burning in billowing black clouds, so the moor seems to make the sky. A hundred furnaces burning the peat into clouds. She takes the coffee as it's handed to her and wrinkles her nose against the bitterness of it. She's no appetite for food.

'Ready Pat?' He is at her heels as always, though he's yawning, and wags his tail. The ride to Mirecoombe only serves to deepen her unease. The world seems hushed. She has to strain even to hear Selkie's hoof steps, her hearing feels dulled. All she hears is the drumming. Louder and louder as she approaches the village. There is nobody about. Houses shut and fires dampened. The drumming is coming from the chapel hill, within the church itself. She can see the quartz that lines the coffin path shaking with each beat. There is another noise, underneath the drums, she had not heard 'til now. A racket of birdsong. Not the trill of songbirds—a thick and tangled cackle. She looks up. The whole chapel roof is black and cawing. A thousand crows. There is a final beat, the drumming and the birdsong stops, and in a single shroud the crows rise in silence, dissipating into the air as the chapel door flies open.

A single bugle call and the drums begin again. No longer the rhythm of her heartbeat, now they beat a dirge. The first to emerge are the wish hounds. Nancy jolts at the sight of the costumes. She cannot see who wears them: each of the four are wearing a mask made from the skull of a fox. From the sockets are iron sconces with tallow candles alight. Their black smoke flames flickering and guttering as the oil spits and crackles. The rest of the costume is a cloak of tattered black, brown, and green strips of fabric knotted into the fleece of black-wooled sheep. The performers twist and writhe, their heads coming to life and scanning about for prey. Nancy wishes now she had gone to a rehearsal. Had known what was coming. The riders come next. Though they look nothing like the wraiths she'd faced they have still, somehow, caught their spirit. There are two, galloping and lilting from the mouth of the church. In one hand they hold a staff topped with a painted horse's head, made from wood and plaster. Black with lips bared over white teeth, their eyes concentric circles. In their other hand, representing the horses' tails, the riders hold leather flails. They have braces on their shoulders, lifting jerkins up above their head and tied tight around false collars, the fronts made from cheese cloth so the riders can see. Around their waists are strung horseshoes that clank as they prance. Nancy knows the format of these parades, those were the beasts, next comes the fool. She feels herself redden as they ride out. Two men, a horse and rider. The horse she recognises as Yestin, who to his very little credit has the decency to look ashamed. He is wearing a grey cloak and is draped in leather straps and brasses. On his back his brother, Luk. A tangled mop of black horsehair on his head, his face crudely painted white, a smear of red on his lips and cheeks and black lines around his eyes. He wears a long green military coat, trousers and boots. It is the least flattering likeness Nancy can imagine, and she is furious, despite herself. She keeps it in check until she sees that on the 'saddle' behind him, is a straw stuffed man with a single button eye.

She starts to storm uphill, a river flowing the wrong way, but an arm on her shoulder stops her.

'Leave them, Nancy.' Abraham Pine-Coffin's eyes are wells of worry and sadness. 'I'm sorry for that, I hadn't seen all the costumes.' He stands with Nancy as a gaggle of children run out in Underfolk outfits. Nancy smiles at them despite her anger. They do look charming. Tattered gauzy wings, faces brightly painted.

'This got away from you more than a little, did it not?' The Reverend nods, eyes fixed on the procession as it is pulled from the chapel door like coloured cloth from a magician's sleeve. He is not smiling. His mouth is set hard against the mummers.

'I left them to it, I'm sorry. I had seen the other but not...'
'Not the foolish Keeper?'
'No. Your grandmother has been helping. I would never have imagined this.'
'My grandmother seeks to teach me a lesson, I fear.'

A string of other animals follows. Less elaborate, for the most part oversized heads woven from wicker and painted. A crow with a beak made from a hunting horn, a curlew with a scythe for a bill. There is a pause in the procession, the children of the village running out with long blue ribbons held between them to form a sea. There are more figures to follow. Horses, cattle, Locryn Calder himself with a bull's head made from cowhide and plaster. The old man moves more quickly than he's done in years, though Cusk is close behind, unadorned, in case his master should fall. Once they are through, the procession stops, the drums too, and all turn to face the chapel. There is a swell of movement inside and people spill out in a flood, crowding around an effigy of their saint. In a raiment Nancy recognises. A version of her grandmother's long black cloak, made from a fabric that must have cost the earth for it shines in the light like a magpie's wing. Into it sewn little mirrored discs that catch the light, reflecting the sunlight onto the congregants and the village in a dance of sunlit freckles. From the collar, a spray of gorse. The golden flowers and green spikes packed into a beautiful, finger-pricking ruff. Atop it a skull. Reagan's, antlered skull. Nancy and Abraham gasp.

'She has the bones.' Nancy looks at the effigy. Sees it clearer now, her grandmother's plan. Abraham sees it too.

'It seems so. Come, we'd best follow if we're to stop this.'

Once the morass of bodies and their saint are free of the chapel there is a drumbeat. Just the one. And on threads the cloak is drawn aside. There is a body beneath woven of willow and stolen bones. Its belly hollow, the weave open, a light burning within. A rushlight in a ceramic bowl to stop the wood from catching. The limbs are ash branches, willow wound round for muscle and fingers, palms open. In the fretwork of wood, the rest of Reagan's skeleton sits, pinning the limbs together. The slender foot bones, the claws, stitched in with golden thread. All present, except Nancy and the Reverend, raise their arms to her. Nancy sees Madge, deep in the throng, her hands caressing Reagan's wicker bird's feet.

Then the music begins.

Horns, fiddles, more drums. A whirling cacophony of exuberant noise, and the congregants begin to dance. Twisting, spinning, leaping into the air from the oldest to the youngest. Nancy sees the faces of Delen Rowe, of Billy Askell in the line and shouts to them but they do not hear her. The procession is moving again. Down along the coffin path, winding through the houses of the village and out, onto the moor. It heads west. Out across the flattened plains at the base of the Queen's Rocks, out past the blue pool. Past the bog where Salan Dell was found. Nancy and the Reverend follow behind. The musicians, the dancers, all are indefatigable. It is the release of a tension that's been mounting for a year, and it comes out in a flood. As the holy well entrance hoves into sight, the dancing slows, panting faces turning forwards. The tall, narrow door stands dark and open, the sound of water rushing up from below. Nancy moves to speak, but the Reverend lays a hand on her arm. Whispers to her.

'This is still mine, in name at least. Let me see if I can quiet it.' Nancy understands, but she is ready for him to fail. It takes a little work for the Reverend to reach the front. People do move to let him pass but they do so grudgingly. Since he lit this fuse, it has remained too far ahead of him to put out, but he will try one last time.

'My friends! Welcome, to this holy place.' He gestures towards the well. 'We are here to give thanks to Saint Reagan, patron of this parish and to God, his son, and the holy spirit.' He does not have them; he can feel it. They are water, he is a net. He tightens the weave. 'I know this valley has seen division. I know it has felt a thing broken apart. I understand the desire to fix it. A first step, the reconsecration of the well, please be silent as we recite the psalm.'

Abraham, head bowed, begins to speak. His voice is soft and gentle, unlike Cleaver whose sermons had been a castigation, Abraham's soothe. And it is working. The villagers, stirred to frothing by the march turn their heads to him. Lower their arms, their flails and torches.

'… Lift up your heads, you gates;
be lifted up, you ancient doors,
that the King of glory may come in.'

As he speaks the last line there is a commotion, a frantic whisper, a declaration spoken in a clear and measured voice.

'Well spoken, Priest, but I will take things from here.' Meliora Ray has arrived.

'Grandmother?' Nancy does not know what to do, does not know which way Mel desires to take this, caught on the cusp of trust. Her grandmother is magnificent. Her cloak has been turned inside out so the magpie feathers shine like spilt oil in the sun, her crimson dress beneath giving the impression she is a flayed bird, her sinews and muscle exposed. At her collar her wide silver gorget. In her hair a hat that Nancy realises with growing revulsion is made of crow's wings, their flight feathers pointing at the sky. Her face is painted, black ash covering her forehead and eyes, and her cheeks and jaw powdered white. Abraham, ever the optimist, extends his hand to shake. It is disregarded. Nancy waits, will give her grandmother the benefit of the doubt. Though she sees that, once again, Knot is missing.

'Friends! As you know, we are here to welcome the Mother,' Mel pauses, briefly, 'to rejoin her with Reagan and ask her to watch over this valley. I would like to help you with this. I am her mouthpiece; I am her devoted acolyte. We offer you true power. Love, sickness and death are all at our disposal. We see no point in judgement. Your consciences are your own. She is two, saint and goddess, and in her division comes your unity. No more worry, no more choice. Today we lead this ritual to bring Her two faces together. Reagan, the Mother, we will join her as one and I will take Her into me. You will not have to fret, any longer, which altar to kneel at. You will kneel to me.'

Nancy shivers as the final nail is driven in. She sees now, with cut glass clarity, the path her grandmother walks. Still, she does not believe it. An accident. A blindness that can be cured. She cannot move, heavy with thoughts of fixing it. Can only listen, as her grandmother casts her spell.

'Some of you, I know, have been blessed with her message. To prove her love is strong. Step forwards.' Delen Rowe, Billy Askell, Madge and the three Calders all step forwards. A handful of others besides.

'Come, you may meet her. You too, girl,' she nods to Nancy, 'and you, Priest.' Those left behind form a corridor for the chosen to walk down. The effigy of Reagan handed to Billy as he passes. Cusk attempts to force his way into the group but Locryn Calder himself bars entry.

'No, my friend. This is my reward not yours.' As he watches his friend walk away, Cusk sees a lifetime of wasted years go with him. Nancy falls into step with Abraham.

'Pantomime, that is all. Once this is done, I will talk to her, straighten it all out. Trust me Abraham, she means to help. She has taken a misstep, that is all. We just need to talk to her.' Abraham smiles sadly at her.

'Nancy, I have seen fanaticism before. And coups. This is both.' They reach the bottom of the well in silence and take their places. Meliora lifts the effigy, leans it gently in a corner and steps lightly over the running water. Faces peer down from the doorway at the top, jostling for a view of the going on beneath.

'Can everyone hear me?' All nod. And it is true, Meliora's voice carries clarion up and out of the well; *every* ear can hear her. 'Good. We welcome the Mother, Reagan, back to us, though she has been long gone. Trapped beneath the name of a saint.' Meliora shoots an accusatory look at Pine-Coffin. 'Today we excavate her, bring her forth, Mother!' Meliora shouts, eyes to the roof of the chamber. 'Wake! Allow me to guide you so you can rule this valley again!' There is the briefest pause then the chamber shakes.

'Reagan! Wake!' Meliora shouts this with less gusto, but the chamber shakes far more than before. The witch's mask slips and Meliora looks unsure for the briefest moment. Then, from the doorway of the well a shadow falls.

'You call, Daughter! Your Mother is here! This valley must pay for its denial of me!'

The figure in the doorway is a woman, her face wreathed in smoke, two antlers breaking through. It smiles and a grin of quartz and copper clink in the dark. All part for it. Meliora kneels. Locryn Calder begins to weep. Nancy stays standing, silent, she catches a whiff of the familiar.

'Forgive the impudent child, my Mother!' Meliora rasps, pulling at the hem of Nancy's coat, but the Keeper ignores her. She'll watch this play out, but she'll not take part.

'Why do you not bow?' The Mother raises her arms, and the room shakes again. Underneath the masquerade, another voice.

They mock me.

Nancy lowers her head and does, now, kneel by her grandmother.

'Mel, stop this. You've woken more than a story here.'

Mel, talking from the side of her mouth, whispers back.

'I told you, girl, if you couldn't play along, I'd play without you.'

This will not stand. This must stop, now.

As the voice speaks, the well walls shake and Nancy catches Mel's look to the "Mother".

'You are right, Mel, I will not play along. This needs to stop.' She stands and begins to walk up the step. Ignoring the whispered fury from behind her. Abraham, looking nervously up, stands to walk beside her, she catches him take his whaletail firesteel from his pocket, and slip it over his knuckles. When she is a foot from the Goddess, Nancy unsheathes her riding crop knife.

'I know your husband, I have stood in His hall, as close as we are now.' The Mother gulps and steps forwards, stage whispers from the smoke.

'Mine Nance, it is I!'

Nancy rolls her eyes.

'I know it is, Knot.' Nancy is swift, she grabs an antler as she digs the blade into the Mother's bare thigh and twists the screaming goddess to the ground. 'Mother, Reagan? Whatever you are I am stopping this.' In a zoetrope flash, Knot flickers into his usual shape and runs whimpering to Meliora's side.

'Mel, you need to trust me. This story has grown too big. Something else is telling it. Listen, can you not hear her?'

They must see me.

Nancy turns at Her voice, the imp's blood dripping from her knife onto the wicker body of the saint.

'Please, they do not know what they do! Mel, can't you feel her?' Nancy's voice cracks and she looks pleadingly at her grandmother. Meliora thinks for the briefest of instants. She tips her head, scrunches her brow as though listening, and when she speaks again it is to someone not present.

'Yes, I understand.' She looks across the chamber, scouring each face. 'A Test! It was a test. She is ready, but She would see Her people prove their love! Who will be the first to cleanse themselves before Her? You, perhaps?' She extends a finger to Madge, who steps closer to the water, though a little of the spell is broken.

'Nancy?' Madge's voice is reed thin and the Keeper takes a step to her friend but is pushed aside by Locryn Calder. Meliora's grin is a sickle.

'Ah, Locryn, old friend. You always thought fondly of me. You, though, Margaret, you did not. You chose him.' Madge starts to speak, her voice a stutter of excuses and apologies. 'Hush, now,' Meliora's eyes are closed, 'it is done. And it was not your fault. You were swayed by the Keeper, by Pel. They are agents of suppression, the Keepers. Even her.' Meliora's look cuts Nancy deep. 'Their time is done. His too.' It is Abraham's time to blanche. 'It is right that you are her chosen, Madge. You are to be our offering. Our salvation.' Locryn Calder, crestfallen, begins to mutter in the crowd. He's drowned out, however, by those not touched by Knot's instigations. A rumble of memories filled with Nancy's help, Pel's too. Nancy sees her chance to bring round the crowd. Locryn's madness falls over him again like a caul. His eyes darting at every sound.

'Enough! Grandmother, this stops now. Whatever this is. You've woken something you did not mean to. She thinks you are poking fun! Tell me, who gave Abraham the sight? Who gave the Murmur the power to fix what it breaks? Who did Knot wake?' The Keeper faces the Witch. Granddaughter and Grandmother. Meliora looks worried, briefly, then the mask is back in place. She leans close so only Nancy hears her whisper.

'Enough of this nonsense. This is pageantry, you know this. Bread and circuses. You know these folk, Nancy. They are easily addled. Don't tell me you are too. I need them with me, completely. They won't follow unless they see blood in the water. Madge will be fine.' She moves her cloak aside to reveal a small vial of red, viscous liquid. 'Lamb's blood. A bait and switch, that is all. Hold firm, girl.' Meliora whips around to face Madge Gould, edging towards Nancy. 'Madge do not waver. You must make amends to Her. To me.' Meliora locks Madge in place with a glare, the flash of a wand unsheathed. The landlady looks to Nancy for help.

'Do as she says, Madge, it will be all right.' Madge's eyes, tear filled, nod.

'I trust you, Nance. I'm sorry I was... Pel told me I would see him again.'

'And you will!' Mel raises her hand, slips the vial of blood into her palm but is knocked aside by Locryn Calder. His madness crowning, his zealotry at its peak. The old man barrels Madge Gould into the freezing water and holds her down.

'My Mother! If it is to be her then take her, but it will be I who sends her to you! Rain down your love! My Mother!'
Yes.
The rocks shake as the old man bellows. 'My Reagan!'
YES.

A split appears in the stone and copper shines through in the torchlight. Nancy leaps to Calder's side and wrenches at his arms, desperate to free Madge from the water. Locryn still screaming two names and the rock still splitting around them.

'Locryn, enough! Mel tricked you! There is nothing, please do not speak Her name!'

Mother Regan sees you, old man. I accept your offering.

All hear the voice. Nancy looks to her grandmother. Meliora is silent, dazed. She gives one last look at her granddaughter and starts to back from the chamber, Knot at her side.

'Damn you, then! Yestin, Luk, help me!' The younger Calders wade in alongside Nancy and pull at their father's arms but the man has the strength of a bull, a lifetime's hard work still remembered by muscle. Nancy tears at him, pulls the grey hair from his head but still he holds Madge down, her arms flailing. From high above, Cusk's shouts echo down but his friend will not be stopped. Nancy reaches for her flowers, but though she rains sparks and fire on the back of the old man, nothing seems to work. He still calls to the saint as he works. The rock splits again, and sparks fly from the stone, catching on the wicker body and its bones, setting it aflame.

Nancy is blind to it.

Madge is still now. Her body limp and Nancy cannot see for tears, she can feel her heart as it tears, and her body fills with the heaviest grief. She screams and uncages the birds. Just as her grandmother had shown her. The Murmur swells, shakes the granite sides of the well and an ossified joist cracks and falls. The ceiling screams and showers rocks onto those below, Yestin catches a stone on the chin and falls down bleeding, those on the stairs suffer broken bones.

Hush, daughter. Let him send her to me. I will hold her safe.

Nancy feels something new, alongside the same change of direction that had allowed her to knit the moor back together. A pushing back, a resistance. She focuses, shakes the floor beneath her feet and lets the Murmur flow into her. She places her hands on the shoulders of Locryn Calder and lets the Murmur out. The chamber fills with the sound of a body's worth of bones breaking into dust. Locryn Calder falls in on himself and is washed into the dark.

I accept your offering.

Nancy, blind to all but her friend, pulls Madge from the water. There is a flicker there, the faintest ghost of life and Nancy holds her tight. Draws on flower after flower to save her.

I said, daughter, that I accept.

She draws on yarrow, to keep Madge warm and watches in horror as the green and black ink is scoured from her, the image of the plant on her forearm lost to the water. She calls on mustard, to shock her friend awake but it burns too. Nancy can feel the tattoo peel from her ankle. One by one, spell by spell, all she might do to save Madge is taken from her until her garden of ink is ravaged, bare skin where help once sat. Nothing left but spells that hurt. Spells that bind. Desperate, she drags Madge further up onto the cold stone steps. She is too late. Madge is gone. Her beautiful face empty of *her*. Nothing left but a body and even that, gods even that, is taken. Madge's frail and quiet form soaks into the stone like a blood stain. Until all that is left is a pile of damp clothes and a smell, Madge's smell of beer and pasties and stables, of home. Of *home*. Already fading. Nancy scratches at the granite until her nails bleed.

Then the spell is broken. The world floods in. From the water's edge a scream.

Luk Calder flies at Nancy and would see her dead, but there, in front of him, Abraham Pine-Coffin. Whaletail steel across his knuckles and a mean right hook and Luk is reeling clutching a broken jaw. The crowd above jostle, the news is passed along, and confusion reigns inside. Delen Rowe and Billy stand woken from a dream, staring at Nancy in disbelief.

'You see?' Meliora's voice echoes from the moor above. 'Your Keeper cares nothing for you, she has killed Locryn Calder! She is in league with the priest, you saw him assault this man. What is that?' She pretends to listen again to a voice in her head and shakes it in mock sincerity. 'She has spoken, she will not appear today, not after this! Come, back to the village. I will tend to those hurt. You,' she points to Luk, 'help cover the well. Leave these two here. We will decide their fate when we have helped the others.' Luk Calder is snarling, but he has been leashed. He submits gladly to a new master and does as he is told. Meliora ushers the bystanders out, then turns.

'I am sorry, girl, I have come too far to go back. The Mother is here? Good! She will help me. She will see what that father of yours has done. She will see what damage he has wrought. Together we will burn it all. A fire for every sister lost. A fire for every year I was trapped. A fire for every betrayal.' She pauses, looks to Nancy with tear glazed eyes. 'You should know, I would have taken you with me. Had you wished to come. I am glad to have met you, Nancy. In another life we could have been family.'

Abraham races up the steps as granite slabs are dragged back in place. Defeated he kicks the flaming bundle of wicker, bone, and blood into the torrent, watches it wash into the stone.

Nancy sits on the shore, cradling the body of her friend, and sings to herself in the dark.

It is done. Blood. Fire. Bone. I am reborn.
I am coming.

STONE PARSLEY

THE DARKNESS OVERWHELMS her. Inside and out. She feels it running through her, she is no impediment to it at all.

'Madge, please, don't leave.'

Abraham feels for her in the ink, lays a hand on her shoulder. He knows better than to offer words, but hopes his presence, his sorrow, is felt. He leaves her to her grief and scrabbles along the walls for a candle. The strike still in his hand. It takes some time, but he finds one, and in two spark-filled strikes he lights it, then the others. The flames low, lacking oxygen. The candlelight gives the well chamber the pallor the vigil deserves. Abraham moves back alongside Nancy.

'I am sorry. If I had not begun this, I—'

'If nothing else is clear today, Bram, it is that my grandmother is to blame for this. All of it. And I for releasing her.' Nancy's voice is thin, as ragged as a windblown thrush. As light as air. She presses her face to Madge Gould's neck and breathes in the last of her scent. The smell of polished glassware and spilt beer, the smell of sawdust. Her voice turns in, so only Madge can hear. *I am sorry I left, Madge, that you were not enough. I should have stayed beside you. What is wrong with me that I only see my family for what they are when I hold their bodies in my arms?* Still sat where Madge's body had lain, Nancy drags her hand through the stream and knows immediately where it leads: a passage to the Undermoor. She can feel the dead drawing the water in like chains. 'You should have seen Pel again, Madge. Your father too. You deserved more than this.' Nancy can feel the tears in her eyes, but they do not fall, she lacks even the strength for that.

'Oh, Gods Madge, where did She send you?' She traces the cold stone and the last of her foundations fall away. The job begun a year ago is finally complete and Nancy crumbles. The sobs wrack her body, and she howls into the stone, the Murmur wails with her, shakes the tomb well and dims the flames of the candles.

Abraham sinks into a sit beside her and wraps his arms around her.

'I know it feels like the end of it all, Nancy, and I know I have not known you long.' He pauses, picks over his words, 'but I promise you. I will be with you in the dark until you remember there is light and together we will find it. I will be by your side when you stand in the sun again.' She moves to hold him, lays her head on his shoulder. 'Not the actual sun, I hope we will see that soon enough, I mean figuratively...' he can feel the smile, small though it is, pressed against his chest and it warms him. 'We will get through this. I will help, just tell me what to do.' Nancy pulls away from the priest and his smell of cedarwood and coffee grounds and wipes her tears away. Takes her grief and presses it down into the box she has kept for Pel. Bolts it shut.

She looks again at the dark water that took Locryn Calder's body away.

'Abraham, Locryn was a churchgoing man, would you speak for him? There is nothing I can do for Madge; I can at least send one soul to its rest.'

'Of course.' Nancy sits and hangs her legs in the stream. She can feel the magic in the cold of the water. It renews her. She motions to Abraham, and he sits too. The stream runs through a narrow channel, Locryn Calder somewhere beyond the black. The Reverend looks into the water to speak.

'He is the resurrection and the life, they that believe in me, though they are dead, yet shall they live. And whosoever believes in G—whosoever believes, shall not die forever.'

Nancy lets a tear fall for the man she has killed, then stands.

'Thank you, Bram. I am sorry, Locryn, you were not a friend to me, but you did not deserve that.' She pauses, then whispers to the dark. 'Mother. Reagan. If you exist at all, hear this. I am ready for you. And I am coming.'

Abraham lays his hand on her arm once again.

'What's done is done, Nancy. To be dealt with later. Now we need a way out of this tomb. The way it was done, the shaking, the stone... can you do it again, to free us?'

'Yes. I can.' It's true she is exhausted, but the Murmur feels stronger than it ever has, here underground, and it has miles left to run.

'Good. Nancy, I do not know what's happened here today, but it is clear we were right. Something is awake, Nancy. Not who your grandmother or that creature intended, but something else. Who did they reach?'

Nancy stands silent in the dark, taking in the peace of it, then exhales with a sharp breath. Speaks to herself.

'Come, Nance, let's get to it again.' Nancy draws the Murmur out. She feels her birds in the stone and sends them flying down veins of quartz. She feels the rock, feels the fissures and gaps and when the Murmur reaches the granite covering the entrance, she lets it fly. The heavy slabs shatter into sand as the vibration is released from the stone surrounding them. The rays of the setting sun set the chamber alight and Nancy steps up into the fire.

OXLIP

The village sits in pews in the chapel, eyes on the only one there who's sure of themselves. Meliora Ray has the village in the palm of her hand; they wait to see if she'll squeeze.

Fifty years in a box and nothing but thoughts of freedom. Of her plan. Her plan that has not quite gone as she had thought. She will have words again with Brock, on the dangers of initiative. It is not that she has qualms. Nancy and the priest damned themselves, her granddaughter chose her side, which stings.

Locryn and Madge, though.

She regrets that. She does. Cusk the only one to remember her that remains. And how long can such an old man last, anyway? He stands at the back, a masterless servant and a heartbroken friend and stares daggers at her. It matters not. She plays the hand she is dealt, and she has been dealt, it seems, a goddess. Truly.

'Friends.' Her voice booms from the pulpit, it ruffles the feathers of the golden eagle lectern. 'You all saw what happened at the well. The Mother's judgement is swift. Few of you remember me. I used to serve you, for a hundred years I served Mirecoombe! But I was cast out, your last Keeper attempted to have me killed. He feared the freedom I offered.' A grumbling from the crowd. Nancy has fought hard this last year to win back their affection, but it has come at the cost of any lingering love for Pel. His daughter's strengths only serving to highlight his weaknesses. 'And now, your present Keeper has shown herself as cruel as her father. Poor Locryn Calder felled, Madge too. He was doing as instructed, Madge Gould would have emerged reborn had he been left to it. The Mother told me so. Nancy Bligh,' Meliora pauses, in for a penny, 'is a poison. She corrupted your preacher. You saw him strike this fine young man.'

Luk Calder nurses the bruise on his cheek, the imprint of a whale's tail rising in a welt. His face still smeared with make-up from the parade.

'Perhaps, and, who am I to say? Her mentor corrupted your last Reverend, too.'

That wound has barely healed but in she sticks the knife.

'The Mother has returned to you. Your blessed Saint Reagan who suffered for you, moons ago. Whose body was lain under this very chapel.' Mel leans into this new truth. 'Both her names scrubbed from the stone. But I have re-written them. She spoke to me, in my internment. Asked me to come and save you. I know she spoke to others too. Those she blessed with her words, step forwards.'

Delen, Billy and—in lieu of their father—Yestin and Luk Calder.

'You girl, did she not heal the division in your heart?'

Delen nods, white as sheet and shaking from the turmoil at the well.

'You, have you not been shown magic?'

Billy, hands fiddling with the cuffs of his shirt, agrees.

'Boys. I am truly sorry for your loss. But did She not give your father back that which he had lost, his faith?'

Only Luk nods, Yestin scours Meliora's face for answers.

'The voice our father heard didn't sound like a saint.'

She holds his gaze and narrows her eyes, clenches her fist. Yestin feels a pressure on the backs of his legs, and he falls to his knees. She has magic enough for him. Only Cusk sees the wrinkled sneer Meliora lets slip as he drops.

'And what does a saint sound like? You are an expert, are you?' Luk kneels beside his brother and jabs him hard in the ribs. He speaks over Yestin.

'Our father was happy, before that witch killed him.' Meliora winces at the word but lets it pass. She has greater fish to fry.

'Do you see? All I had promised—certainty, freedom, peace—would be yours now, had the well ceremony been completed, but alas. It was not.' Meliora waits, lets the news settle over the crowd like a film of dust before continuing.

'No matter. She is coming. She will be united in me soon, we must only wait. In the meantime, I will attend to you. Not as Keeper, but as a friend. Not as reverend, but as a minister. Please, give only what you feel is owed. I have not the limits, the shackles, on me that your Keepers or churchmen had. I'll not stand here and lecture from the back of a tin bird.' Meliora shoves the lectern to the floor, denting the eagle's beak.

'I bring you honesty. Truth. Here…' she waves a hand towards the altar and Knot shimmers into sight. His eyes wide, posture a crouch of hangdog piety. 'Nancy told you the Underfolk were real and asked for your trust. I show you they are and ask only for your… well, whatever you may choose to give.'

There is a shifting in the pews. A burden lifted, replaced with another, and not one man is sure of the weight.

'I have sent men to fetch your Keeper and your priest from their cell. We will decide what to do with them together, when the Mother returns.' She has barely finished speaking when the door of the chapel pushes open, three men standing cap in hand in the light. 'Where are they, I told you to bring them here?'

'I'm sorry, Meliora,' the first man takes a tentative step towards the witch. 'They were gone. The stones are gone, the whole entrance is gone. It is sand.'

Meliora shakes her head.

'I will deal with them, with the Mother's help. Worry not.'

The second man steps forwards, childhood stories of the Coffin Witch rising like bile.

'My—' he does not know what to call her, 'Meliora. There was a message, in the rock at the shore of the stream. A seam of gold, run into the cracks.' His voice falters as the third man steps up.

'I am coming.' His face is white, eyes wide, 'it said, "I am coming."'

Meliora reaches for the lectern too recently overturned. With nothing to lean on she makes a staff of fury and with a fling of her hand the three men tumble backwards out of the church.

'Go now, back to your homes, all of you! I will think on what to do with the Keeper and the Priest. You will know Her, when she visits us, when she comes to make this valley new. I will see you all when She calls us. For now, please, leave me be.'

Pew by pew, Mirecoombe files out. Not quite sure what they have signed up for. The masks and costumes discarded piece by piece throughout the day now litter the village. Make up rubbed clean with the backs of hands and doors quietly shut behind each and every person. Thirsting for a drink, but nowhere to go.

Alone, Meliora lets out a ragged sigh and sinks a little on her podium. She moves her hand inside her cloak, takes a badge between her fingers and presses it tightly, so the image is indented in her skin. She had taken each charm as payment. Some reused from pilgrim's trails, some fashioned just for her. A practice she had stopped when she had lost any pride in her work, lost the belief she should help. When the world turned against women like her. She had always thought she would burn, that they would melt alongside her and be sifted from the ash. They were kept now as a reminder that she had had not.

'My Queen!' Knot has dropped his masquerade and skips about the chapel, leaping onto pew ends, swinging from votive candle holders. 'It worked! You have done it! You have done it. The whole valley, yours,' he giggles, 'Hers, that is.' Meliora climbs down from the pulpit and gathering up her skirts sits on the altar steps.

'Enough, Brock.' The imp does not stop scampering, and she grabs a foot as he passes, hurls him to the back of a transept in a clatter of iron and wax.

'Enough!' The shout rocks the font lid. 'She should not have been able to do that, the way she killed Locryn. When I met her, she could not.' Limping from the shadows, Knot takes a seat beside his mistress and waits. 'That Murmur, that power of hers. I had thought it was the same as mine, *my* grandmother's. It is not. She controlled the grasses, Brock. Living grasses. And in the well, she took it *into* herself. Do you understand? That should be impossible. We are keys to a lock. The knife that cuts the trebuchet's cord. We are not the stone missile. She was stronger once we were back on the moor, stronger again in the well.'

'Does it matter? They all saw her kill the old man. Saw the priest strike his son. Who cares if she is strong. They hate them both.'

'Are you stupid?'

This knocks Knot from his perch, he sinks wounded, to sit at Meliora's side.

'The priest, the sight he gained. Those bones. Your stupid, mindless prattle! You woke her up, you imbecile. She is real, Brock. The Mother is real.'

Knot looks confused, turns furrowed brows to his mistress.

'Is that not a good thing? Is that not what we wanted?'

'She was nothing, Brock! A memory of a memory. A fairy tale for fairies. A myth for creatures long banished to legend. If I had thought, for a second, she was anything but that I would not have gone this route. Not risked it. It is *your* fault. Your ignorant efforts of help. Even you, even a creature as dense and useless as you, *knows* how much power is in a name! But no! Like the giggling halfwit you are, you shout "Reagan! Reagan! Reagan!" from the rooftops even as the echo of your "Mother! Mother! Mother!" dies away.' Meliora's face is frantic, eyes darting and her hands tapping the slate tiled floor.

'No matter. No matter. So, she is real. Then the stories are true, my power is hers. She will *know* me. Will choose me. Recognise me in her. Will give me the power I need to set this wretched valley right. To see me sat on the throne I deserve.' Pushing hard on the floor Meliora stands. Throws her chest out and head back. 'Meliora Ray, Queen of the Witches? Thrown over for a Keeper? Never. Still. That girl has something in her. Too much by far, we must get there first, seize the reins. Come, Brock. We have a goddess to win over.'

Meliora strides from the chapel, Knot bounding at her feet, and as she slams the door behind her she cracks a diamond pane of glass in the newest window. Saint Reagan's mouth shatters into a grin.

* * *

DEEP BENEATH THE earth a polyphonic voice weeps with joy. A King resets his crown and laughs as the tumour he's been afflicted with heals.

Riding through woodlands, that crash with the sound of the sea, a Hawthorn moves past her kinsmen, goosebumps on her skin. She spurs on a heavy horse to galloping.

On an Island, that floats unmoored, beneath the hall of ghosts, something shifts. An eye that's not opened since the world began, flits beneath its sleeping lid.

The Mother is Coming. Be ready.

CROW GARLIC

ABRAHAM PINE-COFFIN SITS by the fire, idly stroking the top of Patroclus' head. Nancy sits opposite and stares into the flames, as though the reflection of them in her eyes can burn away the memories of the day. They have been sat like this for an hour. Abraham has not found a single word that can break through, so he's turned his attentions to the dog. The brownies make themselves busy in the corners.

'Good boy, Patroclus, was it? A good name, boy.' Patroclus whines, he is worried for his mistress. Once he had seen her leave with the festival procession, he had ambled home to find the brownies keening in the porchway. He'd not been able to settle until he'd seen the two figures stumble home. A final pat and the Reverend stands. Moves to the sheafs of drawings on the table. He traces with a finger the portrait Nancy has drawn of Colenso, her name written beneath, and those of Baz and Meliora. This final one holds his gaze.

'You captured the glint. There,' he places a finger on one smudged eye, 'I am sorry, Nancy. I know the sting of familial betrayal.' Nancy still does not look up, but she drops her hand so the dog can lick it, place his head beneath it an ersatz stroke. 'I have many of these books.' Pine-Coffin gestures to her piles of half-read folklore, 'if your grandmother is the witch in half of them, she has had quite the life. If your father is the Pellar in the rest, well, you're a rich brew, Nancy Bligh.' The young man continues in his wonderings, Nancy's head shifts slightly at the sound of his rummaging.

'It was an accident, Nancy.' He has watched her, this past hour, seen the balance of her grief. Madge weighs heavy, it's true, but the death of Calder will sink her. He can see it. 'I have not known you long, Nancy, but I do not peg you for a killer.'

'He saw it in me.' Nancy reaches for a drawing of Pel and Pine-Coffin places the ceramic owl he holds in his hands carefully on the table.

'He warned me about this,' Nancy lifts her hands, the charcoal worn into the grooves of her nails staining the cuticles black. 'About using the Murmur. He *knew* where it came from. Whose heirloom it was. He was right. Colenso was right. Madge was right. All of them were right. I swung a sword I could not hold, and Locryn Calder is dead because of it.'

'He should not have been doing what he was.'

'It does not matter! He should not have died.' Nancy stands, turns, and as she does so she rips the sleeve from her shirt, exposes her shoulder wrought in a garden of weeds. The bare skin where her spells were taken bright in the firelight. Abraham does not turn away, nor does he stare or blush. His golden eyes find the green of hers and lock them tight as she speaks. 'I have, I had, a thousand spells, Bram. A hundred ways I could have stopped him. Instead, I use a tool I know can bring a tor down in a cavern!' She tears her face away, her cheeks wet with tears and her mouth a smile twisted in half with regret. Laughter weeping from it like a cut vein. She raises a hand and without a thought, twists it into a shower of light. A palmtop storm. Closes it and throws a ball of fire into the grate.

'See?' He does. 'Or, I could have done as you did. I can fight, can I not?' She reaches to her waist and flicks a knife into the skirting. Pulls the blade from her crop and stares into the shimmer from the fire as it dances on the metal. 'I have failed and lost them all, Bram.' Her face on his again, a tragedian's mask, the feelings writ large enough to reach the gods. 'I killed a father, a friend. An innocent man. Drove a grandmother I had only just met to betray me and caused the one I already had to drown. I was so cruel to Madge, Bram! A spoilt child.' Abraham walks forward slowly, his eyes still with her, and takes the knife from her hand. Lays it on the table and pulls her into him, squeezes her tight, a hand on the back of her head. His mouth by her ear and tears in his eyes.

'Might I tell you how I see things?' A movement he cannot parse as a shake or a nod, so he continues. 'You, Nancy Bligh, are quite the remarkable woman. You have stepped into the shoes of a father, to a role always held by a man. You have been betrayed and you have lost a dear friend. I have read Cleaver's diaries. I see you in them. Between the lines. I see the shadow that you lived in, that you overcame. I have seen nothing, in Cleaver's words or the tales your community has told me, that shows you to be anything but good, Nancy. Nothing. You made a mistake. So have we all. Perhaps if you are lucky, one day I will list off mine. It may not count for anything; I speak only for myself. I would call you my friend, Nancy Bligh. And be proud to do so.'

It carries no weight. No expectation. It is enough. It is too much. Nancy sags under the weight of his kindness and he helps her to the chair. She grabs the portrait of Colenso on the way and stares into the charcoal eyes.

'She told me not to give my heart to Mel. I didn't listen. I lost her too.' She is about to throw the picture onto the fire when the door opens, and a forest walks in.

'Oh Nancy, you couldn't lose me if you tried.'

RAGWORT

* * *

ABRAHAM LEAVES THE two to talk, exits on the pretence of walking the dog. Nancy pours herself into Colenso's arms and lets the mess of the last four days unfurl. Colenso is a sponge. When Nancy is done, she leans in and kisses her on the forehead, strokes her hair. She leads her to the spare bedroom and lays her down, undresses her and pulls fresh covers over her. Nancy draws her knees up, turns on her side and stares into the light of a candle on her bedside table. Colenso climbs into the space next to her and strokes her hair.

'He seems like a nice man, the priest.'

'He is.' Nancy's voice is a galaxy away, barely audible.

'He was right, I heard him from outside. You are a wonder, Nancy Bligh, a bright and burning light. Don't let this dim you. Don't snuff yourself out over a mistake.'

'I thought I had lost you.'

'I was angry, true. You needed space. I knew Mel would tip her hand in the end. Though I fear I ought to have come regardless.'

'I am glad you are back. I do not know how to fix this.'

Nancy pulls up the sleeve of her shirt, shows Colenso the bare skin where tattoos once bloomed. Colenso lays a hand over it, pulls the sleeve back down.

'You don't, Nancy. Some things can't be fixed. You can keep going though, put the valley right and show the moor you're not one action, you are a million, until one mistake is hidden in a bushel of help, of success. They need you, Nancy. More than they ever have before. The world needs you. I felt it, miles away and I felt it. She is coming. I do not know how, but She is. Meliora will not stop her, that woman would burn the world if she looked good in the firelight. You'll see a way through.'

Nancy turns to face Colenso, her eyes ringed with dark shadows and her nose red from crying.

'What if I can't?'

'You can, Nancy. You've got friends to help you. Now rest.' She sweeps her palm over Nancy's face and the air suffocates from the scent of almonds, of hawthorn blossom. Nancy fades into sleep and Colenso steps quietly from the room. Abraham is back from his walk.

'Priest.'

'Miss. Colenso.' She stiffens at the use of her name, but Abraham indicates the drawing on the table, the dryad's name neatly labelled beneath. 'Apologies for any informality. I make a habit of it.' Colenso looks the young man from head to foot. What she sees from her assessment she cannot say but she sits and motions him to join her.

'I hear you have quite the right hook, Reverend.'

'Bram, please. Ha, yes. I am not sure that is what a community looks for in a priest.'

'This community might be glad of it, Bram. I've been coming here for a long time, and it always seems to be in trouble. She can't fight all the battles alone.'

'I'll do what I can.' Colenso sees him look at her, a different look to the one she'd expect. His eyes are appraising, yes, but whatever they are searching for it is not her physical form. She lets him look.

'You are a nymph?'

She lets out a snort of a laugh.

'A nymph? No priest. I have sense in my head.' The Reverend smiles, tries again.

'A dryad.' She nods, impressed.

'How could you tell? Few do. Nancy didn't.' Abraham leans back to revel in his deductions. A vice he indulges in often.

'Your hair, it is not quite copper, there is green in it. When the light hits it right. Your scent, of course. No perfume could match that smell so perfectly. And your eyes.'

'What of them?'

'They are too old. They have seen too much for a girl your age. I've read enough to have a few options at my disposal. Had I not struck on this one I might have guessed you were Irish royalty, of the *old* families you understand. Perhaps some form of Rusalka. I came across people who spoke highly of them in the Baltic.'

Colenso sits quietly for a moment. She takes the pin from her hair and lets it fall over her shoulders.

'A good guess. The eyes, I will give you, the scent too. The hair though, that you should not be able to see. I do not think even Nancy sees that. You have the sight, Reverend?'

'A recent gift. Given by Reagan. The Mother, as you call her.'

Colenso starts.

'I call her nothing. As we all should. She ought not exist, let's not continue giving oxygen to her names.'

Colenso and Abraham stand in the fading firelight.

'Let's hope you live long enough to enjoy your gifts, let's hope we all do.'

The fire burns down to an ember, and the sun rises with trepidation to begin the day.

BLOODY DOT

THE UNDERMOOR is busy with guests. A river not used for centuries and before then, rarely, has begun to deliver its cargo again. The ferryman, long retired, not ready for their arrival. Locryn Calder stands blinking under the rippling moon, hanging in the watery sky. For the first time in a decade standing tall. Clear headed.

'Dad?' Jan Calder stands watching his father, his body remade, a little piskie, cap in hand. His father kneels to see him but has no time to answer. The pool he stepped from boils, steam rising from it in iridescent clouds. A figure, a wicker woman, emerges. The wood ablaze it burns the very air around it. As the willow burns away a woman emerges. Her skin the colour of an autumn sky, mottled with the fingerprint marks of a leopard picked out in white. Her hair a mane of black. Her horns, which are growing, are those of a stag and beneath her knees she has the legs and talons of a bird. From her shoulder blades wings unroll, those of a lacewing. She extends an arm, and a staff appears, a stave of whitebeam. From its top jangle silver bells in the shape of a bushel of apples. Finally, from the water beneath her, a column of liquid gold. It wraps around her foot like a snake gaining hold and coils around her, finding a point between her breasts, and burrowing deep. It makes its nest in her ribcage where it beats itself into the shape of a heart.

She stands blinking in the moonlight, watches as the Underfolk funnel from every rill, every path. Amongst them striding the God of the Mire. Out of his chamber for the first time in centuries and back cracking as it straightens, his tattered robe disintegrating at the touch of the light.

The King wades through his subjects like they're leaves.

'Mother.'

He kneels and creaks like a tree in the wind. The Mother, Reagan, regards him impassively. The King is about to speak when a ghost interrupts him.

'Reagan! Saint Reagan!' Pel, quite comfortable as orator, addresses the presence before him. A plan that only calcified as he ran here. He looks, sees the confusion on the faces of the Underfolk. Hears the muttering of Mother, over and over again. 'Yes, Sainted Reagan. Hear me, please. Reagan. Saint of Mirecoombe. Protector of Mirecoombe. I too, have held that role, though not for the last year. My daughter, Nancy, perhaps you have met?'

The addled ghost turns.

Nancy.

'Yes! She is my daughter.'

My daughter.

'Yes, quite, please. You were not supposed to wake. Not supposed to hear what you did, you need to sleep. Reagan, listen.'

Reagan.

She tips her head, as though listening, to the echo perhaps of her twin names as they fall through the floor of the chapel. She is caught between them. Pel watches, eyes wide, as she considers both. Then the chanting begins.

MOTHER. MOTHER. MOTHER.

Every spriggan, every piskie. The witches, the hounds, the

riders, all chant her name. The God of the Mire chants her name. He has lost her, Pel sees it. The God, the God he has been tethered to this past year brushes him aside to stand before Her.

'Mother. That is who you are. This wretch lies. He has infected this place. Infected me. Remove him, I ask this of you.'

Pel starts, raises his hand.

'Listen, I—' he is stopped by a pain. Something he had been sure he'd left behind, that doubles him over in agony. The Mother, head cocked, is staring at him, at the King. She lifts her hands, places her palms together and points at the pair before her, then she pulls her hands apart. Pel screams and the moon above flickers as a ghost is torn from the mind of a god. When it is done, as Pel lies panting on the floor, the God of the Mire stares at him.

'There. Lord Hunt. It is done. I am myself again.' He turns to face Her, whoever She may be, and inclines His head. 'Thank you, Mother. We are ready to follow you, to the world above. To reclaim what was once ours.' He raises his enormous, branch-like arms above his head and claps. Once. It sounds a war drum. A sky breaking thunder that sets the moon to rippling.

In the distance, heavy footsteps break into a run as every creature, beast, and spirit of the Undermoor races to welcome the Mother home, to join her in her return to the surface.

On the floor, Pel whispers to himself.

'Oh, dear friend. I hope you did as you were asked.'

Yes, every creature races to Her. Including a giant who's thousand head of cattle, with gold on every hoof, race with him. Hooves that spark as they hit the granite. Spark and light the tallow wedged in every fissure and crack.

Hilla's smoke billows and boils from the ground. An army of monsters felled by sleep. A father and a son who go into the dark together. Pel smiles even as he fades to sleep with the rest of them. Whispering as he does.

'You are Reagan, confused one, Reagan. Not the Mother.' He sees, just before his eye closes, that She has heard. Then Gogmagog, standing before the smoke can reach him, lifts Her high above the fug. As he stands, he grows, his head hitting the ceilinged sea and breaking right through in a tsunami of moonlit rain.

LOVE IN A TANGLE

SPRING RAIN. EVERY drop of water warmed by the sun it falls through. The ruins of Echo Tor stand tall against the clouds, its crenelations fallen, its top a sandcastle trampled flat. On a natural plateau Meliora Ray stands reinvented. Her red dress gone, she wears white today, though the cape remains. She has a wreath of blackthorn on her head, a careful graft of thorns so well cut that the flowers still bloom, bees still feast on the nectar. She is barefoot, and in her hand, she holds a stave cut from the same wood as her crown. Knot stands at her side, chest pressed out and beaming, though he flinches each time Mel's hand draws close.

Before her stand the village. The madness of the day before has faded, and they have woken to another tragedy. Not for them the post storm quiet, they rush from tempest to tempest. The Nest is closed, so they cannot even drown their sorrows. They wait quietly to do as they are told.

'Friends! Good morning. You feel her too, do you not? Today we rise anew.' Meliora throws the cape from her shoulders, a few white feathers shaking loose as it falls. 'Your former protectors run from you, they would not face you yesterday and,' she scans the crowd, 'they will not face you now. I will face you. I will seize Her light and shine it on to you. Mother Reagan.' She smirks at the contraction.

'She will give her gifts, to you, through me.' There is a hubbub building from both ends of the crowd. The front lean forward to receive their gifts, just as the back split apart. Meliora frowns at the cleaving. Three figures walk steadily through the crowd. Abraham Pine-Coffin wears his bands of office, a neat, pressed cassock and his wide brimmed hat. He has his satchel, his tinder box and strike inside, and a flask of altar wine for courage. Next is Colenso, wearing a green satin bodice and a gathered bunch of skirts. Barefoot with one hand at her side and the other in Nancy's. Nancy Bligh who comes dressed, once again, for a fight. Though in a new garment. Pel's coat at home, she wears a loose gansey sweater, recently knitted from grey-green wool and covered in hanging knotted threads. Her black hair kept up with the blackthorn pin Colenso had given her a year before and a green ribbon tied around her neck. Nancy lifts her thumb, presses the base of Colenso's hand, before letting go.

'I've shirked nothing, grandmother. Nor has he. I will speak for the both of us.' Nancy walks up the hill and stands by Meliora. In voice only two can hear Nancy Bligh whispers,

'You are making a mistake, Mel. The wasp's nest you have been shaking was not dead. It had a queen inside. Sleeping deeply but now awake.' Meliora smiles wide enough to show teeth.

'I know.' She laughs at the worry on Nancy's face then turns to snap at the crowd.

'My loves! I promised you fairness, did I not? No dictate, no proclamations. I keep my word. A reminder, first. Step forward, Her acolytes.'

Once again Delen, Billy, Luk and Yestin stand forward from the crowd. Only Yestin's eyes don't shine with fervour. His eyes are pinned to his feet. Nancy tries again.

'Are you this arrogant? You saw Reagan's bones, they were burnt through, Mel. If your story is true, then what if it all is? You think to persuade Her to what, reside in you? She'll burn you out.' She is ignored.

'As the chosen four, you will represent this valley. I ask you. Has the time for Keepers ended? Can this girl lay down her burden?'

Delen Rowe steps forward.

'Aye. Nancy, please forgive me but perhaps it is for the best. This valley needs unity, not division. It is being given to us freely, do not stand in our way.' Nancy stiffens against the betrayal. Luk is the next.

'End it.' A man of few words, Luk's eyes bore into Nancy's. His brother stays put.

'Two left. Come, boys, why dally?' Meliora's focus is on Yestin, Nancy's too, so much so neither notice Billy Askell step forwards. Nancy grimaces in surprise.

'Billy? Why?'

'You promised to keep me safe, Nancy, and you have. She will give me magic. I will be magic. I can help you.' Nancy is furious.

'Your life was mine to direct, was it Billy? You would be *dead* if I had not stepped in. You are a fool, more now than ever before. You think she will give you magic? She will blind you with stardust and leave you begging in the dark.' Billy moves to speak but Nancy has turned to Yestin. 'Go on then, follow your brother.' Yestin stays put.

'No, Nancy. I'll not be a part of this. I do not believe an angel, or a saint, spoke to my father. I saw what you did, what he did. Nobody in that well was blameless. I'll not be the end of this valley.'

Meliora rolls her eyes.

'A noble but fruitless stand. Well done. It is three to one, does anyone else in the crowd disagree?' Cusk raises his hand but is disregarded. 'Good. Raise your hands then, we must ask the Mother what the punishment will be. All those present lift their hands, close their eyes, and pray to the promise of a goddess.

Abraham Pine-Coffin prays to God, then prays to Saint Reagan, asks for her aid again.

Colenso prays to a bedtime story.

Nancy prays to the moor itself.

All of them answer and the world ends, in an Amen of dirt and light.

It begins as a tremor, the whole moor become a quaking mire. The centre of the quake is the cap of the Queen's Rocks. The Queen's Rocks that are being rent apart. The sound the earth makes as it splits is deafening. Behind the crowd Mirecoombe trembles, slates and chimneys fall. It is only the boundary trench, mitigating the tremors, that saves the whole village from falling, but the lightning blasted tree finally releases its hold on the long house, tearing the building apart as it goes. Every nesting bird, every falcon and hawk and owl screech up from the grasses and trees. Fox and rabbit race, blind to each other, towards stable ground. The two sides of the hill separate by a foot, then two, then a chasm. Great fingers finding purchase on stone and driving the two halves of the hill aside. There is the sound of grunting, of a burden being shouldered and as a head of blood red hair breaks the surface the clouds themselves part to let him pass.

Gogmagog is risen again.

'The sky is dry; can you believe it?

The sun strips the moonburn away.'

He stands tall, the rent in the earth at his waist, his head blocking out the sun and throwing those present into shade. From the sides of the pit, arms reach then fall as the Undermoor's army falls asleep, Hilla's smoke curling from the hole and halting the sea of monsters. All the help an old ghost could give.

It was the least that he could do.

Gogmagog rights himself, then begins to change. His already pallid skin turns grey, his veins fill with quartz and tourmaline. The giant is turning to stone. In a bid to escape, the two halves only recently joined struggle to tear apart, two faces screaming out of one head. They manage, at last, to separate but it is too late, and whether by accident or design the Queen's Rocks are now an echo of Echo Tor before its destruction. Two stacks where there once was one, the two hills switched, each side bearing the chiselled face of a giant that misses its brother. In between both, hanging in the air, is the Mother. Reagan.

The Mother who is coming.

Saint Reagan who is here.

Nancy loses all sense of herself; she feels as though she is floating. The Mother swells until she is twelve feet tall and lifts into the air, feet pointed down. One hand raised in twisted benediction, the other gripping her staff.

'Mel!' She shouts to the woman muddying her white dress, kneeling in the mud. There is a manic smile on the witch's face. 'Mel, you did this, help me stop it!' Her grandmother turns wild eyes on her.

'Quiet, girl!'

Standing, Meliora Ray walks towards the vision of the Mother, waves of light and energy pulsing from her. Already the Mother is losing her form, her body slipping, reforming, then melting again. The truth of her scrabbling for purchase.

RAGWORT

'My Mother! I am your servant, Meliora Ray, Queen of the Witches, and I kneel to you. Offer myself as host!'

Nancy shouts up, through the rain.

'Mel you don't need to do this! You made this story up, she doesn't need a host, she doesn't exist! If you stop telling the story, we might have a chance!'

Meliora smiles, hungrily, sadly at her granddaughter and reaches out for the goddess.

As she does, the pulsing stops. The moor falls silent. Nancy curses.

'Reagan! I offer myself! Nancy Bligh, Keeper of the High Moor I...'

She does not finish, Knot barrels into her, knocks her flat and any hope of a choice is gone as the Mother turns to Meliora. She rises, turns into a shining cloud, and funnels into the witch's open throat, dropping her staff to the floor. Mel buckles at the heat, her skin blisters, blackens and cools back to ivory. She stands, slowly, looks at her hands, the magic seeps from them like water from moor stone.

'Yes! Thank you, my Mother. I should not have doubted you. Mirecoombe! Do you see? Kneel for your Queen. Kneel for your Mother!'

Nancy takes her grandmother by the shoulders, she's hot to the touch.

'Meliora, this is too much, let Her out, please. She will kill you.'

'Jealous, are you, granddaughter? You think yourself special, I have been bound for fifty years! No Keeper, blood of mine or not, could stand against me in my prime. I am renewed and I will have my due.' Meliora draws her wand, her silver ragwort stem, and watches in awe as it blossoms. Nancy takes a step back.

'Mel, you can't control Her, She's raw magic, it is too much. Let Her free, let Her fade away. Let her sleep.' Mel turns and Nancy could swear for a moment she looks into two sets of eyes.

'No. I can do this. Brock!' She calls over Knot, who scampers to her side. 'You've not been yourself, *look at you*. All rotting wood and moss. Where is that wonderful face I knew? Would you like it back?'

Knot nods and Meliora splits his skull in two like a horse chestnut shell, pulls the skin from him. Nancy gags as Knot screams out, as his muscles meet the late spring air. Red sinews that Meliora plucks like piano wire as she flays him. When she is done fine tuning, Meliora places a hand to Knot's chest and pushes him backwards, knocking him off balance. He lands, tumbles and though it's hard to say how as he comes out of the rolls, he is changed. His skin regrown. He is taller, too, as tall as a man though his proportions are odd. As he stands, shakes himself out he stares at his hands, his paws. At his shaggy coat of grey, white and black hair. Wrinkles his long snout and bares sharp teeth. A badger standing tall as a man.

'Thank you, Meliora.'

'Thank you, Brock. Now, come with me. Our new home awaits.' Meliora has barely taken a step when she falls to the ground. Everyone feels the burst of magic, it explodes like a quarry bomb and Delen Rowe screams with a voice the scent of spring.

The girl's eyes are blank, and as she screams her skin cracks. Forms into the shape of daisy petals that peel one by one from her face. The screaming changes into a howl and the rest of Delen Rowe uncoils like an anchor rope, its weight kicked into the sea. Chains of flowers, stem through stem, until nothing of the girl is left but a tower of seeds. Meliora straightens, clears her throat, and uproots a stem of ragwort. Straddles it and begins to rise. No need of her salve now.

'Grandmother, stop, you aren't in control of this!'

Billy Askell's skin bubbles and boils under some internal heat, and then he is burning. His ashes and the sparks of his life heading heavenward.

'Meliora Ray, you know who I represent, don't make me visit them!' Colenso, at Nancy's side, raises her voice but still sounds gentle as a breeze. It matters not.

'Nancy, this sapling needs cutting down. You'll get splinters if you're not careful!' Meliora reaches out to Colenso and sharp thorns pierce the dryad's skin. At the first sign of blood Nancy lets loose her birds.

'You should not have taught me I was in control, grandmother, let her go.' Nancy takes every beating bird in her Murmur, winds them like a coiled spring and launches them at the witch with the power of a shooting star. The ground splits and a shelf of granite knocks Meliora from her perch, sending her tumbling down the bank, the grass turning to copper as she hits it, the metal tearing at her skin. Nancy does not see; she is at Colenso's side.

'I am all right, Nancy, after her.'

Nancy reaches the base of the hill as Meliora rises higher; the pulses are quicker now. At the next there is a bellow from the throat of Luk Calder, whose slack, broken jaw clicks back into place as it lengthens, whose forehead splits at each temple so the horns can grow. Whose brow stretches and deepens, whose throat expands into a wattle of folded muscle and flesh, his eyelashes lengthening around baleful eyes. Luk Calder has the head of a bull. He charges Nancy, horns down, they catch on the edge of her jumper and tear right through.

'Luk, if you are in there, enough!' Nancy doesn't have time to play toreador with him, Meliora is back in the air. Luk cares not.

'Enough!' Nancy raises her hand, crackling with the harebell fire, waits for Luk to charge. He does, head down, until his brother stands in the way. Luk clatters to a halt, Yestin's hand on his nose. He stands panting and pawing in the sun.

'I have him, Nance, go.'

Nancy follows her grandmother by the trail of the changed. A girl turned, in a flash, to a charm of goldfinch who bully each other into the sky. A man now nothing but worms in an apple. Those that are passed over stare with wide eyes at the new world. There is no pattern, no control. As Nancy passes a sheep it twists, grows a shell and scales, begins belching fire. In the stables, horns drive bleeding from the brows of the horses. The ground itself changes. Splitting and spewing black tar from the wounds. Granite rocks become quartz; slate becomes obsidian. Birds fall from the sky, their wings turned to arms.

Meliora has reached her goal, the Mother's staff still lying on the floor. She lifts it, shakes the silver apple bells and the noise from them seems to wrap itself around the world. A peal of birdsong with the echo of thunder. Those unchanged, Nancy, Meliora and the rest clamp hands over their ears.

'Please, Mel. Let Her go. We don't need Her.'

The Witch's eyes turn to Nancy and for a moment, Meliora seems to truly see her granddaughter. Nancy who is silent and shaking, and for the briefest second, she seems to consider it. In the distance, Colenso and Abraham take a step forward, but Mel raises a hand and stops them in their tracks. Feet bound to the ground with grasses. The air pressure changes, and it feels as though a vice holds Nancy's head.

'Nancy. Don't make me hurt you.'

The pressure in Nancy's skull intensifies then stops, as though a pick has been driven in to relieve the pressure, and Mel starts screaming. Nancy can see her grandmother's skin light up from the inside, can see every vein, a shadow play of blood. Every muscle in Meliora's body tenses. Nancy cannot bear to watch her writhe and reaches out. The movement triggers something within the witch, she stiffens, clenches her fist, and bites her mouth shut against the screams, as though swallowing foul food. When she speaks it is through clenched teeth.

'Get back. She is mine. She is mine.' By some superhuman control Meliora draws the Mother deeper in and her skin returns to porcelain, freshly fired. Glazed with sweat. Her eyes, that have been clamped shut, open and Nancy recoils. They are dulled and milky. Her grandmother is blind.

'Mel, your eyes…'

'Mean nothing, Nancy. Nothing means anything now I have the power to change it all. Watch.' Meliora raises her hands and covers her face. When she removes them there are two eyes crudely painted onto her eyelids. Nancy watches open mouthed as the pigment sinks into the skin, filters through pores like rainwater into turf and when Mel opens them, her eyes are whole. Brock, who has cowered and hidden since his rebirth, moves nervously into the open. Meliora smiles at the sight of him.

'Come, Brock.' Meliora extends a hand to the creature, and the two rise on a sudden influx of warm air, a wind that seems to herald an early summer. 'And you? Help your friends. Those you have left, at least.' Meliora raises a hand, and the ties binding Abraham and Colenso begin to pull them below the moor.

Cursing her grandmother, Nancy races to her friends, calls on her twine of ivy to raise them up and out of the clutches of the roots. By the time she is done, Meliora is away over the top of Echo Tor. Over the fractured husks of Gogmagog, over the trench still spewing monsters onto the grass. Past the meadow that once was Delen, and the electrically charged air that was Billy. Past Luk Calder bellowing at the sky as his brother tries to lead him home. She flies up the chapel hill, into the church, the heavy doors swinging shut behind her.

ALL SEED

IT HAD BEEN a struggle, getting her home. Once Meliora had left, Abraham and Colenso had raced to Nancy's side. The moor, Mirecoombe, was a mess. A nightmare of bodies and blight. Nancy immobilised in the face of so much that needed fixing. In the end, they had dragged her, one arm each, across the fields to Nancy's cottage, Patroclus barking at the door to greet them. At the sight of her dog, Nancy had fallen, wrapped her arms around his shaggy neck and pressed her face to his fur.

'Oh Pat, you're not changed!' The dog had barked, cheerfully, and turned inside as they bolted the door. They sit, now, around a brownie-built fire and try and drive away the chill. It is Abraham that breaks the silence.

'Well, I came here to find the unbelievable, so I only have myself to blame, I suppose. Nancy, might I ask your brownies for that wine they make?' He laughs nervously. Nancy ignores him, but the brownies fetch it anyway. She has turned to Colenso.

'What is Meliora now, Col? Can we stop her?' The dryad is staring into the fire. Watching the kindling as it burns.

'I'm sorry, Nancy. I should have taken her more seriously, and her stories.'

'You knew this could happen?'

'Of course.' Colenso catches herself. 'I don't mean to be glib. I'm sorry, love, it's one of those things. Our things. We take it for granted, I suppose.'

Nancy pushes herself onto her feet, wraps her arms around herself and stands with her back to the fire.

'Your things?'

'You know what I am. A creature of myth, a folktale. A story told at bedtime. We are all of us strengthened by the telling.'

'You're more than that.'

'Am I? What are any of us but stories' Colenso stands and takes Nancy's face in her hands. 'It's a magic, of sorts. Stories stoke the fires of us. Gods and their believers, monsters under beds. Offerings left on the moor. Tales told by firelight. Pel knew it, more than most men, did he never explain?'

Nancy pulls free.

'What do you think? Why didn't you tell me?'

'It takes time, Nancy. A long, long time. It never crossed my mind Mel could conjure a goddess. Even in the years she's been gone. I'm a fool, I let her tell you, tell everyone about the Mother. Spin her yarn. If I had thought something would hear her stories, answer them? I'd never have let you come back here.'

'I don't know, I think I might still have come.'

Abraham, on his third glass of gorse wine, giggles.

'Yes, me too.'

Colenso turns to the Reverend.

'Abraham Pine-Coffin, you have a remarkable knack for trouble.' He has the courtesy to blush. 'Perhaps place that glass down now, though, if you don't want that trouble catching up with you.' He does as he is told, and Colenso turns back to Nancy. 'I don't know Nance, I don't know if we can stop Her. If it is as you believe, if she is the echo of Reagan, brought back with stories, I do not know how we could stop Her. Mel, perhaps we stand a chance with.'

Nancy looks to the window. To the storm clouds raging outside.

'Can She be reasoned with?'

'No. If She believes the story then it's as good as true and the story has her a goddess.'

Nancy begins to pace, frantic, bone tired. Chewing on her fingernails as rings run round her eyes. Colenso grabs her as she passes.

'Stop, Nancy. For a moment. Take a breath.'

'Not until this is done, Col.'

'You've lost more friends in two days than most do in half a lifetime. Nancy, please, just stop for a moment.'

Nancy brushes Colenso from her and paces the room. Rattles out questions.

'She went into Meliora. Why? Answer. She was invited.' Nancy frowns, turns her worry and frustration to the job. 'She's following Mel's story, Col.'

'Then we change it!' The Reverend is on his feet, a finger pointed to heaven, knocking over the wine at his feet. Colenso might be worried, but he cannot resist the game and stands rosy cheeked as the wine pools at his feet. 'She is following Mel's story, not Reagan's. I have her hagiography, Reagan was good person, she healed and helped, she lost her head, we tell her that one. Make her see. She is a ghost with two stories in her head. We must make ours the better one.'

'That's all well and good, Reverend.' Colenso waits for him to sit. 'But first we must get close enough to tell it.'

Nancy stops pacing. Picks at the threads of her sweater.

'We remind her who she is. The girl that died for this valley. Who lost her head.'

Abraham smiles.

'You read the books, Nancy. Yes. That's when the horns appeared, when the teeth changed. Supposedly Reagan carried her head with her to the hill, then directed the digging of her tomb and the building of the chapel above her. Then, when they were done, she lay in her coffin and died.'

'They built a church on her. How much must she have heard, in all those years?'

'A great many things. More importantly, a great many versions. I gave you the hagiography I first found, more arrived from Exeter. These stories, they were copied over and over and each time the scribes added things. Bored, they would embellish, elaborate or just plain change things. If this, are we sticking with ghost?' The assembled group nod. 'Very well, if this ghost imagines herself to be Reagan, she has heard far more stories in her head about her than the Mother. Your grandmother, those creatures and people she has swayed, are just the loudest voices. We need to be louder to change the story.'

'But softly.' Colenso is stood leafing through books. 'It can't be a wrench; we can't just swap the tales. We need to merge them.'

'So, what do we do, I'm not dying telling her bedtime stories. Can we separate her from Mel? Starve her of a host?'

Colenso looks at the floor, face pale.

'We offer her a better one, Nancy, we offer her you.'

THE BADGER BROCK does not know what to do. He cowers above the rood screen amongst the carved creatures and wrings his paws as the chapel writhes beneath him. The golden eagle lectern flaps heavy wings, beating the metal on the floor and letting out screeches that sound like tearing steel. The lead in the windows melts and runs in rivers, the panes left behind fusing together the images moving between each window, and on the walls the fresco subjects tear themselves from the gesso and dance through the knave. Meliora sits on the large carved chair by the altar, knuckles white and gripping the armrests, and eyes clamped shut. Every few seconds a grunt or yelp of pain escapes her, and some new atrocity happens.

'Mel, I—'

'Quiet! I have Her under control. She just needs time, so settle—argh!' Another scream and the wooden creatures that Brock sits amongst start to paw at his fur. Finally, Meliora's grip on the chair relents and she forces herself to stand.

'I can feel Her, Brock, Her power. I need not have worried about my granddaughter, or Pel or any of them. If I had known she was really here, under my feet, I would have run to her a century ago. The world is mine to shape, little one. I gain a little control every time, soon I will be able to direct it. And we will never be stopped.'

Brock shakes but nods his head and swings himself down to the floor. He can hear the bodies that lie beneath rising, beating bony fists on the stone.

'Your granddaughter—'

'Let her try, Brock, I will not hurt her if she gives me no cause to. There is no need for her, for any of them any longer. I am all this moor needs. I am what the world deserves. Come. Gather the Underfolk, the giants, gather the villagers and the monsters and bring them to the moor. I would speak with them all.' At the doorway, Meliora doubles over, hands shaking, and the carved faces in the arch of stone drop one by one to the floor, grinning as they roll about the witch's feet. In the churchyard the stone effigy of the Reverend Cleaver turns over in his sleep.

'GO! Brock. Now!' The badger lumbers down the hill and wonders as he goes if there is anything left to pray to. Anything at all.

SKULL CAP

THE BATTLEFIELD IS waiting. The sky is on fire and the rain tries hard to put it out, grey clouds marching on the sunset.

It sets the drops to burning.

The hills that roll out from the village are covered in the bodies of the transformed. Of the calf whose head grew so large it snapped its own neck. Of the lamb whose wool is now golden snakes that twist and burrow in on it, devouring themselves a coil at a time with the hiss of coals dropped into water. Meliora Ray rises above it. Her cloak fluttering in the wind. Her ragwort steed turned to filigreed silver; the starry flowers beaten gold. An echo of her wand. She grips the stem tightly in her hand, the waves of power from the being she has caged threatening with every falling raindrop to escape. This is her battlefield. It is her castle she defends.

From the foothills of the Queen's Rocks comes rebellion.

Nancy has ridden to the fight. Selkie dressed for battle, her faceplate fixed. Behind her stand the Reverend, Colenso, and Patroclus. Behind them the moon is rising, to watch the lunatics fight. Nancy's gansey sweater is snug under Pel's old coat that billows around her, whipping in the wind. In her right hand is the eel glaive, the long-handled spear that Busker had stuck her with. Another legacy of Eythin. Around the haft end Nancy's tied ribbons that flutter in the gale.

RAGWORT

'Face me!'

Meliora turns on an eddy of air and rides her bushel of ragwort down. Drawing level with her granddaughter.

'Go home, Nancy. I am not something to fight. Not anymore.' Nancy glowers at the witch.

'I am not talking to you, Mel. I'm talking to Her. Reagan. That's who you are, St. Reagan. Healer of the sick, saviour of the valley. Who lost her head when it came to it but didn't let it stop her.'

The moor shakes like a meteor's hit it. Meliora doubles over in pain, shoulders hunched, but she stays astride the ragwort. Forces herself back upright and speaks through gritted teeth.

'She is mine, Nancy. You had your chance. The Mother chose me.'

'Reagan! Which story should I tell? The one, perhaps, where you found a lamb lost in the fellmire? That you pulled from the jaws of a wish hound?'

'You think you can trick Her?'

'I'm not talking to you. I'm talking to Reagan! Perhaps I should tell the story of your teeth? How to save the moor from famine you plucked out your teeth, tore them from your jaw and planted them in the soil where they shot like lightning into the earth and showed the miners where to dig for hidden veins of ore? Your teeth replaced with the minerals you found for them. Or when you saved a devil from the beast of the moor and were given horns for your trouble. Or perhaps, the time you joined a Keeper? When he made space within his body, the better to do good.'

Meliora folds again, the moorland shakes.

'Lies! She's telling you stories!'

'Yes, Reagan! I am. Trust me. Leave the witch and join me. She means harm unless she's paid to help! Join me and we can do right by the valley. You spoke to me, did you not? You gave your sight to my friend here. You helped me tame the gift you gave me.'

Nancy smiles, eyes wide, and releases the Murmur, lets her birds arc up and around Meliora, down into the earth. When they emerge, they do so a wing at a time. Caught on roots that wrap around the ragwort stem her grandmother rides on. Tipping her from it like a bucking horse. She lands, and the grass boils like pitch. Meliora's eyes burn with rage and Nancy can feel the heat from meters away. Still, Nancy knows she has Her.

'Join me, Reagan.'

In the books Nancy reads, battles have direction. There is an order to it. This is not like that. Meliora strikes without speaking. She lifts her fine-wrought ragwort and rises again into the air. She reaches into her cape that billows around her and brings out a small, feathered object. Nancy can barely see it.

'You're speaking to me, now, granddaughter.' Nancy can see the effort it is taking Mel to hold Her in. Sweat beading in every pore. 'Here, Nancy. Catch.' Meliora throws the object down and Nancy reaches for it, it is only as it is nearing, she sees what it is. A starling with its eyes put out. She pulls back her hand and as the bird hits the grass there is a smell of sulphur, of wood burning and the sound of slate shifting on a slope. Selkie rears, and Nancy is thrown. She lands hard on a patch of granite and hears her ribs crack. Colenso rushes to her but is stopped with a look. Nancy rises alone. Reaching into her pocket, Nancy draws out a glass bauble, hurls it at the witch. Meliora flaps her magpie cape, avoids the projectile but as it shatters below her a shower of sparks rise upwards, catching on her feathers, the keratin smouldering. Meliora struggles to free herself of her cape before the whole thing goes up, falling in flames to the floor, filling the air with the smell of burning hair, her charms and tokens drops of molten lead. They turn to gold as they hit the grass.

'How many spells have you lost with that, Grandmother?' Nancy has a smile on her face. It does not last.

'Plenty, Nancy. You've freed me up though, I'll be faster without them.' She swirls the wand over her head and as she brings it up shards of slate burst from the grass in a line, racing towards Nancy who dives as it reaches her. She can feel the broken ribs grinding against each other as she lands. Without rising, Nancy holds her flowers in mind, conjures the net that held Stag all those months ago and hurls it at Meliora. It catches—she can see the witch writhe. Stag was weak, it won't hold Mel for long. Nancy takes the time to stand, hauls herself up with the glaive, reaching for the set of knives strapped to her side, the shining daggers flying from her hand like diving kingfishers. One grazes Meliora's cheek, drawing a thin line of blood that runs down the side of her face. Another catches in the woman's skirts. The third Meliora catches, mid-flight.

'Enough!' Meliora Ray throws the knife back at Nancy who steps aside to let it pass. 'I will blow you away, girl.' She reaches to a pocket sewn in her dress and pulls out a length of knotted rope. Nancy at least knows what this does, though she cannot think of how to avoid it. Mel unties the first knot and the wind begins to howl across the moor; it blows birds from trees and tears earth from rocks. Those able to do so flee. The villagers turn home to hide in their cottages, the animals seek the shelter of the tors. Nancy leans into the gale and takes step after heavy step forwards, hauling herself on with the spear.

'I am grateful, grandmother. For what you have taught me.'
Another step.
'About family, and what that means.'
Another.
'About the prices we have to pay.'
Again.
'But as is often the way, it's the practical lessons that stay with you.'

Nancy reaches down to her gansey and unties knot after knot after knot. With every loosed thread the wind changes direction. Blows harder. Soon it is a vortex of rushing, howling air. A spinning maelstrom. She has knitted the winds into her gansey. A hurricane of them. Nancy waits until she can barely stay standing then steps astride the glaive.

'Thank you for teaching me, grandmother, thank you for teaching me to fly.'

Nancy rises, the glaive soaked in the salve Meliora had taught her to make, up into the spinning winds and lets them twist her round, lets them point her like a weathervane. Then she feels her grandmother's Murmur. Her bloodied water. The earth shakes below her, and a stone lurches from the ground. Nancy drifts in the wind and it sails on by. Her grandmother has the advantage, but she can fight the shaking of the ground. Closing her eyes, she releases her birds.

She can feel them rise, dive, work their way through the earth. She can feel the resistance from her grandmother's magic. Her Murmur hits it like molten metal hits water. It evaporates against the beat of the Murmur's wings. Since Meliora, since Reagan, showed her that she could—Nancy, eyes still closed, smiles at the mistake that must feel—she has had more control, more power than she had ever known. She grinds her grandmother's magic to dust, winnows the

Murmur through the rabbit runs and feels for something she can use. She pulls on roots, twists the bones of the dead until she finds what she needs. Nancy's eyes open.

'Mel, please just stop. Give Her to me. It's over.'

'No. Now move asi—' Mel is cut off as a boulder of quartz is shot from the earth beneath her, Nancy has pulled roots into a coiled web around it and squeezed the earth, pushing the boulder like a pebble from a sling. It catches the filigree tail of the ragwort stem and shatters the silver and gold like glass. Meliora hits the floor and snarls as she rights herself. Nancy does not let her speak. The earth beneath her shakes into sand and the witch sinks to her knees in it. Granite works itself around her feet, locked in place by grass and peat. Meliora scowls, closes her eyes, and hands the baton to the Mother.

Meliora shakes as the Mother takes control, the ground around her turns to ash as she steps from it, firming once she is free. A throng of ragwort rises around her and, plucking a stem, she is up in the air again.

'Reagan! Listen to me.' Nancy is on her tail, emptying her pockets swiftly, hurling baubles and cantrips into the swirling air just ahead of her quarry, but the Mother steers Meliora through the torrent with ease. Nancy thinks, back to the sea, back to the tunnel in the Brine. Her Murmur should have failed her, but it didn't. It won't now. As before, she draws her birds together, more than she has ever held before, the Murmur straining at its leash. The moor drifts away from her, a hundred feet below, and the pulsing magic from the Goddess ahead threatens to unseat her with every beat. Around her birds pop in and out of existence, gain wings, lose them. The buttons on her coat start screaming with little brass mouths. Still, Nancy waits. Until the air is thin. Then releases the birds. It should not work this high, this far from the ground, but as it worked below the waves it works in the clouds. It is the smallest of stones that she calls, from the moor below. A piece of flint sunk in the peat for five thousand years, but it hits Mel's chest like the arrowhead it is.

It is enough. Mel, the Mother, is knocked off balance and spirals down in the tornado towards Echo Tor. Nancy can't help but crow.

'See? Take me, Reagan. Leave me. I do not care. I have power enough. I don't need yours but if you must rest somewhere, rest here. Take me, hollow my bones, but leave the moor alone. I am Nancy Bligh; Keeper of the High Moor and I will not allow you to hurt it.'

The witch crashes into the Queen's Rocks, into the cleft between Gog and Magog's stone faces, her ragwort ground to paste. She pulses, turns, but Nancy is above her and the Mother screeches at the sound of rockfall. The split halves of Echo Tor shake and grind as the chasm closes, the rocky shape of Gogmagog re-joining with it until the hill is whole and capped with towering granite stacks once again. Meliora and the Mother trapped within.

'Nancy, stop, please.' Nancy turns at Colenso's voice. Distant. Worried. She can see her, Abraham too, sheltering in the lee of the Nest, but she shakes her head.

'Not until it's done, Col. Trust me.' Nancy has barely turned back when the rock starts to tremble. Nancy raises her Murmur again and grinds it tight. Only when she can no longer feel the pulse of the Mother's magic does she tear the hill apart again. Her grandmother lies broken at the centre.

Seeing her knocks the wind from Nancy's sails and she glides to a stop beside her. She hurriedly unties the rest of her threads, and the storm stops.

'Mel, do you hear me?'

Around her grandmother's body are fragments of stone, changed to moss. The Mother's attempts to keep Her host alive. It has worked, just. Mel coughs blood and smiles.

'That's my girl.' The smile fades as the Mother, as Reagan, leaves her host. Rises again as a gilt cloud before pouring into Nancy.

It is like swallowing mercury.

Liquid silver filling every vein. She lifts a hand, it shines out, lit from within, and Nancy marvels at her network of veins and bone. She feels herself warm, a little at first and then as though she is covered in nettle stings. It builds, nettles become burns, burns become the most intense pain Nancy has ever felt, but each time she tries to scream nothing comes out. She tears her coat away, pulls her jumper over her head, stands in her shirt and watches as her remaining tattoos, those not lost in the well, lift from her skin. Feels tendrils from inked vetch work their way from her collar and coil around her throat. She can smell the eyebright, the violets, the foxgloves. Can feel the scratch of dogrose thorns dig into her back. Her flowers are alive. Her friends are weeping. She wonders why. Lifting her ragwort again she glides to the valley floor, walks to a pool, every nerve alight with pain. She gazes in and wonders how she was not aware her eyes are burning. They flicker with a bluish green light, like marsh gas set on fire. She raises her hands, and they are a tangle of weeds, her skin shining out beneath them. She barely has time to consider it before the flames go out, and she passes into darkness.

REST HARROW

Darkness reigns, the world has gone. There are no lights in the blackness. Until.

Pop, pop.

The sound of gas igniting, and Nancy sees again.

'I did not know you'd be so...' Nancy stops, the world does not exist. Reagan shines before her, a face in the darkness. The face of everything; as though her portrait was painted on water, and every moment that passed someone drew their hand through the pool and a new face emerges. The face of women and men, but of beasts too. Of robins and wrens and weasels. Of the wish hounds, of piskies and spriggan. The face of the God of the Mire and the Empress of Salt, of Busker and Colenso. Of Pel. Of Madge. And millions more, never resting on one. Every face that has told Her story. Every face that has heard it.

Nancy.

Her voice is rockfall, the song of the shore, the rising of larks.

Who are you, Nancy?

A question Nancy has asked often enough of herself yet has no answer to. Keeper of the Moor, Daughter of the daughter of a witch. A killer.

'A girl, Reagan. Who wants to do good. Just like you.'

Who am I?
'A story.'
Tell it to me.
'You were a girl. Who lived and was loved. Who had brittle bones but a heart of gold and a stubborn head.'

Reagan's laugh is like the ending of the world and Nancy can feel the tears burn as they fall down her face.

'Maybe you were magic, maybe you were a saint. Maybe you were something more wonderful entirely. You were loved enough to be lain beneath the church. To have it named for you. For the village to grow around you. Then you slept. For a long, long time. Until a man who'd lost his son called you. Until a foolish girl broke your house. Until other stories were told to confuse you.'

I've hurt people.
'We all have. It's time to stop, though, I need it to stop.'
I could stay with you.
'Can you bring back the friends I've killed?' Nancy feels them behind her. Delen, Billy, even Luk. A sea of other faces too.
No.
'Then I've no use for you.'
Where will I go?
'Oh, I have a plan. Some friends and I have been reading the books. But there's some things we must do on the way.'

Nancy rises, Reagan lifts her, and together they sweep the moor. As they pass the creatures that were changed, they do their best to help them, but both are tired. Nancy exhausted from the fight; Reagan not as powerful a story as the Mother was. Her's a softer magic. The snake-wool lamb is shorn of its fleece, that writhes on the moor by its side even as fresh wool grows, white and wiry, from its skin. The broken necked calf is beyond their help, but they calm it as it dies. Some of the villagers, their bodies twisted, can be returned. Those are gently smoothed into shape. Others are too far gone. A group of six sit in a circle just outside the village, their bodies breaking under the forms inflicted on them. One, who wished for wings, lies barely moving, her first attempt at flight nearly breaking her in two as incompatible musculature fought for space within her.

Nancy knows what to do, she whispers it to Reagan.

The stone circle will stand as memorial, as warning, for a thousand years. Some they find other ways to help. Luk Calder is too far gone to return to himself. Yestin stands by his brother's side, arm on shoulder in a desperate bid to calm him.

'Nancy! Please, fix him, he's all I have.' Nancy looks at the final Calder, the closest she came to a friend in that family. She can see, however, that Luk cannot be put back. He was too much a bull to begin with. There is only one way that she can help.

'I'll not leave you alone, Yestin.' Placing a hand between Luk Calder's horns, Nancy soothes him. Concentrates. Luk falls to his knees and begins to bellow as his body cracks and breaks, lengthens. As his ankles snap into hooves and hocks. His clothes break around his swelling body, his uncurling tail, and when he stands Luk Calder is a prize beast of a bull. Yestin looks at Nancy with confusion.

'It's all we can do, Yestin. He will live, that must be enough.' She leaves before Yestin can think of a reply. As she passes the patch of daisies left by Delen Rowe she pauses. There are fireflies hiding in the petals, waiting for the night to shine.

'You are a fool, Billy Askell. I hope there is comfort wherever you are.' She touches the daisy tattoo at her wrist. Holds her lost friend's face in her head. Picks each daisy and makes a chain that turns to silver in her hand. She plucks a single firefly, encases it in amber and adds it to the necklace. Hangs both friends around her neck so she'll not forget the weight of them.

They heal the land too, combining the Murmur and what remains of Reagan's magic to sew the ground shut and stem the bleeding. She can feel the Murmur has been strengthened by Reagan's presence. It will take future experiments to see by just how much her flock of birds has swelled.

By the time they have reached the Queen's Rocks, there is only one problem left to deal with.

Meliora lays where she was left, Brock cradling her in his lap.

'Hello, Mel.' Her Grandmother, broken and bruised, lifts her head.

'She's still with you, isn't she?' Meliora closes her eyes against the tears.

'Yes. For now. She isn't meant for either of us. I saw you, Mel, you barely contained her; she'd have burnt you out. I can feel Her, burning me.' Meliora Ray laughs, raises herself onto a hip and turns to her granddaughter.

'You don't understand, girl. I would have embraced the fire. If you'd let me. At least I would have died shining. You've left me broken. How is that better?' Nancy kneels by her grandmother's side, noticing for the first time the skewed angles of her legs. 'Go on, girl. Do it.'

'What?'

'You know what they say, thou shalt not suffer a…'

'Enough. I am not you. I'll hang no wolves as warnings. She's with me. We can mend you.'

'Then you are a fool who's learnt nothing. I will not stop. I promise you, when I am healed, I will take this moor from you. As he took it from me.'

'Why? It is done, Mel. All that was done to you, also. Don't let your past stain the future. You can recover, stay with me.'

Meliora pushes herself to sitting, and Nancy hears her ribs crack with the effort. The old witch lifts her hand to cradle Nancy's cheek.

'Darling girl. I am proud to call you kin. What future we could have wrought! You are young, though. In time you'll see. The world does not change. Not for us. You can tell yourself they need you, want you. Can tell yourself that tree of yours will love you to the end but they all leave. They all let you down. Will hunt you, burn you when their fear outweighs their need of you.' As she speaks, Nancy feels Meliora's hand slide down her cheek, around her throat. Until she has her in a choke. 'Let me live, Nancy, and I promise I will kill you. Love you, though I do.' Meliora's eyes are a flood. Her grip holding Nancy's head above water. 'And I do love you, Nancy. Believe me. I am so pleased we met. But I cannot stop. I have lost too much to let it go. And if I cannot burn this world, for what it did to me?' Meliora releases Nancy's neck with a push and turns to the doleful creature beside her. 'Brock, my faithful familiar, it is time. Do it.' The badger, tears matting his fur, closes his eyes and grips the sides of Meliora's head. Nancy screams, leaps for him, but it is too late. Meliora's neck cracks and the world is still. She sits, immobile, as Knot stands.

'Leave her to me, Keeper.' He kneels and scoops Meliora up, lifting her easily. Nancy moves to help but he shakes his head.

'No need, Keeper. You saw Reagan; you said it yourself, the Mother burnt through her.' He walks away, not turning his head to finish speaking. 'Her bones are hollow, Nancy. She weighs no more than a bird.'

Nancy watches the badger as he leaves. Stares after the family she's risked the world for.

Nancy.

Reagan's voice is soft.

It's time. Take me where you need me to go.

IT IS BARELY a blink, but they are there. The Fellmire falls below them, the water lit a thousand fathoms in the moonlight that breaks through clouds and is fractured in the misting rain.

Nancy moves towards the centre of the water, alone, and speaks to the voice in her head.

'One last thing, Reagan.'

Of course.

'My friend, Madge. The woman who died in the well. What did you do to her?'

For the first time in their fledgeling relationship the voice of Reagan waivers. Splits. Becomes a chorus of two.

I was not myself. I was my Other.

The words run together, and Nancy waits. When Reagan speaks, She is Herself again.

She is everywhere. We made her the moor. She is in the air. In the earth. In the stone. She runs in the rivers. She falls with the rain. She is caught in the cycle, is eternal.

Nancy traces the surface of the Fellmire with her foot, lifts her face and closes her eyes against the gently falling, mizzling rain. Smiles. Let's a hard, knotted feeling go and turns back to the ritual.

Colenso had suggested it.

Nancy lifts a stone, catches the newt that lies sleeping below it, and blows. Reagan flows from her in the same burning stream that she entered. She pours into the open mouth of the newt and Nancy braces against her blistering lips. It can't work, she thinks, this animal cannot hold her. It does. She has read of cousins of the creature that are born in fire; this one seems able to bear the flame. It lights up from the inside and with two crackling pops its eyes set to burning. Colenso's voices startles Nancy from the glow of it.

'You're ready?'

Colenso and Abraham stand at the edge. Nancy had not heard them arrive. She nods and waits for Abraham Pine-Coffin to open the ivory box. The reliquary he had found in the chamber under the chapel. Bone and cornered with gold. A reliquary waiting for the return of its relics. Nancy drops the newt in, and Colenso adds the last fragment of hollow bone, the creature curling round it like a stuffed toy. Abraham closes the box and together they ride to the chapel. Lay the box on the shelf where Reagan's body once lay. Where the Murmur still yearns to roost. Nancy lifts the lid, looks down at the creature still coiled there.

Promise me something, Nancy.

Nancy closes her eyes, sore and still burning, and nods.

Visit me sometimes. Tell me a story.

She closes the lid, feels the world slip, and all is darkness.

DYER'S GREEN

NANCY WAKES TO the smell of frying bacon. Smiles, stretches, and pats the space beside her. Still warm and sweet with almonds. She swings her legs from the bed. Checks, as she does every morning, that her tattoos are still just pictures. They are. She moves to the mirror and faces herself.

Not a mark on her.

Except for one eye. The left remains the same, but the right is almost black. The iris so dark it merges with her pupil and no vestige of white remains. Bright veins of gold run through it, as though it is an ember cooling. Reagan's parting gift.

'I think it's quite beautiful.'

Colenso wraps her arms around Nancy's waist and pulls her from her reflection.

'Come on, I've made breakfast.'

Nancy quizzes Colenso with a raised brow and the dryad laughs.

'I'm quite capable of frying eggs!'

IN THE KITCHEN of the cottage, Colenso plates up the bacon. Lays a pile of broken eggs besides it.

'Fine. Egg frying is a skill I have not learnt, I'm not a patch on Madge—'

She freezes.

'Nancy, I am sorry, I spoke without thought.'

Nancy looks out of the window as she cuts her bacon, looks at the day breaking softly across the moor. At the stream running by.

'Don't worry yourself, Col. You are quite right, though, this isn't even close to a breakfast at the Nest. Thank you though, love.'

She sits beside her.

'Big day, today. You're sure you want to go?'

Nancy nods with a mouthful of breakfast.

'Yes. Where's Bram?'

Colenso looks out of the east window, to the chapel on its hill.

'He's getting ready. We told him she wouldn't want all the pomp, but I don't think he's doing it for her.'

Nancy pulls on her boots, buttons her shirt and wavers between her gansey and Pel's jacket.

'There's a breeze,' Colenso shouts from the doorway, 'wear both.'

Nancy wraps herself in magic old and new and shivers under the weight of it.

SHE RIDES SELKIE to the village, Colenso sat behind her with her arms around her waist. They pass the Nest. Closed until further notice. They pass the field where Yestin Calder pulls on a golden ring, threaded through his brother's nose, as he tries to move him to water. They pass Cusk keeping an eye on both. Most men and women nod as they pass, the villagers having seen what happens when left to their own devices, they have broadly returned to the way things were. Some at the chapel, some not. Though more than in Cleaver's time. Thanks, in main, to their new priest's… laxity. It is to the chapel that Nancy and Colenso ride.

It waits where it always does. Though it seems more alive. As they dismount, walk under the carved stone doorway, they look at the masonry. The beasts and plants that coiled and snarled during the fight, that simply turned back to stone when Reagan fell asleep. Inside, too, the rafters and pew ends have set in the most incredibly realistic scenes. The creatures carved there stare back with looks of genuine surprise.

Abraham Pine-Coffin, dressed in his priestly finest, is stood in the centre, righting the golden eagle which now soars from the lectern—even with a dent in its beak—and he turns as they approach. Sees them looking at the woodwork.

'I'll never be able to explain to visitors how we made everything so life like. It is time, then?'

TWO LOVERS, THEIR friend, and a dog leave the chapel. Walk beneath the lychgate and follow the coffin path the wrong way to the top of the Queen's Rocks, the space between the giant's heads filled with bracken and briar. A wild and woody byre. Knot kneels besides it, stroking Meliora's hair.

'She was made into this. She was so much brighter, once.'

Knot does not leave Meliora's side.

'It does not matter. It is done. For what it is worth, mine Nancy, she was sorry for your part in this. The plan was made before you were born.'

'Would she have changed it, had she known?'

Knot shakes his two-tone head.

'No. The things that happened to her. The things the world did…' He pauses. 'Do not mourn her, Nancy. The woman

I loved is long since gone. She was already dying when that bastard locked her in that box. He simply hastened the end. I thank you, though. For showing her the sky again.'

Abraham steps forward, opens the book he has brought. Not the one he ought to. Though this one has better stories.

'We are here today, to share the tales of Meliora Ray. Queen of the Witches.' He opens the book and reads a fairytale of magic and starlight. Of a woman who bottled the sky. He passes the book to Colenso, who reads a story of a woman who tricked a lighthouse keeper into piloting a ghost ship safe into port. The book goes round the circle. Story after story is told. Nancy tells her own, of a grandmother she is grateful, after all that's passed, to have known.

Far, far below, a one-eyed ghost tells a tale of a sorceress who pulled a lordling from the sea.

And faint though it is, two giants whisper a story of dreams and sunlit skies. Passing the fragments back and forth between two stony heads.

When all are done, Abraham passes the book to Nancy.

'A gift, from the library in Exeter. Well, a loan. But they're used to mine running overdue.'

The book is bound in yellow cloth. The title stamped in red. *The Ballads of Old Mel Ray.*

Nancy holds it close.

'Thank you, Bram.' She turns to Knot, to Brock, who had told a tale of kindness and mischief.

'You will not change your mind?'

The creature shakes his two-toned snout.

'No.'

He stands and strikes the byre alight. Lifts Meliora in his arms, wrapped in the remains of her cloak, some lead charms still clinging to it.

'I've burnt for you once, Mel, let me do it again.'

The tears burn into Nancy's cheeks, but she will not look away. She watches as the flames take them both. Burn the last of her blood family away. Watches Mel and her oldest friend rise, up into the sky. Black ash swirling. Like starlings.

When the flames have died down Nancy shivers, pulls her coat around her shoulders, straightens the necklace at her throat. Looks to her friends. To the family that remains. She draws them close. Looks out at the broken moor.

'I can't believe it, Col. All this, all that has happened. What a tale it will make.'

Colenso pulls her close.

'Be careful when you tell it. Stories are too powerful for us, Nancy. They always have been. They're too strong of a draw. Mel told herself her story so often, trapped in her coffin, that she forgot the light. Repeated the worst of it over and over until nothing was left but pain. Pel wrapped himself up in stories of adventure and moralistic saviours and it killed him.'

Nancy sighs, looks out to the glint of the Fellmire.

'I thought he might have shown himself. I'm amazed he could resist the spotlight.'

Colenso squeezes her arms.

'He did his part, I'm told. Those tales will make their way to you soon enough, and Pel will be more than happy as stories. He's made of little else. Don't fall into that trap, though, Nance. Don't pin yourself down with words. You can be anything you wish to be. You are all that you are. Stories are tempting, I know that. But they always wind up the same way.'

'How's that, my love?'

Colenso leans in to kiss her, and Nancy understands. She watches the sun catch on the fire as it sets. Watches the glow until the dark takes it. When all is darkness and starlight she straightens her coat. Takes her crop.

'Come then, all of you, let's get to it again.'

WOODEN SOLDIERS

THE STORY ENDS. The story begins. A world wakes from sleep.

Pel rises from a tangled heap of piskies. Walks long-legged through the Undermoor stepping carefully over a sleeping God. His mask slipped, His dog-toothed divinity showing. Pel walks to the top of the hill where the chapel sits and walks to the throne. Lays his hand on the weathered stone.

'It's too large for you.'

Pel turns and smiles at the shadow in the doorway.

'Do you think so, Jacob?'

'Your God or mine, their boots are too big for us. Our place is outside.'

Pel walks to his friend, takes him by the arms and draws him into an embrace. Holds him tight to hide the tears that stream down his face.

'She is safe, do you think?'

Jacob Cleaver does not mention the fact he can feel Pel crying. Simply holds his friend.

'She is, Pel. I believe she is. You've helped keep her as safe as a father can. It is never as safe as we'd like.'

They stay, for a moment, locked together. A lifetime of friendship and heartbreak and forgiveness passing between them. When they separate, all three eyes are wet with tears but both faces are smiling. Pel walks to the doorway and looks out at the Undermoor.

'Your son?'

'Is sleeping. For a long time, I hope. He has a great many nights to make up for.'

Before them, the inhabitants of the Undermoor stir and shift. The moon above them ripples. The grass below them is combed by the wind.

'Well then, Jacob, it is us two alone, together then?'

'Indeed it is, old friend.'

'What trouble can we get into, I wonder?'

'Oh, more than enough, I've no doubt.'

They walk together, down the hill, and into another story.

ACKNOWLEDGEMENTS

WRITING AN ACKNOWLEDGEMENT for a second book is a tricky thing. On the one hand, all of those people who were so instrumental before still are and must be thanked again. I would still not be able to do any of this without my partner, Bex, whose unwavering support has given me the space and confidence to create this book. My parents and brother, all of my family, who have been the most wonderful cheerleaders. My incredible agents, John and Julie who, miraculously, have remained enthusiastic even as I send them new and unasked for book ideas (and often fully written books) that are niche even by my standards. I can't wait to see what you do with them.

My editor, Amy, who took what was a far less polished proposition than *Gorse* and showed me where it might shine. Her notes and suggestions have been so important in the shaping of *Ragwort*, I'm eternally grateful.

My cover artist, Veronica Park, has once again delivered the most breath-taking creation. Her covers are so good I worry they have given me false expectations for all future books that might never be lived up to.

I also, wholeheartedly, thank the wonderful people at Solaris not only for helping bring this book to fruition, but also for all their hard work making sure *Gorse* got into so many hands. Special thanks to Jess and Natalie for their incredible promotion, wonderful and creative ideas and constant support as I travelled about and talked nonsense about fairies.

I've also met so many wonderful friends that have helped shout about *Gorse* and share in the joys and anxieties that came with it. I look forward to returning the favour.

Finally, because Bex told me I ought to, thank you to our dog, Bron. She is neither as steadfast nor as useful as Patroclus, nor as loyal or sensitive but she has made sure I've gotten out of the house and onto the moor and for that—and her approximation of faithful hound—I'm grateful.

FIND US ONLINE!

www.rebellionpublishing.com

/solarisbooks /solarisbks

/solarisbooks /solarisbooks.bsky.social

SIGN UP TO OUR NEWSLETTER!

rebellionpublishing.com/newsletter

YOUR REVIEWS MATTER!

Enjoy this book? Got something to say?

Leave a review on Amazon, GoodReads or with your favourite bookseller and let the world know!